Based in the Blue Mountains of Australia, Peter Hill is a former professional writer, now first time novelist with his debut epic tale about books and intrigue. In his spare time, Hill is also an award-winning fine art photographer with many exhibitions under his belt. And it was whilst on one of his photography expeditions to Iceland and other parts of Europe that he was inspired to write the story of *Finder, Keeper*, a book written by someone with a love of books, especially old books, and an inquiring mind.

Finder, Keeper

Peter Hill

ISBN: 978-1-922788-70-2
Published by Vivid Publishing
A division of Fontaine Publishing Group
P.O. Box 948, Fremantle
Western Australia 6959
www.vividpublishing.com.au

A catalogue record for this
book is available from the
National Library of Australia

Table of Contents

Dedication

Finder, Keeper is dedicated to the memory of my good friend Michael Nagy (1957 - 2020). After I had started the journey which produced this book, and when he was already suffering from the illness which a few months later took him away from us, Nags informed me that in a previous life he had been a scribe during the Middle Ages. I thought at the time he was half-joking, but then again .....

Acknowledgments

It is a bare-bones fact that *Finder, Keeper* would never have been finished without the unwavering support, encouragement, and input of my partner in life, Tatiana, who told me I needed to go to somewhere in Europe for six months and finish writing what I started in Iceland in 2018, otherwise I would never finish it and would always regret it. She was right. It was Tatiana who also supplied the Russian translation for dialogue in Chapter 12.

I am extremely thankful also for the support and encouragement of my children Louise, Christian and Dylan. In particular, Christian provided me with great assistance in how to best communicate in writing dialogue involving the Deaf character in *Finder, Keeper* — Finn Mackie. It was Christian who also came up with Finn's 'sign name' of Numbers Man.

My gratitude also extends significantly to the following friends.

To Marco and Fabiola Tanganelli I extend my eternal thanks for looking after me during my six-month stay in their beautiful Pienza in Tuscany in 2020 to finish my first draft. It was only after they got me settled into my little stone tower that began the crisis for Italy, and the rest of the world, that was the COVID pandemic. Their generosity of heart and concern for my wellbeing during a difficult time for Italy, especially during the initial ten-week lockdown, will always be remembered, as will Federico's at *Idyllium*, Roberto's and his family at *Latte di Luna*, and all the support and friendship from the townspeople in that small but incredibly inspiring Renaissance marvel.

To Matt and Dina I extend my deepest thanks for their friendship and support during my six-week stay in 2021 on their beautiful farm near Dorrigo to finish my second draft. I thank also Dina for her honest feedback on the first four chapters.

Last but definitely not least, to my stepson, Tim Sviridov, I extend my great appreciation and thanks for his intensive and detailed editing of my final manuscript before printing. Without his many hours of concentrated effort, the book you are now holding and about to read would be less than something I am proud of.

Chapter One

The Diamond That Cuts Through Illusion

"General," he said, "if you want to know how I know about every book here, I can tell you: Because I never read any of them... The secret of a good librarian is that he never reads anything more of the literature in his charge than the title and the table of contents. Anyone who lets himself go and starts reading a book is lost as a librarian," he explained. "He's bound to lose perspective."
Robert Musil, *The Man Without Qualities*, Part II – Pseudoreality Prevails, 1930

6:12pm, Thursday, 15th November 2204

Mads Ingridson, the tall, sprightly, and straight-backed 96-year-old chief librarian of the world's largest library, The Bibliotek, stood alone in the black-walled room of the Central Repository reserved for the oldest and rarest of the library's Chinese Collection. He was one of only three people ever allowed to be there.

That was partly the reason he was alone, but in any event, it was how he preferred his occasional visits to the Central Repository to be. The fact that the room he was standing in was surrounded by darkness, as a matter of routine, and was 52 levels below Ground Level, did not perturb him. On the contrary, being alone with such treasures all around him was just the temporary escape from the vicissitudes of office Mads needed from time to time, especially on this occasion given the duties he was soon to perform. As was the case this evening, such visits always reminded him of what The Bibliotek had come to represent, and that was something Mads felt privileged to experience yet struggled to fully comprehend the enormity of. Not for nothing did Mads appreciate the affectionate nickname his close friends had long ago given him – The Book Keeper. It and its often-shortened version – Keeper – helped him stay grounded.

Not for the first time the Second Bibliotekar, as Mads was formally known to distinguish him from his predecessor and mother, the First Bibliotekar, carefully held the world's oldest *existing* copy of a dated and complete printed book in his sterile-gloved hands. It was a Chinese translation of the Sanskrit *Diamond Sutra* and had been produced in 868 during the T'ang Dynasty.

The *Diamond Sutra* was originally created as a scroll, about five metres in length, by woodblock printing seven sheets, all the same

1

size, and gluing them together to form a book. A fragile thing it was; but nevertheless, a book, a wondrous book. A bibliophile such as Mads did not normally consider any *one* book to be his or her favourite, but the *Diamond Sutra* was close to being Mads'. That was why he had returned to this room, to this book. He had somewhere else to be, according to expectation, and soon he would be there. But for now, Mads needed to again feel that wonder that he knew so well.

Despite the precisely controlled air temperature, pressure and humidity within the room Mads now stood, or maybe because of those things, the *odeur* of the *Diamond Sutra* and its pages was pungent and unmistakable – a sharp, strong and indescribable mixture of a thousand exotic scents. A smell that no-one but Mads had experienced for many years. It was intoxicating and he loved it, and holding (and smelling) the *Diamond Sutra* now, deep within the far-removed world of the Central Repository of The Bibliotek, as always, fuelled his imagination like no other stimulant could come close to doing.

Once again, Mads resisted the temptation to *inhale* too deeply lest he inflict upon himself some ancient spell or malady. Once again, as he felt the book's almost weightless perfection, he marvelled at the craftsmanship in the making of the 1,300-year old exquisite artefact of human creativity.

Once again, the thought occurred to Mads that the world as it had existed when the *Diamond Sutra* came into being was simply beyond his learned and experienced comprehension.

Once again, he stared intently at the book's frontispiece. Alongside a few lines of text which gave instructions about the chanting of devotion required of the reader was an exquisitely detailed and fine woodcut illustration of the disciple Elder Subhuti addressing the Lord Buddha, and the worried face of one the latter's attendants stared straight at Mads as before, mysteriously the only visage of many on that page to look at the viewer. Every other face was looking to the left, at the Lord Buddha. Mads identified with that singular face. The longer he performed the role of Second Bibliotekar, now into his 55th year of doing so, the more remote Mads felt from many around him, especially a few of his colleagues on The Bibliotek's Governing Council. Even the expression on the face of that one attendant made Mads feel some kindred connection.

He knew that the sermon contained in the remainder of the book — the sutra — began with the words *Thus I have heard,* as all sutras did, followed by the pronouncement that the sermon was first given by the Lord Buddha in a large park in northern India which was attended by a thousand monks, the disciple Elder Subhuti being one of them. It was Subhuti who had asked the Lord Buddha how to achieve enlightenment, and that question was partly the essence of what drew Mads back to the book time and again. The other part that drew Mads back was the Lord Buddha's answer: that learning four lines of the sutra and imparting them to others was more meritorious than filling 3,000 galaxies with treasure then giving it all away to the poor. Mads liked to speculate that the book's creator, Wang Jie, was motivated to do just that, and that many thousands of others were similarly motivated, thus creating the impetus for the development in China of printing techniques centuries before the rest of the world.

Once again, Mads quietly marvelled at the irony of the book's history. He knew from the entry for the *Diamond Sutra* in The Bibliotek's Master Catalogue that, for many centuries, the book had been secretly sealed within a hidden room in one of the 492 caves making up the holy site that stretched along a long cliff wall which for a millennium had been called the Caves of a Thousand Buddhas, situated at the eastern end of the ancient Silk Road, in the Dunhuang province of China. In that secret room it had remained sealed for centuries with many thousands of other books and manuscripts dating from the 4th to the 11th centuries, all long-forgotten until discovered in 1900 by a Taoist priest by the name of Wang Yuanlu. Exactly when and why the items, collectively known as the Dunhuang Manuscripts, were placed in the room before it was then sealed, were questions for which answers were not likely to be ever known. But Mads liked to speculate that the 'why', the purpose, was the very same overriding purpose The Bibliotek was meant to perform — that of a repository. A place of safekeeping.

He had said as much during a speech he once gave to the new intake of students at The Bibliotek's Academy as his Annual Welcome Speech. The irony, as Mads had also noted in his speech, was that the central tenet of Buddhism was that the material world was an illusion, and that, therefore, there existed no individuals or objects. Yet here the *Diamond Sutra* remained safely in The Bibliotek, where it played the role of a beacon of human history and thought amongst many millions of other books, young and old, though none quite so old. As for the Cave of a Thousand Buddhas, it had been bombed out of existence before the Great Holy War had ended in 2092. Now, in 2204, the *Diamond Sutra* was again residing in a repository — another sealed cave — only now not veiled by secrecy and dust.

As Mads contemplated that worried visage of the Lord Buddha's attendant, his recently-appointed personal assistant, Nils Larkin, an ambitious young neophyte who did not yet have Mads' complete trust, pinged his data pad a second time about the dinner in the Great Hall of the Academy of The Bibliotek about to start and which Mads had been eagerly waiting for some time. Larkin may not have earned Mads' trust yet but Mads knew he was efficient. That much he could not fault, and he had delegated to Larkin the task of organising this important event on that basis. That second ping to Mads meant he was due to make his welcome speech to the 500 assembled guests in 45 minutes.

With unhurried care, Mads returned the *Diamond Sutra* to its exclusive position in the small pine and glass cabinet where it prominently resided, took off and discarded his gloves, then exited the room after its glass door slid to one side, and resumed his seat on the travelator, which began its journey back to the start of the five-kilometre-long West aisle of Level 52 devoted to the rest of the ancient books, manuscripts and other printed material from China held by The Bibliotek - the soft cream muted lighting progressively turning off just behind his egress - stepped off the travelator and exited the tunnel, the humidity door sealing off the tunnel behind him with a quiet hiss, then walked to the lift that was waiting to take him back up to the Central Repository's Ground Level, next door to the Academy within The Bibliotek precinct, at the foot of a mountain range near Helligskogen in remote northern Norway.

As the lift ascended, Mads sent a message to Larkin via his neurophone that he was 20 minutes from arriving at the Great Hall, and sent a note to himself to ask Kaitlin Drummond, The Bibliotek's Head of HR and who had assigned Larkin to his office two months previously, when Mads had been on leave, what she had based her decision on. Despite his efficiency, there was just something about Larkin that made Mads dislike him, and that was causing the trust issue. Perhaps it was his youth, maybe it was his overt ambition, or both. After that note, though, Mads pushed aside his concerns and focused on the night ahead.

To Mads' thinking, it was apt that the 1,000,000,000[th] entry in the Master Catalogue of the Central Repository was a book that had been procured for The Bibliotek by his long-time friend Rafe Nagy, who so far had held the title and role of Rafe the Finder for 63 years. So much so that he made sure it happened that way.

Naturally, as the Master Catalogue's magic billionth entry figure approached, everyone at The Bibliotek became aware of it, and so in accordance with a directive from the Governing Council, Mads had approved the preparations for a formal function to mark the event, which was occurring in the 103rd year of The Bibliotek's operation. A date was set in advance once the magic number became imminent. There had been hopes that the magic number would be reached in the 100th anniversary year of The Bibliotek, and indeed there had been made a concerted effort for a few months to make that symmetrical coincidence happen, but when it became clear to Mads that compromises were being made at the expense of acceptable levels of quality outcomes, he had put a halt to it. Symbolism had its benefits, but it also had its limits, even for such a person as Mads who lived and breathed its place in history, and, for that matter, everything else connected to history itself.

Notwithstanding the importance of the milestone to The Bibliotek, the organisation of the night's function was a challenge that Mads expected Larkin to be able to handle. He had accepted the delegated task without hesitation, but his overt keenness irked Mads. What had been a challenge though for Mads alone, was silently and secretly ensuring that, behind the scenes, the one billionth entry in the Master Catalogue was indeed a book secured by Rafe. That took some doing. Several favours had to be repaid or renewed but Mads achieved his aim without it being generally known he had slightly 'fudged' the numbers to ensure it was Rafe the famous Finder who would be making the keynote speech. That was the kind of symbolism that Mads was happy to orchestrate, given Rafe's many important contributions to the Central Repository over the years as a result of his undisputed expertise as The Bibliotek's best Finder.

Upon reaching Ground Level, Mads exited the lift bay, returned to the waiting security guard the locator that had been on his wrist during his trip 'downstairs', and walked with purpose out of the Central Repository.

By the time he arrived at the main entrance of the Great Hall a few minutes later, Mads could see that most of the guests were already seated. He could see Larkin standing in the middle of the Hall, between tables with data pad in hand and directing the various wait staff to the tables with pre-dinner drinks. As usual, the slightly-built thirty-something Larkin wore his light grey Bibliotek uniform with skin-tight precision and creases, his taut, clean-shaven immaculate face matching the formal impression his clothing and style gave. His heightened formality in dress and visage seemed to Mads to be a robotic-like façade, but one which he had yet to penetrate to see what Larkin was really like, as a person.

Mads paused at the open doorway and quickly scanned the seating plan on the holographic drifting above the main entrance foyer but didn't see the name he was looking for. It then took him a few minutes to wade through the gaps between the tables on his way to the main table on the stage, where the VIP guests were seated, as he stopped at each table to acknowledge those attending who he knew and shake the hands of several more. Along the way he stopped beside Larkin. "Everything okay?" he asked, leaning into Larkin to make himself heard above the din of several hundred conversations.

"Yes, Bibliotekar, everyone found their seats without too much drama. There's been a bit of seat swapping, but not at the VIP tables and nothing to waste time on sorting out," replied Larkin, without diverting the remainder of his attention from the surrounding hurried walks of the wait staff.

"Seat swapping? That's *not* good" he sighed. "We spent so much time on seat allocations," Mads complained to Larkin.

"Yes, Bibliotekar, understood. I did have a word each to them, but I also stopped all table swapping."

"Okay, we'll leave it at that then," accepted Mads. "No issues in the kitchen?"

"No, I just checked the meal status. Entrees are basically ready to go out, they're just waiting for my signal, and no dramas with the mains — all on track."

"Good. When the time is right you need to hover near the VIP tables to make sure they get served first after the main table, okay?" checked Mads.

"Yes, Bibliotekar, I was planning on doing exactly that," replied Larkin, a little put out.

"Okay. Now, remind me where my old friends the Conservators are," said Mads.

"Ah, just let me check," replied Larkin, looking at his data pad. "They're all on those tables over there," said Larkin, pointing to a group of tables on one side of the Hall.

"Hmmm, that's a bit further than I realised. Do you have a guest with the Chief Conservator?"

"Yes, Bibliotekar — one from the UN contingent. I've spread them around."

"Okay, good. From here on in it's your show, Mr Larkin. Any decisions to be made, any fixes needed, you make them," instructed Mads. "Sorry, but you don't get to relax tonight."

"Not a problem, Bibliotekar," replied Larkin, perfectly serious and still miffed at being told the obvious.

Staring at him, Mads nodded then resumed walking. As he neared the stage Mads could see that the Chair of the Governing Council was already seated, as was Rafe, who looked younger than his centurion age. Mads was envious because Rafe even looked younger than him, helped somewhat by the fact that Rafe's closely-cropped beard and moustache only held small hints of grey amongst their black hairs. Fit and slightly muscular, with piercing brown eyes, Rafe was happy for people he met to underestimate his nous and intellect — he spoke several languages proficiently, including Latin, and held an encyclopaedic knowledge of books and their history. Looking now at his body language, it occurred to Mads that Rafe was pleased that Mads was to be seated between him and the Chair.

Danuta Thurldottir, the stony-faced and heavy-set woman who had been elevated to the Chair a few years ago as the outcome of an unsavoury 'boardroom coup' within the Council, did not like Rafe and made no secret of it. For his part, Rafe usually did his best to ignore Thurldottir at formal events such as this one, and given his general antipathy towards rules, especially those rules ostensibly applying to his travel and expense accounts, this lack of respect only added to the Chair's hostility towards him. For reasons Mads was yet to fathom and had all but given up trying to discern, Thurldottir also did not like Mads, but with him she was more politic, astutely aware of the need for her to avoid overt antagonism. She was the Chair of the Governing Council but that did not make her Mads' boss, though she did behave more often than not as though Mads did report to her instead of to the Council. This behaviour she exhibited by making semi-regular intrusions into Mads' operational management of The Bibliotek. This was not welcomed by Mads, was resisted by him, and was associated with her persistent adoption of an abrupt if not rude demeanour towards Mads (and indeed many others), the level of which sometimes prompted him to consider why she had wanted the position she had fought for and obtained.

"It just had to be Nagy, didn't it!" quietly rasped Thurldottir, leaning into Mads at their places at the head table as he sat down, adding when he didn't respond, "you couldn't resist it, could you?!"

Contemptuous of her bleating indignation, Mads nevertheless responded to the 86-year old Thurldottir — who looked so much older that Mads believed she consistently lied about her age — with restraint, "Rafe is our most experienced and senior Finder," he replied, irritated that she seemed to be implying that Rafe's 'selection' was a deliberate slight aimed personally at her. She was being, it seemed to Mads, a little too conceited. "He deserved it. End of story," he quickly added.

That said, he rose to make his speech at the lectern in front of the main table. Whilst he waited for silence to prevail, he firstly checked the lectern's holographic screens to make sure his speech was on them and scanned the audience as he took a sip of water from the champagne flute he had arranged to be placed on a stool beside the lectern. Mads looked at the faces but could not see the one person he was looking for. He hoped she was there. For a brief moment he thought about messaging her to confirm she was somewhere in the audience.

"Welcome, staff, friends, and guests of The Bibliotek," he began in a measured tone, only slightly raising his voice as he knew the sound system had been tested. "It is wondrous to see you all here for a shared and special celebration, and I particularly want to thank Olaf Hendriks, the Prime Minister of Norway, Hilda Jenkins, the President of Finland, Floki Magnusson, the Prime Minister of Iceland, and His Excellency Boris Rudenko, the Deputy Secretary-General of the United Nations, for each accepting our invitation to be here tonight," Mads continued, turning and bowing slightly at each guest as he named them. "I also wish to acknowledge the presence here tonight of Danuta Thurldottir, the current Chair of the Governing Council of The Bibliotek, and Paul Bradshaw, the long-standing Deputy Bibliotekar." Again, Mads turned and bowed slightly to each of his colleagues as he named them, knowing that his respective use of "current" and "long-standing" would rile each of them, but that reflected how he felt about them: not altogether collegiate and positive.

Mads turned back to his audience and continued. "Many of you here tonight are able to recall the occasion of the one hundredth anniversary of The Bibliotek and how we chose to mark that auspicious event. And I daresay the rest of you who were there are not able to recall it," joked Mads to muted laughter. "Tonight, we are here to mark and celebrate something arguably more significant than the age of The Bibliotek — the one thousand millionth entry in the Master Catalogue. And as our special guest tonight we are joined by Rafe the Finder, he who procured that entry." At this, Mads turned and motioned to Rafe as the audience cheered and clapped, prompting Rafe to give a little wave. Out of the corner of Mads' eye as he turned back to the audience, he noticed Thurldottir sitting resolutely still, not clapping, just glaring at Rafe.

"One billion is a big, round, number," continued Mads. "It is almost too large a number to fully comprehend. But it is not just a very large number. It represents the size of The Bibliotek's responsibility. As such, it is a powerful demonstration of the success of the aims for the Central Repository held by the founder of The Bibliotek, Siegfried Sorenson. The Bibliotek is very much the main repository of human knowledge, thoughts, and experience in print. It plays this role with strength, with resoluteness, and with clarity, and will continue to do so. You are all part of the success of The Bibliotek and that equation.

"On *this* auspicious occasion," Mads continued, "I feel we need to be reminded of the reason our monumental task is so important. And there is no better way of doing this, in my opinion, than to re-acquaint ourselves with the arguments made against the preservation of books by the uniquely-named Rahul Ramsay, a former student at the Academy." At his mention of Ramsay's name, Mads perceived Thurldottir shifting in her seat slightly, probably tensing. This he had expected, but he was not concerned. His audience was 'captive'; Thurldottir had no choice but to sit, listen, and appear impassive if not interested. He continued. "As most of you know, Ramsay's arguments had started as innocent fun, as part of the case for the Negative in a debate as to whether or not books were of any value, held in 2183 by an Archival Philosophy class of undergraduates at the Academy. As a class exercise, it was meant to be a resounding victory of the Affirmative argument that, yes, books have value. But, again as most of us know, this did not happen. Rahul Ramsay, the leader of the case for the Negative, took it upon himself to be erudite and convincing during his opening argument. Forget what you've perhaps heard, this is what he *actually* said:

"Books have no value;" started Mads, changing his tone slightly, "they are a burden to mankind. They are a burden from the moment they are created until the moment... *they are destroyed.* The older the book, the bigger the burden of its preservation. The older the book, the less likely it is *to be opened*, let alone *read*. The longer a book remains closed, the greater the decrease in the value of its contents to mankind, until, eventually, it holds no value to mankind.

"An unopened book is an object of zero utility. Zero. The same goes for unread manuscripts and every other item of printed material. But what about their contents?" you ask. "Should not a book be kept for its contents to be used some day?

"Fair question that. Say you are a theatrical producer. Allow yourself to be a renowned one. You come to me and say "Lowly vassal, I am wanting to put on a play, Shakespeare's 18th — *Much Ado about Nothing*. Get me the script." Excited, do I immediately start to ponder how I am to procure for my renowned master the original 1598 manuscript in Mr Shakespeare's hand? No. I am going to firstly ask you: do you want a fresh copy of the *Olde English* original 1598 script? Or perhaps a copy of the 1792 *New English* version of the 1598 script? Or maybe the screenplay for the 1968 UK television adaptation? Or perhaps the 1992 USA adaptation? Maybe the 2056 Swedish adaptation?

"With so many copies of the original, and more choices from adaptations, do we need someone to be safely keeping the very original? We have the content, what is the point of the thing? My point is that The Bibliotek has more than 800 million books — and counting — that it is preserving for... what purpose? If it is for nothing but preservation, is that a purpose? I say no.

"What is the human fascination, society's obsession, with books? My colleague for the Affirmative said "Books are our connection to our heritage. Lose them and we lose a piece of ourselves." I say that is rubbish. I say that whatever value stems from having a heritage, it is not connected to the objects of print we fastidiously keep, but instead to their contents. The words, not their place or means of holding. Whatever meaning or 'value' printed words have, it is always going to be more than their cover or means of holding them in place.

"I say the preservation of knowledge by The Bibliotek long ago became an end in itself. I say the inherent assumption made by Siegfried Sorenson after the Great Holy War that The Bibliotek was necessary for the future of mankind was merely a hope when it was made and a current theory that has not been proven. And never will be proven.

"Books are accumulated and venerated by the literate solely as symbols of status and wealth. For many centuries they were also venerated by the illiterate as symbols of something powerful beyond their grasp, mere words on sheets of paper.

"So much money pours into the purse of The Bibliotek yet nothing worthwhile to mankind can be seen to flow from the costs we all have to share, and that is why I say books have no value."

Mads paused, took another sip of water, and continued in a different, more measured tone. "Ramsay's emotive rant won the day amongst his classmates, and I don't know why no-one on the Affirmative team wasn't able to counter his arguments, or, should I say, argument. Because from where I stand, it is easy to do so. This irks me. It did then, and it still does. But, once it had been delivered, Ramsay's singular contribution to the debate fed student dissent against the accepted narrative. Unfortunately for Ramsay, his little victory went to his head, and without any apparent sense of irony, he caused a much-expanded version of his short speech to be published in the University's student newspaper, a copy of which is, unsurprisingly, stored in the Central Repository. After that, and as you know, the arguments he had made continued on their own, without Ramsay, to be taken up by young people far more radicalised and marginalised than him. All he ended up achieving was the honour of being expelled from the Academy for pursuing his debating argument as if he firmly believed it.

"Some of you may be asking yourselves why I am giving air to what Ramsay said. After all, is this not essentially the doctrine of radical groups opposed to the concept of keeping books, in particular those misguided souls comprising the Present Sect? Yes, it is, it is all that and more. I raise it here, on this occasion, as a reminder that we cannot sit here tonight with nought but lofty airs to sustain the very principles, the very ideals by which we work and live in The Bibliotek. Every one of us needs to know why Ramsay got it wrong; why the Present Sect has it all wrong; and that is why I am talking about the value of books.

"Had I been on that Affirmative team back in 2183, and acknowledging I am now speaking with the great benefit of hindsight, I'd like to think I would have had the presence of mind to respond to Ramsay's argument with a counter-argument along these lines..."

Again, Mads paused for few seconds, then, altering his voice to a more resolutely confident tone, he began. "With no book to show me, where is your proof of a written word? A written sentence? A written page?" Mads asked, pausing again. "Show me a digital version, or a screen full of words from of one of our aged manuscripts, any copy of your choosing, and I could ask you, "Where is the proof? Is this real?" But I do not ask this question because I have no need to ask it. I know the original manuscript is held, safe and secure, by The Bibliotek in the Central Repository. Were it to be left to the Negative side in this debate, this would not be the case. There would be no way to prove the digital copy was in fact a copy. How then are we to give certainty to anyone, at any time, that any copy is real without the original? We cannot. On that score alone, the argument the Negative team is making loses credibility. Books give us certainty. Certainty of the written word, the sentence, the page, *and* the book is something that has and will always have value. That certainty validates original thought, our learning, and our contemporary view of the past.

"If it was left to the Negative team to decide to do away with paper altogether, I would say this: a book provides us inquisitive beings with something a digital screen can never do, and that is what I call the capacity for *real reading* and what others call *deep reading*. This reality is not something new, but what is new is its collective outcomes for humanity. How often have we seen unilateral decisions made by a few and based on digital snippets adversely impacting the many? Access to digital information is just as much about abuse of power as it is empowerment. We have seen this truth demonstrated so many times since the start of the digital age. It reached a crescendo before the Great Holy War and was the partial cause of that terrible conflict.

"A book is truth. Not always truth as an absolute — indeed rarely is it so — but the truth as being what the author wrote. Digital content, whether it be a digitised version of an actual book or content generated by a software program such as the ubiquitous *iWrite2*, can never be accepted at face value as such an absolute truth. Show me a so-called digital truth and I will show you an imperceptibly different version. And another. And another. As many different versions as I am wanting to create, all false yet all facilely true. Society has already been down that road, and as we all know, it was a dead end from which we had to turn around. Just today I was reminded of this aspect of the truth of a book when I inspected The Bibliotek's sole copy of *The Diamond That Cuts Through Illusion*. It is not the original book that is more commonly known as the *Diamond Sutra*. But it's colophon has been translated as these words: "*On the 15th day of the 4th moon of the 9th year of the Xiatong reign period, Wang Jie had this reverently made for universal free distribution on behalf of his two parents*" and that tells us the book was produced in 858, using the Common Era Calendar, and this makes it the oldest date and printed book *in existence*, as far as we know, and I can say this because we can accept the truth of that publisher's statement without having to accept the truth of the sermon the book contains. Indeed, I accept neither the truth of that sermon nor the basic tenet underpinning its message — that nothing is real.

"Naturally, for the purposes of study, research, and contemplation, The Bibliotek prefers that the digital copy of the *Diamond Sutra* be utilised and not the book itself. But the fact that we *have* conserved and protected the actual book from which the digital copy was made gives that copy the *status of truth* as I have described it. Rid The Bibliotek and the world of that book and every other book and we can prove nothing."

Mads paused again and took another sip of water, before continuing. "Up to this point I have focused my argument on the content of books. That is to say, the content of books written with human hands and human minds. As you all know, The Bibliotek does not concern itself with computer-generated content — artificial books, as I have always called them. But books themselves, *real* books, written by *real* people, have value, the sort of value that a digital copy can only hint at and a digital transcription can **never** hint at or hold. Deep reading is enhanced when a book is real, not a printout. Real books, especially hand-made books, tell us a lot about the society that created them. The *Diamond Sutra* is an example of this fact. We can credit Wang Jie's desire for enlightenment for its creation. Indeed, we can credit the advancement of the printing process in China centuries before Europe on that nation's collective desire for enlightenment and acknowledgement before the eyes of Buddha. We can look at the artistry of books published before the *Gutenberg Bible* and wonder at their hand-created beauty whilst gauging their makers' devotion to *their* god. A book is a relic, a tangible trace, and so long as the lessons and value of history are considered relevant and important to those of us in the *present*, so will a book.

"In a simpler time, in 1995, as a heartfelt warning, Professor Jon Thiem wrote a futuristic satirical essay about a 'Universal Electronic Library' — the UL — which "came on-line in 2039" and which held the sole purpose of being a world repository of all humankind's digitally-stored books. Thiem outlined the nature of various sects targeting this global-scale abrogation of keeping actual books, adding a 'postscript' discussing the impact of the attack on the UL by one such sect, the Luddites, which completely erased the UL's database, thereby rendering, in one fell swoop, the entire digitisation philosophy moot. As a consequence, said Thiem, "the return of the reader may be imminent.""

Here Mads deliberately paused for effect. "A book will always shine a solitary yet bright light on those things to guide us. As a great librarian, Archibald MacLeish, once said late in his distinguished life, "a true book is a report upon the mystery of existence; it tells us what has been seen in a man's life in the world — touched there, thought of, tasted.

"MacLeish said those words during a speech in 1972 at the opening of a new library and soon he found himself in the midst of a debate about the role of all libraries. He had railed against intellectuals who considered a library nothing more than 'a sort of scholarly filling station', contrary to his belief that libraries are academic facilities at the centre of our intellectual lives. One of those intellectuals, Charles

Martwell, himself a librarian, responded to MacLeish that intellectual life was centred not in an amorphous institution such as a library but primarily within one's own being. He said 'we, as individuals, give libraries their life. As we learn and distil from the latent treasures housed in libraries, we transform the static store of information into a vital and meaningful reality. The impersonal values of bureaucratic institutions should not be the mainspring of our spirit or the spokesperson for our philosophy.'

"I think there is a lot about what The Bibliotek stands for and how it goes about it in Martwell's words. But, fortunately, we in The Bibliotek don't need to linger too long within the constructs of what our purpose is. For that we have our creator, Siegfried Sorenson, and his Three Tenets to thank. The world is a different place to what it was when librarians and intellectuals argued amongst themselves about the role of libraries. I know what my role is, and collectively we all know our role, and with our one billionth entry in the Master Catalogue, we are succeeding in that role. Thank you."

Mads looked around his audience. They had listened intently to his words and now began showing their appreciation.

After the applause died down, Mads continued. "Well, that is enough from me, I am sure you are all hungry. Dinner will now be served, and in a little while," Mads paused to glance and, smiling, make eye contact with Rafe, "our keynote speaker, Rafe the Finder, using his renowned wit, charm and insight, will enlighten us with the story of how he procured the billionth book for The Bibliotek."

With that, Mads resumed his seat, receiving an even stronger round of applause. Then several hundred conversations resumed in the hall, creating a cacophony that allowed him to talk freely with Rafe whilst he waited for his meal which, according to tradition, was served to Mads and all the guests at the main table before anyone else. But before he began talking to Rafe, Mads waited for Thurldottir to pass comment on his welcoming words.

"An interesting speech," she turned to Mads and said quietly, almost too quietly to be heard by him. "I don't think I could have been as knowledgeable on the subject."

"Thank you, Chair Thurldottir," responded Mads with a nod, but he was not sure there wasn't a backhander in her comment. Thankfully, Thurldottir had then immediately turned to the UN Deputy Secretary-General on her right and begun engaging in conversation with him, thus avoiding any further discussion of the topic Mads had chosen to talk about in his speech. He turned to Rafe.

"Thanks for the wind up. Not. I gather the Chair is not pleased it is me making this speech," Rafe offered to him.

"Don't worry about her, Nags. You found the billionth book, so it is you telling the story, by necessity," replied Mads.

"Yes, I accept that. But what I am wondering, Mr Book Keeper, is how *lucky* I was to be the one who procured it," Rafe countered, in a slightly ironic tone. "Let's just say I am not certain it was pure luck," he added conspiratorially.

"Let us indeed," said Mads. "My goodness, this venison is tender, isn't it?" he smiled.

Mads had been looking forward to Rafe's speech. He knew it would be an engrossing and witty telling of how he had procured for The Bibliotek a certain ancient, rare, and exquisite book.

But Thurldottir had something she wanted to discuss with Mads, and she wanted to discuss it as soon as Mads returned to his seat after finishing his meal and after introducing Rafe and his presentation. Her timing was intentional, as was the perception it would create that she cared nothing for what Rafe had to say, as he made his way to the lectern, trying not to look as reluctant as he was feeling.

"Phicom is concerned about capacity," she whispered to Mads as she quietly moved her chair closer to him as soon as Rafe began talking.

"How so?" whispered back Mads in an irritated tone. Irritated by the interruption and irritated by the obscureness of what she had just said. Phicom was the Philosophy Committee, which was one of only two committees of The Bibliotek that reported directly to its Governing Council, but which Mads did not sit on. As the Bibliotekar, however, he was required to put into practice any resolution of Phicom, which was chaired by Thurldottir. The other committee was Adcom, short for Administration Committee, which Mads chaired and which concerned itself with the day-to-day running of The Bibliotek.

"Your last report from Adcom on utilisation capacities. There is an across-the-board concern," continued Thurldottir.

"My report didn't raise any such concern."

"Yes, but a trend is discernible."

"How so? I have shown a manageable trajectory."

"Be that as it may, you must admit that capacity will become an issue in the foreseeable future."

Mads reluctantly turned away from looking at Rafe and looked at Thurldottir. He did not want to continue this conversation, but at least the large frame of Rafe in front of them largely obscured from the audience the fact they were having it. Before he could answer though, she continued, "Phicom is also concerned about security."

"You're not referring to The Present Sect, are you?"

"Yes, I am. The threats are becoming more strident, more specific. The bodies, shall we say, are being hung closer to home, their faces becoming recognisable."

"Where is this..."

"We think there is a legitimate need to begin preparations for the eventuality that The Bibliotek's capacity will need to be re-established elsewhere," interrupted Thurldottir.

Mads looked back at Rafe continuing his speech and waited until his friend had made the audience laugh again before he turned back to Thurldottir and asked, "we, as in Phicom? There's been no elevation of this to Council, as far as I am aware. In any event, this seems to be an issue for Adcom to raise, not Phicom."

"And that is why we are having this discussion."

But why now? thought Mads. "The enormity of what you're suggesting is enough to warrant discarding it, surely," he quickly whispered.

"No. We are not necessarily talking about moving the entire Bibliotek. It could involve just moving the most valuable content and archival material in the Central Repository to a dedicated remote facility. All staff and current infrastructure could remain here, to deal with current and future material. This alone would free up an enormous amount of space, the long-term cost being reduced accessibility of material barely accessed for useful purposes."

"I'm not convinced such a project is warranted, or indeed will be supported by a majority on the Council."

"That is why I'd like Adcom to initiate it. Or, more correctly, an investigation into the potential need and feasibility of relocating the whole or a part of The Bibliotek, or, more specifically, the Central Repository. If such an investigation happens, you can be sure that the Council will agree to funding it."

Mads wasn't ready or willing to agree to her so-called suggestion. It was almost a standard response from him to anything suggested by Thurldottir, but there was also something else playing on his mind; something he had not the time to think through, just yet. So, he stalled. "In view of the fact that my utilisation reports are on the record, it would be out of place for me to initiate such a project in my capacity as Chair of Adcom, much less as an advocate in my capacity as the Second Bibliotekar. The request has to come from you, in writing, as the Governing Council Chair."

"As you wish but bear in mind, I will be imposing milestones which I will hold you accountable for, personally," rasped Thurldottir.

"As *you* wish," replied Mads, pausing for a second. "One last thing though; where does this fit in with the Secondary Repositories issue?" asked Mads, referring to the handful of repositories maintained by The Bibliotek at various sites in Europe, as 'back-up' to the Central Repository.

"It doesn't," rasped Thurldottir. "The two are to be kept away from each other, is that understood?"

"Perfectly," Mads answered, curtly. It was true, he understood perfectly Thurldottir's directive, just not its reason. Essentially warehouses, the sole purpose of the Secondary Repositories, as they were known within The Bibliotek, was to hold whatever copies of original books and other records the Bibliotek came into possession of. Having the copies 'in reserve' dictated the creation of separate sites for them as insurance. The whole concept of the Secondary Repositories was created by the Governing Council in the early life of The Bibliotek when procurements of entire libraries were common. Often it was a case of accept everything or accept nothing, which meant that The Bibliotek was taking on the responsibility of preserving books it didn't need. At first, it wasn't necessary to physically separate collections, but after a few decades it became obvious that the Central Repository needed to have all copies of original books removed and stored elsewhere. Capacity wasn't the issue, it was merely management of the books that actually mattered. The Secondary Repositories were neither accessible nor made known to anyone outside The Bibliotek. As far as anyone not connected with The Bibliotek was concerned, they were merely noted as "storage facilities" in The Bibliotek's financial statements. They were not quite a secret but secrecy was encouraged given the point of maintaining them.

The problem was, however, that the very existence of a formal means of holding *copies* of things in the Central Repository contributed to their growth in size and number and, as a result, their cost. Some housecleaning was well overdue and Mads had been glad when the Council resolved at its most recent meeting that Finn Mackie, the General Manager of Facilities at The Bibliotek, be tasked with undertaking an audit — still in progress — of the Secondary Repositories. Many people, including Mads and several members of the Governing Council, considered their existence to be technically outside the scope of The Bibliotek's purpose, and Mads was hoping that Finn's audit would provide the impetus to the Governing Council to finally and decisively act. Finn's brief had been comprehensive. He was not tasked to do a mere stocktake of each Secondary Repository — there were currently ten, including four in Oslo and three in Frankfurt — the audit was to encompass a full cost analysis, diagnostics on the condition of the books at each repository, current and projected capacities, security issues, and whatever recommendations Mads, in consultation with Finn and the remaining members of Adcom, felt appropriate to make to the Governing Council.

Though important, the issues with the Secondary Repositories were not exactly forefront in the collective mind of the Governing Council so no timeframe had been set. However, Finn had made the audit his priority and with no deadline imposed by the Governing Council had been allowed to perform it *quietly* during the last few months.

Mads was about to ask Thurldottir why the issues with the Secondary Repositories could not be taken into account by Adcom in performing the task of examining the capacity of the Central Repository when he realised by virtue of Thurldottir turning her face away from him that their muted conversation had come to an end, somewhat to his relief. He was then able to listen to what was left of Rafe's speech, only his mind would not let him. His mind was trying to process the ramifications of what Thurldottir had just told him about the relocation proposal and to understand what was behind her request.

He was still in a fugue when Rafe finished his speech and resumed his seat. Mads had heard it but had not listened to a word of it, so when he stood to thank Rafe on behalf of everyone he kept it short but, he hoped, no less enthusiastic than had he actually known what Rafe had said.

His mind was still on Thurldottir's request for the remainder of the evening and his formal duties as host of the dinner. It made him angry that his attention had been hijacked.

9:21am, Friday, 16ᵗʰ November 2204

By the next morning, the dinner itself had become a blur to Mads. He felt it had been a success, and at least Nils Larkin said as much when Mads strode into the reception area of his office, albeit uncharacteristically late. Checking the time just beforehand, Mads hoped the person he had arranged offline to meet some 20 minutes' prior was still waiting for him. Mads was not in the habit of being late for anything, especially not this late, but 'she' had made getting out of bed on time this morning more than a little difficult.

"Congratulations on last night, Bibliotekar. Everyone said it was a special night, and for once the food arrived on everyone's plates promptly and hot," said Larkin.

"Thank you, Nils, and thank you for the work you did in making sure it all went smoothly," Mads replied. He did not want to admit it, but he had been impressed by the way Larkin had handled the dinner's organisation. Delegating it to him had been a test, and he had passed it. "No problems with the guests' accommodation last night?"

"None whatsoever. I've made sure their respective departures this morning have gone smoothly, and I have already received several messages of appreciation on your behalf," offered Larkin.

"Excellent." Without averting his gaze from his now-standing personal assistant, Mads could see from the corner of his eye a figure dressed in pale blue, also now standing.

"What does he want?" he brusquely asked Larkin.

"Dr Foote says he has something important and urgent to show you," he replied.

Mads looked across at Justin – Dr Foote. He was already advancing towards him, with a dreaded Pink File in his outward hands, like an offering, and before Mads could utter his displeasure, he said, "I do apologise for coming without an appointment, Bibliotekar, but

I've encountered some anomalies in the employee fixed overhead data sets presented at the last Adcom meeting — material anomalies — and I thought it best to brief you before I sought clarification from..."

"Stop right there," Mads interrupted, holding up his hand. Turning to Larkin, he asked "My next scheduled meeting is in..." Mads paused to check his data pad, "fifteen minutes, yes?"

"Yes, Bibliotekar," he responded, "with..."

"No need for that." Mads stared at Larkin. He should have known better than to volunteer information to his visitor. Turning to Justin, Mads said, "Come in and present your report. You know how long you have."

Immediately the door to his office slid closed behind them, Mads turned to his visitor, smiled, and said "Anomalies in the employee fixed overhead data sets, eh?"

Justin returned the smile. "It was the most inane and innocuous thing I could think of, Bibliotekar." He was a short, stocky, man with an unassuming demeanour. Very smart, but in a quiet sort of way, and exceptionally competent. Officially, Justin was an Associate Director in Personnel, which is exactly where Mads needed him to be. Unofficially and unbeknown to others, Foote was his preferred go-to person when Mads needed assistance on off-the-record confidential issues. Justin fulfilled that role with the utmost discretion and care — he knew his way around The Bibliotek's systems, much better than Mads did, and Mads knew it. Two days earlier he had asked Justin to see what he could find out about the whereabouts of Councillor Metcalfe.

Thomas Metcalfe was 154 years old, and close to retirement from the Governing Council and all active assignments. Mads had known him for many years - since he was a young boy — and Mads had always liked him ever since he realised his mother — the First Bibliotekar — did as well. Moreover, Mads knew she trusted Thomas. She had told him as much shortly before she died and had implored Mads to keep him close. Thomas was very much looking forward to spending his final active years as a Professor Emeritus at The Bibliotek's Academy. But Mads had now not heard from him in thirteen days and had last spoken with him just before he left for Arcadia on a routine inspection and test of the backup mainframe facility. Arcadia was in the Alpha Centauri system and the Norwegian Government had leased part of its allocated territory to The Bibliotek for the purposes of its Disaster

Recovery Plan. The amount of data stored by The Bibliotek was literally astronomical, and its Master Catalogue alone was the largest such system in history. Since that last conversation Mads had had no report or contact from Thomas apart from a short message after his apparent return to The Bibliotek on the day before he was last seen that he needed to talk to Mads urgently.

"Absolutely," Mads responded. "Now, tell me what you've found out."

"Councillor Metcalfe is missing," Justin began. "He is not currently in the Locator as being anywhere in The Bibliotek precinct, but his absence has not yet been formally recognised. I have not been able to locate his neurophone or his data pad, and neither is showing up on the Locator. What I can confirm is that he went to Arcadia, completed his work there and returned to The Bibliotek on the same day - the eighth of this month. After that, there is nothing, I'm afraid, apart from some lectures he missed giving at the Academy. There is a record of some data being sent from his data pad to The Bibliotek's file system shortly after his return, which might have been his report on his Arcadia trip, but the actual entry is missing and there is no record of any such report on the system. I haven't made any enquiries or raised any flags about it, so anything more would be mere speculation. The fact some data was sent from his pad after he got back is an isolated piece of information. That concludes my report, and, if you permit me to say, I have concerns, Bibliotekar. Members of the Governing Council do not ordinarily go missing."

Mads looked at him for a few seconds, pondering a response. "Thank you, Justin, I share your concerns, hence my reason for asking you to do some quiet digging. I'll now make my own inquiries to see if some light can be shed on this. But for now, I need you to return to your normal duties."

"Do you wish me to reduce my report to writing?"

"Yes, but do it off-line for now and send me a paper copy only, in a sealed envelope, just like a normal confidential report from HR."

"Shall do, Bibliotekar. What about Security? Do we alert them?"

"Not just yet, Justin, let's give the Councillor a few more days to show up," replied Mads, in a way that sounded to Justin as if Mads retained hope there was a simple and innocuous reason Thomas could not be located.

Mads walked with Justin to the door and waved the Pink File Justin had brought into his office. "Thanks again for this," he said after Justin left the reception area, and then handed the file to Larkin. "Here, file this with the minutes of the last Adcom meeting, after agenda item five." Mads didn't need to look at its contents. They were certain to be a report on some anomalies, just as Justin had said, and which he cared nought about.

Returning to his office, Mads sat down at his desk and tried to think of a reason for his friend's apparent disappearance. He didn't want to admit to Justin that he couldn't. Then, on impulse, he tapped his neurophone to call Thomas. He knew it was probably futile, but he wanted to be sure.

But his call *was* answered. "Hello," a male voice said, a little hesitatingly.

END OF CHAPTER ONE

Chapter Two

Rafe the Finder

"A library represents the mind of its collector, his fancies and foibles, his strength and weakness, his prejudices and preferences. Particularly is this the case if to the character of a collector he adds — or tries to add — the qualities of a student who wishes to know the books and the lives of the men who wrote them. The friendships of his life, the phases of his growth, the vagaries of his mind, all are represented."
Sir William Osler, Introduction to *Bibliotheca Osleriana*, 1929

Saturday morning, 6th October 2204

Rafe was generally recognised by all at The Bibliotek as being a particularly good Finder, if not the best. Rafe held that status partly because he could not conceive desiring doing anything else and always rejected suggestions and offers to do something else, and partly because he was an expert sleuth, an attribute unfortunately not shared by many others in his cohort. Rafe loved his job because he loved the hunt itself, and the prize at the end of a successful hunt — a new and hopefully valuable addition to The Bibliotek.

A Finder's main task was to scour the part of the Earth each was allocated for books and other records that The Bibliotek did not already have, and to procure them for The Bibliotek's Central Repository. This included finding earlier editions of books already in the Central Repository, making first editions the most prized Finds of all. To assist the Finders a team of List Compilers maintained a list for each Finder comprising books known to exist and which were waiting to be found and procured. Although none would admit to it, some Finders were known to devote their entire search efforts to sources on their respective Lists and not bother doing their own research. But Rafe did otherwise, and this was another reason why he was good at his job, because it was often the case that a find by Rafe that was not on his or anyone else's List held at least one reference, if not more, to other sources also not already on it, and that was the sort of information the List Compilers yearned to obtain.

Rafe's designated territory was Europe. His success rate was not only consistently higher than all other Finders, but was also significantly higher than the other Finder who had shared the territory of Europe until she was fired eighteen months ago, and who shall remain nameless for a reason that will become apparent in the telling of the following search Rafe carried out near Roccascalegna, a remote mountain village in the Abruzzo, Italy, region.

Rafe had travelled to Roccascalegna in a hired hovercar, his usual mode of transport within Europe, on the strength of a tip from an antique book dealer in Naples that a monastery not far from the village retained a "small library of ancient religious books, and a few medical texts." His former colleague, acting upon a reference in her List to an incunable printed by Lucas Diminici in Venice in 1482 of which only five copies were known to exist, none of those then held by The Bibliotek, had travelled to the monastery a few years beforehand and was successful in obtaining the said book, *Sermones* of Pope St Leo the Great (440-462). But given what Rafe had gleaned from his own research he felt there were possibly one or two other Finds still to be had at the monastery. And given what he knew of his former colleague, it would be no surprise to Rafe that she had missed them.

Not long after sunrise on this particular day, but before the sun was anywhere near reaching the top of the mountain range overlooking the village, Rafe set off for the ancient monastery. He had been told by Bernardo, his host at the old locanda, that it was atop a hill in a small gorge up the valley behind the village, approached via a dirt path, and that he would first see the monastery after walking for about two hours. Rafe had thought it was an interesting way for Bernardo to describe the distance to the monastery, but he had made no comment.

Rafe was not in his usual austere monotonic grey garb, the unofficial uniform of Bibliotek staff, but was instead trying to pass himself off as almost a local in his choice of attire, being a loose oversized white cotton shirt, loose-fitting, flowing tan pants and thick sandals – his 'rural look', topped off with a mangy old beret. He carried in his old leather satchel not only his usual materials, including his data pad, but also a large wild boar salami, a round and pungent slab of cheese, a small loaf of bread, fresh apples, and several bottles of Cerasuolo, a *rosé* wine. It was all local produce. The items were not for Rafe, but he hoped they would serve as tokens for entry beyond the wall of the monastery, as Bernardo had also given him the information that Monsignore Matronola, the sole remaining monk and therefore effectively the full-time caretaker of the monastery, had not come down to the village for nearly a week due to persistent storms and would be missing his usual fare and favourite wine.

The path Rafe found himself on looked tired and worn, though more from age than use, and it was at risk of being covered by the vines, branches, and foliage edging over it like scraggly fingers which silently bent to Rafe's passing body. "Two hours my arse!" he silently scoffed to himself, just as he rounded a bend and was stopped by a sight that betrayed an audible gasp.

There in the near distance sat a circular stone tower, five storeys high, perched atop a massive rock outcrop a hundred metres or more high, spearing out and up into the landscape towards Rafe, at an angle that seemed to mock gravity. *Whoever decided to build a monastery atop this monstrous monolith certainly achieved their aim*, thought Rafe, *if their aim had been to make a grand statement.*

Returning to a more immediate and practical matter, Rafe wondered: how did one access this place? He kept to the path, though it appeared to meander away from the monolith now looming over his head. But as he rounded its apex, the path turned to follow the other side of the rock and Rafe then saw that the path stopped at the start of stone steps which slowly, rather than steeply, ascended, whilst hugging a stone wall abutting the monolith.

As he got closer, Rafe began to discern not steps, but uneven rows of flat stones with their rough sides facing outwards and upwards, each row slightly higher than the one before it. Even though the steps, for want of a better description, were wide enough for a horse and cart, it seemed too steep, far too steep, for either, and this perplexed Rafe. *If you have flat rocks suitable for steps, why put them in at an angle?* he thought. He looked up and saw a wooden door with a curved top at the end of the steps, far above him. On either side of the door the monolith gave way to high stone walls which seemed to rise directly out of the stony crag. They were pitch perfect in a near-straight drop.

Rafe adjusted his grip on his satchel and climbed the steps. They were dastardly and made it difficult to maintain an even pace. They required his constant gaze to avoid tripping. He tried to reach the doorway in one stretch, but failed, and as he paused for a while to catch his breath he looked up, away from the doorway, and thought he caught a glimpse of someone's face, which he assumed to be that of the monk, peering out of a window high above him in the stone wall before it retreated inside.

He continued on and a few minutes later finally made it to the doorway, and as he was about to lift the doorknocker — a rusty steel likeness of what looked like a demon pointing its tongue at him — the door creaked open and a white-haired and much-creased face with slightly bulbous but intensely bright eyes appeared from behind it, followed by most of the bent over figure of an old thick-set man of average height in a dark robe, tied at the waist.

"Buongiorno Monsignore," Rafe said.

"Buongiorno," the old monk replied stiffly and quietly. Still stooping, he looked at Rafe's face, then down and back up. "You are not from here," he said a little louder. "Who are you and what do you want?"

Rafe slowly opened his satchel, took out an apple without taking his eyes off the Monsignore, took a big bite and slowly began to eat it. The Monsignore peered at Rafe even more intently, his eyes narrowing, but he said nothing more.

"My name is Rafe, and Bernardo asked me to bring you your usual. I think he said he was worried about you. Nice apple. I was heading this way, so it was nothing for me to agree."

"Heading this way? Why would you be doing that?" enquired the old monk.

"Well, to be honest, I was coming to the monastery to see you. If you let me in, I can give you the things I brought from Bernardo and we can talk about it." Rafe could see that the Monsignore was in two minds, but he had deliberately not told him what the things from Bernardo were, making it difficult for him to ask Rafe to give them to him and just telling Rafe to be on his way. "I promise I won't impose on your time too much or your hospitality at all," Rafe added.

"You are already imposing on the one and I suspect you will also impose on the other, given you have begun eating what I also suspect is one of my apples" grumbled the Monsignore.

With those words, the old monk slowly and with some effort completed opening the enormous, heavy, aged door, stepped to one side, and motioned Rafe to enter. That was when Rafe noticed the old monk was almost barefoot. What passed for sandals seemed long overdue for falling apart.

Immediately on stepping through the doorway, Rafe extended his hand to the old monk, who obliged with his own, podgy, heavily calloused hand, and gripped Rafe's like a tightening vice. "I am

Monsignore Matronola," he introduced himself with a hint of displeasure, and, still holding Rafe's hand in his, said "But you already know that. And I already know that you are not being as honest as you claim and are in fact a liar."

"A liar?" Rafe said, slightly hurt, whilst retrieving his slightly crushed hand, also slightly hurt. "How so?" he responded.

"Bernardo has never worried about me, or anybody else, in his entire life, apart from himself. So now I know two things about you: you are a liar and you are not from these parts. And given you are a liar, I think perhaps that you do not normally wear such clothes as you are wearing right now and are thus from another country, if not planet. But I am curious. And I am hungry. So, come with me and no more lies from you, if you will."

"I believe I can manage that, Monsignore," Rafe responded crisply.

"And no more patronising me, Mr Rafe. I am old — too old — and I have not time nor patience for such treatment, especially from a stranger. And I am still hungry." With those words, he turned and slowly pushed the door closed, and locked it. Then, with Rafe following, he continued up the pathway, to another doorway. The old monk seemed to Rafe impervious to the irregularity of the stonework in the path; he obviously knew its worn surface well. Rafe, on the other hand, had to watch each step he took lest he trip. That was the last thing Rafe wanted the monk to see.

"I must say," he offered, "this monastery looks more like a castle."

The Monsignore stopped and turned around. "I see you have good eyes and use them, Mr Rafe. What you are looking at was intended to be a castle by its builder, Baron Corvo de Corvis, but he was killed one night by some of the Roccascalegna village people, and the unfinished castle was then occupied by our Order, the Augustinians, and used as a monastery. That was in 1572."

Before Rafe could ask his next question the Monsignore had resumed walking up the pathway, but he could see why the location was considered suitable for a castle. Even from where he stood, Rafe could see that the monastery commanded an uninterrupted view to the Majella Mountains on one side and the Adriatic Sea on the other.

The Monsignore came to yet another doorway, took out a band of keys from a pocket in his tunic and used one to open it, beckoning Rafe to step through before him. This Rafe did, and found himself in a small grassed courtyard, bounded on three sides by stone buildings each comprising two levels, and on the remaining side by a small stone wall. Rafe peered over the waist high parapet and straight down to the rocky ground far below. The question occurred to him: how many heathens had been pitched off the walls to the rocky ground far below? The Monsignore joined him.

"You know, Mr Rafe, it is said that if a monk or, er, *noviziato*, er... neophyte..."

"Novitiate," corrected Rafe.

"Yes, thank you. If a monk or novitiate committed the sin of suicide in the monastery, his body was thrown from the highest part of the wall," offered the Monsignore, looking at Rafe and sensing his thought. "Burial was not for them. Fortunately, not that many poor souls suffered from this policy, but it is certain that the first body to be thrown was that of the Baron, probably from this very parapet."

"I meant to ask you, why was he killed?" asked Rafe.

The old monk smiled and asked, "Have you heard of *jus primae noctis*, Mr Rafe?"

"Yes, it means the *right of the first night*, whereby a lord had the right to sleep with a local bride the night before her wedding," Rafe replied.

"You know your Latin, Mr Rafe, so you would also know *ius primae noctis*."

"I admit I have not heard of the *law of the first night*," said Rafe.

"I am not surprised, and nor had the local villagers heard of the *right* being *law* before the Baron introduced it. And that is why he was killed, by a bride-to-be plunging a dagger into his heart when he tried to invoke it."

"Oh, I see..." said Rafe, his voice trailing off as he watched the Monsignore walk across the courtyard.

"Come Mr Rafe," the old monk said without turning, "come into the kitchen."

Rafe followed the Monsignore across the courtyard, through another doorway — open this time — and into a large room which held a long solitary bench table with a few chairs. To one side, between two narrow, tall windows from which streamed the midday sunlight, was a large wood-burning stove, which was lit and warming the stone-paved room. On the opposite side of the room sat a large old wooden sideboard and a slightly battered tin food chest. After closing the door behind him, the Monsignore beckoned Rafe to sit at the end of the bench nearest the stove. "Please you to sit down and rest your feet," he said.

Rafe emptied the contents of his satchel onto the table and sat down. He then took one of the bottles of wine and began to open it with a corkscrew the old monk handed him from a drawer in the table they now shared.

"Ah, the Cerasuolo," said the old monk. "The body of a voluptuous woman with the soul of a vixen. A potent combination, not least in wine. Or so I have been told," he quickly added in response to Rafe's glancing query, smiling for the first time since Rafe's arrival, which had the effect of making him look like a newborn's grandfather instead of a cranky old monk. Rafe now also observed that Monsignore Matronola possessed a perfect set of pearlescent teeth, though he assumed the teeth were artificial as they sat in sharp contrast to the rest of his body that extended beyond the strained confines of his robe.

"Well," said Rafe as he poured the wine into two tall-stemmed bell-bottomed glasses that were already on the table, a silent fact that had not gone unnoticed by him, "this *rosé* is certainly a darker red than any other *rosé* I have seen, so I can perhaps agree with you as to the body."

"*Saluti,*" said the old monk with another shimmering smile, holding up his glass.

"*Saluti,*" responded Rafe, with a small chink of their glasses.

The Monsignore proceeded to take a rather large gulp of wine, then, placing the glass back onto the table, let out a sigh. He was still smiling. Rafe however swirled the wine in his glass and took a few samples of its aroma before taking a sip. "Hmmm, that's quite alright for thirty Euros."

"Ha ha," the Monsignore laughed softly, "Bernardo charged you thirty Euros for each bottle, did he?"

Rafe did not answer, he did not need to. The question was rhetorical: the old monk had just informed Rafe that he had been charged too high a price. Rafe did not otherwise react either, he just let it go.

"Now, Mr Rafe, it is only just noon as I speak. I should not be drinking this wine without eating something as well so please join me." With that, the Monsignore set about slicing the bread, the salami, and the cheese straight on the table with a knife he took from the same drawer. To Rafe's slight relief he then got up and took two ceramic plates from an old wooden sideboard along the wall facing the windows.

For a while they sat together eating and drinking in silence. Rafe could tell the Monsignore was very hungry, but he could also tell the old monk was trying not to his hunger be obvious, so he decided to keep quiet as well and let him eat in peace. And also drink — the contents of the bottle were disappearing rather quicker than Rafe was used to. He did not try to keep pace.

"Your methods are subtler," the Monsignore said as he finished his third thick slice of bread with equally thick slices of salami and cheese, "but I believe you are another borrower."

"Sorry... borrower?"

"Borrower, looker, finder, seeker, or some such nuisance."

"I am a Finder, Monsignore, but I try not to be a nuisance."

"You are failing," the old monk said matter-of-factly.

With that warning, Rafe took care with his next words. "I am from The Bibliotek and am called a Finder, but in truth I find only what I seek; and in seeking I look for the truth. I never borrow."

"You are none of that," the Monsignore responded quickly, "But you are a man who sprouts riddles that I care not to entreat. Do you have what was borrowed from me by she who came before you?"

"I'm sorry, Monsignore, but as you can see, I have brought nothing with me apart from your food and wine which, by the way, I am grateful for its sharing, and a few personal items. And I'm not sure what you mean by 'borrowed'. I am aware that the person you are referring to *procured* a book from you; The Bibliotek does not engage in borrowing books," said Rafe with a slight measure of uncertainty mixed with concern. He had a suspicion, given what he knew of his predecessor, but he didn't want to show it.

The Monsignore took up his glass and leaned forward towards Rafe. "She said she wanted to borrow it. To study it. That is what she said to me, Mr Rafe. Are you saying she was not being truthful with me?" He took a long, slow, sip without taking his eyes off Rafe.

Rafe returned his gaze without responding for a few seconds. The old monk's demeanour had suddenly hardened a little and Rafe was struggling against the urge to say exactly what he was thinking: that his predecessor was someone he never trusted and who was eventually dismissed from The Bibliotek after it became an undisputed fact that in her dealings with Bibliotek staff and with outsiders she was at various times a consummate liar. Rafe thus had no doubt that what the Monsignore had just recounted was true. But he could not fathom, then and there, why she had lied about 'borrowing' the book she procured.

"I don't know why she told you The Bibliotek merely wanted to borrow your book, Monsignore Matronola, but I can tell you that it was received by the library in good faith as a procured addition to its collection. I can also tell you," Rafe paused, "that my colleague is no longer in the employ of The Bibliotek and that, consequently, she is no longer a colleague."

All this time the Monsignore had maintained his gaze at Rafe, but now his eyes narrowed to an almost squint for a few seconds. "I see," he almost whispered, with resignation in his voice. "Well then," he continued after a pause, "perhaps you can tell me what exactly did happen to my book."

"With pleasure," Rafe replied, taking out his data pad from his satchel. He quickly keyed a few strokes, then placed the pad on the table, facing the Monsignore. "These are the photographs of your book that were taken for the purposes of the Master Catalogue. They are the standard type of images taken for each record procured and held by The Bibliotek; in this case, being a book, its cover, its spine, photographed vertically, its frontispiece, and any material or unique features, such as gilded page ends or bookplate."

"It looks... clean," the Monsignore ventured after looking at the photographs.

"Standard practice is to clean and, if necessary, repair and restore any book coming into the possession of The Bibliotek," Rafe paused. "By whatever means. We have quite a large team of conservators who are all expert at their craft and use the latest technologies."

"You do all this even to the ones you merely borrow?" the Monsignore asked wryly.

Rafe then showed him an entry in the Master Catalogue for his book. "This is all the information about *the* book we now hold, starting with the basic data of title, author, publisher, year of publication, edition number, and all the information we have about this particular copy, for example, who the previous owners were and how it came into our, um, possession, plus internal details of the conservatory work performed on the book and who carried out the work, and all relevant dates."

"I see," responded the Monsignore, with faint disinterest and without really looking at what Rafe was showing him.

"For security reasons, the Master Catalogue is an intranet-only database, so I am showing you offline samples I prepared beforehand for this very purpose," Rafe explained to the Monsignore. "The more sophisticated the Master Catalogue becomes, the more real-time information it provides, the greater the need to keep it in-house only."

"I see."

Rafe persevered, explaining that only a small amount of basic information was duplicated for the purposes of The Bibliotek's on-line public database, including the digital copy of each item. There was no security issue involved in giving on-line access to the digital copies and, besides, it was a mechanism to keep Access Requests to the original books at a manageable level.

"That is not correct," the Monsignore said after a few moments of finally reading his book's entry. Rafe assumed he was referring to that part of the Catalogue's entry that related to the book's procurement, as opposed to it just being 'borrowed'. "Which part?" he asked.

"It is not the original first edition. It is the revised version. Eight years later."

"Oh, but how do you know that?"

Given the look that now appeared on the Monsignore's face, Rafe knew he had just asked a very ill-informed question. The look was enough to serve as its answer, as the Monsignore remained silent.

"One moment, Monsignore. I will make a note of that correction." Rafe quickly typed and sent a note to the Conservation Department at The Bibliotek requesting further investigation of the book.

He then showed the Monsignore the Record of Access. This was the official register of all who had sought and been given access to the book or other item. It was blank. Nobody had examined the book since its addition to the Catalogue.

In accordance with The Bibliotek's protocol, Rafe did not mention or show the Monsignore the Record of Denied Access for the book, even though it too was blank. That information was confidential.

Lastly, Rafe said he wanted to show the Monsignore where exactly in The Bibliotek the book was being "held". He consciously avoided using the word "stored". An important component of the intranet-only database was the real-time tagging facility. Every item held by The Bibliotek and listed in the Master Catalogue was physically 'imprinted' with a unique identifier. Much like a bar code only not visible to the human eye, the identifier could only be accessed by a Bibliotek Scanner. Also unseen was the constant auto scanning of every imprinted item, many times hourly, with the result that the Master Catalogue was not only able to show exactly where in The Bibliotek an imprinted item should be found, it also showed where an item actually was to be found. In this manner, the Master Catalogue was also an important component of The Bibliotek's security system – it monitored all movements of catalogued items and thus could immediately flag any such movement that was not authorised.

Rafe brought up on his data pad's screen a 3D holographic diagram of The Bibliotek's entire collection, with every single one of the hundreds of millions imprinted items 'pinned' by a light green marker. Of course, at the scale of his data pad's screen, the collective green pins formed a large green blob, so Rafe zoomed in on the section of the level of the Central Repository where the book was housed. The Monsignore could see that the pin for his book was highlighted. It was surrounded by many other green pins.

"What are those green blinking lights?" asked the Monsignore, who had noticed there were two such lights to the side of the screen.

"A blinking green pin designates a book that has been temporarily removed," explained Rafe.

Rafe told the old monk that there was a variety of legitimate reasons for any imprinted item to be elsewhere than its normal place. "For example," he said, "at any given point in time, thousands of items could be going through their bi-annual health check, or being repaired, or translated, or taken to a Reading Room for an authorised inspection or study. So long as a removal is authorised, its imprint will blink as green."

"And what if a person just takes a book?" worried the Monsignor.

"If a book is not where it should be, it will blink as red," replied Rafe, "but as you can see," Rafe zoomed the holographic back out to show the complete collection, "there are no red pins."

"That is all impressive," offered the Monsignore.

"Thank you, and yes, we think so too. A lot of thought went into the structure and processes of the Master Catalogue," responded Rafe, with a small smile.

"Hmm, yes I see that. Have some more wine, Mr Rafe," said the old monk as he poured some more of the Cerasuolo.

They sat in silence for another while, each in their own thoughts. Rafe was wondering when he should broach the reason for his visit, but he was in no hurry and did not want to upset the old monk by suddenly doing his job as a Finder. He need not have worried.

Finally the Monsignore spoke. "You know, Mr Rafe," when I die, which feels sometimes to be coming sooner than later, the monastery will be left to rot and crumble, but not before the Prelate, that idiot, will send some novitiates here to retrieve that which I alone have kept safe for three decades and more."

"Now who talks riddles, Monsignore?"

The old monk peered at Rafe wearily. "My books, Mr Rafe, my special books. They number seventeen; all to do with, how you say, the anatomy of the human body," he said softly.

His expression must have betrayed the astonishment Rafe felt, for the Monsignore continued, "I will show you these seventeen books, Mr Rafe, but not before we finish the wine, because I feel I cannot reveal them to you without its help."

Rafe slowly poured most of the remaining wine into the Monsignore's glass, and the rest into his. "You surprise me, Monsignore, I was hoping to find one, perhaps two, books here, but certainly not seventeen. That would be news to both me and The Bibliotek." This was true. It was the reference to "a few medical texts" in the message from the dealer in Naples that had aroused his interest, as monasteries were not known for being repositories of books of such type, but he never imagined it referred to anything like seventeen books.

"And so it should be," said the Monsignore, with the merest hint of a smile on his face as he placed his glass in front of it and peered into the contents, "As well hopefully as the fact the books are the only survivors of the Giordano Collection. I think you would know of these books, Mr Rafe," he added matter-of-factly.

Rafe peered at the Monsignore closely for a few seconds, his glass in his mid-air hand, not sure if he had heard him correctly. Shock mixed with excitement mixed with a rising sense of the need to adopt caution. The Monsignore returned his gaze, but with a slight nod of his head as he put down his glass.

"Yes, Mr Rafe, the Giordano Collection, what is left of it. It is here and has been for some time. I imagine The Bibliotek would like to have it, all seventeen books, yes?" stated the Monsignore, again matter-of-factly.

Suddenly it occurred to Rafe that he had been played the fool since the moment he had arrived at the monastery, if not even before. Davide Giordano was one of the founders of modern surgery in Italy, if not the world, and more importantly, to Rafe and The Bibliotek at least, one of the greatest historians of medicine. During his tenure as Chief Surgeon of the Municipal Hospital of Venice in the early 20th century in particular he established a collection of rare medical books and treatises from the late 16th to 17th centuries, and then, shortly before his death in 1954 he donated the entire collection to help establish the Library of the History of Medicine of the Scuoloa Grande de San Marco, only for it to be lost in the Great Earthquake of 2046 that struck Venice, causing fires and untold damage which was closely followed within days by a record two metre *Acqua alta* that finished off the city and any building still standing.

Rafe finished the contents of his glass and proceeded to uncork the second bottle. Aggressively.

"Correct, Monsignore," he curtly responded, "but by all accounts, the Giordano Collection was lost forever, either burnt to a crisp or sunk, or both, when Venice was destroyed."

"Now, Mr Rafe, I ask that you not be angry with me. I wanted to be sure you were the man I had been told about — never mind by who — so I had to play my little game. Surely you will forgive an old man his small pleasures?" he rhetorically asked, quickly adding, "It is true that the Library the collection was housed in was destroyed by the earthquake that was the death of Venice, but it is also true, but not known by any but a few, that a young friar of our order, one Federico Tanginelli, was on a sabbatical at the church next door to the Library, the Basilica of Saint John and Paul, and had rushed into the Library after the first tremors and rescued all the books he could before it became too dangerous to remain. It seems he had only been in the Library the day before and had been quite taken by their beauty and their significance."

The Monsignore paused and beckoned for his glass to be filled, which Rafe obliged, in silence, his mind racing.

"But for reasons that I am unaware of, Tanginelli did not reveal his deed to anyone at the church, and in time, he was evacuated with of course many others, carrying the books he had saved as his only possessions. I can only but speculate on his motives, but I think it can be suggested he was so enamoured of the books, he saw an opportunity and took it, so to speak."

"I am prepared to accept what you say, Monsignore, but how did the collection end up here?" asked Rafe.

"That part is easy, Mr Rafe. This..." said the old monk, waving his outstretched arms once, "is the monastery from which Tanginelli was taking a sabbatical from. He simply returned here after being evacuated from Venice, with the books in a chest."

"But that was over one hundred and fifty years ago. Surely the secret became known at some stage?" asked Rafe.

"That is a fair question, Mr Rafe, but I do not have a definite answer for you. All I know is that the fact the books were from the Giordano Collection, and indeed were all that was left of it, was never disclosed by Tanginelli before his death many years after he left Venice, and long after it had generally become known that the entire collection had been lost in the Great Earthquake and fall of Venice. He kept quiet about it. As far as I know he told no-one. Even back then our numbers were in decline so there were not many inquisitive minds to question the status of these books as being anything but Tanginelli's personal collection of old books. Until I was sent here that is, some forty years ago, because as soon as I saw the books, by then gathering dust, as you would say, in our library, I felt they were something special, and when I opened the first one I knew straight away what they were, for there on the inside cover was the unmistakable bookplate of the famous Davide Giordano, inscribed with his motto *Lucerna oculorum meorum solatium et laborum*."

"Lamp of my comfort and work" translated Rafe.

"Correct, Mr Rafe," the old monk smiled, once again impressed with Rafe's grasp of Latin. "You would like to see the Collection, no doubt?"

"That would be the case, of course."

"Yes, well, as I said, let us finish the wine first and then I will show you your prize. You like the wine, yes? My brother's wife's family has been making it for many years, many generations. I asked Bernardo to make sure it was this fine Cerasuolo you brought with you. It is the best in the valley. It is made from the Montepulciano grape, which is why it is a very dark colour for a *rosé* and is macerated for less than a day before the pressing. Someone once asked me how long they should cellar it for and I said, 'why would you want to do that!?' Ha ha!" the Monsignore slapped his thigh after telling his little joke.

The Monsignore watched as Rafe twitched in his chair as if he had just come out of a trance, pick up his glass of wine and drink its entire contents in one short series of gulps. "Now who is thirsty, Mr Rafe!" roared the Monsignore with a hearty smile, before taking his own, but far gentler, drink of the wine. "Well, perhaps now is a good time."

Rising slowly, the Monsignore took a huge iron key out of a pocket in the fold of his tunic and beckoned Rafe to follow him as he made his way through the kitchen door and back into the courtyard. Rafe obliged, taking his satchel, the third bottle of Cerasuolo and both their glasses with him. Turning to his right, the old monk shuffled to the next door, which was shut and locked with a huge padlock. The old monk thrust the key into it and turned it with vigour. The padlock opened with a loud click. The Monsignore took it off the door latch, opened the door, and stepped into the room's mild darkness beyond it.

"*Un momento*," he said absentmindedly.

Rafe obliged and waited outside whilst the Monsignore negotiated with a stubborn kerosene lamp. "Come in," he beckoned to Rafe after he succeeded in lighting it.

The Monsignore shuffled to an ancient wooden chair by the small, solitary, grime-covered window and sat down. The chair protested noisily but held the Monsignore's frame. Rafe could see a wooden desk and stool but not much else at first. The lamp though lit was showing its age and its wear, the glass had obviously not been cleaned for some time. He did not shuffle like the Monsignore, but he more than less reeled across to the stool and sat down with a thump; the Cerasuolo had certainly done its work on Rafe just as much as for the Monsignore. He sat facing the old monk, and gradually his eyes adjusted enough for him to discern a single, solitary, glass-encased towering bookcase beside him, next to the window.

"When I see the future, Mr Rafe, I am not in it," said the old monk. "Not because I am dead, though I probably will be, but because..." He paused to glance at some far-off thing beyond the window, then lowered his tone and continued with slow feeling, clearly convinced of his words. "It is a world I no longer like. It is a world no longer content but filled instead with cynicism and expediency. Everything said and done is second-guessed by a pervading wall of negative thought and action. When I see these things, I turn to the books, Mr Rafe," he said, turning his head ever so slightly to the direction of the bookcase, before resuming. "They remind me of a different world, a world I sometimes wish I had lived in. I find them comforting, even though I rarely open them and when I do, I never read them enough to turn the page before closing them again. Just looking at them, holding them, feeling the weight of them, smelling them; all these things are enough, I tell you. Do you understand what I am saying, Mr Rafe? I think you surely do."

"Indeed, Monsignore, I do," replied Rafe. He noticed that the old monk was talking more freely now, probably due to the wine that was again fast disappearing from the third bottle. And just as he also realised that he was beginning to take a liking to the Monsignore the thought suddenly occurred to Rafe that to his near left, just within reach, was the Giordano Collection, or what was left of it, just as the Monsignore had said. The collective body of the seventeen volumes was becoming more distinct in the corner of his eye because they were all bound in the same pale cream pigskin hide. It also occurred to him that he was not in that much of a hurry to hold and inspect the books, as he would usually be, being quite content instead to continue sitting there and listening to the Monsignore being more and more philosophical the more they shared the wine. But he also knew time was dragging on, and he was so close.

"And when I see the future, Mr Rafe, I do not see these books either," continued the old monk, again motioning towards the bookcase. "You know of Eustathius of Thessalonica? I presume you do," he said. Without waiting for an answer, the old monk continued his story. "Or perhaps you do not. I will tell you about him. Eustathius was a twelfth-century archbishop of Thessalonica, and a scholar. He was also unique in that he had a love of books, Mr Rafe, and he detested their treatment by illiterate monks. He once wrote a story that one day he was visiting a monastery plagued by illiterates because he had been told that he would find there a certain volume of Gregory of Nazianzus known as a masterpiece of calligraphy, but when he arrived and asked to see it, he was told it was no longer there. Why was it no longer there, he asked, and where was it now?" the

Monsignore asked animatedly, before continuing without a pause, "and that was when the abbot of the monastery told him it had been sold for a handsome sum, adding "what use was it to us?" You may be surprised, Mr Rafe," chuckled the Monsignore, "but I would not be surprised at all if that idiot Prelate did the same thing with these books. *And that*," he stressed, leaning across to Rafe, "is something that I will not let happen."

The Monsignore relaxed again in his chair, which squeaked with his movement.

"You still have a Prelate, Monsignore?" asked Rafe.

"In name only. These days he acts as the legal owner of all that is left of our assets, such as this monastery, and little else.

"Now, tell me about this great library of yours, Mr Rafe," said the old monk, changing the subject after a pause. "How far away is it? Do you go there often?"

"No, not often, and that's just how I like it," replied Rafe. "A good day for me is when every decision made is mine. The Bibliotek has rules, many rules, and I am not known for always fitting within the narrow confines of their parameters. No, it is best that I keep my distance as much as possible, and besides, every day spent at The Bibliotek, which is far away up in the mountains of northern Norway, is a day spent not being productive."

"*Bene...* ah, sorry.... good", said the Monsignore.

Rafe continued, "The Central Repository is where the books are held when they are not in the hands of the conservators. It is a massive underground complex, a large portion of which had already been excavated, during the Great Holy War, as some sort of bunker network. But the needs of the Central Repository necessitated a great expansion, with much more digging. More and more levels underground, each one several thousand metres in four separate directions. Filled with bookshelves. And books. All in a secure and carefully controlled environment. Above ground there are the administration and other buildings associated with the workings of the library including the Display and Reading Rooms and the Conservation Department, the apartments and other facilities for the employees stationed at The Bibliotek, and the Academy – the university – and its student housing. The whole Bibliotek takes up quite a large area above ground."

"So, nobody is allowed to see the books?" asked the Monsignore.

"Well, the Central Repository is not open to the public, that is true. We restrict access, but depending on the book and the person, it is possible. On any given day, there will be any number of books, many books, being studied and read by academics and others in the above-ground Reading Rooms. The books are brought up from the Repository only when requested. Other books, however, the exceptionally rare, fragile, or just exceptional books — are not allowed to be moved. They stay in the Repository. Access may or may not be permitted, depending on the book, and any conservation work is performed on them *in situ*."

"But, Mr Rafe, does that mean that there are other books kept just for the purpose of... being kept?" asked the Monsignore.

"In a physical sense, yes," responded Rafe. He had been asked this question many times before. "But in another way, the way I prefer to think about it, the collective body of all those books, and the ones that nobody ever seeks access to, that we now protect and preserve serves to represent our very soul, in a very tangible way. Just contemplating the minds of humanity that toiled to produce the thoughts behind the words in those books gives me a connection to the essence of humankind that sustains my wellbeing and my hopes for our future. Is that not enough, Monsignore?"

"My dear Mr Rafe, you are not only a Finder, you are a... forgive me if I use the wrong word... a Philosophical Finder. And a worthy one at that. I wonder if that will apply to any of *these* books," said the Monsignore as he rose from his chair. Rafe watched him in silence as he shuffled to the door of the bookcase and opened it. It was only then that he noticed several chains inside the bookcase.

"This was a chained library?" asked Rafe.

"Yes, it was. But that was many, many years ago. You would not think so for a monastery would you, Mr Rafe? But it seems some of its visitors could not be trusted. Fortunately, their necessity had diminished by the time young Tanginelli arrived back from Venice with the Giordano books, so they remain as they were when first placed in this bookcase. I just have not been bothered to remove them."

With that, the Monsignore stood back from the bookcase, and with a small wave, said proudly "Well, there it is, Mr Rafe, the Giordano Collection. You may inspect." He watched Rafe remove some protective gloves from his satchel on the table and slowly and carefully stretch them over his fingers, first his right hand then his left.

Rafe now stood up and approached the bookcase, facing the books. There were a few scrappy looking volumes, mostly bibles, on the shelves as well as the Giordano Collection, but Rafe had eyes only for the latter. "One, two, three, four…" he quietly counted to seventeen. Looking at their spines he could see they were all single volumes. And he already knew which book he was going to examine first. Whilst sitting and listening to the Monsignore philosophise, in the corner of his eye it had literally stood out from the others, being of folio size. But that was not the primary reason for his interest, rather it was the hope, if not suspicion, that the book would prove to be the fabled and exceedingly rare 1619 first edition of Johann Remmelin's *Catoptrum Microcosmicum*, which just happened to be the only book from his study long ago of the Giordano Collection catalogue that Rafe could remember.

With great care, Rafe lifted the large book from its place in the bookcase and placed it flat on the table. He quickly looked at the Monsignore, who was smiling at him and faintly nodding his head in acknowledgment of Rafe's choice. He looked back at the book and carefully opened it. There it was — Giordano's unmistakable bookplate — on the left inside cover. And on the frontispiece, there was the title of the book — confirmation of Rafe's hope and suspicion.

Rafe looked back at the old monk, "Monsignore, you do realise the significance of this book — Johann Remmelin's *Microcosmic Mirror*?"

"I gathered it was special, but I am not a book scholar, Mr Rafe. Perhaps you can illuminate me."

"*Una momento*," said Rafe, a little tipsy. Taking a deep breath he said "I just want to check something first." With that, Rafe carefully opened the book further, searching for a particular page. He quickly found it. On the left, the page was filled with nine columns of Latin text, but on the right-hand page was an exquisitely detailed engraving of a young naked woman, surrounded by various detailed drawings of various internal organs and, in the lower left corner of the page a drawing of a snake protruding from a human skull holding a representation of the Tree of Knowledge in its mouth. And there they were, the famous flaps; the little pieces of cut-out page at various positions on the woman's body that were designed to be lifted back to reveal the respective part of the female anatomy. Remmelin was not the first to create such pictures in a book, but he had taken the concept to the 'next level' in producing a book of this size and its lifelike, detailed, drawings. Rafe lifted back the cut-out of the woman's lower abdomen, to reveal not a vagina but a representation of the Devil. This feature alone was the proof that Rafe was looking for. He could barely restrain himself from dancing a jig of excitement.

"Monsignore, you see the Devil here?"

"I see the Devil everywhere, Mr Rafe," the Monsignore quipped as he lent towards the book and peered towards where Rafe's finger was pointing.

"Quite," Rafe resumed. "But this particular Devil was only present in the 1619 first edition. It was only in later editions, after Remmelin's death in 1632, that the Devil was replaced by the original drawing of the woman's... ah... private parts. And that is what makes this volume significant. For a start, The Bibliotek does not have a first edition, it is exceedingly rare. Many different copies were made during the seventeenth century after his death and right up to the late 1700s, but to have Remmelin's original text is quite special, more so because this particular copy appears to have all flaps, intact, on three different and distinct pages."

"I agree the book is quite special," responded the Monsignore, resuming his seat, "just by looking at it, but I did not know just how special. But who was this Remmelin? Where was he from?"

"He was a doctor in Germany, originally in Ulm, but later in Augsburg where this book was printed. He was still practicing medicine in Augsburg when the Black Plague arrived in 1628," explained Rafe.

"So this book he made for students to study?"

"No, not really. The text is conversational, not formal, so it is unlikely he intended it to be a textbook. This was the Renaissance period, so the book is an expression of the metaphysical and the theological just as much as the anatomical, a blend that evidences the concept of Natural Philosophy, not science — that came much later — as the prevailing view of the world, where God and man were not divisible or separable. So this book, in revealing to its reader and viewer the secrets of the human anatomy, is enabling that person to know the mind of God. That was the accepted thinking when it was first published. It was therefore considered a book of empowerment."

"I understand that, and you say your library does not have it?"

"Not the first edition, no. We do have a digitised version but not an actual book."

"But how can you have one without the other?"

"That is a very good question. We *think* the digitised version is of the 1619 first edition, but we can't be sure. Coincidentally, it was created by Canada's Osler Library of the History of Medicine in 2019 and then placed in the public domain. Unfortunately, the book that was digitised was subsequently destroyed, along with many other irreplaceable books, about ten years ago in an attack by members of the Present Sect who turned out to be students at McGill University where the library was housed, but by then the digital copy had already been downloaded around the world so it survived," explained Rafe.

"You are very knowledgeable about this book, Mr Rafe. I am impressed," the Monsignore said, then paused. "You said 'coincidentally'?"

"Yes, the Osler Library and the Scuoloa Grande Library in Venice had each been given thousands of historical medical texts by eminent doctors. In the case of the Osler, the donation constituted nearly eight thousand books and in fact was the foundation of the library's creation. In Venice it was Davide Giordano and in Quebec it was Sir William Osler, and it just so happened that both those collections included an original first edition of Remmelin's *Catoptrum Microcosmicum*. I don't know how Giordano acquired his copy, but I do know Osler acquired his during his tenure as the Regius Professor of Medicine at Oxford University in the early twentieth century."

"It sounds like you have been searching for this book, Mr Rafe, ever since one was destroyed by the Sect."

"That I have, Monsignore, that I have been," nodded Rafe, without lifting his hypnotised eyes from the Remmelin.

After a few seconds of gently tapping his fingers on its cover, Rafe turned his attention to the other sixteen books. As he expected, they were also all first editions. Giordano collected nothing else. They included William Harvey's *De Motu Cordis* (1628), a ground-breaking study of the flow of blood in the human body, and several works by Andreas Vesalius who, unlike Leonardo di Vinci before him, was credited as one of the two founders of *scientific* human anatomy. The other founder of the move away from Natural

Philosophy was Bartolomeo Eustachi, and the collection now before Rafe included his greatest work, *Le Tabulae Anatomiche*, which wasn't published until 1714, at the personal expense of Pope Clement XI, some 140 years after Eustachi's death. Rafe also quickly identified Gabriele Fallopio's *Anatomy* (1561), the only work of his published in his lifetime, and Leonardo Fioravanti's *Del compendio de i secreti rationali* (1566).

By the time Rafe had finished photographing and recording all the details he could about the books in his data pad, the sun had long disappeared behind the valley wall. All that time the Monsignore had sat watching Rafe with a faint smile, only occasionally offering his thoughts on particular books as Rafe examined and processed each one in turn.

"So, Monsignore, just to be formal for a moment," said Rafe, "I need you to sign our standard form here on the data pad, attesting that you, Monsignore Matronola, are the custodian, if not the owner of the books I have listed and that you have agreed to donate them to The Bibliotek by means of handing them over to me, Rafe Nagy, today as an authorised representative of The Bibliotek."

"You are not paying for them, Mr Rafe?" asked the old monk meekly.

"I think you already know the answer to that, Monsignore," replied Rafe, as he watched the old monk sign his data pad. "It has always been our mandate that no direct consideration is to be paid for any books we procure. The Bibliotek has never hidden that fact, and as far as I am aware there have been no exceptions to that rule. Having said that it is often the case that indirect consideration is negotiated, it just depends on the circumstances. For example, it is our policy to offer to any donor of books we accept a Tax Certificate as to the agreed value of said books. This is because The Bibliotek is a non-profit entity and many countries, including Italy by the way, allow tax deductions for any donations a taxpayer makes. And I know for certain that the Italian tax authority — the Agenzia delle Entrate — always automatically accepts without query our Tax Certificates, as do the tax authorities of most other countries. But I daresay you are not a taxpayer, Monsignore, so any Tax Certificate I can give you is actually worthless."

"Ha! Indeed, Mr Rafe. I guess I will have to remain a true donor, and in keeping with that lofty status, you best stay here the night, Mr Rafe, as my guest. There is plenty of room."

"Thank you, Monsignore, that would be appreciated. It's been a long day."

Over dinner back in the kitchen — more salami, cheese and bread, some leftover wild board stew and potatoes, and some grappa the Monsignore had been saving for this very occasion — Rafe and the old monk discussed the logistics of relocating the books to The Bibliotek. Rafe had received a reply to his data entries — bring them all. Once Rafe got to Roccascalegna with them it would not be a problem to get them to Norway and the Central Repository, but the problem was getting them safely to Roccascalegna where Rafe had left the hovercar. Fortunately, the Monsignore still had his horse, which he took to the village once a week for his supplies. He did not ride the old nag, but used him to carry the load, and for this purpose had two huge leather saddle bags within which, apart from the folio sized Remmelin treasure, the books could be securely stored. Rafe would have to himself carry a carefully wrapped *Catoptrum Microcosmicum*. The Monsignore would come with him and use the opportunity to get more supplies. "I will be very sad to see the books go, Mr Rafe, but it is for the best," he admitted.

"But why now, Monsignore?" asked Rafe, "Why not years ago? Why have you waited so long to give these books to The Bibliotek?"

"Ah, that is a good question you ask, Mr Rafe, but to be frank I was hoping you would know by now the answer and not have to ask its question."

Rafe looked at him a little blankly, but mostly impassively. He was too tired to think quickly, tired by the enormity of this Find, and he wanted the old monk to tell him why it was now that Rafe had made it.

The Monsignore shook his head slightly, sadly. "For many years, Mr Rafe, I had thought ill of this grand idea of a world library, but not really a library as I used to know them. More a warehouse, a storage facility. Just some place to dump books. The idea that such a place could be intended to store all the world's books was too fantastic for me to accept. So presumptuous, so arrogant. So... *impossible.* So of course, I kept quiet about my little collection. I felt indignant that anyone else could conceive that the books would be better off elsewhere. Being here the books have a connection with a human being. Someone who appreciated them and knew what they represented. I felt that if they were instead in this world library of yours, they would sit on some shelf somewhere and entirely forgotten by all, just seventeen out of millions and, in effect, lost to the world."

The Monsignore paused, and looked down at the table, away from Rafe's gaze.

"What changed?" prompted Rafe.

"Well nothing, really. Not until today. Wait, that is not quite true. My own mortality came into the picture, Mr Rafe. The realisation that having these books here when I was either no longer able to look after them, to appreciate them, or just simply *el morto* — you know — *dead,* would place them in grave danger, if not from the Prelate, then simply from neglect. I am, after all, the only person who knows the books are here. And there is the irony. Here I was worrying that the books would be lost to the world if they went to your library, when in truth they had been lost to the world for many years. My dreaded thought that they would come to the attention of the Prelate after my death and that he would sell them suddenly became the best possible outcome, as bad as it would be. This is where we are at, courtesy of the Great Holy War. It has been many years since this place was a monastery in more than a name. Many, many years. The thought that I should relinquish the books before it was too late did not make me happy, indeed it makes me quite sad as I have said, and knowing your big library was perhaps the only place they should be sent to made me even sadder. Nevertheless, that is why I gave that woman a book to take to your library. It was a test; I knew she was lying to me. I do not know why she lied to me, but that did not matter. After she left here with my book, I knew I would never see it again, but that did not matter either. I waited for some months then put the word out, as your people are want to say, that there were some old and rare books still here. It was not hard. I have many family and friends spread around Italy and beyond. So, it is true that I was expecting a visitor, who turned out to be you, Mr Rafe. Then today, listening to you talk about books, and listening to you describe how each book is treated by your library and what happens to it, and seeing those pictures you showed me, it has all alleviated a lot of my concern. I feel... not quite *happy* you understand, Mr Rafe, about giving you the books, just... *decided.*"

"I understand," said Rafe, "I do understand."

"But tell me, Mr Rafe, will these books remain as the Giordano Collection?" asked the Monsignore.

"I'm sorry, Monsignore, but normal practice is to break up collections such as this one and incorporate the books into The Bibliotek's own collections."

"That is disappointing. Are there no exceptions?"

"Again, I am sorry, Monsignore, but there are no exceptions. You can hopefully appreciate that with so many collections coming into The Bibliotek, there would be no system to the Master Catalogue, just random collections, many of which would include books with absolutely no relationship to each other apart from the fact they came from the same source or owner. Once at The Bibliotek, books are placed into well-defined and relevant collections of our own, though we don't give them fancy names, just accurate descriptions. I am not sure which specific collection these books will be added to, but I can assure you that if they are not physically kept together, they will be joined by very similar books in subject or some other bibliophilic connection. And don't forget, the entry for each book in the Master Catalogue will naturally include the information that it was not only part of the Giordano Collection but, more importantly, one of its survivors of the destruction of Venice, and stayed in that collection which was donated to The Bibliotek by one Monsignore Matronola. This means that any person wishing to research the Giordano Collection will be able to find out from the Master Catalogue the name of each surviving book and where exactly in the Central Repository they are respectively kept."

"I see, Mr Rafe, yes that does make sense, thank you. And I must tell you, when I spread the word there were some old and rare books here, I got word back from a cousin that someone connected to the Present Sect had heard it as well. That scared me, Mr Rafe. Had I known they were here, in Abruzzo, I would not have been so careless."

"That's unfortunate, Monsignore, and unlucky. As far as we are aware, the Present Sect may be spread wide but thinly; it is not large in numbers by any means. Attacks are therefore probably random and hopefully unconnected, so in theory there is no area or place at greater risk than any other."

Sunday, 7ᵗʰ October 2204

The next morning Rafe, the Monsignore and the Monsignore's horse ambled into Roccascalegna and after helping Rafe unload the precious cargo from the saddle bags and into the hovercar, the old monk bade farewell to Rafe.

"We will not see each other again, Mr Rafe, but that does not matter. I know you will take care of my books. I bid you a safe journey to your library and good health. Goodbye." The Monsignore gripped Rafe's right hand with both of his hands and shook it firmly.

"Thank you, Monsignore, for everything. Take care," Rafe replied, and with that the Monsignore turned and led his horse to Bernardo's locanda. Rafe patted the packages of his treasure, then hovered out of Roccascalegna and onto Rome.

8:36pm, Tuesday, 9ᵗʰ October 2204

Rafe did not do it often with his Finds, but on this occasion he personally delivered to The Bibliotek the books he had procured from Monsignore Matronola. It was the first time in almost a year that he been there. And waiting at The Bibliotek's maglev station for him and the sealed crate Rafe had brought with him all the way from Italy which contained his latest, and perhaps most glorious Find, was Mads, who excitedly shook Rafe's hand as he alighted from the high-speed maglev train.

"You look good, Nags. It's been a while, old friend," said Mads. "We've been looking forward to this ever since we got your notes. So, tell me, which one of the seventeen books do we need to give the most attention to?"

"You're looking much older than me, as usual," replied Rafe. "Do you mean the book needing the most work done to it by the conservators or the most important book in the collection?"

"The latter."

"That would be this one," said Rafe as he extracted and carefully held up to Mads the *Catoptrum Microcosmicum* in both hands, still in its wrapping.

"We will make sure this one is processed and entered into the Master Catalogue before the others," a wide-eyed Mads said to Rafe and to his staff present. "And that means I can offer you my congratulations for procuring the one billionth book for the Central Repository," shaking Rafe's hand again.

"Oh, thanks. Does this mean I have to make a speech?"

"It does indeed mean that," Mads replied with a conspiratorial smile.

END OF CHAPTER TWO

Chapter Three

A Book is Judged by its Cover

"[A library] is an achievement in and of itself — one of the greatest of human achievements because it combines and justifies so many others. That its card catalogues and bibliographical machinery are useful no one doubts: modern scholarship would be impossible without them. That its housing and safekeeping arrangements are vital, essential, necessarily goes without saying. But what is more important in a library than anything else — than everything else — is the fact that it exists. For the existence of a library, the fact of its existence, is, in itself and of itself, an assertion — a proposition nailed like Luther's to the door of time."
Archibald MacLeish, "The Premise of Meaning", *The American Scholar*, Vol 41, No 3, 1972.

9:44am, Friday, 16th November 2204

Mads was stunned. "Who is this?" was all that he could muster at hearing a stranger's voice answer Thomas's neurophone.

There was a silent hesitation on the other end, then, "I'm sorry, but I need to authenticate this contact, as you initiated the call and your number is not showing on my screen. To whom am I speaking?" said the stranger in an officious tone.

"You are speaking with Bibliotekar Ingridson," said Mads in a reciprocal tone, "and I do not like having to repeat myself. What is your name?"

The person with Thomas's neurophone did not reply, but instead terminated the call. Mads immediately rang the number again but he knew it would be in vain. The phone was now off.

2:10pm

Mads rang Rafe. "Nags, where are you right now? Are you still at The Bibliotek?" he asked.

"Yes, but I am about to share a heliojet to Moscow, what's up?" replied Rafe.

"Moscow? Again? Is this the Vatican thing?"

"These things sometimes take time, you know that Mads. It *is* the Vatican thing, but I'm following a lead,"

"Fine. The less I know for now the better. Anyway, I'm just letting you know that Thomas has gone missing."

"What? When?" Rafe was incredulous.

"He was last seen in his office at the Academy two weeks ago. He has missed lectures and a catch-up meeting with me. I'm ringing around trying to find out if anyone has seen or heard from him since."

"You know Thomas, he has a habit of 'disappearing'. Perhaps he's on another bender," offered Rafe.

This was potentially true and Mads had had the same thought, but now he was certain this was not the cause. "No, not this time, this is different. Someone has his neurophone. It was on, but I couldn't get a fix on it before it was switched off," he told Rafe.

"That's a worry. Do you think something has happened to him? Like, bad, I mean," offered Rafe.

"I hope not Nags."

"Well, I can tell you I haven't seen him in a while, much longer than two weeks. And I haven't spoken to him at all in that time either. When was he supposed to have caught up with you?"

"I got a cryptic message the day before he was last seen. He'd just got back from Arcadia and all he said was he needed to talk to me."

"Arcadia? What was he doing there?"

"Just a routine test of the DRP."

"The what?"

"The Disaster Recovery Plan, surely you've heard of that?" said Mads, a little agitated. Sometimes Rafe's aloofness and penchant for ignoring the wider organisation of The Bibliotek got to him.

"I confess I haven't, Mads, but it sounds important. Maybe Thomas being missing has something to do with Arcadia?"

"I can't see how. He did return in one piece, I'm told."

"If I hear from him I'll let you know. Got to go, they're boarding my flight," Rafe said, ending the call.

Mads pondered what Rafe had said, trying to dismiss the suggestion that Thomas going missing may have something to do with his trip to Arcadia. But there was also the missing report. That was the thing that was out of place. Thomas had either not done a report at all before he went missing, or he did prepare a report and sent it but it was intercepted. Mads hit the intercom.

"Larkin, it has just occurred to me that I am waiting on a report from Councillor Metcalfe on the outcome of a DRP test he performed recently. Do you recall seeing it?" he asked.

"Ah... no Bibliotekar, there has been nothing come through for you from the Councillor for some time. Do you want me to follow it up with him?" replied Larkin.

"No, I will deal with it. Thank you."

"Oh, Deputy Bibliotekar Bradshaw is here and wants to know if you have a minute,"

"Yes, send him in."

Paul Bradshaw was a solidly-built 68-year old Oxford-educated Englishman. He had the body, the face and the demeanour of a bad pugilist. As Deputy Bibliotekar he was supposed to be Mads' 'right-hand man', but his increasing abrasiveness was precluding this from being both the perception and the reality. Mads had promoted him to his current position twelve years ago. That had been a mere two years after Mads had recruited him from the British Library not long after The Bibliotek had procured the *Diamond Sutra* and the rest of the Dunhuang Manuscripts from that institution. He had been impressed by Bradshaw during the negotiations and had gotten along very well with him. But in the last few years Bradshaw had become increasingly surly and demanding of Mads, to the point where Mads had to counsel him about some instances of stepping beyond the boundaries of his role, and not fulfilling other parts of it. Mads had the impression that Bradshaw had not fully accepted that Mads' response was justified, if at all, so in an honest attempt to placate him Mads transferred to him some responsibilities a year ago. But his negative behaviour had continued, which in turn fractured their relationship to the point where Mads had made up his mind not to appoint him Bibliotekar when he retired. Instead, Mads was now silently waiting for a transgression from Bradshaw that would precipitate his sacking. Tired of trying to work out what made his Deputy tick, his patience was at an end.

Mads had barely finished speaking with Larkin when Bradshaw opened the door to his office and strode inside. Neither was interested in any greeting, so Mads motioned to his Deputy to take a seat across from his desk. As he complied, Mads could feel the aura of hostile tension Bradshaw was becoming known at The Bibliotek for carrying around with him. "What is it, Paul?"

"This request from Thurldottir, when were you planning on discussing this with me before the Adcom meeting?" asked Bradshaw, a little brusquely. This annoyed Mads. Bradshaw was referring to the meeting on the following Monday of the Administrative Committee.

"Paul, I have simply been too busy to set aside time for a discussion with you about this, and to be honest I want to hear your thoughts in the open meeting. But one thing I was going to tell you before the meeting, which I may as well do now, is that there will be a sub-committee of Adcom established to deal with Thurldottir's request and I need you to lead it. Okay?"

"That's okay with me, of course. It's your prerogative, but I would have preferred that you and I discuss this whole thing in private."

Mads could tell what Bradshaw was alluding to, but he was not going to let him off the hook. He wanted to hear it from him, so he made no response other than look blankly at him.

"What I mean to say is that there have obviously been some discussions between you and Thurldottir that I have not been a party to," continued his Deputy.

"There has been a discussion, but what of it?" said Mads, sitting up straighter now and leaning slightly towards Bradshaw, his voice a little louder than before.

Bradshaw hesitated, then continued. "I think it is important that you and I present a united point of view to the Committee. And may I ask, why would you not lead the sub-committee?"

"That would not be appropriate," said Mads, more than a little exasperatingly and ignoring Bradshaw's 'united' comment, "I can't be seen as having control over or influencing this process. As I am the Bibliotekar, it would obviously be seen as a potential conflict of interest. And besides, you keep harping on about needing more responsibility. Well, now you'll get it, and then some... Is there anything else?"

"No," said Bradshaw irritably, as he got up from his chair and turned and walked towards the door.

"I look forward to your input at Monday's meeting, then," said Mads as Bradshaw left. He did not get a reply.

8:58am, Monday, 19th November 2204

The members of The Bibliotek's Administration Committee – Adcom – were all senior managers of The Bibliotek and the Academy. Its meetings were held in the Boardroom adjoining Mads' office. The Committee members were permitted to bring to the meetings their respective personal assistants, and these attendees sat in chairs surrounding the Board table, directly behind their respective manager. Accordingly, Nils Larkin always attended Adcom meetings with Mads. In practice, members of Adcom always brought their respective PA with them because Mads preferred questions raised in any meeting to be answered at that meeting and not deferred, and it was a standing rule that all neurophones had to be taken off and turned off. By contrast, data pads were compulsory. Unlike all the other PAs, however, Larkin sat at the large rectangular Board table next to Mads so he could enter the Minutes as the meeting progressed, even though all Adcom meetings were recorded. A full complement of attendees numbered twenty – ten members and their respective assistants, but such meetings were not crowded as the Board table was quite large yet nowhere near dominating the Boardroom. Mads always sat at the head of the table, which was made of thick oak, and Bradshaw always sat at the other end, facing him.

Mads was, however, at his desk, making final notes for the meeting, and waiting. Then Larkin spoke on the intercom.

"They are all in the Boardroom, Bibliotekar."

"Good, I will meet you in there."

Mads waited for two more minutes, then got up and walked to the opaque glass sliding door separating his office from the Boardroom. As it opened, he saw that everyone was seated, as well as Larkin. Some were talking to each other or with their assistants, including Finn Mackie, who had already turned on his holographic signing interpreter, which statically hovered above the table facing Finn on the opposite side. Mads walked straight to the chair at the head of the table, sat down, and spoke.

"Good morning all. Okay, I know you are all quite busy, so we'll get started. Standing Agenda Item One is the roundtable. Dom, you first." Mads was now looking at Dr Dominic Coenraad, the Dean of the Academy.

At 163 years of age and thus two years shy of retirement, 'Doc Dom', as he was known throughout The Bibliotek and the Academy, was the oldest member of Adcom. Fit, tall, lean, and sun-tanned, he didn't look a day older than 125, if that, and still placed well in The Bibliotek's annual cross country ski race. He also held the increasingly rare distinction of being at The Bibliotek since it first 'opened for business' in 2102, when he was appointed its first Deputy Bibliotekar. "Thanks, Mads," said Dominic. "The new intake has settled in well. No dramas there. Thomas Metcalfe has missed a few lectures, though. Mads, do you know where he is?"

"I'm looking into that. This wouldn't be the first time. I wouldn't worry about it. He'll show up. Tell him to come and see me when he does," Mads responded briskly. Without waiting for Dom to reply, Mads turned to Rani Sharma, The Bibliotek's Chief Information Officer. "You're next Rani."

Rani Sharma was relatively new to her role as CIO, but had been with The Bibliotek's I.T. Department for a number of years — Mads could not recall how many — and had slowly progressed up through the ranks. She was 65 years of age. "Thank you, Mads. The DRP test went well," she replied, concisely as usual.

"You may wish to explain to your colleagues what this test was, Rani," said Mads quietly.

"Oh yes, sorry," Rani responded, then looking around the table, said "This was a scheduled test of the backup mainframe on Arcadia as part of the Disaster Recovery Plan procedures. The Arcadia end was managed by Councillor Metcalfe on our behalf."

"Where's the report? I haven't seen it," asked Mads.

"I'll follow that up."

"That's not what I asked, I'm asking where is it?"

"Thomas was meant to be filing it. I assume he is just being a little late."

"You did perform The Bibliotek end of the test, didn't you? I mean, personally?"

"No Mads. The protocol is that if I am present at the time of a DRP alert, I initiate it. But I wanted to test the scenario where I was not at the Data Centre at the time. In that event, the most senior I.T. person is meant to initiate."

"And they did?"

"Yes."

"And Thomas, he was at Arcadia doing his end?"

"He was. And the download and transmission went well."

"But you never followed up with a report?"

"I sent Thomas my part of it."

"Whose responsibility is it to actually file the report?"

"That would be Thomas."

"I see," Mads said resignedly. This was typical of Sharma. She rarely showed any initiative and was almost militant in doing nothing but her actual prescribed role. It just would not have occurred to her that perhaps she should show interest in the fact that she had not been sent a copy of Thomas's report in a timely manner. But Mads had to be careful not to press the issue here and now because to everyone sitting at the table except him, it was just a missing administrative report. So he moved on.

"What about the new Master Catalogue software? Have you resolved all of the red flag issues?" he asked Rani.

"Not yet, Mads, but our progress is on track and within scheduled timeframes. I can run through these if you like."

"No, not today. Just send me an update summary please, and cc Paul."

Sharma turned around and whispered something to her assistant, and Mads immediately knew then that she had a summary already prepared, had been waiting for Mads to ask for it, had just asked her assistant to send it, and would now consider that an example of her outstanding efficiency. And her version of showing initiative. To Mads it was just the opposite, and irritating behaviour.

"Finn, you next," signed Mads. He was not very good at Bibliotek Sign Language, especially its grammar, and he knew it, but he tried. BSL reflected the multiculturalism of the large workforce permanently living in The Bibliotek precinct and was a product of the need for signers to move beyond the informal International Sign Language 'pidgin' language which had developed over many years at The Bibliotek and had become a cobbled mess of Norwegian, Danish, French, British, American, Australian and other sign languages. Finn had been instrumental in formalising BSL and its adoption by The Bibliotek's Deaf community. No-one doubted his claim it was better than relying on the informal ISL, not least the many Deaf and hearing Bibliotek employees who used it, including Finn's personal assistant, who had become quite proficient in it since joining Finn's team.

Finn had come to The Bibliotek from the National Library of Australia. He was a tall and lean 54-year old, with a bald head. Profoundly deaf at birth, he had eschewed any implants. Resolutely focused, he had transformed the Facilities Department since taking it over five years ago. Mads considered him one of his most dependable and efficient managers.

"I have substantially progressed the audit of the Secondary Repositories," said Finn through the holographic interpreter, 'who' was an exact representation of Finn himself, apart from the voice, which of course had to be estimated. The holographic had a major advantage over Finn's data pad; it could see Finn's actual signs and so was able to communicate the full meaning, tone, and emotion behind his words. Hearing people at The Bibliotek, albeit used to Finn's deafness, did not appreciate this difference. His colleagues on Adcom, however, did. Although it was always going to be novel for them seeing 'two' Finns at Adcom meetings, they knew they were getting the 'real' version of Finn via the holographic because it would focus on Finn's eyes and face just as much as on his hands and fingers and was thus able to communicate better than a data pad, which could only rely on the words Finn typed.

"Conclusions yet?" signed Mads.

"The situation is getting ridiculous Mads. We risk it getting out of hand and becoming too much of a financial drain. Of the four sites in Oslo, there is only an overall fourteen percent unfilled capacity. For the three in Frankfurt it is worse, at nine percent. The other three sites are averaging seventy-two percent filled capacity. Overall, we are looking at something like twelve percent capacity remaining. I think the final figures, especially the projections, will come as a shock to many, and hopefully that will include the Governing Council."

"Okay Finn," said Mads, interrupting several murmurings around the table, "we'll take this off-line for now. When you're comfortable that the numbers are looking final send me the data sets and make an appointment with Larkin to come and see me in the week before the next Adcom meeting and we'll run through the numbers and your draft recommendations. Allow for an hour."

"Shall do," signed Finn, looking back at Mads after watching the interpreter translate Mads' words to BSL. "But just to give you a heads up, the documentation will be extensive."

"That's okay, so long as it's accessible," replied Mads, who had every confidence it would be. Finn was very particular about his reports.

"When will the rest of us get the chance to have some input, or to at least review the data?" asked Bradshaw.

Mads fixed an impassive gaze onto Bradshaw. "Finn's devoted a lot of time and energy to this project, so the only person reviewing his data and projections will be me. Otherwise we risk there being too many cooks in the kitchen." Turning to the other members of Adcom, he continued. "But everyone will have the opportunity of commenting on the draft recommendations at our next meeting. Just to be clear, though, on this matter the Governing Council is expecting to hear my recommendations, not Adcom's. Now, Bernie," continued Mads, without waiting for Bradshaw, or anybody else, to respond to his answer, "where are you up to?" He was now looking across at Bernadette Collingwood, General Counsel for The Bibliotek. Mads knew she was at least 85 years old, but she had not a single grey hair. Collingwood had been with The Bibliotek for fourteen years after Mads had recruited her from a London-based multinational company directly into the role of General Counsel.

"Two things. First, I received a message from the office of the new President of Iceland that she wants to have a meeting with you in Reykjavik, at your earliest convenience."

"That sounds like a summons. Is this about the *Sagas*?" asked Mads. He was referring to the records of Icelandic history written in the 13th and 14th centuries, completely unknown at the time to most of the rest of the world, and collectively the most important relics of Icelandic heritage. Bernie had been engaged in sensitive and prolonged, but to date positive, negotiations with the Prime Minister of Iceland for their procurement by The Bibliotek, and now the new President appeared to be getting involved.

"I presume so," Bernie answered.

Mads waited a few seconds for her to expand on that, but to no avail. Looking directly now at Bernie, he spoke softly, with some resignation in his voice. "Okay, liaise with Larkin on my schedule and on our heliojet — it should be available. This will have to be a quick day trip. What's the other thing?"

"We've just received a formal notice from the Internal Revenue Service that they are about to commence an audit of our Tax Certificates for the last seven years."

"Great," said Mads, with feigned enthusiasm. "This is the U.S. I.R.S., right?"

"Yes," replied Bernie.

"Is this the Riley issue?" Mads asked, referring to an issue The Bibliotek had had four years ago with the Finder allocated to North America at that time, Reggie Riley. It was discovered shortly before he had been sacked that he had been facilitating excessive valuations of procurements in return for backhanders and other favours. The problem for The Bibliotek was that these valuations were for the purposes of the Tax Certificates it issued to owners of books it procured through the efforts of Riley. And if they were shown to be excessive, it amounted to tax fraud by those owners as they were used to lower their tax bills.

"Not specifically, Mads. The notice we just received is of a routine general audit of our Tax Certificate procedures, but that's not to say the Riley issue won't be looked at," said Bernie.

"Remind me of the total amount of tax we originally estimated as being involved?"

"We are talking one point eight billion U.S. dollars, Mads, give or take a few million," interrupted Michael Huntington, The Bibliotek's Chief Financial Officer.

Bernie shot him a quick glare.

"Bernie?" asked Mads.

"We are *not* talking about 1.8 billion dollars in tax exposure," she said firmly and grimly.

"But isn't that the amount you calculated as being the tax avoided under Riley's dodgy Tax Certificates?" asked Mads.

"That's right, Mads," Huntington said, interrupting again.

"But it wasn't avoided *by us*," said Bernie. "We don't pay tax, so we don't have any tax to avoid."

"It doesn't matter," responded Huntington. "We are exposed to fines for the amount of tax avoided because *our* dodgy Tax Certificates were used for a tax avoidance purpose. That puts us in the frame."

Mads had heard enough. "Let's stop right there. We risk our colleagues falling asleep from all this tax talk."

"Many a true word spoken in jest," commented Dom, eliciting some laughter from his colleagues.

Turning to Bernie, Mads asked "We disclosed all the problem valuations and the amounts involved just after we finished our internal investigation, didn't we?"

"Yes, Mads, I wrote the letter to the I.R.S. myself," Bernie replied.

"Then as far as I am concerned there is no issue here," Mads ruled. "We will adopt our standard full co-operation stance when the audit commences," he continued, looking at Bernie then Huntington, "and for that purpose, Bernie, please extract from your files the current agreement we have with the I.R.S. concerning our Tax Certificates."

"Will do," replied Bernie.

"Now, let's move on," said Mads. He could see Huntington shaking his head in disagreement but ignored him. He had seen it before and it was a typical reaction of the 72-year old CFO – always hanging onto the worst possible fiscal scenario. Despite coming from California ten years beforehand to join The Bibliotek, Mads had little confidence in his knowledge of U.S. tax rules.

"Nikka?" Mads was now looking at Nikka Johannson, Head of Security at The Bibliotek and the only native Norwegian on Adcom.

"Nothing from me," she replied, with barely any emotive change to her taut face.

"Okay. Kaitlin? Alan?" Mads looked at, in turn, Kaitlin Drummond and Alan Murray, General Manager of Admin & Support Services. Neither had any updates to give. Mads now looked at Bradshaw at the opposite end of the table, facing Mads.

"What about you, Paul. Anything to update us on?"

"No, nothing today."

That prompted Mads to ask all the personal assistants, except Larkin, to leave the remainder of the meeting. He occasionally did this when an agenda item was particularly sensitive. After the last assistant had left the room and the door closed, Mads began.

"As you will have seen from the paper I circulated, the Committee has received a formal request from the Governing Council to undertake an important study. It seems there is a concern about The Bibliotek's capacity. You all know its terms, but to summarise them, we've been given six months to determine one broad question: should the Governing Council give consideration to relocating the Central Repository, or some part of it?"

"Mads," said Finn, "if you'll permit me to say upfront, we're nowhere near capacity. What's the urgency? Why now? The rate of new Finds has been on a downward trend for years. Plus, the rate of increase of new additions has slowed."

"That is true, Finn," replied Mads, who could tell that most of the other Committee members agreed with him and had probably already discussed the issue amongst themselves, "and as you know our capacity reports have consistently signalled manageable capacity. But, even though the rate of increase in new additions has slowed, it is still increasing, and given our current capacity level this is what has given rise to the concern, coupled with the understandable desire that The Bibliotek put in place appropriate planning and preparation for an eventuality that definitely will arise at some point in time. After all, The Bibliotek wasn't built in a day." Mads quickly glanced around his colleagues, but none of them got the reference.

Finn looked at Mads. "That is all good and true," he said, "but has anyone challenged our projection that the Central Repository will not reach one hundred per cent capacity for another fifty-six years? Remember..." added Finn as he paused and glanced around the table, "... this is a projection for which we gave a margin for error of less than five per cent."

"No-one has challenged the projections," responded Mads, "but, I repeat, this is a formal request from the Governing Council, and as a working committee of the Council we are meant to basically do as we are told to do. It is not within our remit to pick and choose our tasks and nor is it our role to question the validity of what we have been told to do."

"I understand all that, Mads," persisted Finn, "as I am sure we all do," he said, glancing around the table again but this time with an added wave of his arm. "But the point I am trying to get to is that we don't need six months to consider the essential question you paraphrased from the terms of reference. In my view, we can answer it now, and the answer is that "Neither The Bibliotek, nor the Central Repository or some part of it, should be relocated.""

Mads waited for the others to finish their grunts of agreement with what Finn had just said. "I wish it was so simple, but it isn't. The terms of reference have to my mind been drafted with enough care so as to preclude the mere giving of such an opinion. At a minimum, our response needs to be analytically based for it to be accepted by the Council as fulfilling the terms of reference, and the analytics need to include detailed direct, indirect, downstream, and opportunity costings based on scenario-based projections, with assumptions that can be tested and validated. In other words, the full suite of economic study outcomes," Mads responded firmly. He paused for two seconds before continuing. "I can see already Finn that you won't be volunteering to be part of the team - which I'll call the Relocation Study Group - to perform the task as it's been set."

"Correct. Sorry, but I think it's a huge waste of time, money, and energy," signed Finn with finality, signalled by folding his arms when he finished.

"Nevertheless Finn, I would like you to be part of the Group for the very reason you think the whole idea is premature. Write a dissenting report if necessary, should the Group come to the conclusion that preparations for a partial or full relocation should begin, but I need someone to challenge any findings supporting such an outcome *during* the investigation, not as a response."

"That makes sense, Mads, I'll give you that, but I suspect I am being set up here to fail. That said, I will agree to your request."

"Thank you, Numbers Man," signed Mads, ignoring the criticism, ending with Finn's sign-name which was a typing motion with his left fingers horizontal against the vertical open palm of his right hand. This was a reference to Finn being a numbers man and it was apt.

"Mads," said Nikka, breaking her apparent disinterest, "if I may be permitted to make an observation before we go any further with this request from the Council, the terms of reference do not mention the growing threat posed by the Present Sect..."

"Indeed they do not," interjected Mads.

"But what I want to know," continued Nikka, "as I suspect others here present might also, is whether that threat is the real reason we've been asked to consider relocating the Central Repository."

Again, Mads waited until the murmuring died down before responding. He knew he had to choose his words carefully, because in recent months he had begun to feel as if someone was feeding back to Thurldottir things that passed in Adcom meetings beyond the Minutes, which, as protocol dictated, were rather concise. "I want to address several aspects of what you have just said, Nikka, so please hear me out. First, let's be clear about what we've been asked to do, and that is *not* to consider relocating the Central Repository — that is something only the Governing Council can decide and you can be sure that before such a decision is in fact made the Foundation will want to have its say. What we have been asked to do is evaluate whether or not such a decision should be considered, and the timing of any move. There is a subtle difference which I hope you can appreciate. To demonstrate, we could recommend today that the Central Repository be relocated 120 years from now. The value of such a recommendation is, however, minimal, so we have to work backwards from there to get to a more helpful and hopefully more precise recommendation. Secondly, in lieu of making a recommendation that the Central Repository should be relocated after or by some stated period of time, we have been tasked with considering whether or not *some part* of it should be relocated. Thirdly, *that* aspect of our task implies that we may consider that a particular part or parts of the Central Repository should be relocated, but not other parts. As for the threat the Present Sect poses for The Bibliotek, the terms of reference are silent on that point, as you have noted, but it is my view that we, as in this Committee, would be remiss in our task if whatever recommendations we make do not sufficiently take such a threat into account, in addition to any other factors we consider relevant. By doing that we will be providing the Council with the means to make an *informed* decision. I choose my words carefully because it is far from certain what is factually represented by the Present Sect threat either now or in the potential future. I know, for example, that this Committee is not unanimous in its attitude towards that question, and I also like to remind myself, and others when I get the chance, that The Bibliotek came into being and was constructed at this site solely due to a similar but much more prevailing threat than what I personally consider the Present Sect to represent. But I want to be absolutely clear about this: in performing the task that we've been given, we will need to quantify that threat, and we will need to do so in no uncertain terms."

Mads stopped speaking but did not move. He looked at Nikka but she said nothing. Then he slowly looked around the table. That and the silence that arose told him that he had succeeded in making his point clear. In drafting the terms of reference, the Governing Council had been very cautious not to raise alarm bells and that is why it focused on The Bibliotek's capacity as the concern. It wasn't necessary for Mads to divulge his private conversation with Thurldottir and the fact that she had specifically raised the perceived threat of the Present Sect, and he chose not to. He had just delivered the message himself, and that was all that mattered. And now there was no doubt; he had just released the elephant into the room.

Mads continued to wait for someone to speak. After a few seconds, Dom spoke. "Mads, I think an assessment of the threat to The Bibliotek represented by the Present Sect is timely and were it not for the Council's request I would perhaps have raised it myself as something that needs to happen sooner rather than later, in my opinion."

In response to that suggestion several committee members nodded their heads in agreement, except Nikka who, Mads noticed, sat silently and impassively with her usual taut and expressionless face. He had only been a little surprised that, unlike Paul Bradshaw, she had not sought to discuss the issue with him before the meeting.

Dom continued. "I accept that we need to positively respond to the Council's request, but I am wondering if the issue of the threat can be kept separate from the issue of capacity. What I mean to say is that any threat assessment should not be tainted by having it done as part of a broader issue. It needs to happen as a 'standalone', for want of a better term. I also want to suggest that an independent party be commissioned to examine each issue. Someone or some organisation outside The Bibliotek, with perhaps a member of this committee acting as liaison."

Again, Mads waited. There was more nodding of some heads but no-one else spoke up. It looked to Mads as if the two managers most impacted by Dom's suggestions, Nikka and Finn, were each in two minds as to whether to comment.

Mads then responded. "I think you are absolutely right, Dom. Whoever is tasked to do an assessment of the Present Sect threat to The Bibliotek should not do so in the context of whether the threat is sufficient to warrant considering moving the Central Repository, or some part of it, to, presumably, a safer place, if indeed there is one to be had. The assessment should stand on its own. The appropriate response to such an assessment is, in theory, an entirely different matter. But there are several reasons why I think the task needs to be done in-house and not commissioned to a third party. My primary concern here is the sensitivity of the issue. We don't want the mere fact an assessment is being performed to become publicly known, or even known outside of this Committee for that matter. We have too many ongoing negotiations with various libraries still in progress and, I think Bernie will agree with me on this, the last thing we need for those to progress is to have a perception arise that we have a concern about our ability to provide the safest repository for the holdings of those libraries." By now, Bernie was nodding. "And I don't want the situation to arise," Mads continued, "where any staff member of The Bibliotek or the Academy and its students is given cause to be concerned there is a tangible threat. Another reason we need to keep this in-house is that to be comprehensive, a study of the threat, if it exists, needs to include an assessment of The Bibliotek's responsiveness and defences, and I would be very uncomfortable letting any outsiders privy to such information, no matter how well they could be trusted with it. And for that very reason I think that Nikka should be on the sub-committee and take the lead on that part of its work."

"Okay Mads. Points well taken," said Dom.

Nikka now looked up at Mads from the table. She had been staring at it for a while and now gave a small nod to Mads. It was obvious she was expecting to go on the sub-committee.

Dom continued. "But what about the capacity issue? Don't you think it would be more appropriate for that at least to be done at arm's length to The Bibliotek?"

"As a matter of principle, I agree with you, Dom. But on this occasion, again I am averse to commissioning it to someone outside this Committee. You know, we or anybody else can talk about numbers and what they mean in terms of trends and projections *ad nauseum*, but we and nobody else have been working with these numbers for many decades and we have made all our planning decisions to date based on those numbers, and, correct me if I am wrong, not once have we found ourselves short of resources or space. Sure, there is a risk of inherent bias but that assumes a pre-existing negative stance to the essential question – a question that has not previously been raised within The Bibliotek and certainly not outside of it. Any bias I think would be self-evident from our report and treated accordingly. I really don't want us to be second guessing ourselves here. And there's one more point I need to make. We do not want the Foundation asking difficult questions at the point in time when we don't have any answers, and *that* risk will arise if we commission the capacity assessment to an external party."

"Again, I see your points, Mads. What about you, Paul, what do you think?" asked Dom of Bradshaw.

"I think we should do whatever Bibliotekar Ingridson says we should do. We've discussed this," he replied.

Mads let Bradshaw's comment go. Now was neither the time nor the place to take issue with his tone and choice of passive-aggressive words. "Now", he said, looking around the table, "Does anyone else have something to say before we vote on the establishment of a sub-committee — the Relocation Study Group?"

"Yes, Mads," said Bernie, "You mentioned the negotiations we are currently engaged in with various libraries. Being a party to all of them I must agree that they would be at risk were it to become known by them that we are assessing the threat represented by the Present Sect. But the very processing of that risk assessment will involve some level of enquiries being directed to the countries where those libraries reside, so how can we effectively barricade or insulate our negotiations from those questions or enquiries?"

"You raise a good point, Bernie," replied Mads. "But let me ask you this," continued Mads, "to date, have you mentioned the Present Sect in any of your negotiations?"

"Yes, we have. In all of them."

"And I am guessing you are using the Present Sect as a bargaining chip?" asked Mads, and as Bernie was about to answer, continued, "don't get me wrong, it is only prudent you do, but answer me this: would that bargaining chip be of greater value were you able to be more confident of what that threat actually represented to any given party you are negotiating with?"

"Why, yes, of course, but..."

"But," interrupted Mads, "how are you going to be able to assess the threat for any given library without them getting to know about it. That is your next question, yes?"

"Yes."

"You don't have to."

"I'm sorry,..."

"You don't have to be secretive, Bernie. Instead, just ask them to give you *their* assessment," offered Mads.

"I see your point, but to be honest, the fact the negotiations are dragging on is partly due to these libraries being of the view they are not at risk from the Present Sect, so any answer they give will reflect that view."

"Indeed," said Mads, "But in asking the question for the purposes of the negotiations you place the subject on that table alone, and that's when you then ask the questions you need answered to validate their assessment, thereby allowing you to place a value on it. Basically, any challenge you make about where they stand with the Present Sect threat will be seen by them as a normal part of your negotiations. Am I wrong?"

"No, Mads," admitted Bernie, "you are entirely correct." She could now see other Committee members looking at her, slightly smiling, except for Nikka, who had resumed looking at the table, expressionless. Mads had just indirectly told Bernie how she should do her job, and she had no come-back. But something else was troubling her.

"There is another issue that concerns me, Mads," she said.

"Yes?"

"I think we may need to consider if there are any legal issues involved in a relocation to any degree. I'm referring to any undertakings given or understandings reached with any procurements," Bernie explained.

"I agree, which is why I think you should be on the sub-committee," Mads replied, to which Bernie gave a slight nod.

"Right then, any other comments or questions?" asked Mads of the Committee.

"Yes, Mads," said Finn. "At the risk of stating the obvious, we appear to be conducting another capacity issue; one for the Secondary Repositories, which is well-advanced, and another for the Central Repository. Shouldn't they each take into account the other, if not merged?"

"That's a fair question. Indeed, I raised it with Chair Thurldottir," replied Mads. "The short answer is no; the two projects are to be kept completely separate from each other. We must not taint the conclusions on one with the recommendations of the other, and vice-versa. More than that, the Secondary Repositories audit is not just about capacity, it's potentially about much more than that. There's a different agenda going on here. Is that understood by all?" Mads asked, looking around the table and seeing the nods.

"Well then, if there are no more questions, the motion is therefore that the Committee agrees to form a sub-committee to be named the Relocation Study Group and comprising solely of members of Adcom to undertake the task requested by the Governing Council, with secrecy being paramount. All those in favour make it known in the usual fashion," said Mads formally.

All ten members of Adcom raised their left hands.

"Motion carried," Mads said quickly, motioning to Larkin, who nodded.

"The next thing that needs to be minuted are the members of the Study Group. Finn, Nikka, and Bernie have all agreed to join," said Mads motioning to Larkin, who nodded. "And leading the Group will be Paul." At the mention of his name Bradshaw barely changed his expression and continued to stare at Mads. "Needless to say, the work will require a fair degree of time commitment, and of course the utmost discretion. I also need to make it clear that the RSG is a sub-committee of Adcom and thus it will be Adcom reporting back to the Governing Council."

Mads left that to sink in for a few seconds before he continued. "Are there any other matters anyone would like to raise?"

"Timing," said Bradshaw. "What's our deadline on this?"

"Yes, thank you for reminding me, Paul. I'd like to see interim findings discussed at our next meeting, in two months' time, with the final recommendations tabled at the following meeting. So that's four months all up."

"That's a bit tight, Bibliotekar," said Bradshaw. "I thought we were given six months."

"I agree, Mads. I've still got a lot of work to do on the Secondary Repositories audit," said Finn.

"I appreciate the deadline might be tight, especially for you, Finn, but I do believe it is doable and I have assured Chair Thurldottir it will be done *within* the time frame set by the Governing Council," responded Mads. "But keep me appraised, Finn, if at any stage you feel my confidence is misplaced, okay?"

Finn nodded without looking at Mads.

"Nothing else? Good, now before we wrap this up I just want to reiterate the absolute need for confidentiality. That applies to everyone here, not just the study group. We simply cannot afford to have a rumour mill start at The Bibliotek that we are moving, or that we are thinking about moving, or even that we are working out whether we need to start thinking about a move. I do not need to explain why this is a sensitive issue. I expect everyone to be on top of this at their respective departments. If at any time a question is asked the answer is to be consistent and it is to be this: that we are merely acting on one of the recommendations of the First Review that we improve our methodology for capacity forecasting. That is it. Period. If anyone cares to look at the Final Report of the First Review, they will find that very recommendation. Until now we just haven't done anything serious about it. As for the security component of the RSG's work, that can be sold as being merely a precaution against the threat of the Present Sect, which it actually is. But again, we do not need to broadcast this work and we shouldn't. If any of you hears or becomes aware of any talk of the RSG's work that does not conform to the script I have just outlined, I expect you to notify me immediately." Mads paused for a few seconds and looked around the table. "Any questions?"

There were none.

"Right, then. Thank you all, let's get back to work."

As everyone rose to leave, Mads asked Nikka to stay behind for a quick chat.

"I'm surprised you didn't come to see me before the meeting," said Mads after everyone else had left.

"If I had known the request would involve a threat assessment of the Present Sect, I perhaps would have," she replied. "Now I feel as if I am being told what my job is and how to do it."

"I can appreciate that sentiment, Nikka, so let me ask you this: would I be reasonable in saying that the absence of any alert from you about the Present Sect means your ongoing threat assessment simply hasn't identified a material threat to date?"

"Correct."

"Then isn't the problem just one of communication? And why didn't you give your assessment in the meeting?"

"I almost did, Mads. But do you know what the biggest problem is on my plate?"

"Tell me."

"It's complacency. I am Head of Security for a collection of books. Not gold, not money, not technology, not whatever, just books, damn books. And I have a team of bored goons who think like that, all day, every day. None of them can comprehend actually having to defend the Central Repository, or its staff, for that matter."

"Can I make a suggestion?"

"Please do."

"You occasionally test security protocols with dummy threats, yes?"

"Yes I do."

"Ever fired somebody as a result?"

"No, I haven't. We've had a few instances of laxness, but nothing to warrant a dismissal."

"I suggest you run a test, very soon, of a hypothetical situation of a person attempting to smuggle into the Central Repository the ingredients of a bomb. Any problem with detection resolve it with a dismissal. Instantly, no ifs, no buts."

"That will send a message, but it may backfire Mads."

"I realise that, but for now it will suffice. And I want to make another suggestion."

"Yes?"

"As part of your threat assessment for the Study Group I want you to undertake a background and foreground check of every member of your team."

Nikka looked at Mads for a few seconds before replying. "Reason being?"

"There is a difference between complacency and deliberate complacency."

"But Mads, I've never had cause to make that distinction. Is there something I should know about?"

"Perhaps, but I don't want to taint an objective check of your team by discussing it just yet."

"Can you tell me at least what risk areas I am looking for?"

"Find out if anyone in your team is potentially at risk of being compromised, or worse, has already been compromised. And do it quietly Nikka. This is just between you and me for now."

"As you wish," replied Nikka.

Mads knew he was taking a risk with his request, but he had an inkling that the person who had threatened Thomas and who had answered his neurophone was the same individual and that the person had a security background, and that meant, if true, the person was on Nikka's team.

3:32pm

They were used to seeing Mads in the Conservation Department, despite his schedule and the many other parts of his work domain as the Second Bibliotekar. This was where his passion for books had been nourished before, during, and especially the productive years after his graduation from the Academy. And where he had made the decision that he would remain with The Bibliotek for the rest of his life.

He never needed an excuse to visit, but today he had one. Mads wanted to see the progress of work on Rafe's latest find, the Giordano Collection. And of course, he also wanted to see Violetta, the Chief Conservator, with whom he had been in a relationship for several months. He made his way to the on-boarding room where the collection was being processed, and he knew that once there, someone would alert Violetta that the Bibliotekar was present. He did not have to wait long. Her subtle yet distinctive fragrance always preceded her arrival, like a herald it signalled her impending presence. It was singularly unique in its effect. Mads was silent on the thought but he suspected it was deliberate, and it never failed to hit him with a passionate jolt. To Mads it felt like their time together, when they managed to be alone, was one long private conversation between two intimates. She quickly grasped anything he said with interest and understanding, and that included whatever or whoever was challenging him. She never, however, sought to offer advice, and Mads gathered this was because she felt averse to intruding. He felt their relationship was founded on a tacit understanding that they enjoyed each other's company. Nothing more, nothing less. Upon that foundation, Mads felt that there was mutual trust and respect. And love? Perhaps, perhaps not; it was hard for Mads to say. He never felt compelled to express it, and he never yearned to hear it from Violetta. He did, however, feel that it was shown between each other at times, especially in the heat of passion.

"Hello, Mads. Nice to see you." Violetta's voice when talking alone to Mads dripped with seductive promise, even with the most innocent of words.

"Hello Violetta, likewise. I was wondering how it was going with Rafe's great Find."

"Very well. We processed the Remmelin *Catoptrum Microcosmicum* first, as you requested, and we are a fair way through the rest. They are all in exceptionally good condition I must say. Our repair work has been surprisingly minimal and so far non-interventionist. I can give you a more detailed report if you wish, *in private.*" Those last two words Violetta spoke *sotto voce* at the same time as imperceptibly gently stroking once his exposed wrist with the tip of her index finger, and it had its desired effect.

"I look forward to it," responded Mads, a little less business-like than normal, "The usual time?"

"See you then, Mads. I have to go now."

With that, Violetta turned and was gone, leaving Mads with just the whirling lash of her departing fragrance. He lingered until it dispelled, then left the room and the Department and returned to his office, a happy man.

9:34pm, Wednesday, 21ˢᵗ November 2204

Paul Bradshaw was ushered into a large, almost cavernous, natural-light-filled room that stretched all the way to the floor-to-ceiling windows. There was no meeting table, only a stretch-canvas lounge on one side of the room and near the windows a large glass and steel desk behind which sat Thurldottir. This was minimalism to the extreme.

"Welcome, Deputy Bibliotekar. Please have a seat," whispered Thurldottir, without rising but motioning to one of the two chairs placed in front of her desk.

"Good evening, Chair Thurldottir," replied Bradshaw, slightly nervously. He had met Thurldottir before, but she had not previously taken much notice of him, to the point where she was formally introduced to him twice before his name and who he was stuck. This was the first time he had been to her private suite at The Bibliotek, and it was also the first time they would have anything more than a perfunctory conversation.

"Councillor Carlson tells me he had an interesting chat with you during the recent Bibliotek celebration dinner," said Thurldottir.

"Yes, we did. The Councillor provided a very good ear," replied Bradshaw, still nervous. He had been warned by Carlson, who arranged for this meeting, to expect blunt and forthright questions from Thurldottir and that he was best advised to answer them without hesitation and with openness. He was not to try and second guess Thurldottir with giving the answer he thought the Chair wanted to receive.

"Indeed," answered Thurldottir with a slight hint of warmth in her ice-cold voice. "Councillor Carlson passed on to me some of your concerns, in confidence, of course. The ones that related to the Bibliotekar and the ones relating to your role as Deputy Bibliotekar. These are issues that ultimately are of interest, if not concern, to me as Chair of the Governing Council of The Bibliotek," rasped Thurldottir, raising the tone of her voice. "So I thought it best that you and I have a little, private, discussion."

"Thank you, Chair Thurldottir," offered Bradshaw.

"Oh, don't thank me, Deputy Bibliotekar, I haven't done anything in your favour. Yet, that is. And having a conversation with me does not always produce a favourable outcome," Thurldottir said, now glaring at Bradshaw. She was beginning to agree with Carlson's assessment of him. "How long have you been Deputy Bibliotekar?"

"Twelve years."

"And you feel that you have waited long enough to be made Bibliotekar?"

"Yes. I. Do."

"And you are up to the role?"

"I am."

"I see, but if Mads Ingridson is doing a good job as the Second Bibliotekar, what grounds do you have for being so impatient in being the Third?"

"I don't believe that Ingridson *is* doing a good job. He has been Bibliotekar for more than half a century. He has lost interest in a lot of management issues and he is spending more and more time elsewhere doing other things, such as at the Academy. He does not seem to have any strategic direction for The Bibliotek, and he does not engage with his senior management team as often as is normally required."

"That assessment is merely your opinion, isn't it?"

"That assessment is mine, but I believe it is shared."

"Who with?"

"I,... ah,... I'd rather not say, for now."

"I see," replied Thurldottir, peering at him. "He placed you in charge of the Adcom sub-committee looking at the relocation proposal, did he not?"

"Yes, he did, despite my suggestion he should lead it. To me it is just another example of him losing interest in the job required of the Bibliotekar."

"Do you think Ingridson would have suggested looking at Arcadia as a potential new site for The Bibliotek if he hadn't delegated the leadership of the relocation proposal?"

"No, not at all."

"So then, we are fortunate, are we not, that with you in the role, that very suggestion to look at Arcadia will be made at the appropriate time?"

"Since you put it in those terms, yes, I would agree with that. But it was Councillor Carlson's suggestion. I just listened to him and saw the merit of it."

"And you will put it into action?"

"Yes."

"You do understand why we believe Arcadia to be a location worth looking at if we are to seriously consider relocating the bulk of the Central Repository, don't you?"

"I gathered from Councillor Carlson it is considered the ultimate safe site."

"Correct. If it's not the Present Sect we need to worry about it will be something else, even another global war. To us on the Governing Council it is obvious that we cannot rely on Ingridson to take the initiative and act to preserve the security and the capacity of The Bibliotek. We therefore need this relocation proposal to go ahead, and it should be Arcadia that becomes the new site. Ingridson will of course fight it because, as you say, he lacks strategic direction. This then, is your opportunity to show us what you are capable of. That you are indeed ready to take on the role of Bibliotekar. Do well and you will have our gratitude and, of course, our support. Do we have an understanding, Deputy Bibliotekar?"

"Yes, Chair Thurldottir, I believe we do."

"Good. Now, just to be clear, Councillor Carlson is your go-to person on the Governing Council, is that understood? He speaks for me."

"I understand, perfectly."

"Excellent. Just keep the Councillor in the loop on the progress of the relocation project if you will, as often as you can. He will guide you on what needs to happen and when it needs to happen."

"That I will, Chair Thurldottir."

"*Make* it happen, Mr Bradshaw, would be my advice," ended Thurldottir with the faintest of a smile threatening to crack her face. "There's one more thing. You haven't been attending many formal functions or get-togethers. Why is that?"

"I don't mix well and prefer to focus on my job. I leave all the PR stuff to Ingridson."

"That needs to change, Deputy Bibliotekar, right now. There are members of the Governing Council who do not know you well, if at all. You need to start fostering relationships with these people. Remember, it is their vote that will see you made Bibliotekar in the event Ingridson is removed. There is a limit to my influence. I can understand your reluctance to mingle and press the flesh, but it is something you need to do."

"Yes, Chair Thurldottir, I will."

"Good. I won't keep you any longer. That is all."

After Bradshaw was escorted out of her suite, Thurldottir rang Carlson. He had been waiting for her call.

"The man is a fool," opened Thurldottir. "He's perfect to take over from Ingridson."

"I told you so."

"That you did, and now I've confirmed it. When the time comes, we'll just need to make sure he is fully aware of how he got the job. As long as he understands *that*, I do believe we will finally have someone we can trust at the top."

"I think he will respond very well to inducements, that is definitely what he is seeking."

"Aggrandisement?"

"Exactly."

"Then he is more the fool than I thought. And the easier for us. Too many threats is a lot riskier."

"I concur."

"Find out what he really likes, apart from money, and get him a sample of the best. We'll start that off as a gift, with one of our cards, you know, 'of appreciation and anticipation'."

"Consider it done. I've already got some ideas," replied Carlson. "I'm told he fancies himself as a bit of a whisky connoisseur."

"Good. Let me know how it goes. It will be interesting to see how he handles it. I still wonder though if he really does understand the need for the utmost discretion on his part as much as on ours."

"Oh, I think he does. I am in no doubt he has very quickly realised we are his best chance to get to the head of the table in the shortest amount of time. He is highly motivated."

"Just the same, get our friend in Security to keep an eye on him."

"Consider that done as well," replied Carlson.

"As you wish," Thurldottir said slowly in a voice dripping with menace, before terminating the call.

END OF CHAPTER THREE

Chapter Four

Shadows Form

"If your library is not "unsafe", it probably isn't doing its job."
John N Berry III, Editor-in-Chief, *Library Journal*, October 1999

3:38pm, Saturday, 8th December 2204

Rafe was nearing his destination – a bed and breakfast next to Loch Linnhe near Glencoe in the Scottish Highlands. He was following up on a lead he had been given by its owner. He was only mildly surprised by the slightly cryptic email he had received three weeks prior, as he knew there were many estates tucked away in the surrounding valleys and villages, untouched and largely untroubled by decades of time and troubles elsewhere, all with their own libraries of old and sometimes rare books, and it wouldn't be the first time he had been approached by what appeared to be an intermediary on this occasion. But he was a bit wary, because, like other cultures Rafe had to experience and deal with as a Finder, the Scots were proud of their heritage, and the downside to that pride was a natural reluctance to part with any book having a connection to that heritage merely for the benefit of The Bibliotek. But at least The Bibliotek was not in England, for that would have made for an impossible task and probably a decision by Rafe to ignore the Scottish Highlands as a source of Finds, if not the entirety of Scotland.

Rafe had initially responded to Dylan, the owner of the B&B, that he firstly had to attend to some business in Russia before he could come to Scotland, and after agreeing on a date, Rafe had let him know when he was on his way up from Glasgow Helioport in his rental hovercar. As he arrived, he saw that the house was a well-preserved two-storey Victorian-era stone villa. It had an elevated and uninterrupted view of the loch, which a low, gentle mist was in the process of slowly covering, and Rafe, knowing far worse places to stay, was suddenly looking forward to spending the night there after the journey up from Glasgow despite not yet knowing exactly why he was there. The sun was about to disappear over the mountains across the loch and Rafe was pleased to notice several plumes of smoke slowly curling up out of some of the many chimneys of the house and venturing to join the mist. A tall thin man was coming out the front door to meet him.

The man pointed to one of the parking bays off the short driveway next to the house. "You must be Rafe," he offered as he shook Rafe's hand after Rafe had parked the hovercar and alighted.

Rafe could see that the man was fit, but despite his full, trimmed, silver-coloured beard, he couldn't guess at his age. "And you must be Dylan," he responded with his usual relaxed smile, "but that's not a Scottish name and I'm not hearing a Scottish accent."

"No, you're not," replied Dylan with a smile. "I'm London born and bred. We've been here for over forty years, but we're not yet locals. Come inside and *git yae warm*," he added with his best Scottish accent, which Rafe thought was pretty good.

Dylan led Rafe into the lounge, just inside the front door and the first room off the hallway. Sure enough the fire was lit and robustly burning. "I'm sorry it took me a few weeks to get here," said Rafe.

"That's okay. We're actually closed for the season, as of the end of last month, so you're our only guest tonight," replied Dylan.

"Oh, I'm sorry to impose on you."

"Not a problem. Having one guest is so much easier than eight, and I'm only too pleased to help our mutual friend. Here, would you like a wee dram? This one's on the house."

Without waiting for Rafe's reply, his host opened one of the several bottles of Scotch on a table next to one of the lounges and poured two glasses. He continued, "we have an honour system. You can help yourself to any of the whiskeys you see here. All we ask is that you write your name and how much you've had on this pad and pay on checkout."

"Thank you," said Rafe, accepting the glass as he stood in front of the fire, "I gathered from your email that you were writing on behalf of someone who has some 'interesting books for me to look at', but you say this is someone I know?"

"I certainly hope that is the case, otherwise I may be sticking my neck out," replied Dylan.

Rafe waited for him to continue, to tell him who he was referring to, but he didn't. Instead Dylan stood next to Rafe, leant on the fireplace surround with one hand and, caressing his by now near-empty glass with the other, gazed into the flames. "So hypnotic," he ventured, "I never tire of looking into a fire."

Rafe was happy to do likewise. "Nor I," he said after a while.

Dylan then straightened and turned to face Rafe. "I'm sorry to sound all serious and secretive, but I've been obliged to seek your patience as to who our mutual friend is, for now. I hope you don't mind."

Rafe was intrigued. The thought now occurred to him that he had travelled a long way to get to what was a fairly remote part of Europe, and that now that he was here, standing in front of a log fire on a cold winter's early evening with a very nice dram of single malt whiskey in his hand, he still had no real clue as to why, apart from a vague possibility of a Find and meeting someone he apparently knew.

"Mystery sometimes comes with the job," he replied. "I'm well used to it."

"Okay, then," Dylan continued. "Tomorrow morning after breakfast, which will be served, shall we say, at eight thirty in the a.m. in the drawing room? I will lend you a map and show you where our mutual friend will meet you. I have been assured that all will be explained on your arrival."

"This *is* about books, though, isn't it?" Rafe politely asked.

"Sorry, I was told what to write in my email, and that was all I was told about the email. But what I can say is that this is a matter of trust, and I trust my friend implicitly."

Dylan had done nothing so far to cause Rafe any alarm or suspicion — quite the opposite — so he continued to stand there in front of the fire with his glass of whiskey and started to gaze into the flames alongside Dylan whilst he contemplated what Dylan had just said. "Well, I guess if you can promise me some bacon and scrambled eggs for breakfast with some strong coffee, I'll run with that," he said after a while.

"Excellent! Bacon and scrambled eggs it is, with strong coffee! That's right up our alley. Like another glass?" Dylan continued as he re-filled Rafe's glass, "If you don't mind, I will let our friend know you have arrived here and will be there tomorrow morning. But, first things first. I see you only have an overnight bag. That's good because your room is the first on the left at the top of the stairs, and they're rather steep stairs to be carrying a suitcase. No hurry though, you're welcome to use the lounge for as long as like. Wouldn't be the first time someone has fallen asleep in this chair, if you get too comfortable. Dinner at six, is that okay?"

"Oh, I wasn't expecting dinner. I thought I would check out one of those restaurants I passed in Glencoe."

"No such luck, I'm afraid. They're all closed tonight. Anyway, the wife and I were actually looking forward to you getting here in time to join us for dinner. From what our mutual friend has told me, you are in a very interesting line of work. We'd love to hear about it."

"The absence of choice won't lessen my anticipation. Thank you," Rafe nodded in reply. "And I look forward to the conversation."

At the appointed time and after Rafe had showered and changed, he joined his hosts in their kitchen, where a table was laid out in front of the wood-burning stove. He had not been in a country kitchen for some time, let alone one with the warmth and aromas he was suddenly experiencing. For a moment he barely noticed the middle-aged short roundish woman, with cheery cheeks and long thick hair bundled into a bun, fussing over the steaming pot, of what Rafe assumed to be a stew, on the stove.

"Hello Mr Nagy, my name is Katrina, Dylan's wife. Welcome to our home, and our kitchen. I hope you don't mind having dinner in here. It's so much warmer here than in the drawing room," said the happy woman ladling some thick steaming stew into three large bowls on the table.

"Hello. I don't mind at all. Please call me Rafe, and I thank you for your hospitality."

Dylan beckoned Rafe to sit facing the fire, and then poured him a glass of red wine from a bottle Rafe recognised as Spanish. "I hope you like the stew. Perfect for a night like tonight. It's a good thing you got here before dark, it can be quite tricky driving a hovercar along the loch at night with a breeze blowing across it. Here, would you like some fresh home-made bread as well?"

"Yes, thank you," replied Rafe. Turning to Katrina, he asked "Are you from London as well, Katrina?"

"Indeed, and in answer to your next question London was never the same after the Great Holy War, and that's why we moved all the way up here. And never regretted it. How's the stew?" Katrina asked.

"Divine," answered Rafe. "What meat is this?"

"Goat," said Dylan. "It's a specialty of Katrina's and a favourite of mine."

"I'm privileged then. The meat's very tender," said Rafe.

"Yes, he was a young goat, bred and fed for the dinner table," answered Dylan. "His name was Graeme."

"Ha! Graeme's very tasty!" said Rafe.

"Dylan tells me you are a Finder, Rafe. Is that true?" asked Katrina.

"Yes, it's true," replied Rafe, "for the last sixty-three, nearly sixty-four, years it's been true."

"That would make you, what, late eighties?" asked Dylan.

"No, that makes me one hundred and two, actually. I was a late student at the Academy, almost what they used to call 'mature age'. I graduated at the age of thirty-one."

"You don't look a hundred and two, that's for sure!" exclaimed Katrina.

"I'll take that compliment, thank you. At my age they're all welcome," smiled Rafe.

"What exactly does the job of Finder entail?" asked Katrina.

"Basically what the job title says I do. I find books for The Bibliotek to procure. My territory of operation is Europe, including Russia and the UK. Normally I would share Europe with another Finder, but we are short at the moment. Most of my time is spent on research and negotiation. Research to locate where books and collections are being kept or possibly being kept, even hidden or forgotten sometimes, and negotiations when their owners need to be convinced to relinquish their books. There are still plenty of books The Bibliotek would really like to have. I have a List that is compiled for me, but I tend to do my own research."

"Even now, after what, one hundred years or so since The Bibliotek's been around?" asked Dylan.

"Oh yes, most definitely. The older or rarer a book is, the more the owner prefers not to let it go, I've found. But attitudes do change, and a book owner's death can often tip the scales in our favour. In Norway, for example, a deceased estate is not allowed to sell or auction any book that is part of the estate without first offering it to The Bibliotek. We'd love that to be the case in the UK, but the government has so far resisted introducing such a law, which means I spend a lot of time in the UK tracking down and meeting geriatric bibliophiles. Old colleges and their remaining libraries, especially those in Oxford and Cambridge are another focus for me in the UK."

"You must get around a bit, then?" asked Katrina.

"Oh yes, travel is my middle name. I don't mind. I get to meet interesting people," Rafe smiled, looking at his hosts.

"So who exactly owns The Bibliotek? And thus the books?" asked Dylan.

"Well, technically, The Bibliotek is not 'owned' by anyone or anything. And that in turn is the case with its contents. Ultimate control of the Bibliotek is vested in a foundation which was established under the terms of a multilateral treaty entered into by all remaining member states of the United Nations. The treaty was given the status of law in Norway by the Norwegian Parliament when it was agreed by all treaty partners to locate The Bibliotek in that country. *Effective* control though is held by the twelve-member Governing Council, and operational control is held by the chief librarian – currently the Second Bibliotekar. Officially, The Bibliotek has no commercial purpose and thus is not liable to any taxes in Norway or anywhere else. We are a bit like a university town, only fairly remote. We have the Academy, and at any one time we might have about four thousand people living and working there. That requires a fair amount of infrastructure, including a sizable security force, who are basically our town police but also there to guard the Central Repository, where we house our one billion books."

"One billion? That's a huge number! I can't even contemplate that many books," asked Katrina. "And the Central Repository can handle that volume? I understand it's a huge underground complex. That in itself is hard to imagine."

"Yes, seventy-five levels, all underground. But no actual security personnel below ground level," said Rafe.

"Speaking of security, what about the Present Sect, Rafe? Who are these people?" asked Katrina.

"The group calling themselves the Present Sect pretty much stay in the dark, in the shadows. They're not into publicity. They haven't said much of anything since their so-called *Manifesto For The Present* was sent to the media to publish instead of doing it themselves. They haven't uploaded any videos or audios either. They just put up pithy slogans and randomly act," said Rafe.

"Yes, and act violently when they do," offered Dylan.

"That they have, but here's the interesting part. Their manifesto was sent by email to the media in many countries simultaneously, from one source, which has yet to be tracked down. But the acts of violence attributed to the group so far have been committed across the globe, with no pattern. Just random acts. So, the thinking is, at least at The Bibliotek, that the group's membership is small, but mobile."

"But their manifesto just doesn't make sense to me. What is the problem with books?" asked Katrina.

"I'm not sure they have a problem with books *per se*," said Rafe, "I think it has more to do with their status in developed society. This is all stemming from the Great Holy War. As I understand it, the Present Sect seems to have sprung out of a collective desire of a few to make sure the relics of religion were all destroyed, without exception, so that humankind would be spared the resurgence of religious fanaticism, or indeed the resurgence of religion full stop. The fear that religious mania would rise again was a common fear, but the Present Sect acted on that fear, and of course religious books were an easy target. And the older the book, the more revered it was as a relic, which in turn made it more of a target."

"Yes, I understand all that, but now it's about *any* book, and that's what I just don't get," said Katrina. Dylan nodded in agreement.

"It wasn't too big of a leap. What the Present Sect saw that made them so angry about religion and religious books was the reverence. And when they started seeing the same kind of possessive behaviour bestowed on all books, they started to also see the vast sums of money being spent on storing them and showing them off. And so we saw a progression of the concept of *destroy all religious relics to save humanity* to the concept of *destroy all books to save humanity*."

Katrina looked at Rafe, a little confused.

"Think of it like this. There is a library. It owns one thousand rare first edition books published in the sixteenth century. They are in Latin. They cover a range of topics, such as Greek mythology, natural philosophy, the nature of the Devil as represented by women, the basics of alchemy, the healing powers of powdered animal horns, a whole range of topics with one thing in common — total irrelevance for today's society. But the people who built the library want to make a statement — *we have these books* — so they build a vaulted marble domed hall, with ornate decorations and sculptured ceilings, and it's twenty times the size of the bookcases housing these one thousand books. It is a thing of beauty. And it costs a small fortune. All for books that no-one reads, no-one needs, and no-one is allowed to touch. Now multiply the cost by thousands and you have the Present Sect saying enough is enough. Today's society needs that money to be spent on the present, not a past that has no value. And besides, they say, preservation of those books, if it is to be allowed, can be satisfied by digital copies. Once a copy of a book is made, there is no longer a need or justification to retain the book, no matter how old or rare it is."

"You sound as if you agree with that, Rafe," said Katrina.

"Katrina!" objected Dylan. "C'mon darling, that's a bit harsh."

"It's okay," smiled Rafe. "I've been a Finder for many years, but I'm not obsessive. I'm getting on in years but I still try to keep an open mind about as many things as possible. So, yeah, I do see some logic in the Present Sect's way of thinking. And having seen many libraries in my time I have to agree that sometimes — often — they lose sight of what they are meant to be doing. Many of the libraries that survived the Great Holy War are mere expressions of power and status and little else, meant to shock and create awe, representations of enormous cultural vanity and one-upmanship. But to use that perspective as justification for simply destroying books is a little too facile for my liking. To me it reeks of ignorance, the very thing that a book is meant to overcome. So no, I don't agree on that score. And speaking of ignorance,... " Rafe paused to refill his glass with Spanish red, "keeping books means keeping them waiting. Waiting for the social historians to finish shouting their reconstructed truths, if not tainted by, then just based on ideologies vacant of evidence. Waiting for the seekers of conflict history to turn their pages and discover their own version of reality. Waiting simply to be read and accepted for what they are — purveyors of imagination and thought."

"My goodness, Rafe, you are a philosopher!" exclaimed Katrina.

"Only when I am a happy drunk, my dear lady."

"Drunk? But you're not slurring your words, or your thoughts," replied Katrina.

"Practice maids perfect."

"Funny. Alright, but what about the Bibliotek? Didn't that cost a lot to build, and still costing a lot of money? Doesn't that make it a target?"

"The Bibliotek certainly does cost a lot of money to maintain, but here's the thing. We asked every country in the UN to tell us the cost of maintaining their respective national libraries. The amounts were staggering, particularly for those countries whose national libraries had survived the Great Holy War. We are talking about the combined GDP of several countries, all told. So we said to each, okay, you transfer your books from your national library, pay us ten per cent each year of your national library budget and keep the other ninety per cent for other things. That's a pretty persuasive argument. The key though is that The Bibliotek is not just another edifice. It is not trying to make a statement of any kind. Every cent spent on it is focused on the books it holds. Period."

"So, you're saying the Bibliotek is not a target of the Present Sect?"

"That's hard for me to say. It may well be some time in the future, but for now it seems there are plenty of other targets for the Present Sect, being basically any library or collection still being maintained on its own."

"Then the threat the Sect represents to others is working in your favour, isn't it," pushed Katrina.

"I don't think that's fair darling," protested Dylan.

"In a way, yes," said Rafe, unperturbed. "Some of The Bibliotek's recent acquisitions have come about due to fears of the Present Sect, there is no denying that. But I can see where this is going…"

"It's alright Rafe, Katrina isn't about to suggest there is any connection between the Bibliotek and the Present Sect," said Dylan.

"Oh no, of course not! I'm sorry, but I was just trying to understand what is going on with those people," said Katrina.

Rafe was only half placated. He decided to address the suspicion, not because Katrina had touched on it but because it had also been implied by others in other conversations and it irked him every time he heard it.

"That's okay," he replied. "I will say that the possibility of there being a motive for The Bibliotek to be behind the Present Sect has been raised in the past, including very recently in some dealings I have had, but from where I stand it is only possible to contemplate such a scenario if it is based on a total ignorance of what The Bibliotek and all who work for it stand for, and that is a resolute desire to protect and preserve the entire history of humankind's thoughts and experiences as it is expressed in books, which is the very foundation of The Bibliotek's creation and mission. The Present Sect to me is anti-history. More than that, I often ask: what *is* the 'present'? What does that term really mean? To me 'the present' means nothing; it is but a fleeting concept of the mind. It is an artificial construct, one that pretends to represent a state of society where everything is 'current' and up-to-date and tip top and 'the latest thing'. All meaningless. Everything is past; everything is just varying degrees of elapsed time." With that, Rafe emptied his wine glass.

"More wine?" offered Dylan.

"Yes, thank you. I've seen the slogans. Have you? *The Present is Here! The Present is Now! Are You in the Present? Are You With the Present?* All very pithy and clever, and all very vacuous. Voluminously vacuous, verily! There's *nothing* behind them. Nothing in them. Now there's a concept – Nothing. That's something I *can* understand. But the Present? Oh, spare me. Nothing is Here! Nothing is Now! Yes, I'll drink to that!" Which he did.

Dylan and Katrina looked at each other, and Katrina found it hard to suppress a laugh with her hand over her mouth. Rafe had quite obviously become a little inebriated. But they didn't mind. He was still making sense. A lot of sense. But Katrina wasn't quite finished with her mini-Inquisition.

"I'm just wondering. The Great Holy War changed everything in terms of religion. Zealotry is gone, as are most religions entirely. And the space travel we now do dealt once and for all with the loony Flat Earthers. So, my question is, if religion is dead, why does the Bibliotek bother with religious books? I mean, there doesn't seem to be much point to me, but isn't it also dangerous?"

Rafe smiled. He liked being asked this kind of question, and his answer was well-practised. He looked at Katrina, then at Dylan, who he could tell was thinking the same thing as his wife. Rafe's own thought was that, as practiced as it was, he should oil his answer as well. "That is a very good question, young Katrina. If you will permit me another glass of this fine red we're drinking, I will fulsomely answer it."

Glass refilled again, Rafe was true to his word. "The world has changed a lot since Herr Gutenberg began publishing books by way of movable metal type and a printing press. That was in the mid-15th century, and his invention revolutionised Europe and the world. Before then, books were the realm of monasteries, where monks worked as scribes in hand-making each and every book. This monastic monopoly naturally meant that many if not most books they produced were almost entirely religious in topic, theme and purpose.

And because of the process, an entirely new book was something quite rare. Some monasteries were reproducing the classics of ancient Greece and Byzantium, but only some. What was important was that until Herr Gutenberg and his printing press, books were controlled by The Church, putting aside the various bursts of Iconoclasm. The Renaissance owes a lot to Herr Gutenberg. Suddenly, control over what kind of books were published was taken away from The Church. But, reverence and fear still pervaded for decades afterwards. Gutenberg had borrowed heavily to make a workable printing press, so to repay those loans he used his world-changing invention to publish thousands and thousands of *indulgences* for The Church, all for a tidy fee. And as we all know, the first real book he published with his invention was *The Bible*, of which there were 180 copies made before he died. So this reverence and fear was there also because of the Inquisitions. Some say that Gutenberg and his printing press were the cause for the renewal of that odious process. The Spanish Inquisition, for example, it began a few short years after Gutenberg's press came into being. But, while it was true that the Church had lost its monopoly on books, it was also true that the *Bible*, the *Quran*, and the many other forms of religious texts became increasingly available to the masses. Then we had a period of book production during the Natural Philosophy phase, where the established religious and biblical rhetoric was slowly but politely dissipated until dissolved completely by the New Age of Science, followed by the Period of Enlightenment, all fostered, spread and stoked by books. Then the Industrial Revolution, the Period of Exploration happened, and then the twentieth and twenty-first centuries when it all turned to custard, as my grandmother used to say. But here lies the essence of The Bibliotek. By not having *any* preconceived ideas or policies that in any way served to treat *any* book *any* differently from *any* other, we can show humankind why we are who we are today. We can show the progression of human thought and belief systems over the centuries. The older the book the more likely it will be a religious text, but without those books, we can't demonstrate anything other than ignorance or prejudice or fascism. We won't be able to connect the dots of human development and civilisation. In that endeavour it would be fatal to be selective. That is my answer."

Rafe sat back and waited for his hosts to recover from his monologue. Sometimes he got carried away with his little speech, so he wondered if they had been listening or had switched off and were just being polite.

"Hmmm, I see your point," said Katrina, in response to which Dylan nodded in agreement. "Basically, we can't simply ignore the role of religion in the history of humankind and its development and The Bibliotek adopts a stance of disinterest in the subject."

"That's the nub of it, yes, but we do appreciate the sensitivities and their associated dangers. And that's why we have a well-resourced security force. The longer cults like the Present Sect are around the more polarising the strive to accumulate and store the world's books, especially the religious ones."

"One more question, if I may, Rafe," Katrina asked.

"Of course, pray tell, fair maiden of the loch, spill it."

"Well, it's about morality and ethics. Does the Bibliotek make those kinds of decisions when selecting books to procure? For example, if you were offered a book bound in human skin by the Nazis in the Second World War would you take it?"

Dylan had his face in his hands, shaking it from side to side, but Rafe could see that Katrina had an academic look on hers rather than some mad-as-a-hatter look.

"That is very interesting question, I must say. But first, I haven't been offered such a book, and I never will because you're confusing a book with a certain notorious lampshade, which may or may not exist."

"Oh, so you know something about this?" asked Katrina.

"Yes, I do," replied Rafe, which prompted Dylan to remove his hands from his face. "About ten years ago I was negotiating with the executor of a deceased estate of an exceedingly rich bibliophile who had lived in Paris. The sort of book collector who can and did spend many hundreds of thousands of dollars on buying a rare book if they could. So this collection was of high interest to The Bibliotek as it comprised a number of rare first editions ranging from the sixteenth to eighteenth centuries plus a few incunabula...."

"Sorry," interrupted Katrina, "incunaba?"

"No, incunabula, Latin, plural; incunable, English, singular. It basically means a book published before 1501," answered Rafe.

"Oh," replied Katrina.

"It's a long story in itself. But anyway, where was I? Oh, yes, the deceased Paris collector. After a lengthy negotiation process which, if I remember correctly was mostly taken up with haggling over the value to be attributed to the collection for the official Tax Certificate the estate would receive from The Bibliotek — which they used to reduce the estate's inheritance tax bill — I was there in Paris packing up the books for shipment to The Bibliotek when the lawyer picked up one of the books and said to me "*Monsieur Rafe, faites tester celui-ci avec soin.*"

"Ah, wait, 'have this one carefully tested'?" asked Katrina.

"Yes. I thought little of it. We carefully examine all books on arrival at The Bibliotek. The book in question was a 1543 first edition of Andreas Vesalius's *De Humani corporis fabrica*, which loosely translates as *On The Fabric Of The Human Body*. It's worth over one million Euros, easily."

"Oh no, I can see where this is going," said Katrina.

"Well, yes, and no. Vesalius did not publish any book with human skin binding, that is fact. The problem, as it turned out, was that a Belgian bookbinder by the name of Josse Schavye had rebound the book for the 1867 Paris International Exposition, and for that purpose he had used human skin. When the book was tested at The Bibliotek and the binding was not animal hide as expected, but human skin, it caused a sensation."

"I bet it did," offered Dylan.

"So, what did you do?" asked Katrina.

"It was clear what The Bibliotek was going to do, and we did it. We entered it into the Master Catalogue and placed a permanent embargo on its access."

"So, you actually have a book that is bound in human skin?" asked Katrina.

"We have eleven such books, and all are under embargo" clarified Rafe.

"Oh my god. Eleven! But what does 'under embargo' mean?"

"It means no access is allowed to them by anyone outside The Bibliotek and even then only to those of us inside The Bibliotek by written approval of the Bibliotekar. And they are never to be displayed in public."

"But who does that? Make books with human skin?"

"Nineteenth century medical practitioners, that's who. That's when the practice was, um, practiced by some practitioners, if you'll excuse the pun. And always using cadavers. Coincidentally, I only just recently procured some other books by Vesalius for The Bibliotek, on my last trip to Italy, and I was happy to find they still had their original bindings."

"Where does the morality come into it?" asked Katrina.

"That's easy. It is not the role of The Bibliotek to make moral judgments. My lawyer friend in Paris had not sought to place a 'special' value on the book in our negotiations. That was ethical. At The Bibliotek, we also apply the highest level of ethical behaviour, and that requires us not to make any subjective choices, including decisions made on moral grounds. Our policy on this is quite clear. This particular incident prompted the Bibliotekar to give a lecture on the subject to an Ethics class at the Academy, which I also attended, and a new protocol for the conservators to follow when on-boarding any medical text published in the 19th century that is ostensibly leather bound. Every such book is tested to confirm the nature of the binding. And we've also been undertaking testing of any such book already in the Central Repository, and that's why I know we have eleven human skin bound books. As distasteful as the practice was, it is important that humankind not be deprived of knowing it did exist. So that when we ask ourselves 'who does that?' the answer requires learning about the psyche prevailing in those times. It adds to our knowledge, basically."

"I think I'm going to be sick," said Katrina.

"I think it's time I checked the fire in the lounge room," said Dylan.

"Please not on my account. I think I will retire early, it's been a long day," offered Rafe.

"You're sure I can't tempt you with a dram of the good stuff? I know I need one."

"You have tempted me, but I am going to decline, thank you. So I'll say my goodnights and thank you again for dinner *and* the conversation. I enjoyed both immensely."

With that, Rafe rose from the table, said goodnight, checked that Katrina really wasn't going to be sick, and made his way up to his room. Sleep came quickly and easily, with nary a thought about what could be in store for him the next day.

8:47am, Sunday, 9ᵗʰ December 2204

Dylan came into the drawing room where Rafe was eating his breakfast. He had a map and some car keys and sat down at Rafe's table, opposite him. It was just after sunrise, but the sun had yet to appear above the mountain behind the house. A chill wind was blowing outside and Rafe was glad for the warmth of the log fire burning in the breakfast room. And the bacon and scrambled eggs — they were delicious.

"How did you sleep last night? Were you comfortable?" asked Dylan.

"Slept well, thank you, like a log."

"Good. I'm sorry we gave you a bit of the third-degree last night. But we find the whole concept of The Bibliotek quite interesting," Dylan said.

"That's quite alright, I don't mind talking about it. I don't often get to do it outside the context of a business meeting."

"So, how's the head?" Dylan asked Rafe with a smile.

"Fine, fine, fine. What's with the keys?"

"You'll need to take my car to where our mutual friend is, as the last part of the road is dirt, probably mud, so no hover rails. It's an old four-wheel drive hydrocar — it will get you there and back no problems — but yours wouldn't."

"It's been a while since I've driven one of those. No problem with fuel?" asked Rafe.

"No, we have more than one hydrogen station around these parts. Lots of dirt roads, you see, so hydrocars are still a necessity, even if they're not made anymore."

"And our friend knows I'm coming?"

"Yes, he is expecting you."

"Okay, show me where he is then."

Dylan unfolded the map and traced the route Rafe needed to take with his index finger. "I think it best I don't draw your route on the map," he said, but you shouldn't get lost. There's only two turns you need to worry about. Here's the first one, it's a right turn off from A82," he said pressing his fingernail onto the map. "You would have driven past it on your way here last evening. You have to watch it though because as it's a dirt road it's not signposted. Blink and you'll miss it. You can see it's just past this turnoff to the left. Just stay on that road for a while, I think about sixteen kilometres, until you see this little turnoff over a bridge crossing the River Etive, here," again pressing his fingernail onto the spot. "Now that crossing will take you eventually downstream to this farm, here, but you don't go there. Instead, and it's not marked on the map, there's a gate straight ahead on the other side of the bridge. It will be unlocked. Drive through it, then get out and lock the gate. Follow the track over the hill and you'll see a house way off in the distance. That's our friend's house. You'll be able to drive there, it's no more than a paddock these days, and he'll see you coming. He'll know it's you because he knows my car. Got all that?"

"Absolutely, thanks. I don't think I even need the map."

"Take it anyway," insisted Dylan, "and whatever you do, don't hit any deer. They're about, especially at dusk and late at night."

10:43am

It was bitterly cold and still windy when Rafe set off, rugged up as Dylan's four-wheel drive had no interior heating. He reached the turn-off from the main road without seeing another vehicle. The dirt road from there was muddy but not rutted by any traffic so Rafe had no problem reaching the second turn-off. The bridge was there as Dylan had said, and beyond it the gate. Rafe took care crossing the bridge as it was narrow, crumbling, had no sides and obviously was not used much. Below it, the River Etive raged. There was a padlock and chain on the gate, but it wasn't locked, again, just as Dylan had said. Rafe stopped the car after successfully navigating the bridge crossing, but kept the engine running as he got out and walked to the gate. Looking around, the thought occurred to him that whoever this mutual friend was, they certainly lived in a beautiful place. Some would call it desolate, but Rafe was attracted by its wildness. As instructed by Dylan, he locked the gate after passing through. Driving up over the grassy, tufted hill, Rafe saw in the near distance a cottage. A few seconds later, a figure came out of the front door and stood and waved at him. The figure had a coat and hood on so Rafe couldn't recognise the person. But just as he stopped the vehicle in front of the cottage, he thought he recognised the scraggly little beard.

"Hello stranger," said the old man as he took his hood off.

"Thomas! My god," replied Rafe, as he opened the car door and climbed out. Thomas gave him a big hug and a slap on his shoulder.

"About time you bloody well got here. Good to see you, Nags!"

"What are you doing here?! Mads told me you were missing!" exclaimed Rafe.

"Yes, I am missing, and that's just the way I like it."

"But why? What's going on?

"That's why you're here, Nags. I need to talk to you, then I need you to go back to The Bibliotek and tell Mads."

"Tell Mads what?"

"All in good time. Now, come in, out of the cold."

Rafe followed Mads inside the cottage. It was warm and full of rugs, comfort, and, around the open fireplace raging with real wood logs, two old leather lounges.

"Good fire," said Rafe. "You look more than comfortable here, Thomas, tucked away in the middle of nowhere. How are your stocks?"

"Thanks for asking. I've got plenty of scotch, but probably too early to get out the glasses. Make yourself comfortable and I'll organise some coffee. Did you find the place okay?"

"Oh, yes," replied Rafe as he sank into one of the lounge chairs, "our mutual friend gave me very good directions."

"And I see he lent you his car. That was good of him. Did you lock the gate perchance?"

"Yes, I followed the instructions to the letter."

"Good. Now, I'll make that coffee."

After a few minutes of staring into the roaring fire, Rafe had become quite relaxed and warmed up. He felt even better with Thomas's coffee inside him.

"I'm sorry it took me a few weeks to get here, but I thought it was just another tip about books, and I had already made plans to be elsewhere."

"That's alright, Nags, I needed some P and Q."

"So Thomas. Spill the beans, what's the story? What's behind your sudden departure from The Bibliotek that's got everybody worried?"

"This may sound dramatic, but the fact is I was threatened, as in my life, and I took it very seriously. So seriously that I left The Bibliotek quietly and quickly, telling no-one. And when I say quietly and quickly, I mean immediately, leaving my neurophone and my data pad on my desk, as if I had just stepped out of my office for coffee."

"Or as if you had been kidnapped. Which is one theory Mads has entertained. But you're right, that does sound dramatic. Who threatened you? Why?"

"We'll get to that."

"You say you left your neurophone and data pad on your desk. Was that in your office at the Academy?"

"Yes, why?"

"Your neurophone and your data pad have not been found."

"That does not surprise me."

"How so?" asked Rafe. "Is this the Present Sect at work?"

"No no, the Present Sect? No, why would you say that? No, this is something else. Something that may be more serious than those loons. Something closer to home."

"I'm not following..."

"Someone at The Bibliotek seems to want me dead or made permanently quiet."

"What? That's insane. How can you say that?"

"It's not insane. I wish it wasn't true, Nags, but it is, I can assure you. It's got something to do with the trip I made to Arcadia. My report never made it to Mads. It went to someone else. I was then told in no uncertain terms not to reveal its contents to anyone, least of all Mads. And when I told the person to get stuffed, I was then threatened that I would be, quote, "quietly and quickly dealt with" if I did not co-operate. The fact that my neurophone and my data pad were not found in my office means that someone at The Bibliotek took them, and that reinforces the fact the threat came from someone at The Bibliotek."

"But why? What was in your report to prompt such a response? What was so important as to place your life in danger?"

"That's the part I'm struggling with. I had logged on to review it before sending it to Mads, to work out what was so sensitive about it, but I couldn't find it on the system. Even the log entry for it was gone. And I didn't keep a copy on my personal storage. I always delete it after upload to the system."

"But do you have any idea what part of the report was the problem? Why were you there anyway?"

"All I was doing was a routine inspection of the facility housing the back-up mainframe, plus a planned data recovery drill. The only person I told apart from Mads that I was going was of course Rani Sharma. She had to co-ordinate the start of the drill. At the nominated time back at The Bibliotek's Data Centre the signal to commence the drill was sent and the Commander at the Arcadia facility went into action. Nothing out of the ordinary and nothing to report but all systems and staff operating to expectation. All I added was a note about a geo team that was there as well, taking core samples near the facility, right next to the greenhouse in fact, right at the edge of our site. I just assumed they were doing a routine survey and I noted their presence and did not interfere with the drill. They were not expecting to see me there, that much I do know, and they weren't too happy about it either. They wouldn't tell me why they were doing a geosurvey, but I didn't put any of that in the report."

"Well I don't concern myself with Arcadia, it's literally another world to me, but something doesn't sound right. So, Mads doesn't know you're here; he is quite worried about you. I got a call from him, and he's being ringing around trying to find you."

"And that is why you are here, Nags. You are closer to Mads than anyone else at The Bibliotek. I know there is no-one he trusts more than you. Well, apart from me that is. The point is, I need you to go back to The Bibliotek and tell him face-to-face what has happened. I had to orchestrate you coming here under the guise of your normal work, and I need you to maintain the ruse and not communicate with anyone. In fact, I am going to ask you to file a dummy report that this particular search was not fruitful."

"That won't be a problem, it wouldn't be the first time that's happened. But why did you choose to come here?"

"This house belongs to my brother-in-law's family. I also have a house on the other side of the loch. I am amongst friends but not obviously here if anyone decided to look for me. They may be, I don't know. But I do know that nobody has been snooping around my house. I'd know it if they were. I've known Dylan and his wife since they moved up here from London — good people — so it was easy for me to ask him to get you here."

"Well it worked, and I'm glad to know you're alive and well. But this is all very worrying and, jeez, what are you going to do?"

"I think it best I keep a low profile for a while. At least until Mads can sort out things. I'm really hoping this is all just a misunderstanding. But..."

"But you are not officially missing. If it was a misunderstanding, you'd think your unexplained absence would be public knowledge. But it isn't and no-one is officially concerned or looking for you."

"Correct."

"And that is a worry in itself."

"Correct again."

"So you'll stay here?"

"Let's just say I might, or I might not. There are other places I can go, but if I do feel the need it won't be far from Glencoe, just perhaps harder to find."

"I understand. So, I'll be able to use Dylan as a contact?"

"No, that won't be necessary."

"So, what exactly is the message I'm to give Mads?"

"Tell him everything I have told you, and ask him if he has any way of retrieving or accessing my report, quietly, or otherwise find out what exactly is happening on Arcadia; why all the secrecy, and, importantly who is behind it all."

"Okay, all that is going to blow his mind, I can tell you that right now."

"Now you know why I picked you as the messenger," explained Thomas.

"Quite," replied Rafe as Thomas handed him a slip of paper with numbers on it. "What's this?" he asked.

"I've got a burner neurophone. That's the number and the country code for Scotland. You need to give it to Mads and ask him to arrange someone he trusts, but not you, to act as the go-between Mads and me."

"Got it. And now you have to tell me who it was who threatened you."

"I wish I could, I really do. But all I got was a phone call. He didn't say his name and I didn't recognise his voice, but you know what? He used a voice disguiser, so I'm guessing he thought I may in fact know who he is, and that is what makes me think someone at The Bibliotek is behind all this."

"This is all unbelievable, Thomas," said Rafe, dejected.

"Believe me, Nags, I wish it was unbelievable. I hope I'm not overreacting, but that phone call. That was nasty, and direct. In hindsight, I am glad I did what I did. And now I'm glad you came. Time for lunch. I've got some leftover stew. Hungry?"

"Let me guess. It's Katrina's?"

"Yes, why, have you already had some?"

"Oh yeah, but it was delicious, so I am definitely up for seconds. She puts something in it that gives that goat some real smoothness."

"That would be the nip of Drambuie she adds."

"Ha ha! Seriously?!"

"Yep, a *ye olde* recipe I gave her," smiled Thomas. "Come on, let's go into the kitchen, it's plenty warm there too."

Over their respective steaming bowls, Rafe and Thomas carried on their conversation, with Rafe asking "what did you tell Dylan and Katrina about all the cloak and dagger?"

"I told them there had been a security issue involving the Present Sect, nothing major, but that we were just taking some precautions until things settled down," said Thomas.

"That explains something," replied Rafe.

"Why, what did they say?"

"Oh, they said nothing. Dylan was suitably vague and added nothing to his email apart from the explanation that our mutual friend had asked him to send it. But they managed to pop the Present Sect into our conversation over dinner last night. Luckily what I said aligned with the story you gave them, or at least didn't contradict it. I just acknowledged that, yes, they were considered a threat to The Bibliotek, or words to that effect."

"Good. Oh look it's way past the hour. Fancy a scotch?"

"Was the Pope a Catholic?"

"Ha! I believe she was. Let's finish up here and head back to the fire."

Back in their lounge chairs, Rafe asked Thomas how Arcadia was.

"Arcadia is something else, Nags, it really is. Nothing can prepare you for it, despite it being habitable. It's habitable all right, just not as we know how to live. It's quite surreal, yet... hyper-real would be how I would describe it. I don't know if it's just the senses kicking in and reminding you all the time you are actually on another planet in another star system and you only left Earth a few hours beforehand, but everything you see, touch and feel just seems exaggerated in every way. I don't know if I would enjoy staying there for any length of time or not. I was glad to leave and yet I wasn't. It's hard to explain the feeling..." Thomas's voice tapered off as he began staring out the window. "So. Far. Away."

"I think you need to lower the scotch intake Thomas. Old men such as you shouldn't be so dreamy. Next thing you know you'll be reminiscing."

"Okay, your lack of respect young Nags tells me it's time for you to head back to Dylan's. Time's getting away and it will be getting dark soon, and you really don't want to be on these roads at night."

"I know. There's deer about."

"Yes. Don't laugh. It's a fair warning. I'll come with you to the gate."

"That's a bit of a hike back for you."

"What, do you think I'm too old?"

"Well Thomas, you're not getting any younger that's for sure, and your leg, well..."

"Don't you be worrying about my leg, it's just as good as the one it replaced used to be. I may be nearly one hundred and fifty-five, but I can still look after myself. Besides, I reckon I may well be the oldest person to travel in space. I bet you didn't know that, eh Nags. And besides, I need some fresh air."

"And fresh air is what you'll get, maybe even some snow. We best be off then."

They made the trip to the gate in silence and shook hands before Thomas got out. After Rafe drove through he stopped while Thomas walked up to his window. "When you ask Mads for me to find out what the story is, tell him to be careful."

"That I will, don't worry. He'll shit his pants though."

"Ha ha! That he will!" With that, Thomas thumped the side of the four-wheel-drive with his palm then waved at Rafe as he drove across the bridge. Rafe waved back before closing the car window and heading back to Loch Linnhe.

It was getting dark by the time Rafe arrived back at the villa. He had driven a lot more carefully on his return journey than he had in the morning, but he had not seen a single deer on or near the road. By the time he had parked the hydrocar at the side of the house and walked back around to the front door, Dylan was standing on the threshold.

"How did you go?"

"Fine, thank you. Thomas was well. He said to pass on his thanks, you've played your part well."

"That's no problem at all. We've enjoyed it and your company. Come in and get warm by the fire before dinner. I hope you don't mind, but we need to finish off that stew from last night."

Rafe smiled. "That's more than fine, that's great. It's a lovely stew."

11:37am, Tuesday, 11ᵗʰ December 2204

Two days later Rafe arrived back at The Bibliotek. He placed a call to Mads, but Larkin answered and told him that the Bibliotekar was at the Academy today, but did he wish to make an appointment for tomorrow? Rafe told him thanks, but not to worry and hung up. He then walked over to the Academy's main building where he knew Mads maintained a small office, just like all other offices allocated to senior lecturers. It was unlocked, but Mads was not there.

Rafe decided to wait for him. Whilst he did he filed a nondescript report of his "unsuccessful" trip to Scotland on his Find hunt. Not long after, Mads walked into his office.

"Nags! This is a surprise; you're becoming part of the furniture."

"You won't believe who I bumped into in Scotland," Rafe said flatly.

"Someone I know?"

"I should say so."

Mads peered at him, asking a silent question with his eyes. Rafe replied with a silent slight nod.

Mads went back to the doorway, looked out down the hallway, then came back in and closed the door. He then sat down with Rafe in the other chair facing his desk and leant towards him.

"He's safe and well?"

"That he is, on both counts."

"So what's going on? How did you find him?"

Rafe recounted the method Thomas had chosen to make contact. Then he gave Mads the details of why Thomas had left The Bibliotek so suddenly. Mads was shocked.

"There can only be one explanation for why he was threatened," concluded Mads after he had made sure he had heard correctly what Rafe was telling him.

"Yes, someone appears to want to keep secret the fact that a geosurvey team was on Arcadia at The Bibliotek's site. And the only logical reason for wanting that is that they found something," concurred Rafe.

"Agreed. The problem now is that explanation raises several questions I need answered. And I get the feeling the answers need to be sought quietly, for now. There's more than one individual keeping secrets."

"Agreed," said Rafe, as he pulled out of his tunic pocket the piece of paper Thomas had given him, "And before I forget, here is Thomas's new neurophone number. He told me he left his phone and his data pad in his office at the Academy. He now has a generic neurophone. He asked that you arrange for a go-between to use this number if he needed to be contacted. He won't leave Scotland unless and until he hears from you via the contact person."

"That's a bit cloak and dagger,..."

"Agreed" interrupted Rafe.

"But I guess we should go along with it," replied Mads as he in turn put the piece of paper in his tunic pocket. "I have someone in mind. The same person I will ask to look into Thomas's missing report and its intercept. He's already told me that Thomas's neurophone and data pad are missing, so now we know they were taken from his office."

"That would be Dr Foote, yes?" asked Rafe. He knew Dr Foote, and he knew Mads trusted him implicitly and with good reason. Rafe considered Foote was the epitome of discretion and resourcefulness.

"Yes, but I've decided I need to get to Arcadia myself, and soon, as in this Thursday on the regular fortnightly supply trip. On the quiet, of course. What about you? What are you up to?"

"Me? Well, I need to get back to my real work. This cloak and dagger stuff is not up my alley. I'll be in Pienza Friday night next week. You will be pleased to know I think I may have finally cracked it with Viscount Rossellini."

"You mean he's finally decided to give us his rare book collection?"

"It would appear so. I'll let you know. Just make sure that Foote also gets a generic neurophone just to use to contact Thomas," said Rafe as he rose from his chair and opened the door to leave.

"Shall do. Good luck with Pienza."

"Good luck with Arcadia. Ciao."

END OF CHAPTER FOUR

Chapter Five

Journey of Discovery

Prospero: "Me, poor man! – my library
Was dukedom large enough..."
William Shakespeare, *The Tempest*, Act I, Scene II, 1611

8:00am, Thursday, 13th December 2204

The spaceship Mads was now firmly strapped into at The Bibliotek's spaceport, awaiting take-off any second, was called the *Nostradamus*. This wasn't its formal alphanumeric designation, but nonetheless it was the name everyone at The Bibliotek knew it by. Mads did not know who originally thought of the name *Nostradamus* as being suitable for The Bibliotek's one and only spaceship, but it stuck. For his part though, Mads knew he had not been consulted before it was announced. The irony of the name was lost on no-one, and for that reason Mads made certain that The Bibliotek's copies of the published predictions and prophecies of Michel de Nostradame, to use his real name, were given the 'no staff access permitted' designation in the Master Catalogue and treated accordingly. The Bibliotek's Nostradame Collection was extensive. It included a first edition of his famous 1555 book *Les Propheties*, which contained 942 poetic quatrains, each suggesting a prediction of an event, the sole remaining third edition which contained another 320 quatrains in addition to the originals, an omnibus fourth edition published in 1568, two years after Nostradame's death, and 16 years of annual prediction almanacs he published up to his death, variously titled *Almanachs*, *Presages*, and *Prognostications*.

The Bibliotek did not concern itself however with any copies of the 263 subsequent editions (to date) of *Les Propheties*, because they were universally based on the first English edition of 1672. Mads knew this from his study of the History of Logic during his student years at the Academy, and he also knew that the 1672 English version was replete with errors, very subjective, and somewhat hindsight-influenced choices of translation from the original mixture of Latin, Greek, French, and Nostradame's local dialect Provencal Occitan in a style that was itself deliberately and variously subjective, convoluted, conjectural, vague and barely coherent, and certainly not in any form of chronological order. Deliberate because even though the Holy Inquisition was by then a thing of the past, Monsieur Nostradame had still been prudent enough to avoid being seen as a heretic in the making of his so-called predictions; the more vague and open-ended his so-called predictions, the better. And also deliberate, Mads suspected, so as to be able to be used to 'retrofit' a given prediction into any given future disastrous event and thus, in a mischievous way, trying to be seen as not so much heretical but as prescient in the supreme because the events and things he was 'predicting' were always large in scale. Due to the persistent and never diminishing popularity of the Nostradame, or Nostradamus, myth, which was much to Mads' rationalistic annoyance, there was no small measure of truth to that particular theory.

Another theory Mads sometimes like to entertain himself with, and which he had shared with Violetta, was that his ship's name derived from Monsieur Nostradame's little-known occupation as a necromancer because most people, including himself, could not grasp the 'black magic' of the ship's faster-than-light (FTL) propulsion system. As far as Mads knew, the Alcubierre-Manning Deep Warp Drive — the formal name of the FTL system - propelled the *Nostradamus* by negative matter which compressed space in front of it and expanded it back to 'normal' behind it, which also meant that the propulsion had no acceleration or gravitational forces to contend with. What that negative matter actually was, where it came from, and how it worked, were things he did not concern himself with. Some engineer once informed him it was the nearest possible thing to 'black light', hence making the propulsion system a very big deal. Mads had to accept that assertion on face value because he was not about to admit to anyone, especially the engineer, that he had absolutely no idea what black light was. All Mads knew was that his ship was able to transport him to the planet known as Arcadia as a routine journey almost instantaneously and that the 'almost' bit was because it was still unsafe to plot a linear course to such a far-flung destination. A path of curvature was necessary. This much at least Mads understood without needing it to be explained to him, but still, how exactly FTL travel could take a curved path was, again, beyond him, and he wasted no time in trying to understand any of it.

For this journey *Nostradamus* was 'his' ship, literally; not because he was the Bibliotekar, but because he was the only living being in it. A journey such as this required immense mathematical precision, and the very last thing it needed was error-prone human input or involvement.

FTL travel had the potential to create a new epoch of humankind. That was understood by most people, even those who had no idea how FTL travel worked, and it had transformed all thoughts of the future and what it possibly held for humankind. Nobody currently alive knew the collective feeling of humankind when watching the first landing of men on the Earth's moon in 1969 or the first landing of men and women on Mars in 2037 but if they did, they would know that the current mood created by FTL travel was exponentially greater.

But even though the technology had been first successfully applied forty-two years ago, in 2162, realising that potential was still beyond the persistent efforts of all First World countries. Apart from the cost of acquiring a license to use the technology, FTL travel still required ships and 'conventional' propulsion systems to get any FTL-enabled ship out of the grip of Earth's gravity before the Alcubierre-Manning Deep Warp Drive could be engaged – it's one big drawback - and both the licence and the propulsion system were still enormously expensive. So much so that, in theory, the *Nostradamus* was one of only seven ships with an operating FTL propulsion system. In practice, it was one of only six, and this was because the first ever FTL-propelled ship had successfully engaged its FTL systems but it had never, or at least not yet, returned from its maiden, crewless, journey, to the distant Beta Centauri system.

Despite that setback, subsequent FTL-propelled ships successfully travelled to the much closer Alpha Centauri system and returned to Earth. This activity served to hasten negotiations initiated by the United Nations when FTL technology was first developed, with the aim of creating a convention between all UN-member countries for the exploitation of planets.

As every person knew, Arcadia, one of only three currently known habitable planets in the universe other than Earth, was discovered orbiting the star Alpha Centauri B by NASA not long after the convention was agreed upon and it, accordingly, was the first planet to come under its terms. Thus, the planet could not be claimed by the

United States, but instead it came under the control of the United Nations. The US, as discoverer, was entitled to name the planet, which it did based on Alpha Centauri B's colloquial name of Rigil Kent, — 'RK' for short. Thus 'arkay', and thus 'Arcadia'. The US was also entitled to exploit twice the area allotted to all other UN-member nations and to choose the zone it was allotted before other nations received theirs.

Thurldottir had argued at Governing Council meetings that the discovery of Arcadia and the achievement of subluminal data transmission had paved the way for The Bibliotek to implement the world's first *real* Disaster Recovery Plan. This claim was true in the literal sense. What better way to absolutely guarantee the safety of millions of terabytes of data comprising the entire digital records of The Bibliotek from fire, flood, or deliberate or (unthinkable) accidental destruction than to back them up somewhere *off* Earth and all its attendant disaster risks? The idea had at first seemed fantastic to Mads, but even he had to admit that, logistics aside, it made perfect sense. The development of FTL technology had overcome the single biggest limitation to using wormholes, which was that the energy needed to create one large enough to send a spacecraft through it was more than the entire Earth could produce in a 250 year period. But, a very small wormhole required only a minute fraction of that energy and was all that was needed to send data through; the millions of terabytes of Bibliotek data.

Thurldottir would never have achieved her aim of establishing a base on Arcadia for The Bibliotek had she not orchestrated the coup which landed her the Chair of the Governing Council. After having achieved that, Norway's allocated zone on Arcadia was chosen as the site for The Bibliotek's back-up mainframe as the primary feature of its Disaster Recovery Plan. The Norwegian government was only too happy to lease a chunk of its mostly unexploited zone on Arcadia to The Bibliotek. In return, The Bibliotek allowed the Norwegian government to use the *Nostradamus* to transport equipment and personnel to Arcadia on scheduled flights. Mads had watched these developments though with increasing scepticism. It represented a huge long-term undertaking of The Bibliotek and to Mads it had seemed dangerously close to stepping outside its *raison d'etre*.

Fortunately, the cost of maintaining and operating the *Nostradamus* was partly offset by the semi-regular leasing of it to various other organisations and countries for a lot of money. The demand was there and increasing. The Bibliotek was meeting that demand for FTL travel but imposed stringent conditions on any potential lessee. For example, the *Nostradamus* was not allowed to be leased for any military purpose or use, and there were certain periods when the leasing of the *Nostradamus* was not permitted due to planned usage by The Bibliotek. The particular journey Mads was undertaking was in one of those periods.

Despite the revenue benefits of leasing the *Nostradamus* to outside parties, there was still a lot of internal opposition to its ownership and use by The Bibliotek. But because Chair Thurldottir had championed its construction and had ensured funding was made available, at no small measure of budgetary limitations on normal operating expenses, a cause of significant issues for Mads to have to deal with, that opposition was confined to informal mutterings.

As time went on, those mutterings diminished. This was because the Norwegian government had also made it clear that to protect its tax-exempt charitable status, The Bibliotek had to ensure that any revenue from leasing the *Nostradamus* left over from meeting the ongoing costs of the spaceship was funnelled into meeting its normal operating expenses. Basically, The Bibliotek was restrained from operating any commercial enterprise that was not directly connected to the Central Repository.

Another factor that enabled Thurldottir to push through with the construction and use of the *Nostradamus* was its size. It wasn't that large, only forty metres in total length, with its cargo bays comprising no more than fifteen metres of that length, and it had no escape pod. This meant it was nowhere near as heavy as nearly all other FTL-enabled ships currently in operation, and this in turn meant it did not require as much fuel for its atmospheric propulsion.

Though a smaller planet, Arcadia's atmosphere was very similar to that of Earth's, so much so that humans did not need a protective suit, only a nose-fitted air filter. Radiation levels were actually lower than they were on Earth, but its gravity was what made it unsuitable for permanent habitation — it was just a little bit too much for the human body to cope with, especially for someone arriving from Earth so quickly via FTL-enabled means such as with the *Nostradamus*. The transition, as quick as it was, was not healthy.

Mads had journeyed to Arcadia on the *Nostradamus* several times before. But today's trip was the first time he didn't have an official reason to be there. He was deeply troubled by what Thomas had experienced, but he kept his concerns to himself. He needed to know more before he raised anything with the Governing Council, if at all, and he felt sufficiently worried to keep his journey quick and, if possible, unnoticed. He was thus fortunate in that this trip was a scheduled supply flight by the *Nostradamus*, albeit such trips were normally supposed to be unmanned.

As with his previous times on board the *Nostradamus*, the take-off and thrust-out of the clutches of Earth's atmosphere provided Mads with all of his excitement during the trip. The remainder of the journey, including the landing at The Bibliotek's site on Arcadia, seemed perfunctory by comparison.

Upon exiting the still-glistening silver spaceship, Mads could hear only the beat of automated mechanical noises and was met by no-one. This he had expected, as it was also quite normal. There were only four people stationed at The Bibliotek's facility on Arcadia and Mads knew that two of them would be asleep. Another would be with the mainframe doing his job, and the fourth would be tending to the biological research facility that The Bibliotek maintained at the very edge of its site. Neither of the staff on duty needed to be at the spaceport facility because the unloading of the *Nostradamus* was fully automated, as was its subsequent take-off and return to Earth in three hours' time. And given the extra propulsion needed to lift off from Arcadia and escape its atmosphere, nobody wanted to be around when it happened. That included Mads, who wasted no time in exiting the launch pad and making his way to The Bibliotek's computer facility, a little further distance, because he needed to be back on board and strapped into his seat well before launch of the *Nostradamus* back to Earth..

And as was the case with every other person making their way from the spaceport facility, regardless of whether or not they had been to Arcadia before, the experience was surreal in the extreme for Mads. Humankind had been through so much in its recent history, seemingly trying to wipe itself out at various times, and almost achieving it with the Great Holy War. But walking on Arcadia made all that seem... pointless. It was easy for Mads to contemplate why some people were not allowed to undertake FTL travel, especially to a planet like Arcadia. It was too much for their minds to cope with, the ease with which they were suddenly transported to an alien world, far away from Earth. It was the fact that merely hours after walking on Earth they were walking on Arcadia. It sent these people literally nuts. Only perfectly sane people could appreciate the surrealness, and not let it fry their brains with sensory overload.

A human could breath and survive on Arcadia, mostly just like on Earth, but that was where the similarity ended. The water almost tasted the same but it had a blue tinge to it. The grasses had a mauve hue. There were plants big and small but anything that counted as a tree was spread out on the ground, not into what passed as the Arcadian sky. And not with thick solid trunks but with more stem and tubelike branch systems. There were no birds but there were large flying creatures, more like insects. And more insect-like creatures on the ground, with hard exoskeletons and tentacles that gave them the unenviable appearance of giant cockroaches. No marsupial or mammal-like creatures had yet been found. And, of course, no evidence yet of humanoids, past or present. The air had a pungent odour to it. Not repugnant, but neither was it pleasant like a perfume. More stale than fresh, a sense heightened by the regular winds. The thinking was that this strange environment was a function of the extended daily sunlight, a constant that saw darkness only ever fall for three hours at the most.

Mads knew he would never get used to how bizarre Arcadia was, compared to Earth. Being there never felt as exciting after the anticipation of his first journey there. Being there after that first arrival just felt... strange. So strange that Mads felt like an alien, like he didn't belong there, and this was a feeling he knew others shared. Thomas was one who shared that feeling and he and Mads had talked about the strangeness a lot.

At least The Bibliotek's rectangular-prismed mainframe facility looked familiar in its human origin and construction, but as he approached it, it merely reinforced for Mads the strangeness of Arcadia, because the facility simply did not look as if it belonged there. It certainly wasn't designed from an aesthetic point of view to fit in with the landscape. The same impression applied to the nearby greenhouse. It was a large white dome. Apart from the growing of some fresh fruit and vegetables under Earth-like atmospheric conditions for the facility staff, an open section of the greenhouse was used to conduct experiments on plant growth under Arcadian conditions on behalf of various Earth-based research organisations.

Entering the dust lock of the mainframe facility eased Mads' feeling of strangeness a little. And then a voice came over the intercom.

"Hello, ah... this is Commander Rolf Henderson, Head of Station, I presume you have just arrived unexpectedly on *Nostradamus*. Ah,... can I help you?"

"Henderson, this is Bibliotekar Ingridson. Can you let me in please?"

"Bibliotekar?!... Oh... Yes, Bibliotekar, certainly. I am unsealing the door right... now. It will be accessible as soon as the vacuuming has finished. And I will be there shortly."

Mads knew Commander Henderson would be on duty, and he knew his arrival would be a surprise, but Henderson just had to deal with it. That and the thing about him that Mads had been tipped off about by Kaitlin Drummond and would be raising with him. He continued to take off his boots and jacket and put on the protective suit that everyone entering the facility had to wear. He then engaged the vacuum, which sucked out all traces of dust that entered with him when he entered the dust lock. After a few seconds, the noisy vacuum stopped and the door to the facility proper opened. Mads entered and went straight to the basin directly across the hallway that stretched left and right and began washing his hands. As he did so he noticed a man walking towards him in a bright pale blue protective suit. Unfortunately, the vivid but somewhat dirty blue of his suit clashed visually with his orange hair and beard, both of which were in abundance. Mads suddenly had the bizarre thought that Henderson definitely 'fitted in' with Arcadia.

"Welcome Bibliotekar," Henderson said, extending his hand to shake Mads'.

Mads dried his hands and shook Henderson's hand. "Thank you, Henderson, it's a pleasure to be back."

"You've caught me by surprise, I'm afraid, Bibliotekar. I wasn't expecting you. Please, come to the control room."

"I am not here, officially, is that understood?" Mads told Henderson as they walked along the hallway, side-by-side.

"Yes, Bibliotekar, understood. Absolutely," Henderson replied, then paused because he had no idea what Mads meant. "Well, not completely. I mean, you *are* here. I can pretend you are not, and will do so after you have gone, but you *will* have been here, so..."

Mads stopped walking and interrupted him. "Commander, how long before your rotation back to Earth?"

"Aaaah, that would be forty-six Earth days, fourteen hours, and, um, twenty-two minutes."

"And this is your last posting on Arcadia?"

"Yes, Bibliotekar, that would be correct. No more off-Earth time for me," Henderson beamed.

Mads did not reciprocate the sentiment. "Good," he flatly said, then resumed walking.

The thought occurred to Mads that Henderson had perhaps already spent too much time on Arcadia. It aligned with what Kaitlin had told him about some of the messages Henderson had been transmitting back to Earth.

As they reached and entered the control room, Mads told Henderson "I am just here to conduct an unscheduled test of the DRP, then I will be returning on the *Nostradamus*. So I will need your full co-operation."

"Yes, Bibliotekar, of course," Henderson replied, "but you do realise that we recently had our scheduled yearly DRP test?"

"Of course, I do. This is an unscheduled test and being unscheduled makes it far more critical to the DRP than a scheduled one, wouldn't you agree?"

"Aaah, yes, Bibliotekar, I see your point. Unscheduled, unannounced, not officially here. All good."

"Glad to hear it. I am only here officially if you fail the test to *any* degree. Otherwise, if my presence is made known you will know about it. Is *that* clear?"

"Yes, Bibliotekar."

Mads stood still and stared at Henderson's eyes for a few seconds, for added impact, before he continued. "Firstly, can you confirm for me how long before *Nostradamus* takes off?"

Henderson checked a screen on his panel, then replied, "Take off is scheduled for two hours and forty-three minutes from now. You will need to be on board twenty minutes beforehand, it takes fifteen minutes to walk back to the spaceport, so that leaves you with... just over two hours."

"Good. Now, is the wormhole engaged?"

"Yes, Bibliotekar."

"Show me."

"Okay," said Henderson, pointing to one of the screens in front of him. "This is the concurrent data feed log. You can see the transmission coding is at normal speed, that is, hyper fast. The bursts are running at between... let me see... between twenty-nine and thirty-three seconds, which is within our normal operating parameters."

"And the lags?"

"They're currently fluctuating at between ten and twelve minutes, roughly, with burst sequences running at fifteen to eighteen minutes."

"Wormhole downtimes?"

"Apart from the daily orbital lags, there have been no unscheduled down times in two years, Bibliotekar, with scheduled down times every six months for twenty-four hours. Those have all been carried out, as... um... scheduled."

"Good. Now,... show me your current outwards data log," ordered Mads, now looking intently at Henderson.

"Here it is, Bibliotekar," Henderson said more than a little nervously as he handed Mads a bound printout, which did not go unnoticed by Mads as did Henderson's attempt to hide his nerves.

Mads peered at the outward entries Henderson had been making, and began looking for certain dates, times, and volumes. As Mads had suspected, courtesy of the information given to him by Kaitlin, he found them. He turned and looked at Henderson, whose face had turned a distinctly red shade. Now it was time.

"I would find it odd if you weren't sending personal messages to a loved one back in Norway, Commander, but you seem to be engaged in a private activity that rather goes beyond the allowances allotted to you in the wormhole. Am I right?" Mads said almost rhetorically, in a flat but firm tone that made it clear he wanted Henderson to respond.

"Um, yes, sorry Bibliotek."

"Just how many subscribers do you have to your 'Cadet on Arcadia' internet videos?" asked Mads, just as seriously.

Henderson suddenly looked as if he had been slapped across the face. "Only a thousand or so, I think," he replied meekly.

"Only a thousand or so..." repeated Mads quietly, nodding as if contemplating the number. "Only, that hasn't stopped you from coming up with all sorts of stories about your 'stay' here on Arcadia, has it?" Mads said rather than asking, elevating his voice. This time he didn't bother waiting for a response. "Perhaps I should review your next rotation, maybe push it back six months or so, to provide you with more things to rave about. What do you think, Commander?"

Henderson's face was no longer red but was now white. "I... can... assure... you, Bibliotekar, that... won't... be necessary," he stuttered.

Mads peered at Henderson again for a few seconds. "That remains to be seen. But what I don't want to see is any more videos."

He continued with his stare at Henderson for a few more seconds, waiting.

"I understand Bibliotekar," Henderson finally said, firmly for once and now wide awake.

"I hope you do, Commander. I really hope you do. Now, is that the current time at The Bibliotek?" asked Mads, pointing to a digital timer on the control panel.

"Yes, Bibliotekar," uttered Henderson with as a respectful tone as he could muster, which, for him, was something relatively new.

"Okay, at some time between eight and thirteen minutes from now, the data feed will cease and you will receive the standard alert message that The Bibliotek's systems are down and inoperable due to a Level Three event. Is that understood?"

"Yes, Bibliotekar."

"Good, now when it happens I will be observing your responses, but before that time window opens I want you to show me the Visitors Log for the past twelve months."

"Yes, Bibliotekar." Henderson reached into a cavity in his panel and extracted a bound A4 notebook. It was definitely 'old school' but Mads had insisted on it when the facility had been constructed. It was another means of keeping important information off the electronic automated systems and out of the hands of I.T.. All visitors were required to handwrite their names, the purpose of their visit and sign the date of arrival and date of departure. Mads perused the entries then looked up at Henderson.

"Commander, this log is supposed to contain entries for all visitors to Arcadia and this facility, is it not?" Mads asked.

"Yes, Bibliotekar." Henderson was beginning to sound like a strained recorded voice.

"Then explain to me why there is no entry for the "heavy dudes" who came here recently," Mads demanded.

"I'm sorry, Bibliotekar, I don't follow..."

"You mentioned in one of your Cadet on Arcadia videos that some, quote, heavy dudes, were here doing some sort of geosurvey nearby, did you not?" interrupted Mads.

"Yes, but..."

"You see, the problem I have right now, Commander, is that there appears to be a discrepancy between what you have been disclosing via unauthorised means and what is supposed to be in the Visitors Log, which, correct me if I am wrong, is your responsibility!"

"I can explain, Bibliotekar."

"Please do, and do it quickly," Mads tersely responded, looking at the clock on the console. "You don't have much time before the shutdown signal arrives, and I am running out of patience."

"Doctor Patrick Joyce, the Lead Scientist. He insisted that the geosurvey team members were not required to enter their details in the Visitors Log because they were not going to enter the control facility, and would be working outside, on the edge of our zone. He told me their work was sensitive and we, as in The Bibliotek, did not want our neighbours to get any wrong ideas."

"I see, and did you dispute that?"

"I did not feel comfortable with Doctor Joyce's insistence that the team wasn't required to complete their entries for the log, and I said as much. But then one of the geo team, a rather large and aggressive man, basically told me to pull my head in. Then they walked away and went with Joyce to the greenhouse. After that I only saw them briefly. They seemed to be taking samples near the greenhouse, but after that I did not see them again. But Doctor Joyce did warn me against making a deal out of it."

"Hmm, I see," pondered Mads. He thought for a few seconds. "Is Joyce there now, at the greenhouse?"

"No, he's off duty, probably asleep. It's Doctor Kurosawa's shift now."

"Alright, we'll wait for the signal, you'll do what you are supposed to do, I'll watch, and if there is enough time before *Nostradamus* leaves, I will go and have a chat with Kurosawa."

"I can wake Joyce up if you want," offered Henderson.

"No, that won't be necessary."

1:30pm, Bibliotek Time

As Mads had requested of a surprised Rani Sharma just before he boarded Nostradamus, the Level Three alert signal had come through, springing Henderson into action. Satisfied the backup data transfer was initiated correctly and proceeding, Mads excused himself, much to Henderson's relief, to ostensibly visit the greenhouse and Kurosawa but actually to see if he could find the area where the mysterious geosurvey team had been active.

Mads had no intention of even speaking to Kurosawa. He was aware that Henderson might find it ironic that he had made a big deal about the mystery geo team not logging their details and an equally big deal about him not 'being here' also, but he had no other option. He had to basically threaten Henderson with his job if he chatted with his friends back on Earth about his presence, and to make that threat work he absolutely had to avoid Henderson getting suspicious about the real reason for his visit.

Mads didn't have to look hard to find the spot where the geo team had been. There in a rocky wall behind the white-domed greenhouse, which had been excavated to provide a flat vertical space for the greenhouse's construction, Mads saw the rubble and distinctive pick marks of recent activity. It was here that he found what looked like an ore deposit of a predominantly silvery-white and lustrous metal running through the strata in a thick vein. There were some small scraps of the metal on the ground, and Mads collected a few of them. Instantly he thought how heavy they were. *Really* heavy, which meant the metal's density was extremely high. He took out an old plastic zip-seal bag he had in the bottom of his cluttered satchel and put the pieces of metal inside it, sealed it, then put it back in the bottom of his satchel. Then as quietly and as quickly as possible he walked away from the greenhouse and returned to the launch facility and boarded the *Nostradamus* for the return flight to Earth.

Whilst he waited for take-off, Henderson sent him a message that the DRP download had been completed successfully. Mads was about to reply with thanks but decided instead to message back that he ended up not having enough time to visit the greenhouse, adding "I will treat our conversation regarding Dr Joyce in confidence, Commander, and I expect you to do likewise."

Henderson then confirmed he understood.

"One last thing," Mads messaged again, "when does Dr Joyce rotate?"

"In two weeks, I believe."

"Noted," Mads replied.

"Have a safe flight, Bibliotekar."

"Thank you."

Not long afterwards, the *Nostradamus* took off from Arcadia. As it rose from the grips of Arcadia's atmosphere but before the FTL propulsion engaged, the thought occurred to Mads that he was experiencing the very latest in technology that humankind had ever created in a startling and fantastic way that would have been far beyond the comprehension of the vast majority of the creators of the things his life was devoted to — books. It was a juxtaposition that seemed almost paradoxical to Mads.

10:57am, Friday, 14ᵗʰ December 2204

Larkin paged Mads, "Excuse me Bibliotekar."

"Yes, what is it?"

"Doctor Foote has just arrived early for his eleven o'clock meeting with you, and Chair Thurldottir is on the line," he responded.

"Alright, put her through and ask Doctor Foote to wait. I won't be long," Mads said. He had a feeling he knew the reason for Thurldottir's call.

"Bibliotekar, I see you are back in your office," Thurldottir rasped.

Mads noted the absence of any greeting, but he was used to that by now. He now knew his suspicion was correct. "I am in my office, yes, what can I do for you today?" he replied, ignoring the inference he had just returned from somewhere.

"I understand you have just returned from Arcadia," she said, as a statement.

"I have," Mads thought about stopping there, but he couldn't help himself, adding "is there a problem?"

"Do I really need to remind you? That you are meant to clear with me any travel you undertake outside Norway? I presume you know this includes any travel *off-planet?*"

Mads was expecting this. "I am sorry, but this was a routine trip," he responded in a flat tone. "I was undertaking an inspection of our back-up facility on Arcadia and a test of our DRP."

There was a pause before Thurldottir responded. It was a short pause, almost imperceptible, but Mads had engaged in enough antagonistic conversations with her to recognise it. He also recognised the difference in the tone of the first word she said in response before picking up her usual tone. It was a trait he was sure that Thurldottir did not recognise in her own speech.

"*If* that was the case," she said after that short pause, "if it was a routine trip, why didn't you clear it with me first? Surely you had plenty of time to plan for *that*. And why did it have to be you doing the test?"

"Any Disaster Recovery Plan is only as good as its ability to function on the happening of unplanned events. *That* was the matter of routine. As Chair of Adcom, I am the one ultimately responsible as you know for making sure the DRP performs this function, and that is why my trip was not only unplanned, but unannounced." Mads was speaking quickly now, not giving Thurldottir a chance to interrupt. "*That* is the only way I can guarantee that the DRP works. The more people who know about a DRP test in advance, the less robust the test, the less confidence in a successful outcome."

"You didn't take Sharma with you?"

"No, I didn't. Obviously. As I said, the less people.... And besides, DRP testing, unscheduled or not, does not involve the Head of I.T. leaving The Bibliotek. I needed her to stay and initiate the test at this end at a pre-determined time, which was shortly after I arrived unannounced at the facility on Arcadia to test not just the DRP but also the crucial human element at the facility, namely Commander Henderson. What's the point of doing so if we can't be absolutely sure *he* will do the job he is meant to do? And in that regard our DRP protocol is that the senior employee on station on Arcadia has the task of initiating the DRP download, and on this occasion that was Henderson."

"And did he?"

"Yes, the test went well. There were no issues with any data recovery. You'll have my full report once it passes through Adcom."

"Yes, please do," responded Thurldottir.

"Anything else I can help you with today?"

"Yes. Notwithstanding you wanted to conduct your DRP test on a pristine footing, I am going to put forward the motion at the next meeting of the Council that your Terms of Office be amended to make it absolutely clear there are no circumstances under which you can elect not to inform me of an intended absence outside Norway. Your personal safety is the issue here, and that concern overrides any you might have about tainting a test of the DRP. Is *that* clear, Bibliotekar?"

"Yes, Chair Thurldottir, and I welcome the opportunity to discuss..."

Mads was interrupted mid-sentence by Thurldottir's termination of the call. Mads was used to *that* as well. Now that she had told him his Terms of Office were going to be up for discussion at the next Governing Council meeting this was going to be his opportunity to finally raise the point that Thurldottir was overreaching; Mads was more than confident he was only obliged to *notify* the Chair of any intended absences. She did not have any veto power as such, and, as far as Mads was concerned, nor should she. What worried Mads more, though, was the question of what was motivating Thurldottir's push against him. She had seemed particularly annoyed that he had gone to Arcadia.

"Doctor Foote can come in now," he paged Larkin, putting Thurldottir's call behind him, for now.

His suite door opened, and Justin walked in then waited for the door to close behind him. "You wanted to see me, Bibliotekar?"

"Yes, Justin, come and join me on the terrace," said Mads walking over to the glass panels separating his office from his private garden and courtyard terrace, motioning Foote to join him. Once they were both well and truly outside, Mads told Foote that Councillor Metcalfe was safe and sound and that he knew where he was and so did Rafe. As Mads expected, Justin was visibly relieved.

"And now you are the third person at The Bibliotek to know Thomas is safe and quite alive. But I don't want anyone else knowing this just yet, alright?" said Mads.

"Absolutely, Bibliotekar." Foote wanted to ask why the disappearance and why the secrecy but knew better.

"Here's the thing, Justin, Thomas told Rafe that he had gone to Arcadia to undertake a planned test of our Disaster Recovery Plan drill. But given the nature of DRP drills, the only people who knew about it in advance was Rani Sharma and some senior members of her team. They pulled the plug at our end to initiate the drill, the back-up mainframe worked as expected, no issue with that, but Thomas told Rafe there was a geosurvey team also at the facility taking rock and ore samples nearby, and that he said as much in his draft report, which he never got to finalise and send to me before it disappeared from the system. It appears someone intercepted it because he was then threatened, and that's the reason he made himself scarce."

Foote was stunned. For once he was momentarily lost for words. "Um... ah... sorry, what happens now?"

"Thomas has a bummer neurophone."

"A burner?" asked Foote.

"Sorry, yes, a burner. I want you to get one too, but I don't want it associated with The Bibliotek in any way. Here is Thomas's number. I want you to call Thomas and establish contact. Tell him you are the go-between; he'll know what you mean. Got it?"

"I understand perfectly. This is to be completely off-line. Which also means he is to remain not officially missing."

"For now, yes," confirmed Mads. "And there's a few more things I'd like you to do, I'm afraid."

"I can guess one of them. Find that report."

"Yes, and in your usual discrete fashion, please."

"That won't be a problem, but what about Sharma?" asked Foote.

"What do you mean?"

"If she had not only known of Councillor Metcalfe's trip to Arcadia but was also tasked to initiate the DRP test from The Bibliotek, then would not she have expected to receive a copy of the Councillor's report on the test? And if that is the case, why hasn't she followed up on it?"

"Both of those are very valid questions, Justin. But as you and I both know, Rani doesn't think that way. It's annoying and one day soon we may have to counsel her again about this, but for now let's see what you can find out about the missing report without involving her."

"Shall do."

"Now, another thing I need you to do is a background check on Chair Thurldottir."

"Excuse me?" Foote was taken aback.

"I'm sorry but you heard me correctly," added Mads.

Foote looked at Mads for a few seconds, then decided he was serious. He could see the concern on Mads' face.

"I realise that what I am asking you to do is quite a different matter from every other off-the-record task I have asked of you, Justin, so I am asking you to take a leap of faith on this one," continued Mads, before pausing again to look at Justin. "The fact is I have reason to believe that Thomas's report was intercepted on the Chair's behalf and is in her hands. I'm telling you this because I trust you with that information and because it may help you secure a copy."

Foote didn't hesitate to consider whether or not he would agree to do what Mads had just asked of him, he just needed that disclosure about the report to be certain what his ears had heard. "It will be done, Bibliotekar, with the usual discretion. Actually... sorry... with added discretion."

Mads gave a little smile and a little nod to Foote. It was his way of acknowledging he had never before asked him to do such a task but that he trusted Foote implicitly. "Now, there's this..." Mads said, pulling a small lead box from his tunic.

"What is that?"

"Inside this box are some rock samples I took from the edge of our site on Arcadia. I can't take them out here because I don't know how radioactive the samples are. It's a mineral I have not seen before and it's incredibly heavy. My feeling is someone doesn't want the fact that this mineral exists on Arcadia to be made known. Bottom line is I need to know what these rocks are," explained Mads, holding up the box in front of him.

Foote reached out his hand and took the box. "As it turns out, Bibliotekar, my brother-in-law is a metallurgist with the Centre for Earth Evolution and Dynamics at Oslo University. He can identify them for us."

"Excellent, thank you, Justin. He'll have to check the radioactivity first, but you absolutely mustn't tell him where they came from."

"That goes without saying, Bibliotekar," replied Justin.

"Can you take the box to him personally?"

"Absolutely," asserted Foote.

"Excellent. Now, Justin, I appreciate that all the things I've asked you to do add up to not much time left for your normal duties, so I've had a quiet word to Kaitlin. As far as she is concerned, you are leading a senior recruitment task that reports directly to me until further notice and which is highly confidential. Nothing in writing, okay?" requested Mads.

"Understood."

"I won't keep you any longer lest Larkin starts getting twitchy. Keep in touch the usual way and let me know when you've contacted Thomas."

"Certainly," said Foote, turning to make his exit.

"Justin," Mads added, lowering his voice. Foote stopped and turned around. "Thurldottir knows I was on Arcadia."

Foote pondered that information for a few seconds. "Understood," he responded, then turned and left.

Mads remained outside on his terrace, ostensibly admiring the late-autumn view but mostly trying to process recent events and the last two conversations he had had. He had taken a risk with each. It was risky telling Thurldottir that story about going to Arcadia for an unplanned test of the DRP, but it was calculated. He knew that the only way that Thurldottir could know he didn't go to Arcadia for that reason was if she had Thomas's report. But it paid off; that pause when he mentioned the DRP test plus that lilt in her tone when she said the word 'if' told him she didn't believe his excuse for going to Arcadia. He was certain of *that*. It was then a risk to tell Justin of his *suspicion* she had Thomas' report, but it too was calculated. Justin did deserve to have that information as a measure of Mads' trust in him. In other circumstances he would have held it back so he could compare it with the outcome of the task, but this time was different, and he was certain Justin appreciated the difference.

But now the potential enormity of that difference started to appear to Mads, and he found it hard to suppress his mind from racing away with it. For now, he tried to focus on the fact that he had played a higher-stakes card in his ongoing game with Thurldottir. Mads knew that she in turn knew that he had lied to her as to why he went to Arcadia without informing her. Any more than that would be speculation on her behalf. But Mads also knew that Thurldottir would now try to convert speculation into knowledge, and that would involve finding out from The Bibliotekar's personnel on Arcadia everything Mads had said and done whilst he had been there. And to do that,

Mads also knew she would get someone else to find out that information.

"One step ahead of you," he very quietly said out loud. Then he abruptly pulled himself up. *What's going on?* he thought to himself. Mads liked being the Bibliotekar. Like any other large organisation, office politics came with the job. But lately it all seemed next level. *Why?* he thought, trying to pin down what had changed. It did not take long. The more he thought about it, the clearer the realisation came that ever since Thurldottir had joined the Governing Council several years ago it seemed to Mads that the level of office politics had increased and kept increasing. And now it was all consuming.

More to the point, there were things happening that should not be happening, and they were happening without his knowledge or control. And they were not good things, they were bad things. So now, instead of feeling able to gradually wind down his role and workload towards retirement in a few years, Mads was beginning to feel more challenged than he had ever felt in his entire career as Bibliotekar.

If this continued, still calling him the Book Keeper would seem trite to his friends. Perhaps he had been complacent about Thurldottir and should have been on alert from the very moment it was put to him by Councillor Carlson that she would be a great asset on the Council. He had surprised himself when he had vocalised "one step ahead of you". But maybe saying it had woken him up. Maybe it was going to be like this all the time from now on. Maybe he had to change his mindset. Maybe it was time to be proactive. And act.

Immediately following her conversation with Mads, Danuta Thurldottir, sitting in her office in her chalet on a hillside near Utne overlooking Hardangerfjord, sent an encrypted message to someone in The Bibliotek, "You are meant to be keeping track of our mutual friend's movements, but you failed to tell me about his trip to Arcadia. Can I ask why?"

After a few minutes, she got a reply. "I am sorry, but he did not mention it to me. I was not aware he went to Arcadia. All he said was that he was taking the day off to do some research at the Academy."

Danuta immediately responded, "Let me be clear. You are meant to be keeping track of his movements. That means ALL of them. You should have checked to make sure he was doing what he said he was doing, and then told me he wasn't. I shouldn't have to spell that out. Is this going to be a problem I will have with you in the future?"

"No."

"Good. Make sure of it," Thurldottir typed with finality. She then sent another encrypted message to someone else. "Come to Utne." That was all she needed to say. Its recipient would know she needed to talk to him face-to-face and in private. It would take him a few hours to get there, and this riled her. But she also felt that caution was now prescribed in dealing with Mads Ingridson. "What a prick, you are," she said out loud in her otherwise empty house.

Just over three hours later, the entry panel of Thurldottir's chalet chimed a low monotone.

"It's Smits, Chair Thurldottir," said a deep male voice.

Thurldottir did not reply but buzzed him in. She heard him enter, close the door behind him, then walk up the steps to her office, where she was sitting, waiting, behind her desk. Smits stood several paces away and waited in silence. He knew better than to begin a conversation.

"Ingridson has been to Arcadia," Thurldottir said matter-of-factly.

"I see. Should I arrange for the Arcadia personnel to be... replaced?"

"No, it's too late for that!" replied Thurldottir, exasperated. "Ingridson knows more than he's letting on, and if we clean up Arcadia that will just raise the stakes, and we're not ready to play that game yet."

"Understood."

"Do you? You really do fucking understand that, *do* you?!" exploded Thurldottir. "Tell me this then, did you understand what you were doing when you threatened Metcalfe?!"

Smits had been waiting for something to set her off. "I felt something had to be done, and quickly."

"No shit something had to be done quickly, but you weren't the one to do it! I don't pay you to make those kinds of decisions. I pay you to implement decisions. My decisions! Do you understand that!?"

"I do, yes."

"Then tell me this. Which is better: Metcalfe meeting a sudden, but innocuous death, or Metcalfe going missing?"

"I... ah..."

"Oh for fuck's sake! Nobody looks for a dead body lying on a floor, you idiot. It would have been a whole lot better if Metcalfe had been disposed of. Quietly and quickly. He's getting on in years, it would have too easy to create him dead by some seemingly natural means that would not have raised any questions. Too easy!" glared Thurldottir at Smits, but she wasn't finished yet. "Now we have the Bibliotekar looking for him and sticking his nose into things we'd rather not have him do. All because you decided to *threaten* Metcalfe. I thought I was paying you to be smarter than that. Am I paying you too much?"

Smits hesitated for second, but then said firmly, "no, you are not."

"Good, I'd hate to think Councillor Carlson was wrong about you. So would Carlson. Now, tell me this: have you managed to find out anything from Metcalfe's data pad or phone?"

"Yes, I am certain that he did not communicate with the Bibliotekar between the time he was on Arcadia and when he left The Bibliotek."

"Apart from the report you intercepted?"

"Correct."

"Well, tell me if you know the answer to this: what made Ingridson go to Arcadia on some bullshit DRP excuse?"

Smits did not respond.

"No? I didn't think so. Now go back and do the fucking job you're being paid to do."

Smits turned around without responding — he knew better than that — and began walking out of the room.

"You know... " said Thurldottir with a pause, which made him stop, "showing initiative is only doing something before you are told to do it. Anything else is just fucking up. I suggest you learn the difference, quickly."

Then, as Smits was closing the door behind him, Thurldottir added "*jeg er omgitt av idioter!*"

He didn't understand Norwegian, but Smits knew he had just received another insult.

END OF CHAPTER FIVE

Chapter Six

A Message Delivered, A Message Received

Almansor: "We heard that the terrible Cardinal Ximenes, in the middle of the market, in Granada — my tongue stares in my mouth — the Koran they threw into a flaming pyre!"
Hassan: "That was but a prelude. Wherever they burn books, they will end up burning human beings."
Heinrich Heine, *Almansor*, 1821

8:23pm, Friday, 21ˢᵗ December 2204

Rafe had seen death before. More than once he had seen the slow and expected death of a loved one and more than once he had seen the sudden and unexpected death of a stranger. But he had not seen this kind of death before. Not the sight that grotesquely greeted his entry into the study of the medieval stone villa in the hilltop town of Pienza, southern Tuscany, where the 168-year old Viscount Visconti di Rossellini lived alone. Not here in the beautiful urban Renaissance village of Pienza, his favourite place in Italy. Not anywhere.

He instantly realised that the grotesqueness had been structured. It was deliberate and it was meant to be seen by him and recognised for what it was. Apart from that it was obviously a murder. And it was a message to Rafe. He had been invited to come here by the Viscount. This was his home, and Rafe, as he had done several happy times before, had just driven there in a rental hovercar straight from Rome's Fiumicino helioport that crisp winter's evening.

The message had been delivered by way of an inexpertly performed evisceration of Rossellini, who was lying on his back with his arms and his legs making like a star, and followed up by a now-smouldering little bonfire in his chest cavity fuelled in part by what appeared to Rafe to be torn-up pages from some of the books in the study. From the impassive look on the Viscount's face, it also appeared to Rafe that his gutting had been *post-mortem*. From the discarded bindings strewn on the floor around the body it also appeared to Rafe the oldest books in the Viscount's collection had been chosen for this purpose; the very books that had brought Rafe here, now, to negotiate their procurement by The Bibliotek. All the other books from the shelves were piled into a corner of the study, ripped apart and smouldering. Not from fire, but from... *what was that smell? Acid!* thought Rafe.

For what seemed to him a long time, Rafe stood at the doorway, listening. Trying to calm his heartbeat. Thinking. Rationalising the coincidence of the timing of this horrendous act into a realisation that The Bibliotek's knowledge of his movements may have been compromised, or at least communicated in advance by someone for someone else.

It's a message. Rafe kept repeating that thought with increasing certainty. *It's a message. A message...*

He went to take his data pad out of his satchel to photograph the scene before him, but then stopped, frozen with fear. It leapt into Rafe's mind. It was fear caused by the realisation of the implication for The Bibliotek and his dealings with it. Rafe could no longer trust it. But more than that was troubling Rafe. The perpetrator, or more likely perpetrators, must have known that it would be obvious to Rafe that someone in The Bibliotek had tipped them off about Rafe's movements, about this very meeting. They could not possibly assume that Rafe would not come to that conclusion, and do so quickly, which alarmed Rafe just as much as the sight on the floor, if not more, because it made the murder of the Viscount seem like it was something off-hand, something done with ease and casualness, a means to an end, and thus something far more frightening than a mere murder, if ever a murder could be called that. And then there was the question of why. Why did they not bother about concealing a link to The Bibliotek? This was a question that rose in Rafe's mind and stayed there, unanswered. His mind was shouting its shortened version – *why?* And then another question arose. Why *present* Rafe with a gutted Viscount instead of waiting for Rafe to arrive and *then* do the same to him? Would that scenario not have also served as a message, even more potent in its implications? Why was this an intimately personal message?

After an unknown time just standing still, maybe less than a minute, maybe more than ten, Rafe composed his thoughts. He decided not to enter the study at all. That was the easy decision to make, already half made in the preceding minutes. He also decided to leave the house immediately and without touching anything, and go straight to Florence to the hotel room awaiting his check-in. That was a less easy decision. Harder still, he decided not to inform the police about the crime there and then. He wasn't sure why. It just seemed prudent, if not safer, to keep himself out of any official handling of the scene and its inevitable criminal investigation. But he had to let Mads know. He had to warn Mads that something serious was amiss with The Bibliotek; that it appeared to have been compromised by the Present Sect. *Who else?* The first question Rafe had asked himself that was almost rhetorical. It had an immediate answer: no-one.

Without yet moving, Rafe prepared himself to leave. Notwithstanding the dim light, he slowly looked around the room for any signs of a security camera, or some such, but unless the Viscount had one hidden amongst the shelving, there was not one to be seen. He saw a light switch on the wall to his immediate right, but he decided not to turn it on. Someone outside or nearby might see it and know that someone was in the house, alive. Still without moving, Rafe tried to recall all the surfaces he had already touched in and around the house. All he could recall doing was to cautiously push the already ajar front door open with his leather-gloved hand on his arrival, already feeling then that something was not quite right. The feeling was enough that he neither used the heavy door knocker to announce his arrival or call out to the Viscount or otherwise speak. It was a feeling spurred by the acrid smell that had been wafting from the study.

Rafe listened for any sound coming elsewhere from within the house or the study apart from the steady ticking of the large grandfather clock in the hallway behind him. There was none, so Rafe had one last look at the Viscount's body, subconsciously wondering if there was something else to be seen that he had not spotted on his shocked arrival at the study door, and he once again resisted the urge to take a photograph in order to show Mads. He then turned around and slowly walked to the front doorway. He stepped outside, turned again, and with his gloved hand slowly pulled the door back to near enough its ajar position as he had found it on his arrival. The narrow stone-covered street in Pienza was empty. This being a Friday night that was unusual. Rafe quickly glanced up and around. There were no open windows on any of the nearby houses, and the few lit windows he saw were behind closed shutters. He pulled up his collar and as quietly as possible walked away from the Viscount's house. Rafe being Rafe, his hovercar was parked down the street.

But before he was even a hundred metres away from the Viscount's house, Rafe heard the distinctive siren of a Carabinieri hovercar getting closer. He stopped walking, turned and stepped over a low stone wall beside the path he was on and walked to a nearby tree and stood behind it, hoping above all else there were no dogs around. Within seconds, the police hovercar raced past, prompting Rafe to waste no more time in getting to his. As he approached it he looked around at nearby houses. There were a few with lights on inside, but no doors or windows had opened to the sound of the siren, which was no longer blaring. Rafe knew that soon there would be more sirens, more police, and windows and doors would then start opening, so he quickly got to his hovercar and as quietly as possible opened the driver's door and got in. Now he waited, with the hovercar window down. He waited for the sound of more sirens before engaging the magneto drive, as he wanted to know the direction the new police arrivals were coming from before driving away. He didn't have to wait long, and to his silent relief they were approaching from the other side of the small town.

Rafe tried not to drive fast, not least because the hoverpaths leaving Pienza were neither straight nor made for speed, but also because he had the presence of mind to try to not to be noticed and remembered. By the time he reached the hoverway, the adrenaline had subsided and now anger began sweeping over his thoughts. *Why such violence? Over books!? What was the justification, no, the rationale? Are these people all psychopaths? Or was it a lone wolf? How could such a person infiltrate The Bibliotek? No, wait, can't be sure of that just yet.* He paused. *Get certainty first,* he counselled himself.

Before long, less than hour, but with his mind still racing, Rafe had almost reached the end of the hoverway and the outskirts of Florence. Without really thinking about it, he turned into a disused hydrogen station and parked his rental hovercar to one side, facing the road, and sat staring in the distance, hovercars silently flashing past in front of him. He desperately wanted to tell Mads what had happened in Pienza before he did anything else, but paranoia was holding him back. But after a few minutes his ability to reason came back to him. He realised that if the Present Sect had compromised his network connection it would not matter if he used it to let Mads know what happened in Pienza because they would expect him to. He just had to be careful about what he said.

With that thought foremost in mind, Rafe tapped his neurophone and curtly said "Call the Keeper". (He always liked saying that. It sounded better than 'Call Mads', and much better than 'Call the Bibliotekar'.)

"Hey Nags. How are you?" answered Mads. "Sorry, I can't talk for long, I'm about to go into a meeting. What's up?"

"I'll keep this short," said Rafe. "We've got a serious problem, Mads. I can't explain now but we need to talk, face-to-face and as soon as possible. I'm sorry to sound dramatic but I'll be at The Bibliotek on Monday morning. We'll talk then." Rafe did not wait for Mads to respond, he terminated the call, then tapped his neurophone off.

8:47am, Monday 24ᵗʰ December 2204

When Rafe arrived at The Bibliotek, Mads was waiting for him on the maglev station platform. "This is starting to be a habit," said Rafe, "but how did you know to be here?"

"I am the Bibliotekar, don't forget Nags, and maglev operators can communicate information when instructed to. Now, what's the problem you mentioned? Let's talk while we walk to my office."

Keeping his voice low and measured, Rafe told Mads of his experience in Pienza, with as much calm as he could muster given the people passing them as they walked.

Mads was appalled by what Rafe had to say about Viscount di Rossellini and what had happened to him. "Let me get Nikka to come here now. We need to find out what, if anything, the Italian police have discovered. And Bernie. We'll need Bernie."

"No Mads," said Rafe. "We have a far bigger problem, don't you see?"

"I'm sorry, but what could be worse than what looks like another vicious murder committed by the Present Sect? You're not saying it wasn't the Sect are you? You said they left a calling card."

"Mads, it *was* the Present Sect, and that's the point. They knew I was coming, I'm sure of it. The timing is far too coincidental. Rossellini didn't broadcast his collection. He was intensely private, and I've been courting him for years, had been courting him, sorry, and he always joked about teasing me gently, leading me along. And as you know he finally decided to donate his books. But I am one hundred percent positive he told no-one but me. Mads, they knew I had finally succeeded in getting him to relinquish his collection. The problem is how did they know? Can't you see?"

Mads looked at Rafe as the realisation dawned on him. His eyes narrowed, and he stepped back a pace.

"Yes, you're right. It *is* too much of a coincidence. So who knew about your appointment?"

"Nobody. The only thing I did was input it into my work calendar. It was a scheduled trip. I named the Viscount and where he lived. I always do that, ever since Accounts started hassling me about my travel expense reports. You know I hate paperwork, but I've gotten used to inputting my schedule ahead of time. And this particular trip I scheduled two weeks ago, to the hour and the day. Someone has accessed that information, Mads. Someone at The Bibliotek."

"But hang on, you only scheduled your visit to the Viscount, didn't you? Not the reason?"

"That's right."

"So maybe that part of it was a coincidence?"

"Even so that still leaves the fact they knew I was coming, and when."

"I see that, yes," said Mads, his mind racing now, just as Rafe's had. "But why? Why kill Rossellini just before you got there!?"

"It's a message, Mads. It's a message to me personally. And I read it as 'stop'. Just that. Stop."

"Without knocking you off at the same time? Why make one statement but not the other? It doesn't make sense."

"You know I don't like speculation, Mads, but maybe if we focus on our problem the answer will present itself." Rafe said, just as they reached the entrance of the main administration building of The Bibliotek, where Mads had his office suite on the top floor, eight levels up. Mads stopped and turned around to look at Rafe. There were Bibliotek employees passing them on their way in and out of the building, each one acknowledging Mads, if not Rafe as well. He took Rafe aside.

"Yes, you're right again," admitted Mads in a lowered tone, "absolutely right. Look. Look, I am about to catch up with Justin. I will ask him to look into the data breach. Tonight though, please come to my apartment for dinner, Nags, it's been a while."

"Sounds good, Mads, but just to warn you, I need a drink or five, so can we please have a red or two from your cellar?"

"We can indeed. And it will be two bottles, as we will be joined by someone I want you to meet."

"Anyone I know?"

"That remains to be seen, but please, no word of Pienza or any of this issue tonight. See you at seven."

"Okay Mads. Wait, did you get to Arcadia?"

"I did, and I found something interesting. But I'll talk to you about it later. Remember, nothing about any of this at dinner, okay?"

"Yes Mads, got it. I heard you the first time."

1:30pm

Justin Foote entered Mads' office suite a little quicker than normal, even though he had made this appointment, but as usual he was carrying a folder with papers in it and his data pad. Mads motioned for him to join him at the meeting table, where he was already seated.

"I'm sorry to bother you just before the holiday break, Bibliotekar, but I wanted to update you on a few things before it," said Foote.

"That's fine Justin, I won't be finishing today for a few hours yet. I got your message that you had made contact with Councillor Metcalfe. Thanks for that. How was he?"

"He said he was relieved to hear from me, as it meant you had stopped worrying about him, Bibliotekar. He sounded upbeat and said to tell you he was fine."

"Excellent, now what have you got for me, Justin?"

"Firstly, the mineral sample..."

"Yes..."

"Well, I've got a very excited brother-in-law on my hands, Bibliotekar. He's analysed the samples — they're not radioactive by the way — and they are mostly palladium and some rhodium. Extremely rare on Earth it seems, and both very valuable."

"Valuable? How valuable?"

"The sample you gave me weighed six hundred and forty-eight grams and according to my brother-in-law that equates to a value of about one hundred and fifty thousand Euros, give or take a few thousand, and that's just in their unrefined state. Not that the samples need that much refining."

"Seriously?!" said Mads.

"That was a conservative estimate, so yes," replied Justin. "He also said he had never seen samples so pure, nor in such concentrated form, and never so much in quantity. So naturally he wanted to know where they came from."

"Oh, I see, what did you tell him?"

"I managed to do some quick research before I had to retrieve the samples from him, so I was able to fob him off with the story that I could not specify the location as it lay within the Disputed Territories in the south of Botswana. It turns out most of the world's scarce palladium supplies come from northern South Africa."

"Good, but I'm sorry you had to lie to him, Justin. How did he take that?"

"He seemed satisfied by my answer, but he was also curious as to why I had them, so in that instance I was able to tell him the truth."

"Eh? You said *what*?"

"That I had been given the samples by someone who didn't want the world to know but who knew I had a metallurgist as a close relative who could keep his mouth shut if given the right incentive."

"Ha ha, well done, Justin. How much is this going to cost me?"

"Twenty-five thousand was the figure I gave him."

"Twenty-five thousand Euros!?"

"Yes, Bibliotekar, sorry."

Mads was still reeling from the valuation of the rocks he had simply grabbed from the surface of Arcadia and put in his satchel. But he quickly realised that a bribe of twenty-five thousand Euros to keep that information private was, in the current circumstances, not worth arguing about.

"Okay, but we'll have to keep this off the books, Justin, so give me a few days to organise something. Tell your brother-in-law the money's coming. Now tell me: why are palladium and rhodium so valuable?"

"I hope I remembered this correctly, but it appears that palladium absorbs hydrogen, making it a key element in cold fusion. I don't know how, but the purity of the sample makes it ideal for the process. And the rhodium, apart from hardening palladium and making it resistant to corrosion — hence the quality of the sample — it is used to measure neutron flux levels in nuclear reactors, and, as it happens, is highly desirable in the construction of quantum computers. In short, Bibliotekar, they are both the rarest and most sought-after mineral elements on Earth. Exponentially more valuable than your boring gold, diamonds and such like."

Now looking at the ceiling, Mads was shaking his head and leaning back in his chair, letting this information soak in. "My. Goodness," was all he could muster in response for a few seconds. "Where are the samples now?" he asked, returning his gaze to Justin.

"Buried in my tiny windowsill garden."

"Buried in your garden!" laughed Mads, "I guess that's as good a place as any, for now. Palladium and rhodium. We'll call it P&R okay? This changes some things and makes other things a lot clearer. I'll need to think this through for a bit."

"Yes, of course, Bibliotekar."

"But what you can do is call back Councillor Metcalfe and let him know where I've been and what I found. He can reach his own conclusion as to whether it explains the threat he received and why his report went missing but see if your update prompts him to line up any dots."

"That I will do."

"Anything else?"

"No luck on the missing report I am afraid. Someone knew what they were doing and left no digital footprints or relics. All intra-office communications are encrypted, just as are all inter-office communications, albeit under a different code. Access to those codes, which are not static, is as you can imagine very limited. If I was to push any more buttons or lift any more lids I'd get noticed, and not in a good way."

"That's okay, Justin, that tells me enough to connect that someone with the threat made to Thomas. And what about you-know-who? Any progress there?"

"The person you mention is a mystery so far. I've not been able to find much of anything that relates to the period before this place, beyond the mere fact of where she was working. But I'm still looking."

"Isn't that unusual?"

"Yes, it is Bibliotekar. It is not the norm. People in my job are meant to be able to find out a lot more about a person's background, at least some aspects. To find zero information of any note is exceptional, but I'm still looking."

"All right, Justin, that would be good. Before you go I have a little something to add to your plate."

"Yes?" Justin replied with the barest hint of stress.

"First though, how is Kaitlin handling your unavailability?"

"She seems to be managing okay, she certainly hasn't been asking any questions. But I think she might be a little miffed she's out of the loop on this hush-hush recruitment project I'm supposed to be on."

"Hmm, I thought as much. She'll just have to deal with it I'm afraid. Now, this other thing. Rafe and I have reason to believe his network communications have been compromised. Is there any way of finding out whether anybody's accessed his network account in, say, the last month? And I mean any access, authorised or unauthorised."

"Does this have anything to do with Councillor Metcalfe's draft Arcadia report disappearing from the system?"

"No, but in a way I wish it was. This is something else unfortunately, and for now I can't tell you what, I'm sorry. I just need to know if someone's being peeping into Rafe's communications."

"I'm pretty sure I can do that. I presume this needs to be done very quietly as well?"

"Absolutely. Same drill. And there's some urgency attached to this one."

"Understood, Bibliotekar."

"Thank you, Justin," said Mads, standing up and returning to his desk. Foote also got up and left the office, more measured in his stride than he had been on arrival.

7:02pm

"Rafe the Finder. We don't see you around here much," said Bradshaw as they met in the foyer of the ten-storey executive apartment building allocated to Bibliotek senior management. As the Bibliotekar, Mads' apartment occupied the top floor along with his formal entertainment suites and several apartments reserved for his official guests. "Catching up with someone?" Bradshaw added.

"Good evening Paul. Just the usual with your boss," replied Rafe. He did not like Bradshaw. He did not know why exactly, apart from

Bradshaw's manner at times, this being one of those times. Rafe had been surprised when Mads appointed Bradshaw Deputy Bibliotekar, but had refrained from expressing that to Mads. This was partly because Rafe was confident that by the time Bradshaw became the Third Bibliotekar he would be well and truly retired from the Finder game.

"Well, have a nice evening. And a good break. I assume even Finders have the year-end holiday," responded Bradshaw as he exited.

"Yes, we do, thanks. You too," replied Rafe, almost without turning as he walked to the express lift that only went to the top floor. Rafe knew the access code for the lift, but he waited until Bradshaw was out of sight before he used it.

Rafe had met Mads when they were both first-year students at The Bibliotek Academy. Every student and academic knew that Mads was the son of Ingrid Rolfdottir, the First Bibliotekar, and her fierce reputation was making it difficult for Mads to make friends. Rafe was having the same problem but for a much different reason. Being twenty-seven at the time, he had been several years older than the other first-years, had no connections at all and it was known by all in his cohort, including Mads, that his admission had been by way of sponsorship rather than academic excellence. It was his life experiences that won him the sponsorship, starting with the fact he had been raised by his grandmother in Amsterdam after his single mother had died shortly after his birth.

Despite their polar-difference backgrounds, the two had become firm friends very quickly. They found they shared at least one very important thing — a love of books. For Mads this was despite his mother's personal attitude towards them — she had none. For Rafe, this was because he had spent many hours from a young age buried within his grandmother's extensive library. She had bookshelves in every single room of their tiny apartment in Amsterdam and they were all crammed with books. It was only natural that his first job had been as an assistant in a nearby antique book shop, and it was whilst working there that Rafe first met the bibliophile client who was a few years later to become his sponsor for his acceptance into the Academy.

After they graduated from the Academy in 2133, Mads and Rafe both decided to stay with The Bibliotek. For Mads that decision was for all intents and purposes always going to be the case, but for Rafe it was a decision prompted by events during his studies that had made a return to Amsterdam redundant — his grandmother had passed away and Rafe had had no choice but to sell off all but a few of her books, which he kept for memory's sake more than any other reason, and the book shop had been firebombed by radicals.

Post-graduation, Mads began his Bibliotek career in the Central Repository as a Classifier and Historian. It was presumed by all that this was the first rung in the ladder constructed for him to scale the heights of The Bibliotek hierarchy, a ladder which he never fell from. Rafe on the other hand had started his career as an Assistant List Compiler. His job was to help compile the official lists that Finders used to search for books to procure for The Bibliotek. It was one of the lower status jobs for an Academy graduate but Rafe thought it ideal, and it was only a few years later that as a result of the zeal with which he applied to his tasks he was made a Finder. That and the fact that Rafe was a European polyglot, which included Latin, a talent he discovered he had whilst at the Academy.

Although they took different paths at The Bibliotek, Mads and Rafe maintained their friendship. Over the years it never waned, only strengthened, but Mads was careful not to let his position as the Second Bibliotekar overshadow Rafe's role as a Finder, and Rafe was careful not to let his friendship with the Bibliotekar influence his performance of the role of Finder.

Rafe did not often visit Mads in his apartment at The Bibliotek complex, and that was because he avoided The Bibliotek as much as possible. But each time he did, as on this occasion, he enjoyed being there. And as he always did, especially after any prolonged absence, he stood inside the front door and marvelled at the bookcases that seemed to line all available wall space, and the books within them. Old books in old and ornate wooden bookcases, newer books in leaner, streamlined bookcases.

Rafe knew Mads well enough to know that had he been a first-time visitor, the books on display would be intended by Mads to give something of himself away: that he was not a mere administrator, he was also a bibliophile *par excellence*. And if that first-time visitor cared to look closer he or she would discover something else about Mads: that his books were not just any books, but that they constituted an extensive private collection representing his interest in first editions relating to the British Raj of the 18th to early 20th centuries, Himalayan and polar exploration, and 20th century monochrome photography. Mads even fancied himself as a black and white photographer of local landscapes and abstracts, so if a wall was not covered by a bookcase, it was invariably adorned by one of his own framed prints.

And if that first-time visitor had known Mads' mother well enough to know she had no pursuits or interests other than performing her role as the First Bibliotekar (and raising her son in the context of that role), he or she immediately gained an insight into something else about Mads. It was a conscious tactic of Mads; a silent but immediate and visually strong statement that he may be his mother's son, but he *was different.* Though his mother had been the First Bibliotekar for decades, she had no personal interest whatsoever in books. Anyone invited to her apartment could have been forgiven for assuming she had no interest in anything, apart from perhaps a craving for sparseness. This was despite the fact that the Bibliotekar's apartment was designed for formal entertaining of Bibliotek guests and so contained a separate restaurant-sized kitchen, formal dining rooms of various sizes, and visitor entertainment rooms.

All the books adorning Mads' apartment were the product of allowing himself time away from his duties to search for and find them. That and his photography. And because he never accepted the normal Finder's Fee for locating and procuring a book not already in the Bibliotek's possession, he was able to keep for himself any book that was.

"I can see already you've acquired more books since I was last here," admired Rafe almost immediately he entered Mads' apartment after Mads had opened the door. He also noticed something else that was new. He could hear classical music coming from somewhere; soft and alluring. As was the faint aroma that he suddenly became aware of.

"Well, it's been over a year since you were last here Nags, so what did you expect?" said Rafe, handing him a glass of red as they stood together in front of the new books that Rafe had noticed. "Here's some Poggio Grande Syrah. I'm sorry but I only opened it half an hour ago."

"Hang on," said Rafe as he suddenly noticed a particularly large set of fine printing books. "This is a set of Roxburghe books! How did you get those?"

"Well spotted Nags. The Club finally made me a member. It'd been in the pipeline for a while. They just had to wait for one of the existing members to pass away. You know their rule - they have no more than forty members at any one time. So when it finally happened last year I bought a complete set from the estate of the member whose passing had created a space for me. It seemed appropriate. And on my passing, the set, which I will of course maintain and add to, will go to The Bibliotek. That was the deal."

Rafe was about to make a derogatory comment about the relic of bibliophilic elitism that, in his view, was the London-based Roxburghe Club, but there was a noise coming from the kitchen and he suddenly remembered they were not alone. Then came a female voice. "Mads, what are you two doing lurking out there?" it called.

Before Rafe knew it, a tall, slim, and finely dressed woman was standing in front of him.

"I *finally* get to meet Rafe the Finder, I'm Violetta. Happy holiday! Now, just quickly, do I call you 'Rafe' or 'Nags'? Mads seems to call you Nags all the time," she said with a broad smile, shaking his hand.

"Hello, Violetta, pleased to meet you, and happy holiday to you too. 'Nags' is fine, and so is 'Rafe'. Your choice," replied Rafe, also smiling, albeit nervously.

"I'll try 'Nags'. Now, it's a cliché I know, but it's true — Mads has told me *a lot* about you. Now, please come into the kitchen. I need to keep watch on dinner."

"It's all true I'm afraid," Rafe replied with his characteristic faux wicked grin, following her and Mads into the warm kitchen and looking intently at Mads with a fierce 'why didn't you tell me?' look in his eyes, which got no response from Mads, despite him knowing very well that Rafe did not like surprises.

Rafe then waited until they were all sitting at the dining table eating the meal Violetta had prepared before asking her his burning question. "I was unaware that Mads had *finally* found himself a partner," he quipped.

"To be perfectly honest, Nags, Violetta is not my partner. That is both the official position and the truth," interjected Mads, glancing across at Violetta, prompting her to nod slightly and glance at Rafe. "It is true we have a relationship, but we are careful not to let it be known amongst our colleagues here at The Bibliotek and nor do we allow each other to be a distraction from our respective duties and responsibilities. You see, Violetta is The Bibliotek's Chief Conservator."

"Chief Conservator?" queried Rafe. "What happened to Jimmy?" Rafe was referring to Professor James Wang, who had been Chief Conservator at The Bibliotek for many years.

"Nags, I know you don't read any memos *From The Bibliotekar*," said Mads a little exasperatingly, "but, honestly, you have been away for too long. Violetta joined us about ten months or so ago, directly from Harvard Library where she held a similar position, though obviously on a much smaller scale. Jimmy had finally retired just before then, as he had reached the mandatory retirement age of one hundred and sixty-five, so it was a natural fit and a seamless transition."

"How very formal you are sounding Mads," said Violetta, with a slight smile. Turning to Rafe, she continued. "You see, Nags, I sort of came with the merchandise. The Trustees of the Library apparently stipulated a few conditions when they agreed to give The Bibliotek what was left of its rare and antique book collections once digitisation had been completed, and one of them was that I was to go with the books. It sounds like I had no say in the matter, but after meeting young Mads here and hear him talk about The Bibliotek with so much passion I knew it was the place to be, so I agreed to be donated. I just hope I'm worth it!"

"I think we can be pretty confident of that!" Mads offered with a cheery laugh.

Rafe smiled. "I'm sorry, it really does appear I've not kept up with current events. But at the risk of reinforcing that, ... don't you report to Mads?" he asked Violetta.

Violetta looked at Mads, who answered on her behalf. "Violetta doesn't report to me, Rafe, she reports to Paul Bradshaw. And that's not a veneer created to hide our relationship. It was well known to various Adcom committee members for some time that I wanted to formally change the Chief Conservator's reporting line from me to the Deputy Bibliotekar. Two reasons — I have been spending more time at the Academy filling in for some gaps in Academic lecturing staff on top of my normal allocation of classes, more time with the I.T. Department on the rollout of the new Master Catalogue software they stuffed up, *and* other things that have been popping up, and apart from the resulting need to farm out other work I wanted Bradshaw to oversee the Conservators because the time was well overdue for him to step up to more responsibility. The only reason I had waited to make the change was because Jimmy, as you know, was pretty set in his ways, and it just seemed more appropriate to wait until he retired, and that's what happened. Violetta came on board not long after Jimmy left and has been reporting to Bradshaw since the day she commenced with us."

"Well, I guess I would have met you sooner or later. I used to annoy Jimmy a bit, wanting to know how my Finds were going. It's just nicer meeting you over a bottle of one of Mads' fine reds. I really enjoy helping him get through his collection."

"So do I, I must admit," said Violetta with a conspiratorial glint in her eyes and a small flirtatious smile. "Mads told me you have been a Finder longer than anyone else and by a good many years. Why is that?"

"It's because he can't or won't do anything else, I forget which," interrupted Mads.

"Mads put it bluntly, but yes, I like what I do and I don't think I can say the same about any other potential role with The Bibliotek. Certainly, I don't aim to be a manager of anything, or anyone for that matter. I like working alone, and I like doing something that has a result, an outcome. Even better when the outcome is a Find of some worth, some rarity, something desirable, and especially something in dire need of protection and conservation. Those kinds of Finds are not becoming rare as such, they're just getting more specific as The Bibliotek fills out its Master Catalogue, and the hard yards of searching and researching still produces results often enough to keep me interested. I have always enjoyed a good hunt. And I get to travel — a lot."

"Well, your work certainly paid off with the Giordano Collection," said Violetta. "I thoroughly enjoyed your speech at the dinner. It's not often we conservators get to know the gritty details of Finds, especially not so interesting details as *your* encounter."

"Stuff like that makes me insanely jealous of Nags," said Mads, with a wink to Rafe.

Ignoring Mads' comment, Rafe said, "Thank you Violetta, unfortunately I did not see or meet you there."

"Oh my table was way back to the side," she replied, glaring at Mads, "and I left straight after your speech."

"Don't blame me," protested Mads, "that was Larkin. Blame him. I did look for you."

"But I think you would have approved it, darling Mads," she turned to him. "Anyway, I gather that Find was somewhat unexpected, Rafe," she asked, turning back to Rafe. "I mean, just how many more such collections are there to be found?" said Violetta as more a statement than a question.

"I think if I was to express that as my considered view to Mads, or even Paul Bradshaw, then perhaps The Bibliotek would no longer need to retain so many conservators. I'm sure you wouldn't like that, Violetta. But, yes, I have to be honest, the workload is constant, but Mads still hasn't recruited a replacement for the Finder with whom I shared Europe with. She was fired, what, two years ago, Mads?"

"That is so. But I'll replace her if you want, Nags. I just haven't heard you complain loudly enough."

"Perhaps I will, perhaps I will, especially if you ask me to make another speech. You put me right in it."

"You did alright," chuckled Mads. "I thought it was important for some of our younger colleagues to hear in detail from our most senior Finder about the one-billionth Find and how it came about."

"One-billionth my arse! You orchestrated that, and you know it."

"Maybe, maybe not. Let's just say it seemed apt."

"Your mother would never have stooped to doing that," reprimanded Rafe.

"I'm willing to perhaps concede that comparison."

"What, no 'like mother like son'?" quipped Violetta.

"The Cobra?! Ha, more like 'chalk and cheese'!" replied Rafe.

"Steady on Nags, you know I never used that name to describe my mother," said Mads, indignant.

"You may not have, but everyone else certainly did!" retorted Rafe.

"I'm sorry, why 'cobra'?" asked Violetta.

"Not 'cobra', she was *The* Cobra," said Rafe. "You need to understand, Mads' mother had a stunning figure, from top to bottom. She had a presence that was of the utmost potency because it was a combination of her looks and her strong personality. She was without doubt an Alpha Plus. But many people around her made the mistake of judging Ms Ingrid Rolfdottir by their reaction to her amazing visage, and this had happened so many times as to give rise to and perpetuation of her nickname – *The Cobra* – which, of course, nobody dared to say to her face or within earshot. She did not so much as tire of being patronised by men who could not see past her good looks as developing a tendency to let any perpetrator of such misperception continue to behave with an *entirely* erroneous attitude until there was no way of turning back. Then she would strike like the proverbial cobra, mentally gut and eviscerate them with some well-chosen words, sometimes merely one or two. But she wouldn't then sit back and gloat or otherwise revel in the look on the face of her victim. She wouldn't even wait for them to speak. No, she was too smart for that, our Ingrid, because to do so would have given them some credit. No, instead she would be gone, and that was her very effective way of sending the silent message that she would not waste any more time with the person."

By now Rafe was leaning forward, talking directly to Violetta, whilst Mads continued to eat his meal as if he was alone. He had heard this story before, but he didn't interrupt Rafe because it was all true about his mother, and now Violetta was hearing it from someone other than his mother's son, saving him the trouble of doing so. Now Rafe leant back in his chair. "I saw her in action several times. It was an impressive sight. *The Cobra.* Yep, that she was."

"Have some more wine, Nags. You must be thirsty after that... speech," Mads finally said.

"She sounds like a very interesting woman," said Violetta, who then turned to Mads. "Mads hasn't told me much about his mother. In fact, nothing at all," she remarked, tilting her head.

Mads rolled his eyes and kept eating.

"You know, Mads," continued Rafe, "you can be a cobra sometimes, just like your mother."

"Oh, come on, that's enough!" objected Mads, now irritated.

"I've seen it, Violetta, so watch out!" said Rafe with a conspiratorial smile.

"Nags..." Mads said firmly.

"So tell me, Rafe," said Violetta, "what is Mads' nickname, what do people call him? Cobra Two?"

"No, no, never that. His 'official' nickname, which he knows because he hears it, is *Book Keeper.* We call Mads *The Book Keeper.* Or just *The Keeper.* You haven't heard it?"

"Oh, I have heard it. *Bookkeeper.* I thought people were just talking about some bean counter when they used it," replied Violetta.

By now Mads was shaking his head. He had heard all this before as well.

"There is that," said Rafe, "but we use two words when we refer to Mads — *Book* and *Keeper* — or just *Keeper* for short, which I personally prefer. You know, there are Finders like me, then there's the *Keeper* — Mads. *Finders, Keeper.*"

"Droll, isn't it?" asked Mads of Violetta.

"Not at all, darling Mads. I think I understand the difference. The *Book Keeper* sounds prestigious. You *are* the keeper of books. It is said with affection, isn't it Nags?"

"Oh yes, and with respect. Just like *The Cobra*," replied Rafe.

"Enough is enough you two," sighed Mads. "Nags, you know I don't like talking about her so much."

"But Mads," pleaded Violetta, "this is all very interesting. Your mother was a pioneer. She made the whole concept of The Bibliotek a reality. From what I've read and heard, she turned a lot of the naysayers into advocates."

"That she did," admitted Mads, with resignation.

"So how did she get the gig as the First Bibliotekar? I'm dying to know. If you won't tell me, I'm sure Nags will."

Rafe looked at Mads.

"It's okay," replied Mads, "Nags has said enough. I'll give you a short *accurate* bio of my mother. Siegfried Sorenson, the founder of The Bibliotek, made it known he wanted to be First Bibliotekar. He felt he was the ideal candidate. After all, the whole concept of The Bibliotek was his and his alone. And, to be fair, there was a lot of support for his appointment for that reason. But sentimentality had no place in the decision and, after all, he was one hundred and twenty-seven years old and that definitely counted against him. My mother, on the other hand, was then only forty-seven, and *she* was considered the ideal candidate. She had already demonstrated her worth as a tough operator as the Chief Bibliotekar of the Norwegian National Library, especially in its renewal after the Great Holy War. So she got the nod, and held the position for the next sixty-seven years."

"Wow, and somewhere in that sixty-seven years you arrived on the scene," said Violetta.

"Yes, Mads," said Rafe, "you've never spilled the beans on that little outcome."

"You've never asked me, Nags. It's no big drama, or secret. I was born when she was fifty-six. For my conception, she simply chose artificial insemination. She was the epitome of the working single mother. For my birth, I was told she chose to take six hours leave of absence. I was placed in the care of a wet nurse because my mother had also chosen not to produce breast milk and had been taking the necessary drug to achieve that. And yes, it's true, by the time I was born, my mother had already left her mark on The Bibliotek in ways that still pervade my administration of it today. In positive ways, I must add. Some of that is because she *was* the First Bibliotekar, which meant that many of her decisions were 'firsts' in their own right. But what I started to see as I grew older was that her success, and later her legacy, were due to her *absolute* resoluteness in adopting and following the decisions of Adcom and, more importantly, Phicom. That resolve put her in good stead with the Governing Council and naturally contributed to her long tenure as Bibliotekar. I saw people impacted by her decisions and overall administrative rule rely on her consistency, to such an extent that she came to lead by implied expectation.

"I'm sorry, Mads," interrupted Violetta, "implied expectation?"

"By that I mean it became more and more the case that actual decisions did not have to be made because her subordinates correctly assumed them and acted accordingly. If ever an uncertainty arose her subordinates also knew that any question aimed at removing that uncertainty should be asked of her, and they also knew that she would give a positive and clear response. This policy also meant my mother had the benefit of directly learning who was using her or his brain and who was not. Fortunately, that included me when I started in management roles at The Bibliotek. On that score, I have always tried to emulate her. But..." said Mads, turning to look directly at Rafe, "sometimes I don't recognise an idiot in time."

"Ha!" said Rafe, smiling at Rafe over the top of his wine glass.

"As you said, Vie," resumed Mads, "she was an interesting woman. Many also considered her to be ruthless, and some of those people told me so. But I observed after a while that those who held that view of her were usually the ones who succumbed to the distraction of her attractiveness as a female, which not only did not wane as she aged but increased in its potency as she grew older, even after my birth."

"That's an amazing story, Mads, thanks for telling me. She does sound very different from you," said Violetta, who continued quickly when she saw Mads' reaction. "But I don't mean that in a bad way, Mads. A successor to a job can do it just as well as the incumbent yet be very different in how they do it."

"Totally correct," weighed in Rafe. "You nailed it."

"But Mads, how is it that you appear to be a very different Bibliotekar to your mother?" asked Violetta.

"*Appear* to be different? I *am* different from her. As to why, that's an interesting question, and I'm going to answer it because apart from me, you are the first person to ask it, believe it or not, and I've had the answer ready for some time. So tell me if this makes sense."

"Oooh, this sounds interesting, Mads," cooed Rafe.

"Shut up Nags, and have some more wine," said Mads, in mock frustration. "My upbringing was a bit unique. The Bibliotek was my home before it became my career. It has always been my home. I've not lived in a 'normal' town, ever. Although my adult relationship with my mother seemed to me, and no doubt to others as well, including this person here," he nodded towards Rafe, "more akin to one between a supervisor and her subordinate, and in day-to-day matters that was literally accurate, I always felt a sense of maternalism in her behaviour towards me, whatever the occasion and regardless of whether her words were stern or in rebuke or not. And although I was not conscious of it until her tenure as the First Bibliotekar was nearing its end, my mother's propensity for long term planning was no more evident than in the way she prepared me to take over the role. As a young child, I wasn't even aware of it. There was always something to learn from her. Significantly for me, her success in imparting that knowledge and experience was accompanied by an astuteness in the way she trained me. And that was to ensure I was never allowed to feel the pressure so often felt by someone following in the footsteps of a successful parent, especially such deep footsteps as hers. She never once told me that one day I was going to be the next Bibliotekar."

"Seriously?" asked Rafe.

"Never. And I never asked. At best, it was only ever an assumption that arose when I became her Deputy."

"*Seriously?*" asked Rafe again.

This time Mads did not respond. "Getting back to the story, the respect, and often awe, in which I held my mother as The First Bibliotekar was always tempered by her explicit encouragement for me *to do things differently*. So, the years I spent formally reporting to her were full of opportunities she overtly or covertly created for me to demonstrate how differently I could perform my duties, so much so that whenever some officious Governing Councillor made a comment along the lines that "Ingrid Rolfdottir would not have made such a decision," I could smile and respond with "Correct" or some similar affirmation, and be proud of it. But my mother's success in not casting any shadow over me only really became evident to me during my tenure as Deputy Bibliotekar. I long ago postulated that, subconsciously or not, it was perhaps the main reason I maintained my interest in all things Bibliotek throughout my younger years, never feeling the urge to pursue another career or calling."

"So you never felt the urge to try something else?" asked Violetta.

"What was the point? He wasn't good at anything else," interrupted Rafe.

"Nags, remind me why I invited you to dinner?" said Mads.

"To make sure you don't sprout any bullshit?"

"See this fork? Want to feel it too?"

"Settle down, boys," intervened Violetta. "Come on, Mads, this is really interesting. You never ventured from The Bibliotek?"

"I've travelled the world sure enough, and have seen if not experienced a lot of things I could do if I chose to, but as far as a career goes, no. And I've never had any regrets about that."

Violetta was about to say something but Mads was only pausing. "Just before she died, when I had been Bibliotekar for a mere three years, we had several long conversations, longer than any other we had previously had."

"Seriously?" once again asked Rafe.

"Yes, Nags, seriously. Your word for the day is it? The fact is that it was during one of those talks that she told me that it was not her original intention to raise me as her successor, and that it only became her aim when I was seven years old and started spending more and more time with Thomas at the Academy, always asking questions."

"Sorry, who?" asked Violetta.

"Thomas Metcalfe. He's a Governing Councillor nowadays," Mads replied, without emotion. He could see Rafe was about to say something so shot him a quick glare, which worked. "Those who held my mother's favour all courted mine after I was appointed Deputy Bibliotekar because everyone assumed it meant I was going to be the Second Bibliotekar."

"I remember that," interrupted Rafe again. "You replaced Dominic Coenraad as Deputy Bibliotekar. Until then it was Dom who everyone assumed would replace your mother."

"And that included me," replied Mads.

"So, what happened?" eagerly asked Violetta.

"Dom decided he didn't want to be the next Bibliotekar. He was more interested in being Dean of the Academy, which was not as nearly a robust institution back then as it is now. That is where he found his mark," replied Mads.

"He certainly did, good old Dom the Dean" added Rafe.

"Stop it. Dom resigned to become Dean of the Academy and I became Deputy Bibliotekar, and all those who began courting my favour did so because they knew I was different from my mother. They all knew that current favours would not necessarily work with me."

"How long were you Deputy Bibliotekar?" asked Violetta.

"Eight years. My mother's very last act as Bibliotekar before her retirement took effect was to appoint me as her successor. No surprise. Three years later, as I said, she passed, at the age of one hundred and ten. Retirement had not suited her well but getting ill at such a young age was definitely not part of the plan."

"Yes, it was quite a shock when she passed away. At least she didn't suffer for long," said Rafe.

"Yes Nags, you're right about that."

"I'm sorry I never got to meet your mother, Mads," said Violetta.

"Well at least you got to meet me," he smiled.

"True. Now Nags, any plans for the break?" asked Violetta.

"Not really, apart from catching up on some reports, including the Giordano Find. My least favourite part of the job."

"You're always behind with those, Nags," said Mads, shaking his head in mock disgust.

"Let's not get started on that allegation," responded Rafe. "Besides, it didn't help the backlog having to prepare that speech, you know."

"Ah yes, the backlog," said Mads.

"The alleged backlog," corrected Rafe.

"Would you like some coffee?" asked Violetta, before Mads could respond.

"Yes please, that would be nice," replied Rafe, who noticed Mads looked puzzled.

"Okay, I'll leave you boys to talk amongst yourselves. Try to behave," said Violetta as she got up from the table, collected the plates and went into the kitchen.

"Since when did you start drinking coffee?" asked Mads.

"When do you want to talk about Arcadia?" asked Rafe in a soft but clear whisper.

"Later!" whispered Mads in reply.

"Okay, but how about some Drambuie to go with that coffee?" asked Rafe.

"That's more like it! That's the Nags I know!"

Later, after Rafe had thanked Violetta for the dinner and the conversation and bade her good night, Mads was walking him back to the lift. He quickly told Rafe that he found something on Arcadia that was probably the cause of the threat that had been made against Thomas. "I didn't want to talk about it in front of Violetta before I know more about it. She doesn't need to know about it, so I'm glad you didn't raise it in conversation, Nags."

"Understood. So, what's this 'something'?"

"I arranged for Doctor Foote to quietly have some mineral samples I found at the edge of our site on Arcadia tested. It turns out the samples indicate there is an extremely valuable mineral deposit. Palladium and rhodium, in the purest concentration ever seen. Look them up."

"And this deposit is on The Bibliotek's site?"

"Some of it yes, but most of it adjacent to it."

"And someone's trying to keep this a big secret?"

"It looks that way."

"But you're the Bibliotekar, Mads. So, shouldn't you know? I mean, officially?"

"You would think so, but for the time being, my knowledge is little and unofficial. I need more information before I stick my head above the parapet."

"Who else knows unofficially?"

"Only Justin Foote, but I asked him to let Thomas know about my trip and what I found. He deserves to know and it may prompt some thoughts on the matter. Other than those two it's best we keep a tight lid on this for the time being."

"Absolutely agree with you on that Mads."

"How did you find Violetta, may I ask?" Mads said, changing the topic.

"She has certainly made an impression on you Mads. You looked and sounded a different person with her around. For the better, I'd say."

"I think you're right about that Nags."

"And I take it she sleeps over?"

"You could say that," said Mads, not a little bit sheepishly.

"Well, that's not the Mads I know, good for you," nudged Rafe with his elbow.

"That's enough," said Mads, trying not to smile.

"What about Pienza?" asked Rafe, changing the topic.

"I've asked Justin to look into it. The only person I can think of who may have been the culprit is Larkin."

"Larkin? Why him?"

"I don't know. I just don't trust him. He's efficient, sometimes too efficient, so I can't get rid of him. But there's just something about him that rankles and feels a bit... off. For now, we need to take care, and keep things off-line."

"Agreed. Thanks for dinner."

Just then, the lift arrived. Rafe stepped in, and as the doors closed he added "and tell her from me that you're definitely punching above your weight."

END OF CHAPTER SIX

Chapter Seven

Truth or Dare

"You want weapons? We're in a library. Books are the best weapon in the world. This room's the greatest arsenal we could have. Arm yourself!"
Russell T Davies, "Tooth and Claw", *Doctor Who*, Second Series, Episode 2, 2006

8:00am, Wednesday, 2nd January 2205

Nikka Johannson had been with The Bibliotek for sixteen years. She had come from a fairly senior position in the Norwegian security forces on a recommendation to Mads by her superiors. She had an unblemished record both before and after she joined The Bibliotek, and it wasn't long before Mads had identified her as a suitable Head of Security, a position he did in fact appoint her to eight years ago. Under Nikka's watch, there had been no serious security issues and no thefts from the Central Repository.

Given the special status of The Bibliotek, the Norwegian Government had passed laws contemporaneously to The Bibliotek's commencement of operations that effectively gave the Head of Security the same powers of search, investigation and arrest as the normal Norwegian police force held. In fact, as far as jurisdiction went, Nikka's team held sway over The Bibliotek's precinct to the exclusion of the Norwegian police force. Nikka had earned the respect of her Adcom colleagues, however, for the restraint which she applied to the execution of her role and that of her team. She much preferred to be seen as security for The Bibliotek rather than as policing its inhabitants and visitors. She just wasn't all that friendly to many, who felt Nikka was not much of a 'a people-person.' To them, including Mads, she was also a bit of a 'closed book'. For example, Mads had no idea whether or not Nikka was in a relationship, and all he knew for certain about her was that she was resolutely focused and intent on doing her job, and now she was about to privately brief him on the progress of her assessment of the threat, if any, posed to The Bibliotek by the Present Sect. Mads did not tell Nikka this, but he was working on the assumption that Bradshaw would apply his own thinking to her findings and advice in his briefings as the leader of the Relocation Study Group. And now, in his first meeting after the annual break, Nikka was sitting, right on time, in Mads' office, facing him from across his desk.

"I have examined all the known incidents and crimes that have been attributed to the Present Sect," she began, in her normal, no nonsense, business-like manner and without any preliminary pleasantries.

"Since when?" interrupted Mads.

"*All* of them, Mads," said Nikka. "As I said."

"Okay, sorry, I'll shut up now." Mads thought he almost detected a slight smile on Nikka's face. Almost.

"That is, all incidents and crimes anywhere in the world. They go back to just after the end of the Great Holy War. In examining all of them the first thing I noticed was that there is no co-ordination of investigations of their activities by any police or security force in the world. At various times Interpol and Europol have separately tried to undertake such a task, but neither has gotten anywhere and nor has either allocated any resources of late as they don't view it as a priority."

"That is interesting."

"It's also not helpful. Interpol has given me whatever intelligence they have, but a lot of it is old and what there is isn't very much. Europol hasn't responded to my request, but that's no surprise."

"Why do you say that?"

"In their eyes, I am just a head of private security, not Chief of Police of a legal jurisdiction."

"Is that something I need to follow up on?"

"I wouldn't worry about it, Mads. It's not as if Europol are important."

"Okay, I'll take your lead on that, but let me know if it becomes a problem for you. We do need your wider role to be respected."

Nikka nodded, then continued. "So, the more recent information I've had to source myself. And I can tell you this: it is far from certain where the Present Sect is based, if the word 'base' is relevant, which I'm not certain is the case. Their slogans first appeared in Berlin, but that only implies the Sect originated from there. It is of interest that it was not until the media began reporting these slogans that they began appearing elsewhere in the world. That implies copycats or at least not necessarily the work of the Sect."

"What about their acts of violence and other crimes?"

"These I looked at very carefully. There was recently a particularly violent murder in a small town in Italy that the state police are attributing to the Sect. In view of the spread of attacks in recent years in terms of time, place, and nature, they have the appearance of being random."

"They're random? How so?" Mads hoped his question would hide the fact that his expression may have changed when he recognised the specific recent attack Nikka was referring to.

"No Mads, I said they *appear* to be random. It is my opinion they are not random at all. They don't follow a sequence, a pattern, or a common target, but they don't have to in order to be part of an overall plan. And I believe that plan is centred on making the attacks appear to be random in order to instil the greatest level of fear. They are not random because they are all very targeted. And there is a trend: the more violent an attack the more targeted they are and conform to their central mantra — that books and other icons of the past need to be destroyed."

"Has anyone else come up with such conclusions?"

"No Mads, not even any academics. I guess they don't have the same sort of access to police records as I have."

"So, correct me if I've got this wrong, but we don't know where the Present Sect is, we don't know who they are, and we don't know how many of them there are. All we know is they are violent, dedicated, and probably working to a larger plan."

"That's about the sum of it, Mads. So far, that is."

"What about in the last five years, or even two years? Any developments or changes?"

"The attacks are happening more often, but in more places, though Europe has always been more prone to attack. The attacks are also becoming more violent. Killing people as part of the plan only really started a few years ago, and the one in Italy recently was a vicious example, assuming it was in fact the Sect. Before then, deaths were usually incidental to the plan, as in victims of bombing."

"I was worried that was the case. I suppose this does have implications for The Bibliotek?"

"I don't want to be seen as raising any threat level higher than necessary in order to secure more funds, equipment, personnel, or whatever. I have enough resources. My problem, as I have already mentioned to you Mads, is that my people are complacent. A little part of me wishes we did experience an incident to act against. Just to shake my people up a bit and help them focus. Bottom line, though, is that my assessment of the threat currently presented to The Bibliotek by the Present Sect is that it is material and measures need to be taken. That is what my recommendation is going to be in the RSG's report."

"Just a minute. Has the Present Sect made any threats against The Bibliotek?"

"Not directly, no."

"Not directly," Mads repeated. "Indirectly?"

"It's only a matter of time."

"I see... fair enough. Unless of course some action is taken against the Present Sect..."

"That is true, Mads, but I'm not seeing any concerted effort, by anyone."

"I presume your part of the report will detail all your findings?"

"Of course."

"And assumptions?"

Nikka sighed. "Yes, and my grounds."

"Good, because as we also discussed, the outcome of your part of the study should be considered by Adcom in any event. I'm not questioning your conclusions, Nikka, but you need to be prepared to defend them."

"I'm aware of that."

"Good. Now, an equally important question. Do those measures include considering relocating part or all of The Bibliotek?"

"Absolutely not."

"That's confident."

"Mads, every aspect of the construction and operation of The Bibliotek, especially the Central Repository, was dictated by the core aim of ensuring the books had the benefit of the highest level of safety. Not just from the physical and natural environment but also safety from human-initiated damage of any kind. In short, The Bibliotek is designed for threats such as from the Present Sect because, to be blunt, that's the whole point of its existence. Short of actual war being declared, the security component of The Bibliotek is doing its job. The measures I am referring to are about reviving some security protocols, especially at critical points such as the entries to the Central Repository. You know we scan everyone before they are allowed downstairs, but I will be proposing further restrictions on what can be taken by staff and visitors with them when they go downstairs."

"Okay, good," replied Mads. He knew that 'downstairs' was what everyone called the underground behemoth of the Central Repository, and Nikka had just told him what he had wanted to hear.

"How is the testing going?" he asked.

"I've arranged for three so far. The first was failed and, as you suggested, I fired the person who made the error. He had been with us for fifteen years. The next two tests were passed."

"I'm sorry you had to do that. But it worked, didn't it? It had the desired effect?"

"Yes."

"And the background checks on your team?"

"Still in progress. No issues identified yet."

"Can you complete those before the next Adcom meeting? It's on the twenty-first, from memory, two weeks from now. I want to draw a line though this."

"It will be done," responded Nikka. "But it will make the whole exercise quicker and more productive if you can give me a little context, an idea of what I'm meant to be looking for."

Mads looked at Nikka for a few seconds before responding. He was trying to decide how much to tell her, and he knew he needed to choose his words carefully. "I want to know if anyone in your team has any connection, or connections, with anybody else at The Bibliotek that are not part of their normal duties and responsibilities, or has any undisclosed vulnerability to outside inducements or influence. I know that's broad but it's the best I can do for now."

"Can I ask why?"

"You can, but not yet."

Just then Larkin paged Mads, "Doctor Joyce to see you, Bibliotekar."

"Tell him to wait please. I'll just be a minute or two."

Mads looked at Nikka, who started to leave, saying, "I'll report back later, Mads."

"No Nikka, I'd like you to stay, if you don't mind. You need to hear what I have to say to Doctor Joyce. It may inform your background checks. Please sit here." Mads motioned to the chair on the other side of his desk, to the left. "Okay Larkin, let him in."

Joyce walked in and approached Mads, who was now standing. "You wanted to see me, Bibliotekar?" he asked as he shook Mads' offered hand.

"Hello Doctor Joyce, welcome back. Yes, I did want to see you. Please sit down," motioned Mads to the chair on the other side of his desk, to the right, "Do you know my colleague Nikka Johannson?"

"Um, no I don't believe we've met," Joyce turned and looked a little nervously at Nikka and then back to Mads. Nikka smiled faintly at Joyce but remained silent.

"This won't take long. I know you returned from your first rotation to Arcadia last week, correct, Doctor?" Mads was looking not so much at Joyce but in the space between him and Nikka. Without trying to be obvious he was trying to assess her reactions just as much as Joyce's.

"Yes, that's correct, Bibliotekar," Joyce replied, looking at Mads, then Nikka, a little nervous and confused. Mads had not told him what Nikka's role was and nor had she volunteered it, a point that had not gone unnoticed by Mads.

"Oh don't worry about Nikka, she's all ears about your time on Arcadia, as I am. That's why you're here, to debrief me on your work on Arcadia, and in the greenhouse in particular. What did you do, and how did it go?"

"Well, it all went quite well, actually," answered Joyce, a little less anxious. "The food garden was sectioned off. We had a control section being Earth conditions and soil brought from Earth, we had another section with Arcadian conditions and Earth soil, and we had another section with Arcadian conditions and soil."

"Interesting, and the results?"

"The control section produced good results, with fruit and vegetables of sufficient quality and quantity to feed all staff on station. We were able to grow some from the other sections as well, but they were a bit different in size and texture, more so with the full Arcadian section, which was not a surprise. We're not sure they're edible, just yet, and that includes the products we got using Earth soil."

"Well I'm sure your final report will be an interesting read. Have you submitted it?" asked Mads.

"Yes, Bibliotekar, just this morning."

"Excellent. Did you send a copy to Councillor Carlson?" asked Mads.

"I'm sorry..."

"You were recommended for the job on Arcadia by Councillor Carlson, as I recall. Is that correct?"

"Oh, yes, that's correct, Bibliotekar. I was intending to give him a copy. I hope that's okay."

"I guess so, since we don't have the IP on the research," said Mads, offhandedly. "But you might want to check the sensitivity of the data before you send Councillor Carlson his copy, just to be on the safe side."

"Yes, Bibliotekar, of course."

"Now, there's just one more thing before I let you go," said Mads, lowering his tone.

"Yes?"

"What can you tell me about the geosurvey team, Doctor Joyce?"

"I'm sorry... geosurvey team?" Joyce was rattled, that much was obvious to Mads, and he was now switching nervous glances between him and Nikka, who had begun typing some notes on her data pad.

"I'm still waiting for the report from the geosurvey team on the results of their sampling from The Bibliotek's site on Arcadia, right next to the greenhouse, so whilst I've got you here, I thought you could tell me about the samples they took and if they confirmed what the first geo team had earlier found there." Mads had no idea about any report or whether there had been an earlier geosurvey team go to Arcadia than the one Thomas had encountered, but he had decided to pretend he knew all about it. Joyce was now more than rattled, he was also now confused as well, and he looked it. He glanced again at Nikka, who had stopped typing on her data pad and was now looking intently at him, expressionless. *Classic Nikka*, thought Mads, who was silently waiting for Joyce's reply. After a few tense seconds it came.

"I'm sorry, Bibliotekar, but the geo team opted not to clue me in on their work."

"Oh, I'm sorry, Dr Joyce, but I had been informed *your* role was to ensure that the geo team was given every possible assistance during their visit to Arcadia. That is correct, isn't it?"

"Yes, that is correct, and that is what I did, but that was the extent of my involvement with them," Joyce replied, a little shakily.

"I'm glad you said that, because I assume it was down to you that the geo team did not log their visit, as protocol demanded," Mads said, more as a statement than a question. Silence prevailed. Nikka was now very interested, and looked at Mads. She surmised what was coming.

"Doctor Joyce," continued Mads, not waiting for a response, "you confirmed just a minute ago that it was you who facilitated the geosurvey team's visit to Arcadia, so it was your responsibility to ensure that protocols were followed, was it not?"

"I'm sorry, Bibliotekar, but I find myself unable to respond to that."

"Unable? Why is that? Do you mean you refuse to respond or that you are unable to respond?"

Joyce remained silent. Mads continued, "It's a simple thing to enter your details into the visitors log on Arcadia, Doctor. It's not a life or death situation. It's not even a test or even scientifically relevant. It's just an administrative procedure, an entry attesting to a basic fact. Why? Because it is vital that we are kept aware of all who visit our site on Arcadia and why, and not just for security reasons." Mads did not pause or motion towards Nikka. "But you told Commander Henderson that the geo team was not required to enter their details, and when he asked for the reason, he was told by you not to make a deal out of it. Have I got that right, Doctor?"

"I'm sorry, Bibliotekar, but again I must... decline to answer that."

"I'm sorry too, Joyce, because unless you provide me with an acceptable explanation, all your hard work on Arcadia will count for nothing as far as you are personally concerned. So, again, is what I have said to you about the geosurvey team's presence on Arcadia correct?"

Silence was the stern reply from Joyce, though he was struggling with it. Mads waited for a few seconds, but the silence remained.

"In that case," continued Mads, "you have left me with no alternative to suspending you from all duties with immediate effect, pending a formal investigation into your actions on Arcadia. Your lack of co-operation has already been noted. You are to hand over your data pad to Nikka, who is Head of Security at The Bibliotek, and de-activate your neurophone, both here and now, and await an escort to your lodgings, where you will be confined until the investigation requires your presence."

Joyce, still saying nothing, stood up, as did Nikka, who held out her hand for Joyce's data pad, which he gave her. His face was white, and he grimaced but kept silent as he then de-activated his neurophone.

"Permission to access his neurophone log?" Nikka asked of Mads.

"Granted."

Mads continued, but in a slightly less formal tone. "If you have anything to say in mitigation Patrick, you can say it now, or later, in writing. But I encourage you to speak now, as you will in all probability never see me again."

"Can I sit down?"

"Of course. I am sorry Patrick, but I have no choice. I hope you understand that," said Mads. He then motioned to Nikka with a nod of his head to follow him as he walked to the door. Then, out of earshot of Joyce, who was still sitting at Mads' desk and now staring blankly out the window, Mads whispered some instructions to Nikka, including arranging for one of her team to come and escort Joyce to his apartment, and another security person to go to Joyce's office and secure his computer for a full download. With that, Nikka left Mads' office.

Now it was time for Mads to obtain the information he really needed.

"Patrick, this does not need to be the end of your career in space," he began, as he walked back to his chair behind his desk and sat down. "There doesn't even need to be an investigation. I can turn this around, here and now, into a resignation by you."

Joyce turned away from staring at the garden outside Mads' office and looked at Mads. "I know where this is going."

"And?"

"Yes, it was Councillor Carlson. He not so much asked but requested I make sure the geo team's presence on Arcadia was "kept off the books" as he put it."

"This was the return favour you were expecting at some point?"

"Yes."

"Thank you for finally being honest with me, Patrick." Mads tried to conceal his relief at his suspicion being confirmed, but it was palpable.

"Here's what's going to happen," Mads quickly continued. "Right now, your computer is being taken out of your office and to Security. You will be escorted soon to your lodgings where you will pack your bags, then you will be escorted to the station, where you will board the maglev for Oslo. On arrival, you will proceed directly to the helioport, without contacting anyone, where you will find a ticket waiting for you for a heliojet to Los Angeles. I believe that is your base. Later today your full termination entitlements will be paid into your account, plus two months' salary in lieu. Once back home you will make yourself scarce for a while. Trust me when I say this is for your safety. Okay with all that?"

Joyce looked at Mads with sad eyes. "Yes."

"Good, now to make this all happen, I need you to sign these two documents. One is your formal resignation. The other is a statement attesting to the fact that you were personally requested by Councillor Carlson to ensure no record was made of the geosurvey team's presence on Arcadia, and that you complied with that request."

"You had these all along?!"

"Of course I did. All I needed from you coming here today was your confirmation. And I got it. Your letter of resignation is going to be made public and I will say all the right things about your valuable service to The Bibliotek and space biology research in general, our loss in losing you, and wishing you well in your future career. The statement about Councillor Carlson I am going to put in my bottom drawer."

"You're using me as a scapegoat."

"No, Patrick. I am not the one using you. There is a reason for your actions on Arcadia, I get that. But that does not equate to an excuse. I could have simply fired you, and you know that HR would have backed me up on that. That would have meant no salary in lieu and no termination payment. Breaching protocol on Earth is one thing, but doing it spaceside is another thing entirely. It just cannot be allowed to happen without serious consequences. I think I am being more than reasonable in allowing you to resign and thus retain your career. And you signing the statement is merely agreeing to a fact we both know to be absolutely true."

"I should get legal advice."

"Perhaps you should. But my offer expires in two minutes, so maybe worry about getting some later, once you are back on home soil. If you do decide to get advice, why not suggest duress?"

Joyce looked at Mads and pondered his comment for a few seconds. He then gave an audible sigh, signed both documents, stood up and walked over to the window. Mads gathered up the documents and placed them in a folder he had ready on his desk. He then sent a message to Nikka about the change in plan concerning Joyce's immediate future, as he had whispered to her before she left his office, then paged Larkin.

"When some Security people arrive show them straight in will you?"

"Yes, Bibliotekar. Ah, actually, they've just arrived."

Nikka came back into Mads' office, this time with a stern looking younger member of her team. For a second Mads had the thought she must have been a clone of Nikka from her appearance and manner. *She's obviously someone Nikka trusts*, he thought. Neither said anything but Nikka looked at Mads, who nodded, and this prompted Nikka to turn to Joyce. "Skye here will escort you to your apartment. She will wait with you whilst you pack your bags, then she will escort you to the station and see you onto the maglev to Oslo."

"Is this really necessary?" Joyce asked Mads.

"Unfortunately, we have found in our experience that it is. It is standard procedure. It is not targeted at you," replied Mads. "You may leave now."

"My lawyer will need a copy of those statements," responded Joyce.

"As soon as your lawyer contacts us, I will make it happen. Goodbye."

Joyce turned to leave with his escort, who walked one pace behind him, to the side.

"Don't forget, Patrick, duress. Suggest it to your lawyer," said Mads before Joyce reached the doorway. His shoulders arched in response, but Joyce said nothing.

As soon as her team member left with Joyce, Nikka asked Mads if he had a few minutes to discuss something.

"Yes, of course, Nikka, what is it?"

"It may only be a coincidence, but I think I should mention it. Paul Bradshaw and I had a conversation not long after the last Adcom meeting. He said in passing that if it ever came to needing to relocate The Bibliotek, Arcadia could be the ideal site. I thought at the time it was an odd thing to say, and ridiculous, so I dismissed it. I don't know the background to the problem you had with Joyce but given what just happened I thought it best to let you know."

"Did you tell him it was ridiculous?"

"Not as much, but I was annoyed. I had only just begun my threat assessment and here he was talking as if he was already thinking of a relocation. He sort of backtracked a bit and made some comment about me not needing to do a security assessment on a place like Arcadia, but that just told me he missed the point. The only reason I can think of for suggesting going off-Earth would be if my threat assessment made it viable, if not imperative, and as you know I don't like being second guessed."

Mads was pleased to hear what Nikka had to say but also surprised. Pleased because he now knew with certainty that Nikka was not involved with Carlson or, by implication, Thurldottir. Surprised because of what Bradshaw had said to her. Arcadia? What had prompted him to say that? Why now? Was Arcadia about a secret deposit of valuable minerals or about The Bibliotek's capacity and security?

"So let me get this straight. Paul specifically mentioned Arcadia as a viable option for relocation of The Bibliotek. Is that right?"

"Yes."

"He didn't say it was worth considering to see if it is a viable option, he just said it was a viable option?"

"He said, quote, "it could be the ideal site if it ever came to needing to relocate The Bibliotek.""

"Interesting. I gather that since you do not consider it necessary from a security point of view to consider relocating The Bibliotek that by definition means Arcadia isn't even worth considering. From your standpoint, that is."

"Correct."

"Thanks, Nikka, for that. I may need to have a chat with Paul," Mads said, then, noticing the slight alarm on Nikka's face, added "don't worry, I won't mention this conversation."

"Thank you," responded Nikka.

"Now there's one more thing," said Mads. "We were talking about the background checks on your team just before we were interrupted by Joyce."

"Yes, I said they will be completed before the next Adcom meeting."

"But so far no red flags?"

"No, nothing."

"Now I can help you in terms of what to look for."

"Yes?"

"Identify anyone in your team who has or had any connection or contact with Councillor Carlson."

"Councillor Carlson?"

"Yes, Nikka, Abe Carlson. There's been a few signposts of late pointing to him, and not in a good way."

"Okay Mads, that will definitely help," replied Nikka. After a pause, she asked "does this have anything to do with Doctor Joyce?"

"I suspect it might, but I have nothing solid yet to be any more certain. In any event, if you need to have access to any records held by HR I suggest you deal directly with Assistant Director Doctor Justin Foote. I've already briefed him that you might need his assistance and the reason. And please make time to see me before the Adcom meeting to run through your results."

"Shall do, Mads," said Nikka, who then turned to leave his office.

Just then Larkin alerted Mads. "Bibliotekar, I have Chair Thurldottir on the line for you."

Speak of the devil, Mads thought.

"Busy day," said Nikka as she opened the door to leave.

"Yes, and it's not even nine o'clock yet," replied Mads. "Okay, put her through," he replied to Larkin. He tried to quickly think of the reason for Thurldottir's call but couldn't.

"Yes?" Mads asked, a little brusquely.

"Bibliotekar I have your travel request in front of me," said Thurldottir, testily. "What is the issue in Iceland requiring your presence? I thought we had concluded our negotiations."

Is that all, really? thought Mads. "No, the negotiations have not finished. They are well advanced, but we are yet to reach agreement on the *Sagas*. As you can imagine it's a very sensitive issue in Iceland, especially given that they would be coming to Norway and not somewhere more neutral, shall we say."

"What I know is this procurement has been in the pipeline for some time. It is *because* The Bibliotek is in Norway that we need the Iceland *Sagas* to come to us. This is not just about the books. You should know that."

"I well appreciate the importance of this for The Bibliotek, and I have kept the Governing Council informed at all times of developments, as you..."

"So why are you going?" interrupted Thurldottir. "I thought Collingwood had this under control. She is your General Counsel after all and when I spoke with Prime Minister Magnusson at the celebration dinner he seemed to think the negotiations were almost completed."

"That is correct. However, the new President has inserted herself into the process, apparently, because it was her office that requested I attend the next meeting in Reykjavik."

"I can't see why the President would think she has any say in the matter, but very well then, go and meet her, but if this falls through I will be holding you personally responsible," blurted Thurldottir, terminating the call before Mads had a chance to respond.

Had he been given the chance to do so, Mads would have reminded Thurldottir that as it was the Governing Council he reported to not her, he always welcomed its review of his performance. Mads found it interesting that Thurldottir continued to act as if, in matters relating to Mads' position as the Second Bibliotekar, she held sway over the Council. As far as he knew he still held a majority of support, by six to four. It was only by one vote, but it was enough. But Mads quickly reminded himself that support included the vote of Thomas, who he had not yet reported as missing, as to do so could precipitate Thurldottir orchestrating his replacement on the Council with one of her cronies. And that meant Mads had to be careful to not keep Thomas away from The Bibliotek for too much longer. All it would take for Thurldottir to declare him missing would be one missed phone call from her, one missed meeting with her.

Serendipitously, an encrypted message came through to Mads from Justin Foote just at that moment. It was a short note just letting him know that he had passed on the information about the 'P&R' to the person concerned, and had received the response that the person had felt the reference was vaguely familiar but couldn't pin it down.

That's interesting, thought Mads.

8:10am, Thursday, 3rd January 2205

"Bernie, why am I on this heliojet?"

"I'm sorry Mads, I'm not sure why President Morthen requested your presence for a face-to-face meeting, replied Bernie. "Part of me would like to suggest it's because they want you there when they finally sign on the dotted line for handing over the *Sagas*, but another part of me suspects something has gone wrong. The request from Morthen's office was left-field. All I know for certain is that Morthen has until now not been present at the negotiations."

"In that case, this meeting may have nothing to do with the negotiations, correct?"

"Yes, that may be the case."

"She won the presidential election on a populist platform, I believe?"

"Yes, very much so," replied Bernie.

"I think I'd better take the lead on this one. Now, where is the Relocation Study Group up to?"

"Hasn't Bradshaw been keeping you up to date?"

"Yes, he has, but I want to hear what you've got to say."

"Well, we've had our tasks allocated."

"Such as?"

"He's got Finn doing a comprehensive update and breakdown on capacity or, should I say, utilisation of space. Far more detailed than for our normal Adcom updates. The same goes for the trend analysis. Finn told me he and Paul agreed to the parameters and variables, all the metrics — that took a while according to Finn."

"Why?"

"I gather from Finn that Paul found it difficult to keep up with him."

"I see."

"Finn also said he tried to be as realistic as possible but with a margin of fifteen percent. I have to say, regardless of the outcome of the RSG, he is going to end up with an improved capacity model. As time goes on it will be more and more valuable to us."

"I take it Finn is getting help on that?"

"Yes, I spoke to him yesterday, and he mentioned he had a small team working on it."

"I trust Paul reiterated the need for confidentiality?"

"Well, to be honest, no he hasn't. Or at least not in any discussions Paul's had with me. But Finn told me he had made it clear to his team that the whole exercise was prompted by a desire of Adcom for better and more detailed forecasting."

"Good. And what about you? What's been your task?"

"It occurred to me pretty soon after you set up the RSG that we may have an issue with some of the larger procurements if, can I say, worst-case scenario is that they are moved to another location. I suggested to Paul that I needed to focus my initial work on reviewing their agreed terms, not least because each is usually unique, to see if any presented any obstacles. He didn't seem to think it would be an issue, but he agreed with my suggestion."

"I'm sorry, Bernie, you've lost me. What's the potential issue with those acquisitions?"

"Well, if we unilaterally decide to relocate any given procurement the donor may feel it unwarranted or, worse, in breach of their donor's agreement."

It did not escape Mads that Bernie was anxious to demonstrate she had shown initiative. "I see... Any conclusions yet?"

"For the most part there are no issues in terms of legalities. By that I mean the terms do not drill down to the agreed location of The Bibliotek, and any new or additional site will be part of The Bibliotek. But I'm starting to accumulate contracts where the spirit of the agreement, if not the legal compliance, may be at risk. So far there are not many of these, but if the primary question becomes active, I will be suggesting that some thought will need to be given as to how these particular procurements are handled."

"Am I right in suggesting that the absence of any agreement specifying the location of The Bibliotek is because it is mutually understood to be exactly where it is, now and in the future?"

"Yes, that would be my view. More than that, it is, has been, and continues to be, a tacit understanding."

"Then, for now, I think it best we don't make any noises."

"Yes, absolutely."

"But I want to hear these concerns in the next Adcom meeting, and I want to see them quantified in the draft report."

"Yes, Mads."

"Anything else?"

"If only. Nikka, Finn and I are still waiting for Paul to convene a meeting of the Study Group. That is, a meeting of all four of us. It seems he doesn't think it's necessary to do so — that we all have our individual tasks to do, hence no need to meet. Which is fine I suppose, as long as we are all on the same page, and I would have thought that is reason enough to at least hold a project kick-off meeting."

"Do you think you might not all be on the same page?" asked Mads, already aware that Bradshaw had not held such a meeting and had instead discussed the project with each team member individually.

"I'm not sure. Well, let me clarify. I can assure you that Nikka, Finn, and I are at least."

"I take your point. Thanks for letting me know, Bernie," Mads hesitated. "By the way, has Paul said anything to you about Arcadia?"

"Yes, why do you ask?"

"Nikka mentioned to me that Arcadia had been mooted by Paul as a potential new site for The Bibliotek, and I was wondering if he had mentioned it to you as well."

"He did."

"In that context?"

"Yes, but it was just a passing comment. I just thought he was trying to be original for once and so I dismissed it."

"But the concept is interesting, don't you think?" Mads suspected Bernie knew he was testing her.

"As a concept, yes, very interesting. But practical? No."

"What if Arcadia was mooted as a good place to store our embargoed material? I mean, being embargoed would it really matter where it was stored?"

"Well it would matter, Mads, if my concerns about our contractual arrangements are agreed to be valid. And even if I am wrong and being overly cautious, no it wouldn't matter where embargoed books were kept but that does not necessarily lead to the conclusion that Arcadia is the best place to hold them. It just means the embargoed books would be way more out of reach of anyone, and that may not be a good thing from a legal standpoint."

"Yes, I have to agree with you on that."

"So I am to ignore his stupid suggestion?"

"For the purposes of your work for the RSG you can ignore it, yes."

"Good."

On landing at Keflavik helioport outside of Reykjavik, Mads and Bernie were met by the President's official hovercar and her very solemn driver, who did not wish to engage in conversation.

"Well, at least you get the official car, which is more than I ever get," whispered Bernie as the hovercar sped them to the Althing. "That may be a good thing."

"We'll see soon enough," replied Mads.

On arrival at the Althing, Mads and Bernie were escorted to the top-floor presidential offices. President Morthen was waiting for them.

"Welcome, Bibliotekar Ingridson. May I call you Mads?"

"Thank you President Morthen, you can indeed call me Mads. May I call you Eva?"

"Yes, by all means, please sit down."

"I congratulate you on your election, Eva, I understand it was an overwhelmingly popular vote," said Mads.

"Yes, it was that, thank you. How long are you staying in Reykjavik?"

"Just today. We're flying back to Norway later this evening, I believe." Mads knew this was the case, but nevertheless glanced at Bernie, who nodded to him.

"In that case, we'd best get started, if that's okay with you?"

"Yes, by all means."

"Well then, as you've probably guessed, Mads, it's about the *Sagas*, and The Bibliotek's desire to have them."

Mads noted the words "desire to have them" but resisted the impulse to correct her. "I gathered it had something to do with our proposal, which I understand is close to being agreed upon," he said, looking to Bernie for affirmation and receiving a small nod.

"Prime Minister Magnusson would probably see it that way, but I have to say, Mads, I do not share his enthusiasm for ridding ourselves of our *Sagas*."

"I'm sorry to hear that Eva. That is, I'm sorry to hear of you ridding yourself of anything. That's not what is being proposed."

"I know exactly what is being proposed, Mads, but I have told Magnusson that if he signs the agreement, in its current wording, I won't hesitate to veto it. I am extending you the courtesy of being forewarned."

Mads and Bernie instinctively looked at each in surprise. Mads and Bernie, in particular, had been working with Prime Minister

Magnusson for some time on procuring the *Sagas*. Being so fundamental as a relic of Iceland's heritage, the *Sagas* had necessitated careful consideration on the part of The Bibliotek as an institution promoting itself as the best option for their safekeeping. To be denied sealing the deal this late in the process was a shock to both of them.

"Can I ask why, Eva?" Mads asked after a pause.

"Mads, we are not a populous nation, but we are an immensely proud one. Proud of our heritage. Did you know that more books are sold in Iceland per head of population than in any other country in the world? That more books are written by Icelanders than by any other nationality? We thrive on books. We don't only buy more books than anyone else, our libraries lend more books than libraries anywhere else in the world. We could even say that before the Great Holy War. So, I ask myself, why would we willingly give away our most valuable books — and I don't mean value in terms of money but in heritage — to a library in Norway? Can you answer me that?"

"I appreciate that context all too well, Eva," replied Mads, trying not to be distracted by the President's piercing glare. "But, and excuse me if I am being presumptuous, I believe Prime Minister Magnusson has been acting in good faith in wanting to ensure that heritage was not only secure and safe but also maintained in a cost-effective manner. As you said, you are not a populous nation. As time goes on, the cost of protecting and preserving the *Sagas* is sure to increase."

"Ah yes, the cost. We have arrived ever so quickly at the 'cost'. You know, Mads, when I talk about our connection with books, with our national literature — ancient, old and new — with Americans, the British, and with other people who do not actually know us that well, I get the same old tired joke. That we Icelanders love books so much it is because nine months out of twelve it is so cold and dark outside there is nothing to do but eat, root, sleep, and read books. Not in so many words, but the sentiment is the same. Which you Mads, coming from Norway, must agree with me is ignorant, yes?"

"Yes, I have heard that little joke and yes, it is impolite and ignorant."

"Then you must also understand that when we see the 'cost' of our libraries, especially our National Library which, together with our oldest university, 'securely and safely' holds all our ancient books and manuscripts, when we see those costs in our national budget we look past those numbers because we accept them for what they are. In other words, I am not inclined to seek favour with my electors in slashing those costs, because favour is not what I will receive in return."

"I hear what you are saying, and I accept what you are saying, Eva, but I believe other factors are involved," responded Mads.

"Name them, Mads, I'm listening."

Mads turned to look at Bernie briefly then back at Morthen. "You may recall what happened after the *Codex Regius* was passed onto The Bibliotek as a sort of test by Prime Minister Magnusson." Mads was referring to the 'Royal Book' originating from the 13th century and which was discovered four hundred years later by the Bishop of Skaholt who sent it to the King of Denmark as a gift. The book contained 55 vellum leaves of Old Norse poems which to that day had never been found in any other book or manuscript, thereby ensuring the book's rarity and status. The *Codex* remained in Denmark for over 300 years before being returned to Iceland, but with eight pages missing. After it had been sent to The Bibliotek, Rafe had made it a mission to locate those missing pages and he had succeeded, much to the collective relief of the people of Iceland.

"Yes, I obviously remember that, and we were very appreciative of it being returned to a complete state. But what of it?"

"To put it bluntly, our designated Finder for Europe, Rafe Nagy, can only spare time to search for books and manuscripts for The Bibliotek. If we were to complete our negotiations for the *Sagas*, I can guarantee that not only will Rafe make it a priority to find as much of *its* missing manuscripts as he can, I will allocate him more resources to do so. And as you know, our proposed terms already incorporate a guarantee of access to all the *Sagas* to any Icelandic academic or student in the same manner as their current access rights. The only difference will be they will need to attend The Bibliotek's safe and secure environment. I also believe our proposed terms include funding in perpetuity, at current levels, of your Institute of Icelandic Studies," said Mads, glancing again at Bernie, who nodded affirmatively.

"I have no issue with those terms, Mads, but I am glad you mentioned the safe and secure environment of The Bibliotek. Is that because you don't consider the *Sagas* are safe and secure in Iceland?"

"I'm not saying that at all, Eva. That wasn't a comparison, that was me merely stating a bare fact. But since you raise it, perhaps you can tell me, do you consider the *Sagas* are not at risk remaining in Iceland?"

"Until a week ago I did."

Mads looked at Morthen, waiting for her to explain, but she didn't. Instead she reclined back in her chair and looked at her advisors. She was forcing Mads to ask.

"I gather there's been a threat made by the Present Sect," Mads reluctantly offered.

"Indeed there has, Mads, indeed there has."

"I see."

"I'd like to dismiss the threat as being just that, a threat, and made by a lunatic or lunatics not from Iceland, but I can't really, because it just seems too... how should I put it... coincidental." At this, one of Morthen's advisors took a plastic sleeve out of his folder and put it on the table in front of Mads, who picked it up and read the typed words on the slip of paper inside.

"You see, Mads," continued Morthen, "if I was the Present Sect, I wouldn't bother with a threat such as this, I'd just do it, I'd blow up the Institute. I'm sure if I had the right amount of explosives, the right access, the right placement, the right timing, I could do it. I wouldn't have to broadcast my intention, why would I? Why would I give warning, to allow time to place more guards at the Institute, to maybe put a tank in front of it. Whatever. That does not make sense to me, Mads. It *only* makes sense to me if it is not really a threat at all, but instead an incentive."

Mads said nothing. He held the plastic sleeve and stared intently at the paper inside it, trying to gather his thoughts before turning to respond. His ears were ringing and he could feel his face go red. He flicked the sleeve to Bernie, who picked it up as if in a daze, her mouth open but with nothing coming out.

"Are you suggesting..." Mads began to ask, indignant.

"I am not suggesting anything, Mads. What I am asking is do you see *how* it makes sense to me?"

"I'm sorry, but I don't. It doesn't make sense to me and I like to think I'm a rational person who places faith in logic. It's too easy to put two and two together and come up with twenty-two, when in reality it's only four."

"So you agree it does not make sense for the Present Sect to threaten to destroy the *Sagas* and everything else in the Institute."

"Yes, it is as you say nonsensical. But it is also nonsensical to conclude that the only rational explanation is that therefore it must be a contrived stunt by The Bibliotek to provide you with some motivation. It's just too obvious a connection to be believable."

"Hmm, I admit it is very easy to draw a line here between some big black dots, but... let's assume for a moment that I agree The Bibliotek is not behind this threat — or non-threat. The question then becomes who and why, does it not?"

Mads ignored the who and the why and instead held up the sleeve again. "Tell me, Eva, what did your forensics people have to say about this?"

Morthen looked at her advisor, who spoke. "The paper used is a very common brand of recycled paper. It is A4 in size and the brand sells many thousands of reams in Norway, Sweden, Denmark, Finland and Iceland. In other words, it is untraceable. The font is nothing special, the printer used is also a common brand as was the envelope. It wasn't posted and it wasn't hand-delivered."

"So how was it received?" asked Mads.

"It was found in the in-tray of the President's media advisor, in her office in a building in the city."

"Where I take it there were no security cameras."

"That is correct."

"So, let me see if I have this right, Eva. Someone with great care and skill ensured this nonsensical threat was untraceable?" asked Mads, frustrated at the theatrics just as much as the supposed threat.

"That would seem to be the case," said Morthen.

"Then the only rational explanation is that the so-called threat had a different purpose. Usually the Present Sect takes great care and shows skill in killing people and destroying books."

"Perhaps Mads, to embarrass you and The Bibliotek? Have you been targeted before this?"

"Yes, but I cannot say more on that."

"Hmm, fair enough. Let's close this matter here and now. Let us agree this so-called threat was not the work of the Present Sect, or it is the work of the Present Sect but for a different purpose. Being the politician I am, normally I would use this incident to my advantage. But I don't like lighting a fire if I have nothing to gain from doing so or if I don't think I can control it. Today, both of those conditions apply." Morthen nodded to her advisor, who picked up the sleeve, took out the paper, and, to the surprise of Mads and Bernie, tore it up.

More theatrics, thought Mads.

Damn it! thought Bernie.

"I am glad we have had this conversation face-to-face, Mads. I thought it best to communicate these issues in this manner, so I appreciate you coming, and I am sorry you are leaving with more trouble to contemplate than when you arrived." With that, Morthen stood up to signal the meeting was at an end.

Before they knew it, Mads and Bernie were being driven back to the helioport. They were each in somewhat of a daze and sat in silence. Mads could understand President Morthen's determination to derail the *Sagas* deal. It was a sudden and disappointing development after a protracted period of negotiations but he could think of nothing that could be done to retrieve the deal. He knew that Morthen was well within her rights as President to veto any deal struck between the Prime Minister and The Bibliotek, but the exercise of the President's general veto powers had not been a regular feature of Icelandic politics. It was a very rare thing for the President to do, and she wouldn't be threatening it if she didn't think she had sufficient grounds or support to do it. At least he had been told of the rejection directly and with certainty, albeit not quite diplomatically. But what had shocked him was the threat that had been sent to the President by, supposedly, the Present Sect, to destroy the Institute of Icelandic Studies and everything in it, especially the *Sagas*, if the Prime Minister signed an agreement with The Bibliotek.

The only positive to come out of the meeting that Mads could see was Morthen's candour and seemingly serious offer she made to Mads at its end not to hesitate to call her if he wanted any help in the future. He pondered that comment as he looked at the contact card she had given him whilst making the offer. It had her personal details on it. That was not normal practice for a Head of State.

"Why did she..." Bernie began to ask Mads why the President had the threat letter torn up, but Mads silenced her by raising his hand.

"We'll talk on the jet," he said, looking at their driver, who did not flinch and gave Mads the strong impression he didn't hear him, or Bernie, speak.

In any event, the remainder of the journey to the helioport was in silence.

Later, when their heliojet had taken off, Bernie got to ask her question, adding "we could have used that threat letter."

"It doesn't matter. If Morthen's people couldn't trace it, I doubt Nikka's team could," replied Mads.

He was waiting for Bernie to make another suggestion, but she didn't. She went on to discussing where all this possibly left any future discussions about any other books and manuscripts held in Iceland, but Mads' mind was elsewhere, focused on what Bernie *hadn't* suggested, and that was the possibility that Morthen herself had orchestrated the so-called threat from the Present Sect as justification for intervening in the negotiations over the *Sagas* and vetoing any agreement before it was signed.

However, before their heliojet had landed at The Bibliotek, Mads had already dismissed that possibility as unlikely. The timing was too obvious — that was the key — and Morthen had gone to a great length to explain to Mads her reasons for vetoing any agreement to send the *Sagas* to The Bibliotek, and those reasons alone were sufficient explanation.

Instead, Mads concluded the threat letter was a deliberate mischief, and could quite possibly have been intended to cause The Bibliotek, and him personally, a measure of embarrassment. And it could well be another message. As he was contemplating this last thought, his neurophone pinged. It was Thurldottir.

"I'd like an update, *please*, on Iceland."

Mads had half expected her call, but not before he at least got back to The Bibliotek. He didn't expect her to say 'please' though, as he couldn't recall her ever using that word before.

"The President informed me she intended to veto any agreement we sign with the Prime Minister for the handing over of any of the Institute of Icelandic Studies holdings, in particular the *Sagas*. She had asked me to come to Iceland so that she could inform me of her decision in person, as a matter of courtesy."

"That is very unfortunate. I take it you objected strongly against her meddling and interference with due process?"

"Chair Thurldottir, the President *was* following due process. That is why she is President. And, to be blunt, she did campaign on a nationalistic platform, she won on a popular vote, and so her attitude to The Bibliotek is hardly surprising."

"Nationalism has no place in what we do. There is no room for it or excuse for it. We cannot let governments go down this path, otherwise we fail to achieve our objective."

"We cannot get involved in local politics if that is what you are suggesting."

"Your job is to overcome these sorts of arguments. Anything else is failure. Your failure."

"That is your prerogative to take that stance, but I beg to differ. Let me know if the Council requires my resignation, will you?"

Now it was Mads' turn to terminate a conversation between him and Thurldottir, something he had not previously done. But he felt he could get used to it. He knew Thurldottir wouldn't play that card just for the rejection of The Bibliotek by the President of Iceland. It would seem petty. Mads was glad though that the conversation had not strayed to other things, in particular the so-called threat by the Present Sect. It seemed Thurldottir was not aware of it. But then again, Mads corrected himself, it only *seemed* to be the case.

10:35am, Friday, 4ᵗʰ January 2205

Justin Foote had finished looking into whether Rafe's network connection had been compromised and if so by whom, and rang Mads to discuss what he had determined. It was a short discussion and Mads immediately rang Rafe afterwards, but it was a little while before he finally made contact.

"Nags, I've just been talking to Foote, about our little issue," said Mads.

"And?" responded Rafe.

"He tells me it isn't an issue. There's been no compromise or misuse or unauthorised access. He's one hundred per cent positive about that," said Mads.

Rafe was a little taken aback. "But that's... That just doesn't make sense, Mads. I don't understand."

"Neither do I to be honest. Are you absolutely sure it was a message?"

"Yes, absolutely. Plus the fact that the police arrived seconds after I left. According to the media reports I've read, someone had rung them anonymously and told them there had been a person killed at that address. I'm sure that someone had to have been watching the house and waiting until I arrived. I was very lucky I left when I did."

"But now we have a bigger problem," said Mads.

"Yes, if my data pad wasn't compromised and nothing happened at your end, there's still the problem of how somebody got hold of the fact I was going to be there," said Rafe.

"Agreed," said Mads.

"Did Foote have any ideas on that?"

"None. He is as perplexed as you and I," answered Mads.

"So where do we go from here?"

"I think it best that you stay offline for now, at least. I'm only calling you now because Justin has assured me your network connection has not been compromised, but I won't be contacting you by this means again, and I think you should do likewise. Apart from that I'm out of ideas. Where are you now? Wait, don't answer that. I don't need to know."

"I can tell you I've just had a very productive meeting regarding a Find. Months of groundwork are about to come to fruition."

"I wish I could say that."

"Sorry? What's up?"

Mads told Rafe about his trip to Iceland and meeting with Morthen, including the threat letter she received, supposedly from the Present Sect.

"That's not good at all," responded Rafe, "have you talked to Nikka about the letter?"

"No, I'm keeping this to ourselves for the moment. I'll explain why later. Okay, I need to go, stay safe Nags."

"You too."

END OF CHAPTER SEVEN

Chapter Eight

The Penny Drops

*"History is not necessarily about what happened, it's often about what someone wants you to **think** happened. Or it's about what we **wish** had happened."*
Dr Tobias Capwell, YouTube, 2015

8:55am, Friday, 4ᵗʰ January 2205

Rafe was early for his meeting with Dr Christian Jamison, the Keeper of Special Collections at the Library of the Christ Church College at Oxford, but Rafe often was for these particular meetings, as he always enjoyed walking around the Peckwater and other nearby quadrangles, even on a chilly winter's afternoon such as this day, soaking in the atmosphere. The air on days like this still seemed to Rafe's nose to hang with learning amidst the odour of old oak and stone.

In its heyday, before the outbreak of the Great Holy War, the Christ Church Library had held the largest collection of early printed books in Oxford outside the Bodleian Library, but in recent years it had been struggling on a number of fronts, not least due to the damage its main building and its contents had suffered during that terrible conflict. For some time now Rafe had been discussing with Jamison the possibility of The Bibliotek procuring much of its vast collection of ancient books and manuscripts, which by one dusty estimate, then amounted to about one hundred incunabula, some of which were extremely rare, eight thousand or so other books published before 1641, and another ninety thousand or so published between 1641 and 1801. It had been an estimate because even the Library did not know how many books it had, and this was because it was yet to find the resources to compile an up-to-date definitive and *complete* catalogue.

The discussion Rafe was going to have today was basically the same sort of discussion that Rafe had been having with most of the college libraries spread out over Oxford for as long as he had been a Finder. Many of those other colleges had already made the tough decision to relinquish their antiquity collections to The Bibliotek, especially after the Bodleian had done so, which had been a major coup for The Bibliotek, but Jamison, backed up by the Dean of the College, had always been a hold out, and for many years had refused to even meet with Rafe. But, as was often the case, money starting becoming an issue for Christ Church, or, more accurately, the lack of it, so Rafe had been making a fair degree of progress with Jamison in recent times. And lately he had started to at least consider the idea of The Bibliotek procuring a large part of its antiquity collection. Rafe was a patient man; he had to be to do his job well, but he was finding it hard to put a lid on thoughts of finally succeeding in securing this particular collection. He had always focused on the totality of the holdings as *the* proposition, and not on adopting a piecemeal approach, and this had prolonged significantly the investment of his time on Christ Church.

"Good afternoon, Rafe," Rafe heard from behind him. Turning, it was Jamison walking towards him, with a large envelope in his left hand. "A beautiful day, isn't it?"

"Indeed it is, Christian," replied Rafe, as he warmly shook Jamison's outstretched gloved hand.

"Let's talk out here, then. You don't mind?"

"No, of course not," replied Rafe, as he followed Jamison to an ancient bench on the quadrangle lawn under a towering yet carefully manicured elm tree.

"I gathered from your note that there may have been a change in thinking of late," ventured Rafe, as soon as they sat down.

"Yes *and* no, I'd prefer to say. What has happened is that the study I commissioned, at your suggestion if you recall, has dispensed with the thoughts that many on the Board of Governors had been holding onto. And I have to admit, it became more and more depressingly apparent to me as the study progressed that we are in serious trouble. Once the study placed a figure on the amount of money we would need in order to finish cataloguing, conserving, and digitising all of the *current* Special Collections, attitudes on the Board began to, how should I put it... soften."

"I see, that's interesting. I'm thinking of a few names in that regard."

"That would not be too hard. Plus, you were right about access. That part of the study revealed the fact that the vast majority of access requests to books and manuscripts in the Special Collections were from visiting academics from overseas. So, in a way, what does it matter if the Special Collections are in Norway instead of Oxford? But more to the point, it is costing us a large proportion of our operating budget to manage and meet those foreign requests. Money we can put to good use elsewhere in the Library. It also emerged that a fair number of those visiting academics — I think it was thirty-eight percent or so — also attend The Bibliotek on the same research projects anyway."

"That is even more interesting. Any chance of getting a copy of the study?"

"Here's your copy," said Jamison, handing Rafe the envelope he had been carrying. "I will also email it to you."

"Thanks, Christian," replied Rafe, as he put the envelope in his satchel. As he did so he noticed the blinking azure light on his neurophone telling him he had missed a call. "That figure of thirty-eight per cent is quite telling, you know. It's a reflection of something you and I have discussed before."

"The more collections you collect the more collective your collection?" said Jamison.

"Ha! Yes, you've got it," exclaimed Rafe with a smile. "As we've discussed, it is our belief at The Bibliotek that, wherever they may be based in the world, any given academic can now hold the rebuttable presumption that The Bibliotek has the most comprehensive collection of books and manuscripts in their given field of study. As you can imagine, the ramifications of this for research outcomes are enormously positive."

"Oh yes, I agree with you one hundred per cent on that, Rafe. I just hope that the core purpose of this College, and all universities, being places of learning, isn't being diminished in the process."

"I know that's the view of some of the colleges in Oxford, and that they need to hold onto their collections for that very reason, and I guess that's why, for example, Brasenose College has never permitted any access to its library to anyone except its own members. But I gather that's not something that Christ Church is considering or would consider doing?"

"That's right. We've never been that 'precious'."

"My thoughts on the argument that the scope for learning is diminished by handing over collections to The Bibliotek are clear. I just don't agree with the proposition. For one thing, I have never proposed stripping any library at Oxford, or anywhere else for that matter, of its entire collections and holdings. Our focus is on procuring those holdings of libraries that are at the greatest risk of damage or loss and the most expensive to insure and maintain, with rarity being a factor on that score. Our aim is to be the Noah's Ark of learning if you will - procuring and saving one of everything. At least one copy of every book ever written, made or published."

"You make it sound like the Apocalypse is approaching, Rafe, but I see your point."

"I would also argue," continued Rafe, "that as a direct consequence of our endeavour to consistently adhere to our Noah's Ark aim, the aim of universities around the world to be places of learning is *definitely* enhanced, not *possibly* diminished."

"How so?"

"Well, you said it yourself, the *vast majority* of access requests aren't made by Christ Church students. So, to put it bluntly, would the students even know the Special Collections were there? But they would hopefully notice that, an increasing amount of source material from those collections would become freely available to them in digital format, and rather quickly. And they would also hopefully notice that improvements were starting to be made to the facilities at the college and the library via the improved cash flow. You haven't finished cataloguing the Special Collections, have you?"

"No, as absurd as that may sound, we still do not know how many books and manuscripts we have or what they are all about. The irony is that as time goes on, it is taking us longer to evaluate, treat, digitise and catalogue each item, and the longer we are taking the greater the risk to the remainder."

"So, correct me if I'm wrong, Christian, but the library was started in 1562 and in the six hundred and forty years or so since has simply accumulated 'collections' bequeathed, donated, or bought, to such an extent that every single collection remains intact as originally procured?"

"Yes, that is the case," confirmed Christian.

"And that has helped to make the Special Collections probably the most heterogeneous assortment of books and manuscripts ever accumulated, and with no firm idea of how many?"

"I would have probably expressed it differently, Rafe, but that sounds about right."

"Okay, this must mean then that the Christ Church Library hasn't been able to hold itself out as the key repository of *any* given field of study. For example, I know you have a collection of about eight hundred books from the seventeenth, eighteenth, and nineteenth centuries focusing on Scandinavian and Icelandic literature as a result of a bequest made in 1904 by Frederick York Powell..." said Rafe.

"That we do," interrupted Christian.

" ...but no other books relating to the same topic were owned by the Library before the bequest was made or have since been procured, to date. And another example: you have an excellent collection of eighty-four volumes published in the late eighteenth and nineteenth centuries in Siam, all in the Thai language, donated by the King of Siam in 1925, an alma mater of the College from his student days, but no other books from Thailand."

"Yes, Rafe, what you say is absolutely correct," admitted Jamison.

"And what's more, those two collections I've mentioned are not actually here. They, like other disparate collections of the Library have long ago been farmed out to other Oxford libraries, have they not?"

"Yes, again, you're right."

"You've also lost an unknown number of rare books as 'strays' to other colleges and possibly other countries, and the last time you discarded duplicate volumes was in 1862, when the massive Earl of Orrery bequest was finally catalogued, some one hundred and thirty-one years after the Earl, Charles Boyd, died."

"You've done your research, Rafe. I've told you that before."

Rafe wasn't done yet. "Presumably you can't discard any more duplicates simply because you can't be certain whether any given volume in any given collection is a copy or not of another book in the same collection or indeed another collection you hold."

"You paint a gloomy picture, Rafe, but yes, basically all of that is true."

"So, in effect, were a specialist team from The Bibliotek to waltz in, pack it all up, including all the collections out on loan, take them back to our Central Repository in Norway, unpack them, ascertain the subject of each item, its author, and its publication date, catalogue it accordingly, and then physically place it in the best possible existing 'collection', it could well be the first time any such book or manuscript would be recognised for what it truly is."

"That is quite possibly the case."

"That is staggering to contemplate," concluded Rafe, with an uncharacteristic serious look on his face.

"It would be also something I have always wanted to do, here at the Christ Church Library. But our rate of progress is such that we are actually going backwards. Each year we accept and receive more additions to the Library than we can process."

"What if you were offered the opportunity to do that very thing?"

"You mean, at The Bibliotek?"

"Absolutely. It's been done often enough in the past. We did it with the conservation team at the Bodleian Library, why not with the Special Collections of the Christ Church Library? Just think about it. Instead of all these distinctly unitary collections being held here on the off chance of prompting a visiting academic or, worse, spread out over Oxford, they would be added to existing collections of the same material and subject matter, thereby instantly adding academic value to both."

"Your point is well made, Rafe. It's something I have in fact been contemplating lately because it would provide the Christ Church Library with some space, not just in the literal sense, but also the conceptual. Space to consider where its direction should be. I think for too long we have been happy to docilely accept whatever bequests of someone's personal collecting habits have been with no consideration whatsoever as to whether bringing any such collection is appropriate for the Library and, more importantly, the students of the College. And that is a major reason why most of the access requests we get aren't from the students at all."

"I'm glad you said that, Christian, because I was hesitant to do so myself."

"Okay, let's park the discussion about our cataloguing issues. I want to talk now about The Bibliotek's *Principles of Access* and *Principles of Embargo*. I also want to talk about the offer of digitisation and transcription, and the resources The Bibliotek would apply to the Special Collections in conservation."

Rafe tried not to show he was excited, but it did appear to him that Christian had 'turned the corner'. "I can talk about access and embargo first if you like."

"Yes, that would be a good starting point. How do they relate to each other?"

"The access principles are subservient to the embargo principles, by necessity. That's our starting point. It's sounds negative, but it serves in practice to give certainty one way or another *quickly*, rather than have someone seeking access waste their time in coming to grips with all the guidelines only to find they can't access the book or manuscript they want. In both formulating and applying the embargo principles the aims are to be consistent but also to be cognisant of special cases, with the overriding aim to allow access unless there is a clear and reasonable reason not to."

"So, for example, a book would be embargoed if it is in such a poor condition that damage to it cannot be dismissed as a risk if it was to be handled by someone other than a member of The Bibliotek's Conservation Department. Such a book may only be embargoed in terms of touch. Access may still be allowed in terms of sight, that is, non-intrusive examination by means other than touching."

"Who makes these decisions, and when?"

"The initial consideration of access is made when we on-board each book. That is, during what we call the Induction Process. If we consider for a moment the possible scenario of the receipt at The Bibliotek of, say, ninety thousand volumes from the Christ Church Library. All of them would be unpacked and laid out in our receiving hall."

"It's that big?"

"Absolutely, and purpose-built. The first step is to evaluate the most predominant subject matters and ages so we can allocate specific conservators. In the case of the Christ Church collections I would hazard a guess that this wouldn't be necessary. Only an estimate of the total number of conservators would be needed for a reasonably fluid processing schedule."

"How many do you have?" asked Jamison.

"Oh, you mean conservators? I think the number of full-time staff at any one point in time is around four hundred," replied Rafe.

"Seriously?"

"Well, it's quite possibly more than that. It's been a while since I visited them."

"I can't even begin to imagine that many conservators in the one place. Go on."

"That initial process of resource allocation also allows us to apply a triage process. That simply means that at the same time as allocating specialties we seek to rank each book in terms of need of repair and preservation. Obviously the most in need are given priority. Then our real work starts. No book leaves the conservators and goes into the

Central Repository until a digital copy is procured. That is our strict policy."

"But that can come at some risk, can it not?" asked Jamison.

"Indeed, and that is the paradox. The more damaged a rare book is the greater the risk more damage is caused by scanning and photographing each and every page, but the more necessary that intervention becomes because of its state. We don't try to resolve the paradox. Instead we treat each case on its merits. Sometimes the decision is made to digitise before repair, sometimes during repair, and sometimes after repair. It just depends. For example, in many instances the only real damage is that the paper has separated from its binding, or even has lost its binding. In such a case, it is far easier to digitise the pages before we repair or replace the binding. In other instances, we may need to treat and stabilise the ink on the pages of a book, so it is preferable to wait until that is carried out before we digitise. Bottom line though is that digitisation is firmly ensconced in the conservation process. It's never an afterthought or left to do 'some time later'. We've found this approach to be very successful. It not only forces the conservators and the photographers to work together, it also fosters cross-learning by each."

"That's very interesting. It sounds like the digitisation of any given book being repaired could even be a staggered progress, depending on the repair process."

"You're absolutely correct, Christian. That happens often and is far better than the photographer being handed a book and told 'here, photograph this.'"

"And the cataloguing. When is that done?"

"That is also done at the same time. We don't expect every book's entry in the Master Catalogue to be completed before conservation ends, but we do at least begin the entry at the same time as conservation begins. In this way, we'll also have a reasonably good idea pretty quickly as to exactly where the book will end up in the Central Repository. And when we are talking about a number of volumes that will be kept together, this allows our Librarians to begin making plans to accommodate them."

"Okay, so let me understand this clearly. You're saying that if, as you say, we donate ninety-odd thousand books to The Bibliotek in one transfer, you will repair and catalogue every single book in one go. Is that correct?"

"Correct. I can guarantee it."

"How long would something like that take?"

"If we allocate say, two hundred and fifty conservators, which is a reasonable number, and if we assume the majority of the books are not in need of extreme repairs, then I would estimate the entire process would take between eight and ten months to complete, certainly no more than twelve."

Jamison leant back on the bench, clearly impressed.

"And if you came with the collection, you would be in charge of the whole process," Rafe continued. "All access and cataloguing decisions would be for you to approve. We could even arrange with the College to have you seconded to us for a year for that purpose. We would of course pay your salary, and pay for your lodgings and board."

"And I would be allowed to decide if any of the books could be digitally copied for the Christ Church Library?"

"Absolutely. And free of charge of course. But you would have to review and approve each digital copy, I'm afraid, or delegate the task."

"And the costs of packing the collection and transferring it to The Bibliotek? And the insurance?"

"All on us, Christian."

"Okay, I think we can move forward on this. The Board of Governors is convening in a month's time for its annual review. It's the only meeting on the calendar when all sixty-five Governors are obliged to attend. If I were to send you an email specifying all the matters I would want your proposal to incorporate — basically everything we've discussed today and a few other odds and ends — would you be able to put that proposal together within, say, seven days?"

"Not a problem, Christian."

"Excellent. Just to be clear then if it's not already obvious to you, Rafe, but I have changed my mind about losing our Special Collections to The Bibliotek, thanks largely to the study you convinced us to do but also due to the manner in which you're proposing the procurement is undertaken," explained Christian.

"Yes, I've gathered from our discussion there's been a change of heart," replied Rafe.

"Somewhat, and the annual review is the ideal opportunity to also get the Board of Governors behind it. To that end I have already circulated the results of the study and put the Governors on notice a formal proposal from The Bibliotek is being prepared. It's on the agenda for the meeting, and I will address and support it, and hopefully get a positive vote on it. It doesn't have to be unanimous; two-thirds of the Governors will do it."

"Do I include the offer of your fully-funded secondment to oversee the project?

"Yes please. Anything else?"

"No, that about covers it," replied a happy Rafe.

"Why don't we leave it there then? I will send that email before the end of today."

With that, both men stood up. Rafe shook hands with Christian, who then departed the quadrangle and headed back inside. Rafe sat back down on the bench and retrieved his neurophone. It had been Mads trying to call him, and now there was a message from him to call back as soon as he could. This he did and Mads relayed what Justin Foote had just told him — that his network connection had not been compromised.

Rafe sat for a while after that conversation, his head thumping. He had trouble accepting that nobody had been tampering with his data pad or his communications with The Bibliotek. Surely Foote had missed something, but what?

It was quite a while before Rafe could consider anything else. Then, just as he started doing so, a thought occurred to him. A thought of the only possible explanation for the Present Sect knowing he was going to be in Pienza and visiting Viscount Rossellini at his home. A thought that was diabolical, and wouldn't go away. He tried to dismiss it, but failed. Instead, it and the thought of the consequences it involved, grew and took hold of him.

Finally, Rafe knew what he had to do. He made a neurophone call, then booked a heliojet to take him to Copenhagen.

9:00am, Saturday, 5ᵗʰ January 2205

It was early morning in Copenhagen, a little after sunrise. Notwithstanding it was mid-winter, the Danish capital was free of snow and the early sky was clear, crisp, and cloudless. Rafe stood at the footbridge across the moat surrounding the old Rosenborg Castle, waiting for Justin Foote when he spotted him walking towards him.

"Hello Justin, you're spot on time, how are you?"

"Good thank you, and you?"

"Apart from a thumping headache, I'm fine. Thanks for coming all this way. I hope it wasn't too much trouble, but it was important we meet away from The Bibliotek. And I had some business to attend to over there," said Rafe, shrugging back towards the castle.

"That's fine, the Bibliotekar has me on a secret recruitment project lately, so I don't get any questions about what I do and where I go. I could begin to start liking this, and besides there's worse places than Copenhagen, especially in winter."

"Good. Come, we'll walk this way, there's a great café across the road from the park. The best coffee in Europe. Hopefully it will fix this headache. Did you tell Mads you were coming to meet me?" asked Rafe.

"No, as you asked me not to. But that's not something I prefer to keep doing, if you can appreciate."

"Yes, I can. But it was necessary, this time around, I'm afraid, especially if I'm right about the thing that got you here."

"Go on."

"I've known Mads a very long time, and I know he trusts you implicitly, without question. And we both know that's become very important of late. And now I need to trust you, for Mads' sake."

"Okay, I'm listening. You've got my attention."

"You're absolutely sure my network connection hasn't been compromised?"

"Yes, absolutely."

"So, and sorry to sound repetitive, no-one accessed my calendar entry for a recent trip to Pienza, in Italy?"

"If it was in the last month or so, no-one. I'm one hundred percent positive about that."

"Did Mads tell you what happened on that trip?"

"No, he didn't. The Bibliotekar simply asked me to find out if anyone had compromised your network account and

186

communications in the last month. I asked him if it had anything to do with Councillor Metcalfe's missing Arcadia report and he said no and apologised for not being able to tell me the reason right then. I checked the last six weeks of your network activity to be on the safe... Wait! Did you say Pienza?" Foote stopped walking and grabbed Rafe's arm.

"Yes, I said Pienza. I gather you heard about it?"

"I certainly did. You were there?"

Rafe then proceeded to tell Justin all that had happened at Pienza, confirming what Justin had read about it, except for the part involving Rafe.

Justin stared at Rafe for a few seconds, reading his face. Rafe did not blink. Justin looked away, back in the direction of the Rosenborg Castle, past the tree-lined path and the other walkers, with their dogs and children and prams and laughter. Finally, he spoke. "I read about that murder. The police said it was particularly gruesome."

"They eviscerated him, Justin, and lit a fire in his chest cavity with the very books I was there to finally seal our deal on procuring them."

"My god."

"Not quite. Come on, let's keep walking."

"Yes. Yes." Justin was shaken.

"Now you can understand why I have to be absolutely sure no-one accessed my data pad or my network connection or the network files containing my travel plans."

"Yes, I appreciate that. Give me a minute."

They walked on in silence, Rafe could tell Justin was pondering, thinking. They had reached the end of the park. The café was across the road, on a corner, and it was mostly empty of patrons.

"Good, let's grab seats at the long table." Rafe said, and they crossed the road. He opened the door to let Justin inside. There were a few steps down as the café was below street level, but nevertheless it had light streaming through ground level windows on both sides. Rafe went to the end of the long old oak table in the middle of the café, and motioned Justin to the other side, facing him on the bench seats. They sat down and Rafe pointed out the coffee menu on the wall behind the bar.

"Let's order first," Rafe said.

After the waiter took their order and began preparing their respective choices, Justin spoke.

"I am adamant no-one accessed that information."

"In that case, you can appreciate my dilemma."

"I can."

"Mads has not been able to solve it, and he now has other things to worry about. But something has occurred to me."

"Yes?"

"Are you aware that Mads is in a relationship?"

"I'm sorry, that's something I've not concerned myself with."

"Justin, he is in a relationship with Violetta Simpson."

"What? Sorry, I mean... that is a surprise to me."

"That's good, in a way, because they've been very careful not to advertise it and, fortunately for Mads, her position no longer reports to him."

"That's right, I helped the Bibliotekar facilitate that change in reporting line to the Deputy Bibliotekar, but that was before Ms Simpson joined us from Harvard."

"Exactly, which is why Mads didn't feel uncomfortable about the relationship, and he basically let it happen. And to tell you the truth, I think he is besotted with her."

"You've seen them together?"

"Yes, I had dinner with them shortly after the trip to Pienza, just before the holiday break."

"And you discussed the incident then?"

"No, of course not, and Mads made it clear he didn't want it mentioned, out of concern for her. But, here's the thing, Justin. During that dinner, it became clear to me that Mads talks quite freely with Simpson about work matters, to the definite point of possibly taking her into his confidence."

"I see, so..."

Their coffees arrived before Justin could finish so he stopped talking whilst they were being served.

Sipping his, Rafe exhaled. "Mmm, just what the doctor ordered. Then he continued. "So here it is. I had specifically mentioned to Mads I was going to see the Viscount in Pienza in a discussion we had a week before I went. He knew exactly where I was going and for what reason because I had been keeping him in the loop on my progress with the Viscount, as I do with all my more important Find projects. Not because of any procedure or policy but because he's my friend and he likes to know what's going on in the field. It was a Find, not one of quantity, but of quality — the books the Viscount had in his collection were exceptional in condition and rarity. They were going to be a great prize. To my point, though, Mads was the *only* person I told I was going."

"I think I know where this is going."

"Now, don't hear me wrong, I don't know if he told Simpson about my impending trip to Pienza or not. But given the other things she volunteered innocuously during our dinner conversation, the more I've been thinking about it the more likely it seems to me that she was aware of it, in advance."

"But if that's the case, you are effectively saying she has passed on that information to the Present Sect."

"Yes."

"I see. And I am guessing now that is why we are having this conversation."

"Yes."

"And now you are asking me to look into the Chief Conservator of The Bibliotek to see if she has any connection to a violent group devoted to destroying everything The Bibliotek stands for."

"No, I am not *asking* you to do anything, Justin. I'm just *hoping* you will. And yes, I know it sounds preposterous. But it's the only explanation I can come up with. I'd love to be told I am wrong."

Justin looked pensively at his coffee for a few moments, thinking. Then he shifted his gaze to outside, somewhere far off, across the road and across the park. "I need to do this quietly and quickly, and without alerting either Simpson or the Bibliotekar," he finally and quietly said.

"Yes."

"My god... anything else?"

"There's that word again. No, there's nothing else," replied Rafe. "How do you like your coffee, by the way?"

"It's *okay*, but not something I would come all this way for," replied Justin, ignoring Rafe's 'god' comment. Just to be clear, you're just asking, sorry, no, hoping, I do a background check on Simpson, am I right? You're not asking me to find any evidence of a link between her and the Present Sect are you? Or *are* you?" Justin said firmly, fixing Rafe with a steely gaze.

"Yes, that's right. I'm guessing HR didn't do a background check before she came on board. Mads said she had been part of the deal on the Harvard's rare book collection."

"That's right. Given the agreement that was signed it wasn't felt appropriate to check up on her, or indeed necessary."

"So, basically, all I'm asking is for that to happen now," offered Rafe.

"I get that, it's just the timing that is not normal."

"But it can be done, and quietly, can't it?"

"Absolutely. I just need to be careful as someone may want to know what has prompted this now, well after the event. And say we discover some skeletons or something that's not quite right. What then? That won't be the proof you're looking for."

"We'll cross that bridge if and when we get to it. Let's just see if there are any question marks first," Rafe said grimly, in response to which Justin nodded. "By the way, have you been in touch with Councillor Metcalfe?"

"Yes, twice now. The first time was just to make contact and to let him know you had briefed the Bibliotekar. He was obviously pleased that everyone could stop looking for him."

"But we're keeping a lid on this right? He's not missing, so he's not been found."

"Yes, those are my instructions, but I'm not sure how much longer Councillor Metcalfe's absence from The Bibliotek can be fobbed off."

"Hmm, yes, I guess that's right. No doubt Mads has that under control for now. And the second time?"

"The second time was just the other day, and that was to pass on the news to Councillor Metcalfe about what Bibliotekar Ingridson had found on Arcadia."

"You mean the palladium and rhodium?"

"Yes, the Bibliotekar thought it was only fair that Councillor Metcalfe be made aware of the apparent reason why his Arcadia report disappeared and why he was threatened."

"Just how valuable is this stuff, Justin?"

"The samples the Bibliotekar brought back from Arcadia are worth around one hundred and fifty thousand Euros combined. Unrefined, in southern Africa, the stuff is currently trading at slightly more than four and a half thousand Euros an ounce."

"Are you serious?"

"According to my metallurgist brother-in-law, yes. But the samples from Arcadia are worth much more than that because, again according to my brother-in-law, they are the purest he's seen or aware of."

"That's amazing, it really is. Let's hope you brother-in-law can keep this to himself."

"Oh he will, I can guarantee that, and so can the twenty-five thousand Euros he's been paid for his trouble."

"I bet Mads flipped out," said Rafe, with a knowing smile.

"He was certainly surprised to be told what The Bibliotek apparently has on its hands in Arcadia, but he agreed the payment to my brother-in-law was adequate. From what Bibliotekar Ingridson was telling me, the deposit of what is mostly palladium is very large. The Euro numbers are literally astronomical."

"And how did Thomas take the news?"

"He seemed a bit relieved actually."

"How so?"

"Well, before then he had been struggling to understand why what had happened to him *did* happen, so the news of what the Bibliotekar found answered that question completely and fitted in with what he knew. And then he said something interesting."

"What was that?"

"He said "that word 'palladium', Justin, I think I've heard it before", but that he couldn't remember where or when."

"Did you let Mads know that?"

"Yes, I passed on that comment, for what it's worth."

By now Rafe was staring blankly out the window of the café watching the legs of pedestrians walking past along the intersecting footpaths, and huddle on the corner waiting to cross the intersection. Justin followed his gaze, and then Rafe spoke.

"Something's not right at The Bibliotek, Justin. Not right at all."

"I agree."

"I know Mads will be very cautious about how he proceeds and what he will do with what he now knows about Arcadia, but if I know Mads he will be focused on finding out who is behind all this secrecy and underhanded stuff, and he won't take into account the danger that may represent. When we're talking this amount of money, and it has to be billions if Mads is right about the deposit on Arcadia, ruthless behaviour becomes the norm. I'm just not that confident Mads can match that."

"He *is* being very careful, or has been to date, I can assure you of that at least. So far there's been one sacking — one of the personnel based on Arcadia — he was quite surgical about that. And I think he's been able to rule out Nikka Johannson as being involved, which is a big relief. But you're right, this issue is his focus. The other problem we've got right now — the Present Sect and its message to you — is very worrying to him, but..."

"But it's taken a bit of a back seat, yes?" interrupted Rafe.

"Only because we've been unable to figure out how the Present Sect apparently knew you were going to be in that house, at that time, and for that purpose."

"All the more reason, then, that I need you to be super cautious about what I've asked you to do."

"Yes, I fully agree. Luckily this particular task is what I do. Well, normally, that is, under different circumstances."

10:07pm

In his study in his apartment, Mads found himself with his favourite ink pen in hand and his notebook open in front of him. Not many people wrote on paper with ink because most had neither the need nor desire to do so, or so it seemed to Mads.

But he did have the desire. It made him feel like a writer — a proper writer — and he found it helped him to think through problems and issues if he wrote them down first. He kept all his filled notebooks. They were the combined effort of his penned thoughts, some solving all the problems and issues he had encountered as Bibliotekar and some just capturing thoughts, especially his fleeting thoughts. Thoughts of something or someone or somewhere that would be gone unless he recorded them. His mother had given him his first notebook when he had graduated from the Academy. It was bound in A4, with glorious blank paper, two silk bound bookmarks and two small hinged clamps. The calf-leathered cover was a replica of a design commissioned by the great 16th century French bibliophile and patron of intricate fine bookbinding, Jean Grolier. It was a gold-tooled, marbled brown design with interlaced curving fillets with flower-filled ends of a six-pointed star in the centre of the cover. It was beautiful, so beautiful that it was several years before Mads had the courage to write in it.

When he had left the Academy, his handwriting was rudimentary at best, more shorthand and symbols than grammar and prose, like everyone else's handwriting, or, at least, those who still could be bothered to put pen to paper. So he spent a long time learning and practising to write just so he would not despoil his notebook, and until he did finally pen his first sentences on its front page — a short dedication to his mother - he was contented enough to just *feel* the book and *smell* it and its crisp pages. So content that one drunken night with Rafe, his friend had chided him that he treated his notebook like a virgin. "Nags, many a true word is spoken in jest," Mads had replied.

This particular notebook, now half-full, was his thirteenth. The other twelve were full and standing together in chronological order in one of the bookcases in his study in his apartment, where he was now sitting. They were all the same notebook; he loved his first one that much. And when he found out the company making them had gone into liquidation, he tracked down every last unsold one left and bought them all. He did not admit to Nags just how many; all he would admit was that he had "enough."

In recent months he had been remiss in filling the pages of number thirteen with his thoughts because they had been somewhat overtaken by the impression and effect Violetta and being with her in private had had on him, and more recently his thoughts had been more urgent with problems to be solved quicker than being written about and reflected upon. But now he needed to move beyond the short quaint poems he had penned after his first full night with Violetta. Now the problems swirling in Mads' troubled mind were elevated like none before. He needed to sort them. He needed to write.

He wrote first about his friend Thomas and what he knew about the issue that had caused him to take flight and go into hiding — that Thomas had gone to Arcadia to perform a routine but important task and had encountered a geosurvey team at The Bibliotek's site. There is *no entry in the Arcadia visitors' log for anyone on that survey team.* This was *deliberate* and *cost Dr Joyce his job. Councillor Carlson was the reason for Joyce's behaviour. Thomas mentioned the presence of the survey team in passing in his report of his Arcadia trip. His report was accessed before he could send it and then deleted. His life was then threatened by someone who cloaked his voice.*

At that point Mads stopped writing and looked at it. It was not good. He was writing fast, as if his pen was finally trying to catch up with his mind, not bothering with calligraphic quality but just getting the words down. Dot points, lines and arrows. Like a literary jigsaw puzzle was how these notes were playing out. He continued, lest he lose his train of thought. Thomas — now with a 'T' — then left The Bibliotek ("TB") quietly and quickly ("Q&Q"). *Left his neurophone and data pad,* which *someone then lifted from his office.* Mads *called his number and a MALE voice answered then hung up,* and the phone has been *OFF since then.* Mads *went to ARCADIA to find out for himself what was going on — SECRET.* He had located the site where the survey team had been working and took some mineral samples. They turn out to be *rare and valuable deposits of P&R. Thomas. Not missing* <u>officially</u>, Mads wrote and underlined. *List Thomas as missing?? NO... wait.* He stopped and pondered why he wrote 'wait'. *Wait for Thurldottir or someone else to do it, then reveal Thomas is not missing but on leave?* That thought made him add a question mark after 'wait'. Something to consider. So, wrote Mads, *who is behind all this??* Whoever organised the survey team is keeping this discovery secret. *CARLSON is involved* and if he is involved then *THURLDOTTIR is involved as well, if not running the show. Thurldottir knows that Mads went to Arcadia and knows* his stated *reason for doing so was not true. Thurldottir must also know* as a consequence that *Mads has been in contact with Thomas,* but she *may not know that he has some P&R. Someone in Nikka's team —* the person who threatened Thomas and who was probably the same person who answered his phone when Mads dialled his number — *is also in on it. That's THREE people so far.* Damn it. *Wait,* thought Mads — *BRADSHAW!* He's been *quietly spruiking Arcadia as a potential site for a relocated Bibliotek. Why would he be saying this if he wasn't involved as well?? It can't be just a coincidence. But why the big secret about the P&R? And what would be the connection between the P&R and relocating The Bibliotek? Then there's LARKIN. I just don't trust him,* wrote Mads, but he left a question mark next to his name. That would make *FIVE people involved if Larkin was a stool pigeon. A conspiracy.* Mads didn't like the look of that word after he wrote it, it made him recognise the feeling of paranoia, so he crossed it out, then replaced it with *CONSPIRACY.* He knew of Thurldottir's animosity towards him, but this was next level if all these people were siding with her. And *for what purpose???*

Question marks now dotted the page in Mads' notebook. Question marks and underlined words. And no answers.

Mads was about to close his notebook when he remembered — the Present Sect! Now words stopped inside the point of his pen as it hovered over the page, tapping up and down. *First Rafe is targeted* with a violent message. *Could it really be that someone at The Bibliotek tipped off the Present Sect. Why?? 'No Other Explanation'* was what Mads reluctantly wrote, putting a big star next to that sentence. Another unresolved question. And then *Iceland. What was that about???* Mads put his pen down and lifted his wineglass to his mouth, took a big mouthful of the smooth cabernet and swirled it in his mouth in contemplation before swallowing. That was such a puerile threat, but the timing, again. *They must have known we were so close to signing the deal,* Mads thought and wrote. *BUT, they didn't know Morthen was going to negate it anyway, otherwise why make the threat??? BUT* why make it anyway?? *Morthen said,* wrote Mads, *why not just bomb the Institute? Was it really just to make Mads look bad?* Another big question mark. *Are the two connected? The Pienza message and the Iceland threat?? Both well-timed, both recent.* Mads pondered that for a few seconds then found himself writing down *'Relocation Study Group'.* Then *'Thurldottir'.* This whole Arcadia thing. A string of words flowed from his pen: *Capacity, Present Sect Threat, Relocation, Arcadia, P&R, Secrets, Threats.* Then he drew a circle around '*Thurldottir'* and lines from the circle to each of those words, with a question mark next to each line. Then Mads put his pen down and stared at his diagram.

After a while Mads sensed a familiar fragrant aroma and looked up to see the silhouette of Violetta in the doorway of his study. He closed his book.

"There you are," she spoke with her usual sultry seductive soft tone, strolling into the light so that Mads could see she was wearing only a towel, wrapped around her waist.

"How long have you been standing there, Vie?" asked Mads, still tense.

"Long enough to watch you writing. What are you writing Mads?" asked Violetta.

"Just making some notes. How was your bath?"

"Divine, my darling, just divine. I do like a nice long bath. I just wish you would join me when I have one, your tub is big enough for an orgy! What are you writing notes about? I mean, who even writes?"

"Well I do, I have for many years. You should try it some time. Or maybe you don't know how to."

"Oh, come on, Mads, show me! I haven't seen your writing. Maybe I can even work out what it says!"

"Don't be rude, my handwriting is perfectly legible."

"Are you writing a book or something? Now that wouldn't be surprising. Let me see, let me see it then if its legible."

"I'd rather not. Just some notes about ongoing work issues. It just helps me clear my mind."

"But Mads, you don't need to write to clear your mind. I've got a better way to clear your mind. C'mon, come to bed with me, I'll show you," Violetta walked into the study, lent over Mads, grabbed his arm and tried to pull him up and away from his desk. As always when Violetta got this close to him, Mads found it impossible to resist. He closed the clasps of his notebook, then put it back in the drawer of the desk and stood up to embrace Violetta and her fragrance, before they walked arm in arm to the bedroom.

"Well, whatever's in it, that looks like a very interesting old book, Mads. Full of mystery," said Violetta. Mads just smiled, his thoughts were now on other things. "How come I've never seen you with your mystery book before, Mads?"

"I guess you've kept me away from it."

Much later, when Mads was sleeping heavily and, apparently unbeknownst to him as she had yet to mention it to him, snoring, the lamp on the desk was turned on and the desk drawer was slowly opened. Violetta quietly took Mads' notebook out of the drawer and, placing it on the desk, opened it to the page Mads had been writing on. But after only a few seconds she heard the snoring stop abruptly so she quickly closed the notebook, returned it to the drawer, and turned the lamp back off. She then quietly left the room, went to the bathroom and made the appropriate noises before returning to bed and a sleeping Mads.

END OF CHAPTER EIGHT

Chapter Nine

Adcom Addresses Arcadia

"The Present Sect is the most insidious danger we face today. And when I say "we" I am referring to those members of humankind who possess souls filled with a desire for knowledge and a respect for history and how it has shaped our world. We are many, they are few, but let us not think that fact keeps us and all that we value safe from harm. We cannot argue with the Present Sect and expect them to change. We must exterminate them and render their twisted logic irrelevant and consigned to the dust of the forgotten past."
Professor Ignatius Turner, Head of Conservation Studies, The Bibliotek Academy, 2201

2:27pm, Friday, 11ᵗʰ January 2205

Finn was slightly early for his meeting with Mads. As if he were Scandinavian and not Australian, Finn was always early for meetings, be they with Mads or with anyone else. It was just his way and Mads did not mind. In fact, Mads was always glad to see that the opposite was not the case, that Finn was instead never on time for their meetings. That would not be good. So consistent was Finn that Mads always tried to make sure he was ready for him, but today was different as he had just taken a video call from Nikka — one that he had been waiting for — so he asked Larkin to ask Finn to wait for a few minutes.

"Okay Nikka let's have it," said Mads, bracing himself.

"You asked me to do background and foreground checks on every member of my team. I ended up taking on board your suggestion to ask for Doctor Foote's assistance, as I started with everyone's personnel file. You also asked me to look for any connections with Councillor Carlson."

"Yes, and?" interrupted an impatient Mads.

"And I identified a member of my team with links to the Councillor. He came on board at The Bibliotek from a security company based in the United States. The major shareholder in that company is a nominee trustee of a Bahamas unit trust. The units in that trust are all held by the Trustee of the Carlson Family Trust. That's Councillor Carlson's family trust to be exact," Nikka paused.

"I see." *I knew it!* thought Mads. "That's a very interesting connection. Who is this individual? Was he recommended by Carlson?"

"His name is Rikus Smits. His expertise is in being a thug, basically. I'm not sure why he was recruited by The Bibliotek to be honest. He is a weapons specialist, so I gather he was brought on board in light of the Present Sect. I don't think he was recommended by Councillor Carlson, but I can't be one hundred percent sure about that. There may have been a quiet word in someone's ear."

"When did he start with The Bibliotek?"

"About three years ago."

"You said you weren't sure why he was recruited. So, you did not personally on-board him?"

"No, not directly. He came on board via HR. We had a number of people starting with us within a short period of time and I basically let HR handle all of them. Kaitlin's security industry consultant is top notch and he has never failed me. In hindsight I should have at least given them each the once-over before they were made their actual offers."

"Hindsight is a wonderful thing, isn't it?" asked Mads, "but not something I like to dwell on. You are aware of him, though?"

"Yes, of course, but to date he hasn't given me cause to doubt his expertise or review his performance. I've kept him generally away from The Bibliotek proper as he tends to scare people just by being around them. I've had him overseeing perimeter patrols, weapons training and target practice. I'm okay with him scaring the other security personnel enough for them not to stuff up those tasks."

"Understood. But − and correct me if I am wrong − in the hypothetical situation where a person is working somewhere with an ulterior motive it is best done by keeping a low profile, isn't it," said Mads, more of a statement rather than a question.

"Yes, Mads, you are right about that. I just need to be careful before I starting calling a spade a shovel when it proves to be just a spade."

"I don't know the difference between a spade and a shovel, but I understand your concern. Your Mr Smits, you can access his neurophone records, yes?"

"Yes, I can, but only after consulting HR and demonstrating reasonable cause."

"Okay, I'd like you to tell Doctor Foote that you need to obtain a record of all calls made by Smits in the week beginning Monday five November last year and see if any were made to this number..." Mads gave Nikka the number of the neurophone Thomas was using when he received the threat against his life after returning from Arcadia. "At the same time ask him to do a search for anyone else employed by The Bibliotek coming from that security company, focusing on the periods immediately before and after Smits was recruited."

"Okay Mads, I'll do this, but as I said before, soon I am going to need to know why."

"Once you get back to me with this information, I absolutely *will* give you a complete briefing. All I can say right now is that it is a serious matter. Justin will ask you how soon you want it. Tell him its urgent and tell him I told you to say that. He will understand."

"Shall do."

"Thanks Nikka. Now, I'm sorry but I've got someone waiting for me so we'll end this discussion, for now. I'll see you at Monday's Adcom meeting, okay?"

"Okay, Mads," replied Nikka, terminating the call.

Mads sat pondering Nikka's revealing information for a few moments, then paged Larkin to let him know that Finn could come in.

"Finn, good to see you," signed Mads, as Finn entered his office.

"Likewise," Finn signed back, as he sat down in his usual chair in front of Mads' desk. "Do you mind if I use my other self?" Finn signed as he placed his data pad on the edge of the desk, in front of him.

"Sure, no problem," signed Mads. He knew what Finn meant and so waited patiently whilst Finn launched his holographic interpreter from his data pad, which Finn placed at the side of Mads' desk, facing them both. The positioning was deliberate, because in addition to being measurably faster than any human interpreter, the holographic had less than a 0.01 percent error rate which meant that Finn's trust in it was high, thereby negating the need for him to occasionally look at it whilst signing. Instead he could maintain eye contact with Mads during their conversation.

"Finn, I wanted to have this discussion today, before Adcom meets, to review the progress of the Relocation Study Group and, as you will recall, to review the numbers you've arrived at on the Secondary Repositories audit and your draft recommendations."

"Okay, yes, I understand."

"Okay, good. First, let's deal with The Bibliotek capacity issue. I am going to ask each member of the Study Group in turn to brief Adcom on the outcome of your respective work to date in relation to the reason why I established the RSG."

"Not a problem, I am basically ready."

"What can you tell me — now?" Mads signed.

"Well, if you recall, Mads, at the last Adcom meeting I made the comment that we were more than fifty years away from the Central Repository reaching full capacity, and that that estimate had a margin of error of less than five per cent."

"Yes, I remember," Mads signed.

"The RSG work has basically allowed me the time and resources to work on improving our capacity management methodology, something I've been wanting to do for some time, as you also know. Now I feel much more confident about the numbers, both now and going forward."

"What you decide?" Mads signed badly. Finn was used to it, and he appreciated Mads making the effort.

"As a result of tightening our algorithms and methodologies, I can confidently say we are, at current levels, sixty-two years away from full capacity, Mads, give or take fifteen months."

"That's good to hear, Finn. Very good. So, really, we're about forty years away from having to look for a second or new and larger site, do you think?" said Mads.

"If it's a case of a second site in addition to our current site, I would say five to ten years is sufficient lead time. In the case of a new and larger site, the lead time should be no less than fifteen years, assuming a progressive start-up of a second site, not an *entirely* new one."

"No-one is suggesting the latter," said Mads.

"Well that means a deferral for forty years of any decisions is within our parameters."

"Are you confident in being able to back up your estimates?"

"If the person I need to convince has an understanding of deep and long-term logistical algorithmic-based forecasting, yes, I am confident. If I must convince someone like Paul Bradshaw, then I am not confident."

"Why, what's your problem with the Deputy Bibliotekar?"

"I am sorry Mads, but Bradshaw is an idiot," said Finn bluntly.

"Sorry, what you say?" Mads signed rhetorically, a bit taken aback. Finn had a reputation for being blunt at times. This appeared to be one of those times.

"He's an idiot, Mads," Finn repeated with the same level of conviction. "I've suspected as much for a while, but now that I've been reporting to him for the Study Group, I know it's a certifiable fact. I realise he is the Deputy Bibliotekar and that you appointed him to that position, but I seriously think he's lost the plot and just doesn't understand a lot of things he should be taking on board. Trying to explain to him the underlying assumptions in our new algorithms is like trying to explain to a five-year-old why the Earth isn't flat."

Listening to Finn say that about Bradshaw made Mads stand up and walk over to the window and stare out of it, in silence. He desperately didn't want Finn to see the smile on his face. He should have been angry at his outburst, even precious about the fact that he alone had made the decision to promote Bradshaw to the Deputy Bibliotekar role. But instead he was relieved to hear from Finn that he thought Bradshaw was an idiot. No-one else had had the courage to say to Mads those very words, betraying an assessment that Mads had a feeling others at The Bibliotek, including some of the senior management team, had made about Bradshaw. In many circles, including of late Adcom, it was the proverbial elephant in the room. He could tell Finn was sitting quietly, waiting for him to respond. It took him a while before he could turn and face Finn with a concerned look on his face, albeit feigned.

He walked back to his desk. "I appreciate your candour Finn, and I will admit to having some concerns of late about *Deputy Bibliotekar* Bradshaw, but nowhere near indicating the level of... incompetence you imply, so I need to ask, what has brought on this view of him?" he asked in a quiet, measured, tone.

"Well, first off he tried to tell me precisely how I was to undertake the task of working out if we really do have a capacity issue needing urgent consideration. And he was the one who used the word 'urgent', not me."

"I see. In other words, he tried to tell you how to do the job you've actually been doing for the last twelve years."

"Precisely. I am so glad I have never had to report to him otherwise. It wouldn't be pretty. In any event, I told him upfront that I didn't need him to tell me how to do my fucking job."

"You said *fucking* job?" signed Mads as soon as he saw Finn sign the word, just before he heard it. He knew at least how to *swear* correctly in BSL, thanks to Finn.

"Well no Mads, I actually said *FUCKING JOB!*"

Looking at Finn, Mads thought he was shouting at him and for the first time in their conversation he was prompted to look at the holographic Finn when he heard it. There was still anger in 'his' face. "You were upset then" Mads said after a few seconds, turning back to face the real Finn.

"A little. Well, maybe more than a little."

"I see. I gather he didn't take that well," said Mads.

"No. But not so much angry as hurt."

"That is bad," signed Mads.

"Yes, I would have preferred anger, then we could have argued about it a bit more. Instead he sort of went all quiet and withdrawn."

"Not good. You said 'first off'; there's something else?" asked Mads.

"Yes, the next time we spoke it was if we'd never had that first discussion. He was the same old chirpy Bradshaw. That was strange by itself, but I let it go. Then he said something that reminded me I was dealing with an idiot."

"Let me guess. He said something like Arcadia would be the ideal site to relocate The Bibliotek."

"Yes, Mads, that he did. How did you know? Did Bernie tell you?"

"Bernie told me he had said the same thing to her, as did Nikka, so I assumed he also said it to you. How did you respond?"

"Not well. I told him not to be an idiot and then proceeded to explain to him why his comment was idiotic. And then I made the mistake of asking why he had suggested it and why before we had reached anything near a conclusion that the Governing Council should consider relocating The Bibliotek."

"What did he say in response?"

"He said that I had already told Adcom the Secondary Repositories were a major concern and that something had to be done sooner rather than later so why not wrap up this whole thing with looking at Arcadia? He said it was an ideal site, especially for any item in the Central Repository that was embargoed, in which case the location of such items doesn't matter, so long as it is secure."

"Salient points, Finn," said Mads.

"Maybe, Mads, maybe. I then challenged him as to why he wasn't following your directive — that the work of the RSG was to be kept separate from my audit of the Secondary Repositories."

"And his response?"

"He said the two reports could be kept separate, and should be, but why not at least cover Arcadia in both, since the work I was doing for the RSG could produce results for the audit without any extra effort."

"Hmmm, interesting," pondered Mads out loud.

"But Mads, I still think it is too early to be going down the Arcadia path. I thought it then and I still think it, even more so now that we've firmed up our estimate of when capacity of the Central Repository will be reached."

"Well, perhaps, and perhaps not."

"What do you mean?" asked Finn.

"On the one hand, I tend to agree with you. The Relocation Study Group should focus on the capacity of the Central Repository and not factor in the situation with the Secondary Repositories. We need the relocation question settled first, and it sounds like you at least have answered your part of it. But on the other hand, you have identified the very real and current problem with those Secondary Repositories, so we do need to resolve *that* capacity issue regardless. Agreed?"

"Yes, agreed," replied Finn.

"So, the fact that the RSG is looking at capacity right now would tend to suggest that at some point we may need to also factor in the problem with the Secondary Repositories."

"Possibly," countered Finn.

"Probably, would be my view," responded Mads. "But anyway, let's park that thought for a moment. Let's talk about physicality. My understanding is that to bring the Secondary Repositories up to the physical standard of the Central Repository, ignoring the fact they are all above-ground, would involve a significant amount of up-front capex and ongoing cost, is that right?"

"That's correct, Mads, but it's worse than that. Some of the Secondary Repositories are simply not suitable for an upgrade. They would need to be relocated if it was decided to bring all the Secondary Repositories up to the standard of the Central Repository. So, the initial capex would be higher. But Mads, why are we even talking about bringing the Secondary Repositories up to the Central

Repository's standard? We haven't had a discussion yet about outcomes of the audit."

"I appreciate that, but right now I want some clarity on the relative capex should such a decision be made. So my question is: would such costs be higher than expanding the existing Central Repository?" asked Mads.

"You mean deeper?"

"Deeper, longer, whatever applies to an expansion," responded Mads.

"No."

"Why that?" signed Mads, again badly.

"Simple logistics, Mads. The *deeper* the original construction went, the higher the cost each level became. Everything is extra. Extra extraction lengths for the rubble, extra insulation, extra cabling, extra air and pressurisation tubing, extra everything. The same logic applies to the *longer* each level became."

"So you're telling me that, bottom line, it could be cheaper relocating some part of The Bibliotek to Arcadia than expanding the existing Central Repository?"

"Ignoring the Secondary Repositories, quite possibly yes."

"So maybe we might consider Arcadia?"

Finn looked at Mads for a few seconds, before shaking his head. "I'm not going to agree with that suggestion," he countered, "without the benefit of a site visit to Arcadia. And even then I'm reluctant to basically ignore the fact that capacity is not currently an issue Mads."

"Okay, I get that Finn. I'm not asking you to. Just be aware there are other factors at play here, so coming out of the next Adcom meeting it may just be agreed that you do in fact go to Arcadia to see for yourself."

"I'm fine with that, but would I have to go with the idiot?" Finn asked, and not without a small amount of frustration.

Mads sighed. "Yes, Finn, and I would send Nikka with you to make sure you do the needful and then you *all* come back," Mads replied, with a slight smile.

"Fair enough. But now, what about the Secondary Repositories? Do I need to factor them into my part of the report?"

"No, not at this stage. I am going to address the issue separately at the next Governing Council meeting."

"You mean push it upwards?"

"Yes, they started the problem so they can fix it. I will make some recommendations, but I am expecting some resistance."

"Can I ask what they will be?"

"You tell me, Finn. You've no doubt got a better feel for the situation than me," replied Mads.

"Mads, I'm a numbers guy. This is above my pay grade."

"I get that Finn, and I am not going to hold you to anything, but I do want to hear what you hopefully think about the most appropriate outcome of your audit."

"Okay. I think the first thing we need to do is slow down the rate of procurements that will always end up in a Secondary Repository, if not down to zero. I'm not sure how, but the cost escalations and projections almost demand it, as you've seen from the data sets."

"Agreed. Anything else?"

"Part of the audit involved de-duping the books we hold in the Central Repository that we've placed an access embargo on with copies we hold in the Secondary Repositories. The numbers involved with transferring those copies into the Central Repository so that they can be accessed make it worthwhile in terms of reducing the space pressure on some of the Secondary Repositories, particularly two of the Frankfurt repositories, but without a material impact on the capacity of the Central Repository. So that would be another recommendation."

"That's a good suggestion, but Phicom might have a different view on it."

"I get that, but you did say I wouldn't be held to the idea."

"Of course. I'm just thinking out loud here. Anything else?"

"One last idea. I would be inclined to consolidate the existing Oslo repositories and the existing Frankfurt repositories as much as possible. If we can also transfer copies to the Central Repository as I suggested, and we cease the procurements, we have scope for filling one or more of those repositories and basically sealing them, thus reducing ongoing costs."

"That is definitely something worth looking at, and it falls fairly and squarely into your ballpark," Mads said cheerfully. "And there's a suggestion I'd like to make."

"Yes, Mads?"

"The data you've produced also target multiple copies of the same book. You've even cross-referenced these across multiple Secondary

Repositories. That suggests an absence of control or management, but bottom line is there is no point holding multiple copies. One is enough, two at most. Any more than that and The Bibliotek should not in my view be holding onto them, so there's a question there as to whether we can sell them or otherwise make them somebody else's responsibility."

"That is more than feasible, given the numbers involved," responded Finn. "But what about simply consolidating the Secondary Repositories with the Central Repository? I know exactly the utilised space of each of the Secondary Repositories. It has never occurred to me that we would *ever* consider bringing all the copies into the Central Repository, but it would not be hard for me to evaluate the impact on our capacity if that decision were ever to be made."

"It may be something to think about in terms of the Master Catalogue, but not realistic in terms of physically consolidating all the books from the Secondary Repositories with The Bibliotek. That is definitely something Phicom would have an issue with, let alone the impact on the Central Repository's capacity. But let's keep that piece of information to ourselves for the time being, and I mean just between you and me. Don't involve your staff or otherwise let them know. But it should nevertheless be covered in your audit."

"Understood. Speaking of capacity, what about my report for the RSG?"

"That has absolute priority, Finn. We'll park this discussion of the audit and possible recommendations for now, but we'll revisit it before the next Governing Council meeting to firm up those recommendations, okay?"

"That will be fine, Mads."

"Now, we've still got some time left before my next meeting, so let's have a closer look at the numbers your audit has produced. I really need to get my head around the size of the problem."

"Don't worry, Mads," said Finn as he opened the first folder of tables. "I went through the same process and survived," smiled Finn.

"That's fine for you to say. You're the numbers guy," Mads replied in kind.

9:02am, Monday, 14th January 2205

As was his habit, Mads waited until everyone attending the Adcom meeting was in the meeting room adjacent to his office before joining them. But as he entered the room he sensed a level of tension, which was not normal for these meetings. It made him adopt a measured, business-like, tone.

"Good morning all. As you all know this meeting of Adcom will be discussing the status of the work being done by the Relocation Study Group — this is the halfway point of the project. Given its importance I'd like to suspend the other agenda items so we can focus on this very important issue. In view of that I need to ask all personal assistants to leave the meeting, except you, Nils," Mads said as he turned to Larkin sitting next to him. "I'm sorry you have all come here for nothing, but I only decided to suspend the other agenda items as I walked into the room." Mads didn't often lie, but when he did it was for a purpose, and this morning he wanted the assistants to assume a relocation proposal was on the cards, and that is why he waited until they had arrived before dismissing them.

As soon as the door closed behind the last of the departing assistants Bradshaw spoke up. "Bibliotekar, why are we discussing these matters at Adcom? Aren't they matters for the Relocation Study Group?" asked Bradshaw, looking around the table for support. Out of all the members of Adcom he was the only one not to call Mads by his name. And because of that, his use instead of Mads' title came across to some of the other around the Adcom meeting table as an insult, one that Mads steadfastly chose to ignore.

"Why?" answered Mads, looking directly at Bradshaw.

"Well, that's the purpose of the RSG," he responded. "Is it not?"

"Have you actually held and chaired a meeting of the RSG?" asked Mads.

"No, not yet. It hasn't been necessary."

Mads was by now clearly exasperated, and he struggled against the urge to yell at Bradshaw in front of everyone. But he made it clear that he was not happy when he spoke. "I appointed the RSG to perform a study. That's what the 'S' in RSG stands for. Any *recommendations* in response to the Governing Council's request will be coming from Adcom, and *not* from the RSG. I thought I had made that clear. No decision-making has been delegated to the RSG. It is therefore not only appropriate these matters are discussed at Adcom — it is necessary. And the fact that you have yet to convene a meeting of the RSG after two months, Paul, adds to that necessity."

Mads now turned away from Bradshaw at the other end of the table, looked at Bernie and, without waiting for a response from Bradshaw, said "okay, Bernie, let's hear your concerns."

Bernie duly gathered some papers in front of her and spoke. "Thanks, Mads. Putting aside the logistics of any relocation involving the Central Repository, whether it be to Arcadia or somewhere else on Earth away from The Bibliotek..."

"Wait, what did you say? Arcadia? Did I hear you right, Bernie?" interrupted Dean Coenraad.

"You heard me right, Dom. Arcadia."

Coenraad looked in confusion at Mads, who spoke before Dom or anyone else could ask the next, obvious, question. "It's all right Dom, Arcadia is a Bibliotek site, and it's come up in discussions amongst the RSG members, so let's hear what has to be said. Continue please Bernie."

"As I was saying, putting aside the logistics of any relocation involving the Central Repository, whether it be *to Arcadia or somewhere else on Earth*," emphasised Bernie, "I have concerns about the legality and ethics of doing so."

"Legality?" said Bradshaw. "Are you serious?"

Mads turned and looked down the table at Bradshaw and was about to shut him down, but Bernie got in first.

"Paul, I know you and I have discussed this," she firmly answered. "And I know your view is that I am creating a problem that may not exist, but as General Counsel of The Bibliotek, I have to have regard to the legal issues involved, and I believe risk is the main legal issue and that it is material enough to warrant this discussion."

"Let's give Bernie the opportunity to articulate her concerns, shall we? And without further interruption," said Mads, more as a statement than a question, and more directed at Bradshaw than the other members of Adcom.

"Thank you Mads. The fact is we have many enforceable contracts underpinning The Bibliotek's procurement of a great number of the books we hold in the Central Repository. It is simply not the case that since these books are in our legal possession The Bibliotek can unilaterally decide, for argument's sake, to take them out of the Central Repository either temporarily or permanently. And that includes for the reason of a permanent relocation. This is because in many of these contracts, there are *conditions subsequent* attached to our legal possession. In basic terms that means that if certain conditions are not satisfied or breached in the period, however long defined, if at all, after we acquire the books, our legal possession becomes null and void. I thus cannot guarantee that any given donor will not seek to enforce the right to nullify the transfer of possession on the happening of the condition by way of relocation. To put it bluntly, our donors only agreed to donate their collections on the understanding their books were to be protected, conserved, catalogued *and held here*, in The Bibliotek. We would have to seek and obtain the express approval of those donors if we identified any number of their donated books as being part of any relocation. Otherwise they stay in the Central Repository in The Bibliotek."

Bernie paused to let that sink in.

"Does that apply to any book coming under embargo?" asked Bradshaw.

"I'm sorry but I don't see the difference," she replied.

"What I am saying is if a book is already under embargo from access, what difference does it make where the book actually is?"

"I would have thought it literally makes the world of difference. I would imagine many donors would prefer such a valuable book to remain exactly where it is, in the Central Repository. That is precisely what it is designed to do, and our donors relied on that. And in any event, those conditions subsequent are not dependant on, or subject to, how The Bibliotek unilaterally decides to classify a book. Correct me if I am wrong, Paul," Bernie said, turning to look squarely at Bradshaw, "since the Conservation Department, the Cataloguers, and the Finders report to you, but my understanding is that many books we classify during the on-boarding process as being under embargo once in the Central Repository did not have that or similar status immediately prior to being acquired by The Bibliotek."

She kept her eyes on Bradshaw and waited for an answer.

"I will need to get back to you on that," he answered to the room, making a note on his data pad as he spoke.

"Please do, it would be helpful," Bernie said matter-of-factly. She paused again, then continued. "I also have an issue with The Three Tenets."

At their mention, Bradshaw rolled his eyes and sat back in his chair, demonstrably unimpressed. The Three Tenets were principles that had been drafted by the founder of The Bibliotek, Siegfried Sorenson, when he first proposed the concept of The Bibliotek to the United Nations in 2093. The tenets were intended by Sorenson to define The Bibliotek's purpose and future course, and when the U.N. voted to establish the library it enshrined them into The Bibliotek's constituent documents. This meant that, technically, anything and everything The Bibliotek did had to conform to the tenets.

"Go on," said Mads, peering at Bradshaw with critical eyes.

"In my opinion, any relocation of part or all of the Central Repository will breach one or more of The Three Tenets."

"Here, here," interrupted Dean Coenraad, prompting Mads to move his hand in a downward motion, signalling to all to let Bernie speak without interruption.

"How so?" asked Bradshaw, sitting forward now, aggressively, ignoring Mads' silent request.

"As we all know," continued Bernie, "the First Tenet prescribes that it is the Primary Function of The Bibliotek "to be Earth's main repository of human knowledge, thought and experience in print." At this point she tapped on her data pad and a presentation slide appeared on each of four holographic boards now hovering above and behind each side of the meeting table. It read:

1. It is the Primary Function of The Bibliotek to be Earth's main repository of human knowledge, thought, and experience in print.

2. It is the Secondary Function of The Bibliotek to facilitate appropriate access to all printed material under its management.

3. The two functions of The Bibliotek must co-exist.

Bernie continued. "In my opinion, it was always Sorenson's intention that this Primary Function be conducted on Earth, and that this intention was shared by the U.N. in agreeing to create The Bibliotek and that necessarily applies to all the member nations which voted accordingly."

"Well of course that was the intention, Bernie," interrupted Bradshaw again. He continued, "Faster Than Light technology hadn't been proven yet, so the First Tenet didn't need to mention where The Bibliotek was intended to be. It was assumed by all to be Earth. But interstellar travel was conceivable at the time. Silence does not of itself create a limitation, you know that Bernie."

"In matters of interpretation such as this, Paul," countered Bernie, "if it ever got to a court, the long-accepted principle is that a sentence such as the First Tenet should not be interpreted in isolation from other related clauses. In our case, this means that all Three Tenets must not only be read together but interpreted together, as a whole. The Third Tenet obviously cannot be interpreted at all without reference to the other two tenets. You can't just cherry-pick a Tenet to suit whatever purpose you have in mind. And that, to me, means they can only be applied in practice to a Bibliotek situated on Earth. To argue otherwise would be to say that we are facilitating access, as required by the Second Tenet, by moving The Bibliotek to a planet in another star system, which is... of course... ridiculous."

At her mention of the word 'ridiculous' Bradshaw changed his mind about responding and remained silent. Instead, Mads spoke.

"Bernie, I quite agree that we risk being in breach of the spirit, if not the intent, of the Three Tenets if we were to advocate some form of relocation to somewhere else on Earth or to Arcadia. As for the practical meaning of "appropriate access", Phicom's development of the *Principles of Access* and *Principles of Embargo* has served us well and, importantly, has also been accepted by our donors. But the Principles themselves have been drafted on the presumption they were only dealing with the Central Repository of The Bibliotek as it is currently situated. I don't think we need to resolve this issue just yet, but I agree it needs to be raised in our response to the Governing Council. I also agree that the greater concerns are the contractual terms under which many of our donors have agreed to hand over their book collections. This is, in my view, a real issue that needs to be taken into account."

"But how is it to be resolved, Bibliotekar, if it's a real issue?" asked Bradshaw.

"At the risk of stating the obvious, Paul, the Council will need to decide whether to rely on Bernie's advice and not put relevant contracts at risk, or whether to seek independent counsel's advice one way or another," replied Mads.

"So, this issue will be raised in the report to go to the Governing Council?" asked Bradshaw.

"If Adcom deems it necessary, then yes, but for now let's allow Bernie to complete her assessment for the purpose of the draft report. Now, I am mindful of time, so, your turn, Finn. What is your preliminary assessment of the capacity issue?"

"Thanks, Mads. Right now, I am circulating to each of you our latest trend analysis of the Central Repository capacity for the next five, ten, fifteen, twenty, and fifty years. Obviously, the margins for error increase slightly over those periods of time. You will see however that the current projection is that we will not be nearing full capacity at any stage between now and fifty years hence. In fact, the numbers stretch out to sixty-two years before we reach full capacity. You will also see that the projected decreases in overall capacity levels will become tangentially smaller each year after Year Fifteen. In simple terms that equates to fewer new entries in the Master Catalogue as time goes on. In short, I do not believe there is any case for suggesting that the Governing Council should consider relocating part or all of The Bibliotek at this point in time."

"But it doesn't hurt to at least plan for the future, doesn't it?" asked Bradshaw.

"That's what I do every day, Paul," Finn said speedily with a resigned look on his real face, before anyone else could get in a word. "As you may be aware, for example," he continued, "there are plans to swap some collections on Level Nine of the Central Repository for the Incunabula Collection currently on Level Twelve sometime within the next two to three years given the growth in procurements of incunables in recent years, thanks largely to Rafe the Finder's work in Europe and Julie the Finder's work in America. I make this kind of plan all the time, and most of them are adjusted, some significantly, before they become actionable."

"Yes, I am aware of all that, and that is why I say it doesn't hurt to plan for bigger moves," replied Bradshaw.

"But Paul, if we assume, for the sake of argument, that the numbers I have just distributed are reasonable enough to accept as being accurate, given our new underlying methodology assumptions as I discussed with you before, it would actually be imprudent to plan now for sixty-two years hence, or fifty years, or forty, or even thirty," responded Finn.

"And why should that be the case?" persisted Bradshaw.

"You're not just playing the Devil's Advocate, are you?" Finn said rhetorically.

"No, I'm actually asking the question," replied Bradshaw.

"Didn't you two talk about this capacity issue before now?" asked Huntington, "You both know how important it is for me to provide five- and ten-year budget forecasts that are at least *reasonably* accurate."

"Yes," responded Finn, turning to face the CFO. "And none of what I am saying puts any of your forecasting at risk, Michael. All I am trying to stress to the gentleman at the end of the table is that it is one thing to calculate with a fair degree of accuracy, that is, with an acceptably low margin of error, capacity up to fifty years in the future – those are just numbers – but it is an entirely different matter to actually begin *now* to plan to act on a capacity issue that won't need to be taken seriously for another forty years *at least*. Things change, so what's the point? Where's the pressing need? There's your answer, Paul."

Mads had heard enough. He had let the debate continue just to see if Bradshaw could turn it around to Arcadia, but he had failed the test.

"Finn," Mads asked, "for the sake of argument, putting aside any concerns with capacity, do you think it is possible that constructing an above-ground annex to the Central Repository on Arcadia *could* be less expensive to achieve than expanding the current underground repository at The Bibliotek?"

Mads' question got everyone's attention when some had been switching off, and Finn straightened in his chair and let out a sigh. "Yes, Mads, you've raised that proposition with me and I agreed with it."

"And that's because the deeper and the longer the Central Repository levels go, the higher the construction costs and, as well, the operating costs, isn't it?" asked Mads, almost rhetorically, for the benefit of the others.

"Yes, Mads, that's the reason."

"Okay, for the sake of argument again, let's factor in the Secondary Repositories. As certain as you are of your revised Central Repository capacity calculations, you are equally, if not more, certain that something has to be done about the Secondary Repositories, as in now. That's right isn't it? That's what you told us at the last meeting?" asked Mads, again almost rhetorically.

"Yes, that is correct, Mads."

"Okay, well I think it's time you share with the other members of Adcom your thoughts on the potential for us to bring the Secondary Repositories up to the standard of the Central Repository," said Mads. Now even Bradshaw became interested, he noticed.

"My assessment is that the costs of doing so would be significant," said Finn resignedly. "And that's without taking into account the fact that some of the Secondary Repositories are not suitable or not able to be brought up to that standard. Those we would need to relocate."

"Bingo," said Bradshaw.

Ignoring Bradshaw's comment, Finn went on the front foot. "Without pre-empting the actual outcome of my audit of the Secondary Repositories, which may or may not include bringing them up to the standard of the Central Repository, the suggestion is that I go to our site on Arcadia and make an assessment of its suitability for an annex of the Central Repository or another Secondary Repository, because it will inform Adcom's recommendations to the Governing Council on what to do with the Secondary Repositories, but recognising that it remains my firm view there is no capacity issue arising for the Central Repository for at least another forty years."

"Agreed," said Mads.

"And can we also agree now that Adcom's report to the Governing Council will reflect my unmitigated findings on capacity?" asked Finn.

"Colleagues?" Mads asked around the table, "Anyone have an issue with that?"

"I'm not saying I have an issue, but I would like some time to review Finn's calculations and methodology," said Bradshaw, prompting Finn to laugh.

"Take all the time you want, Paul," he said.

There was an awkward silence at Finn's retort, but it was interrupted by Huntington.

"Mads," he said, "forgive me for asking this, but aren't we supposed to be keeping this capacity issue separate from Finn's audit of the Secondary Repositories? You did say that at our last meeting, I recall."

"Absolutely. A decision on one should not taint a decision on the other. The two reports must be stand-alones, especially given Finn's audit goes way beyond mere capacity issues. It may or may not be a fine distinction, but I do believe that much of Finn's work with the RSG, which has priority, will quite possibly better inform the recommendations to be made as regards the pressing Secondary Repositories issue. Fair enough?"

"Yes, Mads, I see your point," Huntington replied, with a small sigh, meaning he did not quite agree with Mads' point.

"Okay, I think we can move on," said Mads, ignoring him. "Your turn, Nikka. Let's have your initial threat assessment."

"Thanks, Mads. My initial assessment is simply this: the threat to The Bibliotek represented by the Present Sect is real. The most plausible means by which this threat would manifest itself is by bombing. The next most likely means would be a direct attack by an individual or two or three individuals. However, and I want to make this perfectly clear, our assessment is that *any* attack currently possible by the Present Sect is nowhere near representing a risk our current security systems and resources cannot handle," said Nikka.

"When you say 'bombing', Nikka, what do you actually mean?" asked Sharma.

"I primarily mean a bomb, or bombs, physically brought into the Central Repository by an individual and detonated in the Central Repository. That is the location that the identified threat is associated with," explained Nikka.

"But what about the Computer Centre? We're not physically part of the Central Repository. Moreover, we are above-ground," said Sharma.

"And the fact your people are not located within the Central Repository is one of the reasons for my assessment, Rani. But, having said that, I have assessed the threat risk of each sector of The Bibliotek, including the Academy," said Nikka, turning to Dean

Coenraad, "and The Bibliotek as a whole, and my conclusions are the same as they are for the Central Repository."

"What's the likelihood of an attack?" asked Bradshaw. "Should we be at some sort of Threat Level?"

"I am quite averse to placing a probability on the *likelihood* of an attempt, Paul, it is a notoriously potentially misleading and arbitrary percentage, not like one of Finn's numbers," said Nikka, turning to Finn with a smile. "However," she continued, "whatever percentage someone else wants to come up with, I am just as confident of throwing back a higher probability an attack would fail."

"There's no point any of us here challenging the veracity of Nikka's conclusions," said Mads. "To do so would require a critical appraisal of Nikka's draft report on the threat represented by the Present Sect, a copy of which you were all sent by Nikka a few days ago. Has anyone had a chance to review it? By the way, Nikka, I want to thank you for the work that's gone into your draft — it's quite comprehensive, and well-argued."

No-one responded to Mads, but Bradshaw had a question.

"I'm not questioning your assessment, Nikka, but I just want to get clarity on something. Basically, you propose to say in the report to the Governing Council that the Present Sect threat risk is real but that you can handle it. Is that what I'm reading?"

"Yes, that's basically it," replied Nikka.

"So, then, it's really only a question of faith, isn't it? That is, ours and the Governing Council's, in your team?"

"And you have a problem with that? Security is not something you can point your finger at and ask 'look, this is our security, nice isn't it?' Security comes from confidence in your systems, and faith comes from that. If there is some aspect of our systems you don't have confidence in Paul, please, tell me. Tell me now, okay? So we can make an improvement."

Before Bradshaw could reply, Mads chimed in. "You've been conducting blind tests of responsiveness, haven't you Nikka?" Again, this was more a statement than a question.

"That we have, Mads," said Nikka, adding as she turned and looked around the table, "you will see from my draft report that I have made full disclosure of the nature and outcomes of those recent tests, including one outcome which was less than our standard expectation and which resulted in the dismissal of a long-term employee from my team. As a consequence of that failure I arranged for more tests targeting that particular point of security and there have been no more problems. And I will continue to do those tests as a matter of course and regardless of any report Adcom gives to the Governing Council on the capacity and threat issue."

"Thank you again, Nikka, said Mads. "I'd like to make a suggestion for finalising your draft report for the RSG. Since Finn has already committed to go to Arcadia to assess the viability of an annex at our site, I'd like you to go with him to assess the security issues, if any, such an annex may represent."

"I hardly think there'd be any security issues at all for Arcadia," said Bradshaw, before Nikka could respond.

"How so, Paul?" Nikka asked.

"Well it's obvious isn't it. Arcadia is on another planet, and there's only one way of getting there. On the *Nostradamus.*"

"Wrong," responded Nikka, "there are other ships travelling there, Paul. For example, the NASA ship *New Freedom* is pretty much on a constant schedule. But in any event, if you want to question the basis of my security assessment for The Bibliotek, what makes you think someone presenting a risk to The Bibliotek could not as easily get on the *Nostradamus*?"

Without waiting for Bradshaw to reply, Nikka turned to Mads. "I'll go with Finn, Mads. It won't cost any extra and it won't take much time. And besides, I've never been in space."

"Excellent idea, Nikka," responded Mads with a slight but short smile. "Now it is your turn, Paul. I particularly want to hear how you came up with the idea of looking at Arcadia as a possible site for relocating The Bibliotek, especially since, as far as I know, there's been no consensus reached as to the need to consider any relocation, and especially since Arcadia is a long way away from Norway."

Bradshaw's face tightened before he spoke. "I think the work of the RSG has progressed well. Bernie has identified a contractual risk in relation to any relocation, one that I'm not convinced is material or even real, but nevertheless I agree should be confirmed one way or another. Finn has done an excellent job on the new modelling for capacity which will put us in good stead going forward regardless of any outcomes of the RSG and has concluded there is currently no capacity issue. But there is the Secondary Repository issue that is contemporaneous with the work of the RSG, and I agree it's a factor the Governing Council may take into account. Nikka has quantified the Present Sect threat as real and that alone is an issue I look forward to seeing in the report to go to the Governing Council."

"Yeah, but what about Arcadia, Paul. Where did that come from?" interrupted Kaitlin Drummond. All eyes were on Paul now, waiting.

"As for Arcadia..." here Bradshaw paused and began fiddling with his data pad, slowly spinning it with a finger. "It just occurred to me not long after the last Adcom meeting that here we were about to spend a lot of time and effort on evaluating the capacity of The Bibliotek when there is a site, accessible to only a few," he said, looking straight at Nikka, "which has hardly been utilised. I mean, the idea of locating our DRP mainframe there was considered radical when first mooted, but it's working quite well, it's doing the job of the ideal DRP. So, I thought, why not the Central Repository?"

"Just popped into your head, did it?" asked Kaitlin. "And from there it went straight to your mouth and out of it. Don't you have some sort of filter inside your head? Like a brain, perhaps?"

It was no secret to anyone on Adcom, except Bradshaw, that Mads had ignored Kaitlin's recommendation to not promote Bradshaw to Deputy Bibliotekar, and that was because she had made a point of telling each and every Adcom member, except Bradshaw, of that fact. But even Bradshaw knew she didn't think much of him.

"Fuck off Kaitlin," he responded. "It wasn't a proposal, it was just a suggestion, an idea."

"That's enough of that, you two," said Mads.

"But Mads," said Huntington, "this idea of Paul's has turned into something being seriously contemplated before we've even agreed as to whether there's a problem or not. Why are we doing this?"

"I agree with Michael, Mads," said Dean Coenraad. "Tt seems quite pre-emptive to say the least."

"Okay folks, the points are taken, though Kaitlin I think yours could have been better expressed. We don't need to be rude to each other, and that includes you, Paul." Mads paused, then continued. "My strong view is that even suggesting Arcadia as an idea was premature. I would not have mentioned it. Even now it's putting the cart before the horse for the purposes of the RSG. But, the Governing Council is going to have to decide very soon what to do about the Secondary Repositories and they are a real issue. So, it would be prudent for us to look at Arcadia, *as radical as that may sound*, for the purposes of the bigger picture. I want considered answers to be ready. Paul, I want you to go to Arcadia with Finn and Nikka." Mads waited. There were a few shaking heads but no-one spoke up.

Mads turned to Larkin. "When's the next *Nostradamus* flight?"

"Let me just check," replied Larkin, as he tapped his data pad. "This Thursday."

"You three okay for this Thursday?" asked Mads.

"What time is take-off?" asked Nikka.

"Zero eight hundred, sharp," replied Larkin.

"I'm good for then," she said.

Mads looked at Finn and Bradshaw, who both nodded. Then he turned back to Larkin and said "book them on the flight. Given the distance they can fly First Class." Most laughed at Mads' joke. Bradshaw did not.

"Right then, this meeting is ended," Mads continued. "In two months' time we will meet again to agree on the RSG's Final Report to go the Governing Council. In the interim it almost goes without saying that I expect nothing discussed here today leaves this room. Thank you all." With that Mads got up and strode to his office, leaving everyone else still sitting, talking amongst themselves. Just as he got to the door to his office, Mads turned and said, "Kaitlin, can I see you for a minute?"

Once alone with Kaitlin, Mads sat down with her on the lounge and told her that, unless he saw a marked improvement in Bradshaw's performance, he was not going to appoint him as the Third Bibliotekar when the time came for Mads to retire. He also told her that he expected Bradshaw would then resign. And he told her that until that happened, he expected Kaitlin to refrain from ridiculing Bradshaw in such a way as she had just done in the Adcom meeting, lest such behaviour gave rise to legal action by him.

"I understand, Mads, and I am sorry for the outburst, but that last comment he made about Adcom was it for me. I'm guessing now that you made him the leader of the RSG as a test," Kaitlin responded, but it wasn't so much a guess as a hope.

"That I did," said Mads. "And guess what? He failed. Aside from risking the whole RSG exercise by raising Arcadia when he did and how he did, his so-called project management skills have not been in evidence. I mean, not even bothering to hold a meeting with the crew and just allocating tasks is far from prudent."

"But having that meeting by way of the Adcom meeting was setting him up, Mads, you must see that," said Kaitlin. "From where I sit, that also could be problematic down the line."

"Yes, I understand that, but that was deliberate on my part. Call it a blunt attempt if you will to get him to see the consequence of his failure as a project manager. If he's got an ounce of intelligence, which I really thought he possessed when I made him Deputy Bibliotekar, he will now see where Bernie, Finn, and Nikka are each going with their conclusions and realise what he has to do to make sure Adcom reaches agreement on *his* Final Report. Recall he did summarise those conclusions before he explained why he had mentioned Arcadia to each of them."

"Yes, he did do that, and I see your point. But that summary was also a bit dismissive of his colleagues' lines of thinking," said Kaitlin.

"I noted that, Kaitlin, don't worry about that. But now that all those concerns are on the table, he can't ignore them. He *has* to come up with something that Adcom will agree on, and he's just been made fully aware of where the challenges to that happening exist. So I'm going to let him continue leading the RSG for that reason."

"Okay Mads, but a little advice if I may."

"Yes?"

"If you have already decided not to appoint Paul as your successor, from an HR perspective, and potentially legal, you should let him know. He is also entitled to know why," said Kaitlin.

"I'm sorry but I am going to have to disagree with you, Kaitlin. I'm not ignoring your advice, I just don't agree with its premise, which is that the Deputy Bibliotekar, whoever that person may be, is entitled to assume that they will be automatically appointed as the Third Bibliotekar. That's not how it works."

"Fair enough, Mads. I just wanted you to know my position. I do at least agree he is not giving us any confidence he is fit to be your successor."

12:45pm

In her suite at The Bibliotek, Chair Thurldottir took a call from Councillor Carlson.

"It seems our friend Bradshaw couldn't keep his mouth shut and mentioned Arcadia," said Carlson.

"Yes, his timing was stupid and perfect. Just as we had hoped. Now Ingridson is sure to join the dots," replied Thurldottir.

"Looks like we are on track, then."

"Indeed it does, but let's just make sure he does join those dots," said Thurldottir just before ending the call.

END OF CHAPTER NINE

Intermission[1]

A Short History of The Bibliotek

Background

In this first session of the series dealing with the history of The Bibliotek, we look at its beginnings and how it came to be.

In doing so, I will endeavour to adhere to the facts as accepted, but please forgive me if I stray into the sometimes muddy field of personal viewpoints. Anytime that I do, I only ask that you recall the response Edward Hallet Carr gave to the question 'What is history?' He said the answer "consciously or unconsciously reflects our own position in time, and forms part of our answer to the broader question of what view we take of the society in which we live."[2]

It was a man called Siegfried Sorenson who in 2093 wrote the original proposal for the establishment of what he called "The World's Library" – The Bibliotek.[3] It was the bombing and consequent destruction of the majority of the holdings of the US Library of Congress during the initial stages of the Great Holy War,[4] followed by the similar successful attacks on most of the other great libraries around the world before hostilities were ended, that paved the way for the United Nations to agree to consider, and ultimately adopt, Sorenson's proposal. But those singularly destructive events were only the catalyst for action.

Long before the library attacks, Sorenson had commenced developing his plan for a world library out of other concerns. One

---

[1] Paper presented by Mads Ingridson MBS, Bibliotekar, to the incoming class for *Introduction to The Bibliotek*, The Bibliotek Academy, on 9 February 2199.

[2] Carr, EH, *What is History?* The George Macaulay Trevelyan Lectures, delivered in the University of Cambridge, January – March, 1961.

[3] Sorenson, Siegfried, *A Proposal for the Establishment of a World Library - A Report Prepared for the United Nations' Preservation of History Emergency Committee* (2093).

[4] Some academics argue, Maxwell Peters being the foremost (see Peters, M, *Genesis of Grief*, Power Publications Inc, Boston (2107), pp 38-56), that apart from the evangelical purpose in the bombing of the Library of Congress, the event also had two other purposes: (a) instilling fear into the hearts and minds of the American populace, borrowing the tried and tested policy of 'shock and awe' so successfully implemented by the U.S. Government in the late 20th and mid 21st centuries; and (b) prompting that same Government to activate its military forces and retaliate in the Middle East, thus escalating and widening the Great Holy War.

such concern was the trend slowly but steadfastly developing amongst Earth's libraries to cease holding their physical book collections. Starting with the Cushing Academy's Fisher-Watkins Library in 2009, collections were being divested of actual books because they were becoming increasingly expensive to maintain in an era of decreasing utility — for want of a better word — thanks to digitisation and the Internet.[5] In the case of Fisher-Watkins, this meant replacing over 25,000 books and other printed materials with electronic versions and terminals to access them. This growing trend Sorenson believed to be in total denial of the Five Laws of Library Science, as originally enunciated by Dr Shiyali Ramamrita Ranganathan, the Librarian at the Madras University Library, in 1928[6] and universally adopted and developed over time since then, and an abrogation of those laws as they could be applied to digital and real copies of books.

In particular, Sorenson considered the trend of removing physical books from shelves in return for access to their digital copies to contravene Ranganathan's First Law that *books are for use* — they are not meant to be shut away from their users.[7] It was Ranganathan's view that this law was obvious; it was a "trivial truism". In Sorenson's view, removing books from shelves, and thus denying free access, was even worse than the Medieval practice of 'chained libraries', whereby books were literally chained to the shelves holding them, thus preventing access to the books by way of loan or removal to a desk for study but also ensuring, if not facilitating, access by the prevention of theft.[8] Sorenson also believed it was an issue of trust. He asked rhetorically: why entrust the preservation of modern-era knowledge,

---

[5] This trend has been traced and reviewed by a number of academics. See, for example, Murphy, S., "When did libraries stop being libraries?" 16:3 *Modern Thought, Modern Action* vol.34, no.2 (2045) at 65.

[6] Ranganathan, S.R., *The Five Laws of Library Science*, Madras Library Association, Madras (1931). Ranganathan first conceived the Five Laws in 1924, following the suggestion of the First Law by Professor Edward Ross. He then drafted the statements embodying The Five Laws in 1928, before publishing them in 1931. The most concise expression of the Five Laws is as follows: 1. Books are for use; 2. Every reader his or her book; 3. Every book its reader; 4. Save the time of the reader; and 5. The library is a growing organism.

[7] Sorenson, page 5.

[8] This particular philosophical conundrum was discussed in Leiter, Richard, "Reflections on Ranganathan's *Five Laws of Library Science*" 95:3 *Law Library Journal* 411 (Summer 2003) at 414.

with 99.9% of that knowledge in digital format only, to a handful of global technology corporations?[9]

Edifice versus Utility

Another factor highlighted in Sorenson's proposal that won considerable favour with the UN was the concept he formulated and discussed of 'Edifice versus Utility'.[10] Sorenson was ruthless in pointing out the distinction between the two, because it was easy to do. It was simply a case of highlighting the physical characteristics of virtually all of the remaining libraries he was proposing to empty of their collections of books. Without exception, they were enormous and ostentatious buildings; they were deliberately designed and built to be very 'loud and proud' statements, and the more ostentatious they were in their physical characteristics, the less efficient they were in performing their actual role as libraries. And they were getting bigger and louder; the newest edifice always trying to outdo the preceding others in these characteristics. In the prevailing political and social environment, they were also easy targets for physical attack; a point devastatingly demonstrated time and again during the Great Holy War.

Sorenson was also able to convince the UN that the huge amount of money spent building and maintaining these edifices was money not being spent on the collections they housed. As he explained in his report:[11]

"Egypt's vastly oversized Bibliotheca Alexandrina, completed in 2002, is a perfect example of 'edifice versus utility'. It had been a vanity project of then leader Hosni Mubarak, who was struggling at the time to not only maintain his supreme power but who was also desperate to leave a physical legacy of it. His dream had been to recreate a modern-era version of the Great Library of Alexandria. It cost nearly a quarter of a billion US dollars to construct — money that many in Egypt believed would have been better served in obtaining actual books and manuscripts to fill it, for when the Bibliotheca finally opened its many doors to the public, its actual library space accounted for only 8% of its physical capacity and, worse, only 10% of that space

---

[9] Sorenson, page 7.
[10] Sorenson, page 24.
[11] Sorenson, pages 29 to 30.

contained books. Even today, in 2093, its library space remains mostly empty. That is, of course, if you ignore the countless rows of facsimile book spines inserted to make the shelves *look* as if they are in use. The Bibliotheca Alexandrina had no funds to acquire much of anything when it opened, and as of last fiscal year its annual operating budget was 55% *less* than it was than when it opened. For several decades now, any and all books coming onto its shelves have been solely the result of donations.[12] Perhaps it was due to the continual presence of guards armed with machine guns and other assorted weapons and deterrents, the fact remains that the Bibliotheca Alexandrina was left untouched during the Great Holy War. Or perhaps the edifice has remained as is due to its largely empty status.

"Whatever the answer to that question, it is a demonstrable fact that the greater the edifice, the less attention is paid to the books within it by those responsible for the edifice. Tourists used to queue to enter the Great Hall of Austria's National Library. They paid an admission price just for entry. They paid it because that is all they wanted to do (or could do) — *enter* the Hall to *look* at it. The countless rows of bookcases filled with ancient and rare texts completely dominated all available wall space and served only as a textured backdrop to the ornateness of the Hall itself, with its marble, sculptures, massive chandeliers, panelled ceiling and a myriad of other fine accoutrements. No other purpose was served by the Great Hall until it was destroyed in the middle stages of the Great Holy War in 2089."

The irony of Sorenson's 'Edifice versus Utility' argument is not well known, but I wrote about it many years later, just before I became the Second Bibliotekar.[13] At that time, there had been murmurings about the growing annual operating budget of The Bibliotek and I was asked to investigate the physical status of some of the more important old libraries still in existence, just in case anyone pushed for a literal return to the 'old days.' What I found was that, almost without exception, all of those edifices had either fallen into a state of disrepair or were no longer suitable to be used as repositories, let alone libraries, for a variety of reasons. It seemed to me that they had needed their collections more than the collections had needed them.

---

[12] Sorenson, page 47.

[13] Ingridson, M., *The Functioning Status of the World's Surviving Libraries*, a report prepared for the Administration Committee of the Governing Council of The Bibliotek, June 2161 (Not publicly available).

As far as The Bibliotek was concerned, however, my conclusion was essentially that there was no going back. The Bibliotek had become the only answer, the only option, despite the budgetary concerns.

Cost Comparison

Sorenson had only estimated *initial* operating costs in his proposal to the UN.[14] He had either not given thought to *ongoing* costs or simply chose not to discuss them in his proposal, but the UN, for whatever reason, did not undertake its own process of estimating them. Sorenson did, however, compare his projected costs of building and initially maintaining the Bibliotek to a singular example of the enormous costs over a period of time of dealing with rare manuscripts or books needing work on them. This was the tortured experience of various Italian Governments from the 18th century to the 21st century in dealing with the *Herculaneum papyri*, which as many of you would know are a collection of nearly 2,000 papyri scrolls, or, more correctly, what remained of them, from a library within the enormous 'Villa of the Papyri' near Herculaneum in southern Italy. As was recounted by Sorenson in his proposal,[15] the library, the villa, and everything else in the vicinity had been buried under 25 metres of volcanic ash by the eruption of Mount Vesuvius in AD 79, and it lay undiscovered for eighteen centuries until found in 1750 by farmers digging a well. The physical evidence discovered during the subsequent 'formal' excavation, conducted under the auspices of King Charles VII of Naples, determined that the collection had been hastily packed in cases before being overcome by a pyroclastic flow from Vesuvius, presumably in an, ultimately, failed attempt to move them to safety away from the impending doom. Their rediscovery in 1750 was a sensation because for eons before then the only known surviving examples of other ancient scrolls were hundreds of years more recent and those were only a few scraps. To this day, the Herculaneum library is the only surviving complete library of antiquity – specifically the Graeco-Roman period between 332 BC and 395 AD; but there were so many scrolls taken out of the buried library that ignorant Court officials began discarding them, until the King put a stop to the destruction and set up a commission in 1752 to study the papyri.

[14] Sorenson, page 56.
[15] Sorenson, pages 56 to 61.

Foremost to the task of study was not the necessity of preservation because the dry air in the library had done that job for centuries, but more the physical state of the scrolls. They had been charred and carbonised by the eruption, and legend had it that they were initially mistaken for carbonised tree branches or, in other words, firewood, with some suffering this useful but nevertheless unfortunate fate at the hands of those officials. Whether that is true or not, what is known for certain is that Italy has been spending untold sums of money, ever since the scrolls were brought to Naples in 1752, in seeking to unravel the mysteries within the scrolls themselves and in seeking to solve the mystery of how to do so without damaging them. In the early years, this dual aim had been failed. The artist Camillo Paderni was one of many in a long line of interested citizens with hopes of providing the answers. He managed to transcribe several hundred scrolls, but he was stopped from doing more when it was discovered that his particular method, that of slicing the scrolls in half, not only seriously damaged them but also effectively destroyed them. Then in 1756, the Vatican Library's Conserver of Ancient Manuscripts, Abbot Piaggio, invented a machine to carefully unroll each scroll. It worked, but there were two problems: it took more than *four years* to unravel the first scroll and this was because the machine only rotated mere millimetres each day, and as each scroll was *slowly* revealed it had to be *quickly* transcribed because in exposing the hidden text to air, the abbot's machine caused the text to vaporise and disappear, which, needless to say, was another means of effectively destroying the scroll.

As Sorenson recounted, over the following years, decades, and centuries, people persevered. Many people. All failures. Some even tried using Piaggio's machine on the scrolls again; and again, this proved to be just as unsuccessful. By 1950, less than a fifth of the scrolls had been completely unrolled, and only a few more had been partly unrolled. Most of the text of the recovered portions was still to be deciphered, but many of the fragments that had been deciphered were revealed to have been probably written by Philodemus of Gadara, an Epicurean poet and philosopher who had lived in the last century BC. Of the transcribed text, Philodemus had written on such subjects as poetry, music, theology, rhetoric, logic, morality and ethics, and it was he who many believed owned the villa where the library of scrolls was situated.

In the early 21ˢᵗ century technology had advanced enough to enable scientists to extract information from the scrolls without damaging them. It had only taken 270 years of trial and error, and, as I have said, Sorenson noted the huge financial cost of those years by way of comparison to his estimated costs of setting up The Bibliotek, and the fact that by preserving the world's accumulated printed books and manuscripts, the world would be avoiding having to incur similar costs to those incurred on the *Herculaneum papyri*.

However, it is my view that Sorenson had lapsed in his comparative argument based on the experience with the *Herculaneum papyri*. He did not acknowledge or take into account that it was the quest for knowledge of forgotten history that fuelled the desire to transcribe the *Herculaneum papyri*. Initially, destruction of the original manuscripts, the scrolls themselves, had been a secondary outcome of that quest. Eventually all of them would have been destroyed, but for the recognition of the 'need' to protect and preserve the originals in that quest, and it was *that* need that contributed significantly to the costs over all the years. But that point was but a minor glitch in Sorenson's proposal.

Libraries are Targets

Countless people over the ages have written of their personal experiences of libraries as being sanctuaries in their busy, troublesome lives. Where, quietly, knowledge and inspiration have been found. Where souls have been fed. Sorenson was one of those people. By education and profession, he was a historian, specialising in the history of books and libraries. According to the man himself,[16] he was in the perfect position to not only place the destructive impact of the Great Holy War in the context of humankind's historical treatment of books and libraries, but also to demonstrate that there was a philosophical connection between that horrible conflict and the very nature of humankind.

It was that topic which he saved for last in his proposal for a world library. He knew it would have the greatest impact.

Sorenson introduced that most important part of his proposal by citing the inscription on a plaque sitting in a public square in Berlin:[17]

---

[16] An assessment I tend to agree with.
[17] Sorenson, pages 75 to 79.

*That was but a prelude. Wherever they burn books they will
also, in the end, burn human beings.*

As Sorenson noted, the plaque was installed after World War II
and commemorates the public book burning rally that took place in
the square on the night of 10 May 1933. Coinciding with other similar
rallies around Germany that night, it had been organised by the
nationalist German Student Association. Its members comprised
many students from the Humboldt University, of which the Law
Faculty Library was then located, since destroyed, to the immediate
west of the square, and those students had spent four days making a
pile of 20,000 books to be burnt, many of them coming from the
library. By invitation of the students, the Nazi Propaganda Minister
Joseph Goebbels gave a rousing speech to the assembled rabble just
before the pile was lit and the books were burnt; a rabble comprising
not only the students but also members of the Nazi Students' League,
the Nazi Brown shirts, the Nazi SS, and the Hitler Youth. To the
chants of *Heil Hitler!* the flames consumed works of the enemies of
the Nazi State, being free thinkers, Jews, philosophers and scientists,
including Heinrich Mann, Karl Marx, and that notorious subversive,
Albert Einstein.

Sorenson recounted that after that dreadful night, a family of Jews
fled Germany and went to Palestine, and that their son, Micha
Ullman, later designed a sculpture that was installed with the plaque,
in a more enlightened 1995. It consists of an underground square
chamber filled with empty bookshelves — enough space for 20,000
books — which is viewed through a plane of glass set in the square
above the chamber.

Sorenson explained that the inscription on the plaque was not new;
the words had been written in 1821 by Heinrich Heine as a line in his
play *Almansor*. Many would thus assume the words were prophetic,
and, indeed, it is no small irony that Heine's books were also fuel for
that particular book burning in Berlin in 1933. But Sorenson was at
pains to demonstrate that, far from being prophetic, Heine was simply
drawing upon the history of humankind to articulate a known attribute
of humankind's soul — the tendency to target libraries and their
contents. In that context, Sorenson argued that the Great Holy War
and its devastating impact on libraries around the world was but the
most recent exercise of that tendency. Further, Sorenson was at pains

to also demonstrate the history of the destruction of libraries caused by natural forces.

He wrote:[18]

"Not one of the original collections of the world's great libraries throughout the history of Man's learning exists today. Every single one has been partly or fully destroyed, whether it be by earthquake, fire, flood, bombardment, deliberate dismemberment or burning, or they have been plundered and dispersed to parts and people unknown and generally lost to the ages.

"For example, the Great Library of Alexandria, created by Ptolemy, ruler of ancient Egypt, and expanded by his son, Ptolemy II, was intended to be the Library of the World, containing all of its books. Legend has it that Ptolemy went some way to achieving that goal, and the library became renowned as a result. It was accidently destroyed by fire, however, in 48BC when Julius Caesar's navy was trapped in Alexandria and tried to bombard its way out by means of shooting fire.

"The great Emperor's Library of Constantinople was founded by Constantius II in the mid-4th century, and it is from the Byzantine copies made in the library that we know most of the Greek classics today. But after several fires, culminating in a fire in 473, most of the library's 120,000 manuscripts were lost. Then in 1204 the Library was looted and burnt during three days of rioting and pillaging after the fall of Constantinople to the Franks and Venetians of the Fourth Crusade. On the fall of Constantinople in 1453 to the Sultan Mehmed II which precipitated the end of the Eastern Roman Empire, there is no record of the Library yet again being looted or destroyed, but in the lead-up to the end of Mehmed's siege of the city it is recorded that many of the Library's contents were spirited away to the Vatican by agents of Pope Nicholas V or taken by the Emperor Constantine XI's brother, Thomas Palaiologos, the Despot of Morea. Some of the hoard taken by Palaiologos were consequently taken to Moscow as part of the dowry for his daughter Sophia's marriage to Ivan III, and then lost to the world after the death of Ivan The Formidable, Sophia's grandson.

"Then, in the late antiquity period, the Theological Library of Caesarea Maritima in Palestine held 40,000 Christian manuscripts,

---

[18] Sorenson, pages 80 to 103.

rivalling the now destroyed Library of Alexandria in size until it too was destroyed, on that occasion by the Saracens in 638.

"The Saracens also sacked and destroyed the monastery library of Monte Cassino in 884. It recovered, however, and eventually became the greatest library in Europe, with over 250 monks working in the scriptorium translating into Latin and transcribing great and ancient manuscripts until an earthquake in 1349 ravaged the library. Much later, in 1799, during the invasion of Naples by Napoleon's Revolutionary Army, its collection was sacked again, with its most precious manuscripts being sent to Paris and parts unknown. This was all before the infamous decision in 1944 of British and U.S. armed forces to drop over 1,100 tons of explosives on the monastery, almost destroying it in the process. There are unconfirmed reports that, fearing the destruction of the library's collection, several German Army officers colluded with the remaining monks to secretly transport the most valuable manuscripts and books to Berlin 'for safekeeping' before the Allies wreaked their bombs on the monastery, but no such items have ever been recovered.

"Then there was the Bibliotheca Corviniana. It had been established by the King of Hungary between 1458 and 1490 in Buda Castle, and quickly became renowned in the Renaissance world until it was completely destroyed by the Ottoman Army in the Battle of Mohacs in 1526.

"Another example is the Royal Library of the Monastery of El Escorial, established by King Phillip II of Spain in 1592, largely by donating his own private collection. It lasted less than 80 years before a fire destroyed most of its holdings in 1671. Following the Spanish Succession War (1701–1714), the new French monarchy then began to systematically loot the remainder of the library, which also suffered more fires in 1731, 1763, and 1825.

"Then there is the Royal Library of Portugal, which was begun in 1712, quickly rising to a status of magnificence thanks to the concerted patronage of King Joao V, only to be almost completely destroyed by the earthquake, tidal wave, and fires that hit Lisbon on All Saints Day in 1755.

"Let us not forget the bibliomaniac Queen Christina of Sweden. She, like many other rulers were want to (notably Napoleon Bonaparte amongst them), instructed her generals to confiscate as many books as possible from Prague and other cities during their battles, most notably in her case the battles during the Thirty Years War (1618 to 1648). Thus was created the Royal Library of Sweden.

It too would have been destroyed by the fire which consumed the Royal Palace in 1697 had not the entire collection been acquired by Pope Alexander VIII on the Queen's death in 1689.

"Although the US Library of Congress no longer exists, it is also a fact that its original collection of 3,000 books was destroyed by the British Army in 1814 when it burned the Capitol. Following this singularly devastating act of war, the library's second collection was then mostly destroyed in 1851, this time accidently by fire. Of the 40,000 or more books destroyed in that disaster, over 6,000 had been sold to the library in 1815 by Thomas Jefferson to 'restart' the collection after the British Army had done its work. As it is well known, the Library of Congress was again destroyed, this time just three years ago during the Great Holy War.

"In August 1914, shortly after the outbreak of the war that would become known as the 'Great War', German troops moving through Belgium on their way to invade France took affront at perceived threats and hostile action from Belgian local forces and, in reprisal, burnt to the ground Belgium's greatest library, the Louvain University Library. Its entire collection, comprising over 300,000 books and at least 1,000 incunabula, was destroyed. The incident was widely-reported and was used by the Allies as a propaganda message deriding Germany's *Kultur*. It became so notorious that in the aftermath of Germany's eventual defeat in 1918 the Treaty of Versailles specifically included, in Article 247, the promise by Germany to provide the university with "manuscripts, incunabula, printed books, maps, and objects of collection corresponding in number and value to those destroyed in the burning by Germany of the Library of Louvain." The U.S. took it upon itself to raise most of the funds for the reconstruction of the library and in 1928 a 2 million book capacity new building was completed. Twelve years later, during World War II, Germany bombed Louvain and destroyed, again, the library and almost all of its contents.

"By the late 1890s, the National Library of France held the title of the largest repository of books on Earth. This was in no small part due to the acquisitive habits of Napoleon Bonaparte's armies. During World War II and the occupation of that country by Nazi Germany, however, it and many other libraries in France were, ironically, decimated through systemic looting of their collections. It is estimated that over 2 million books and manuscripts 'disappeared' during this period.

"The University Library of Leipzig was established in 1542 but was mostly destroyed during World War II, when it lost more than 75% of its collection, much of it through pillage. This included a rare two-volume paper edition of the *Gutenberg Bible,* which was stolen by the Soviet Army, then stolen again from the Moscow State University in 2009.

"The then largest library in Italy, Florence's National Central Library, was severely impacted by the 1966 flooding of the Arno River, the worst flood that the city had experienced in 400 years. Over 1,300,000 books and manuscripts, comprising nearly one-third of its total collections, were seriously damaged, and restoration work continued for half a century. The same flood severely damaged or destroyed the collections of many other archives and libraries in Florence, including the entire collection of the Gabinetto Vieusseux Library — some 250,000 volumes.

"By the time Imperial Japan surrendered to Allied forces in 1945, bombing raids by the U.S. Air Force had destroyed all but 5,000 of Japan's millions of books and manuscripts.

"The National Library of Cambodia, established in the 1920s, was occupied by the Khmer Rouge army during that country's civil war in the 1970s. After implementing a deliberate policy of destroying almost all of its collections, the library was converted to a residence for members of the then-ruling Pol Pot regime.

"Until civil war erupted in 1992 in that country, Afghanistan's National Library, located within Kabul University, held over 200,000 books, thousands of which could be classified as 'rare', and several thousand ancient manuscripts. During the war, however, the library was basically decimated by large-scale pilfering, which saw most of its collection being openly sold in markets and by more discreet means, or simply destroyed.

"Between 1968 and 1978, the National Library of Denmark saw not only one of the largest book thefts in history, but also one of the longest undetected thefts. It was years before it was discovered that, over that decade, someone had managed to steal some 1,600 historical books worth more than $50 million. The thief turned out to be a long-serving senior employee at the library. Another notorious example of an 'inside job' at a library was the plundering of the Girolamini Biblioteca in Naples, which was plundered over a period of several years by its then Director Marino Massimo de Caro before his arrest in 2012.

"Iraq's National Library and Archives once held nearly half a million books, thousands of periodicals dating from the Ottoman period, and many thousands of rare manuscripts. That all changed when the U.S. invaded the country in 2003. Forces loyal to the Ba'athist regime of Saddam Hussein and other factions, plus desperate gangs, looted and destroyed most of its collections, including the oldest known copy of the *Quran*. This all happened despite the fact that U.S. forces were at the time stationed across the road in the Ministry of Defence building; the lack of preventative action being in contravention of the articles of the Geneva Convention regarding the 'protection of cultural property'."

Sorenson continued his discussion of the history of the destruction of libraries and books for many more pages. Too many to continue to recite here, but hopefully you understand Sorenson's message.

All of this terrible history goes to show that there is nothing more prone to loss or destruction than a book.[19]

And it was *that* part of Sorenson's proposal that was the final push for the United Nations to in-principle approve not only the concept of The Bibliotek, but also the funds necessary to complete its initial design features proposed by Sorenson.

But one thing that irked me about Sorenson's proposal to create The Bibliotek was that, without making the distinction, the design features proposed by Sorenson for the physical Bibliotek were nothing short of monumental, in the true sense of that word, and they were underpinned by Sorenson's absolutist and utilitarian approach — from start to finish the design and construction of The Bibliotek was focused on its intended contents and how best to hold them. Cost seemed secondary, as did accessibility design — both to the building itself and to the individual books and other items — after completion.

The benefit of those design features was that no-one questioned Sorenson's logic to ask: how does placing many collections into one mega collection make their contents safer from harm or loss? Is not the risk increased? As far as Sorenson was concerned, the answer was a definite "no". The Bibliotek was always intended to be a safe and secure alternative. Its size may be monumental, but it is not an edifice. An edifice soars and spreads, it is meant to be seen and admired, it is meant to be a symbol of power, status, and wealth, whereas more than 99% of The Bibliotek cannot be seen by someone standing outside it

---

[19] Sorenson, page 105.

at ground level. The Bibliotek is literally buried treasure. The fact that most of The Bibliotek and all of its collections are housed below ground sufficiently negates the chance of many of the fates suffered by libraries occurring. Then there are the many and specific design features of the underground levels that serve only one purpose — the protection of the collections and the minimisation of all known risk factors. In terms of the human risk factors, such as direct attack, security and defensive measures were created within the design features of The Bibliotek from the start. They are not focused on entry points but encapsulate a 'whole of entity' approach which, to date, no testing has been able to breach or find fault with.

As for what drove the decision of where The Bibliotek should be, there were several factors contributing to the decision to locate The Bibliotek here in a remote part of Norway: its stable government, its decades-long experience with tunnel-building, and its geology being the main ones. There is no doubt its location and situation contributes greatly to minimising the multiple risks of damage to its contents. Global academic politics was of course another factor, and a large amount of the details of that activity will never be known, partly because many governments considered the 'honour' of their respective countries being the host of The Bibliotek to be instead a *poisoned chalice*. In any event, the announcement of Norway as the site of The Bibliotek received little criticism. Construction took 14 years to complete The Bibliotek in its entirety, but it was operational 9 years after construction began because of its modular design. Basically, the design allowed for the underground levels to be completed one after the other in groups of five, thus allowing each such group to begin full operation as soon they were finished and construction moved down to the next five levels and so on. By the time all of the levels were completed, The Bibliotek has already been operating for some.

Library or Repository?

But operating as what, exactly? As I have discussed, Sorenson's proposal for 'the World's Library' was partly motivated by what he believed was the growing trend of libraries to depart from the long-accepted *Five Laws of Library Science*. These were principles by which a 'true' library was meant to operate; or at least the 20th and 21st century versions of a library.

The Bibliotek is styled — and I use that word carefully — as the World's Library, but in truth is it a library? After all, tucked away here in a remote mountain in Norway, are we even pretending to be a library that the good people of, say, the mountain town of Dorrigo, in Australia — the literal opposite side the planet — can walk into and read and borrow a book from The Bibliotek? No, of course not. We do not even pretend that anyone from Oslo can do that, or Bergen, or from anywhere else in the world for that matter.

So, by the mere fact we do not allow any book to leave the premises, or The Bibliotek precinct, can we truthfully call ourselves 'a library', albeit not a public one, as that concept is known and understood?

The answer — *my* answer — is that we call ourselves The Library — The Bibliotek — because that is the term that humankind is not only comfortable with, it also gives humankind comfort.

Deep down, physically *and* philosophically, The Bibliotek is a repository. As a starting point, and thanks to the Three Tenets conceived by Sorenson for the functions of The Bibliotek, as part of his proposal to the UN[20], that is its primary function.

As you should be aware, the Three Tenets are as follows:

1. It is the Primary Function of The Bibliotek to be Earth's main repository of human knowledge, thought, and experience in print.
2. It is the Secondary Function of The Bibliotek to facilitate appropriate access to all printed material under its management.
3. The two functions of The Bibliotek must co-exist.

Expressed so succinctly, the United Nations had little difficulty in taking them on board as written, and we have been stuck with them ever since. I am sorry if that comes across as being less than enthusiastic about the Three Tenets, but I can't help wondering if Sorenson knew or had even any inkling of the behemoth institution The Bibliotek would become when he wrote them in 2093.

Indeed, the longer I am Bibliotekar the more I feel disdain for Sorenson's statement of the Functions of the Bibliotek, and that stems more from what the statement *doesn't say* rather than what it *does say*.

---

[20] Sorenson, *Recommendations*, page 125.

It seems to me he deliberately made it immutable. To me, the lofty statement exists in a vacuum; where the concept, constraints, and practical reality of time are irrelevant. This much is also a generally-accepted fact, as was noted in the First Review of The Bibliotek – and, I remind you all, to date the only review – carried out by a panel appointed by the Governing Council. And as the First Review also noted in its Final Report in 2197, since the 'body' of human knowledge in print has, for the most part, exponentially expanded since humankind first had an individual thought, the Primary Function of the Bibliotek is thus, as it has always been, a task with no end, with the Secondary Function being akin to a pillion passenger, along for a very long ride. However, were it not for the Secondary Function, The Bibliotek would be engaged in a singularly pointless endeavour. So yes, the two functions co-exist.

To fill the practical gaps, the *many* practical gaps, in the Three Tenets, the main role of the Philosophy Committee – Phicom – has been to lay down principles by which The Bibliotek has been able to operate. We will cover these principles, and more, in the next session dealing with the history of The Bibliotek.

END OF INTERMISSION

Chapter Ten

Rafe Runs into Ruben in Ronda

"Germany undertakes to furnish the University of Louvain... manuscripts, incunabula, printed books, maps, and objects of collection corresponding in number and value to those destroyed in the burning by Germany of the Library of Louvain. All details regarding such replacement will be determined by the Reparation Commission."
Treaty of Peace with Germany (Treaty of Versailles), Article 247, 28 June 1919

5:45pm, Monday, 14ᵗʰ January 2205

Rafe walked into the spacious room decorated with twelfth-century furniture and which included a large four-poster bed, set down his bag and satchel on the ancient tiled floor, walked straight over to the window doors, opened them, stood at the wrought-iron balcony and breathed in the cool early-evening mountain air. He had been looking forward to returning to Ronda, the largest of the 'White Villages' in southern Spain, to this hotel, the Hotel Montelirio, to this room, to this view, for almost as long as his absence from it had been. It did not matter to Rafe that it was winter and the off season. What mattered to him was that the Hotel Montelirio never closed.

The view he was now savouring again, as always, never ceased to take his breath away. On his immediate right was the Puente Nuevo, the 'new' stone arch bridge stretching over the sheer 120-metre walls of the El Tajo canyon to the other side of town, and to the left of the bridge, across the gorge in front of Rafe, was the promenade where in warmer months the tourists normally strolled all day to and from Aldehuela, the clifftop lookout where they, and Rafe from his side of the gorge, could look out over the immense Guadiaro and Genal Valleys and the Serrania de Ronda mountains beyond. The massive bridge was over 400 years old, but it was still referred to as the 'new' bridge so as to distinguish it from the 'old' bridge it replaced just upstream on the Guadalevin river which flowed through the narrow canyon, bursting out as a waterfall immediately below its highest arch. It thus also served to distinguish itself from the earlier 'new' bridge it had replaced that had collapsed into the canyon in 1741, only six years after it had been finished, taking fifty Ronda residents with it to their deaths.

It had taken Rafe a few visits before he truly understood the reason the view of the 'new' bridge was so alluring. It was made from the very same stone of the Tajo canyon itself and it seamlessly joined each side of the canyon walls. Over the ages it had thus become part of the canyon itself, and this was no more evident than in the light of the setting sun which turned both canyon wall and bridge the same warm golden hue.

It was one of Rafe's favourite views in Europe and he never tired of it. But Rafe was himself tired, very tired. He had told nobody he was coming here, even to Spain, and he had not typed his destination into any memo or message or email. He had booked a heliojet to Lisbon, and then, at the helioport, changed it to Alicante and from there he had hired a hovercar for drop off to Seville in eight days' time. It was normally a five-hour drive to Ronda and now he was here, in his favourite hotel, a converted 17th century Moorish mansion right on the clifftop with only nine other rooms, after only four and a half hours, courtesy of a new hoverway, a fast hover rental, and a manic non-observance of any speed limit, even on the hoverway. Here to rest, relax, and recuperate. Without telling anyone, he was having a break. He felt it was well-earned and he was beyond caring about it appearing on his expense account. The thought had occurred to him that after a few days of doing absolutely nothing but sitting on the lounge just in from the balcony soaking up the view and the atmosphere, eating olives, cheeses, fresh bread, and swathes of local Iberian hams washed down with copious amounts of *gran reserva* tempranillo, he might, just might, make an effort to concoct some kind of story about some kind of Find he was looking for in Ronda. But deciding whether or not such an effort was worth the trouble could wait.

"I am here to rest, relax, and recuperate," he said out loud to himself as he de-activated his neurophone.

But then, standing at the balcony he stopped admiring the view as other thoughts came to mind. Rafe admitted to himself that his decision not to tell anyone of his destination was really because he did not want to experience a repeat of Pienza. He knew that his 'escape' was more about trying to get some space to work out what was going on at The Bibliotek than a need to recuperate from work.

6:16pm, Tuesday, 15th January 2205

For dinner on his second evening in Ronda, Rafe had booked a table at the hotel's restaurant downstairs for just before sunset. It may have been one of the few restaurants in Ronda still open at that time of year, so his choices were limited, but he had requested a table right next to the balcony so he could continue to enjoy the same view he had upstairs in his room. In the early afternoon he had napped then showered, and on arrival at the restaurant felt fresh, but nevertheless Rafe was pleased to see the gas heaters on their stands had already been lit to offset the early evening chill despite the fact that there were no other diners yet, as was normal. For Rafe it meant he could enjoy a meal in peace and quiet yet without feeling lonely given the view across his table.

But not long after taking his seat and before he had a chance to order anything — let alone a much-desired drink — a well-dressed and tanned man strode into the restaurant, said a few passing words to the *maître d'hôtel*, and then walked straight over to Rafe's table, all the while looking directly at him and smiling.

"Good evening, Señor Nagy," the smiling middle-aged man said with precise politeness as he arrived to stand beside Rafe's table. "My name is Ruben Javier Garcia Rodriguez. May I sit down?"

"I guess so, Señor," Rafe replied a little hesitantly without getting up from his chair and with a hint of suspicion in his voice, for the name sounded familiar to him, as he shook hands.

"Forgive me for intruding on your meal, Señor Nagy, but I was hoping to have a conversation with you."

"I see," said Rafe, less hesitantly but now more suspiciously. "And you are..?"

"A dealer in rare antique books, Señor Nagy, for many years and one who has known about Rafe the Finder for almost as long. I am so pleased to finally make your acquaintance."

"A dealer in rare old books you say," replied Rafe, contemplating. "Now I remember — you are *the* Garcia Rodriguez who was once arrested for attempted fraud, yes?"

"Oh yes, Señor Nagy, that was me!" said Rodriguez, who followed his reply with a hearty laugh. "Yes, I was arrested. But Señor Nagy, that was a long time ago and I have never been *convicted* of attempted fraud, or any other crime. This is an important fact, you agree?"

Rafe nodded in agreement that that was an important fact whilst being struck by another fact; that his new friend was completely unfazed by being reminded of his arrest for allegedly trying to sell a forged 18th century rare book, a rather unique crime if it had been committed as charged. Rafe found himself taking a liking to this interesting Spanish gentleman. He now wanted to know more. "I haven't ordered yet. Would you like to join me? I'd like to hear how you came to being *almost* convicted for attempting to sell a fake antique book."

"Thank you, Señor Nagy, I would be honoured to join you. Now, please call me Ruben. My name is a mouthful, my parents were traditionalists you see, so I am happy with just Ruben."

"Please call me Rafe then, Ruben."

"Rafe and Ruben, it has a ring to it, no?"

"I guess so. Right now though I need some wine," said Rafe as he picked up the wine list.

"*Asi sera!* Do you mind?" beckoned Ruben to Rafe to hand him the list.

"Not at all, shall we order a *vino tinto?*"

"*Si si un momento.* Ah! Yes, they still have it!" Ruben exclaimed, stabbing the wine list with his index finger, which drew the solitary waiter, who had been standing still at a respectful distance, to come to the table and take the order.

"Wait, isn't that a fifteen-hundred Euro bottle you just ordered?" asked Rafe.

"*Si si* Rafe, it is indeed. This is a momentous occasion. We need to celebrate! But — *no hay problema* — I will be honoured to pay for our celebration. And besides, Rafe, the Dominio de Pingus is the best tempranillo in Spain, in the world. When we finish that we'll have the second best, a Teso La Monja."

Rafe had an alarm bell go off in his head at hearing that his meal would be paid for, with expensive wine thrown in, because it was a classic set up to create an obligation. But Rafe was impressed by Ruben's selection of wine and not a small part of him was mildly excited at the prospect of trying it. And it occurred to him that he now had a name he could drop into his otherwise fictional trip report. "Ruben, I will accept your hospitality, but on one condition, okay?"

"You do not want me to try and sell you a book. Yes, I understand. Again, *no hay problema!* This is strictly a social occasion, *si!*"

241

Rafe smiled and a little bit more of his guard came down. "Perfect. You read my mind."

"Let us get this de Pingus breathing first, then we can think about some food, *si?*"

With that, Ruben began conversing in Spanish with the waiter, who had returned and was now nervously cradling a dusty bottle which he showed to Ruben. It appeared the waiter had never opened such an expensive bottle of wine before, so Ruben took over the task and did so as if he were uncorking a bottle of house wine. Bottle opened, he held the cork to his nose and closed his eyes. His smile was enough for Rafe to know the wine would pass muster.

"Why are you standing there!?" Ruben said to the waiter in Spanish delivered with the rapidity of a machine gun, so fast that Rafe could only catch a word here and a word there. "Get a decanter!"

Wine finally sorted, Ruben lent over the table towards Rafe. "Do not order the sea bream my friend, for Juan Carlos does not cook it right, he merely waves it over the stove for a few seconds. Trust me!" Ruben whispered with one hand on the side of his face. "He thinks it is the modern thing to serve near raw fish. Maybe in Japan, but not here, Señor!"

"Noted."

"Can I suggest? Can I order for you, Rafe? Now the grilled beef Juan Carlos does *perfecto*. This is what you must have, okay? But the soup first, then the artichoke stuffed with Iberian ham and shavings of foie, then the beef. *Si?* You are not a vegetarian, I hope?"

"Sounds good, Ruben, and no I am not a vegetarian or even a vegan," Rafe replied. Since Ruben was paying, he wasn't going to insist on ordering himself. And besides, his selections did sound good.

"Good, because it is a waste of a palate to be here in Ronda and not eat our meats. So Rafe, what brings you to Ronda? A book or two perhaps? I may be able to assist, I know every bibliophile within a hundred kilometres."

"I will tell why I am here if you first tell me how it is you knew my name and how it is a coincidence that you just be happened to be here the same night, the same time, as me," replied Rafe in his best sceptic's voice whilst waving his arm at an otherwise still-empty restaurant.

"Oh, Rafe, that is easy. This is a small town. Your past visits have not gone unnoticed; and when I heard the famous Rafe the Finder had come to Ronda more than once, I had to meet you. So I asked Manuel the concierge to tell me the next time you came. He told me when you arrived last night that you had, you know, arrived. I said to him, Manuel, please you to tell me when and where Señor Nagy goes to eat dinner, because I want to meet him. Tonight, Manuel came to work just when he saw you walk into the restaurant here at the hotel, so he called me and here I am. Easy. No coincidence."

Again, Rafe was impressed with Ruben's candour. His explanation was so logical and obvious as to make the question rhetorical in hindsight.

"I see. Well, to be honest I am specifically not here for any books. I am here for a few days for some respite. And just the view from my room upstairs and here now from our table does that job. I like Ronda."

"I am glad you have come to Ronda, Rafe, but I find it hard to believe a man like you can switch off like that. Once a hunter always a hunter I say. Anyway, you have been here before, yes? Why have we not met before? I am the most important — the most experienced — book dealer in town. Me."

"How many dealers are there in Ronda?"

"Just the one," smiled Ruben. "The climate here suits my books and most of my business is done internationally. When I need to I can be in my office in Sevilla for any clients. Some even come all the way here because, like for you, it is pleasant to be here."

"So tell me about the spot of bother you had with the *policia*; you were charged with attempting to sell a collector a fake antique book, weren't you?" asked Rafe.

"*Si*, Rafe, that was what the *policia said* I had tried to do."

"And?"

"Do you know the book in question, Rafe?" asked Ruben.

"I don't recall. In fact, I don't think the report I read even mentioned the title of the book. But I do remember reading about your arrest and thinking it was odd, that someone would try to pass off a fake copy as a genuine and famous book published hundreds of years ago. That is what I remember."

"*Si si*, that is the very question that should have been asked by my accuser, but he did not."

"Well, what was the book?"

"It is a beautiful book. Spain was blessed to have in one of the sons of King Carlos the Third a most intelligent and educated young man. His name was Gabriel Antonio Francisco Javier Juan Nepomuceno José Serafín Pascual Salvador... "

"That's a handle and a half!" interrupted Rafe.

"Yes, a consequence of tradition, Rafe. We Spanish are very big on tradition. We were, that is. Each of those names had an important familial connection. But, of course, to make things easy he was known as the Infante Gabriel of Spain. So, this young man, when still a teenager, set to work on translating from the Latin, into Spanish, two famous works of Sallust, the great historian of ancient Rome. One, *The Conspiracy of Catiline*, which was Sallust's first historical work, written late in the First Century BC. The other he wrote a little later, *The Jugurthine War*. They are the only two of his works that have survived the ages complete."

"And our young prince translated both?"

"He did, Señor. And his work was published as one book, called *La Conjuracion de Catilina Y La Guerra de Jugurta*, in 1722, just before his twentieth birthday. His twentieth birthday, Señor Rafe, can you imagine that! And a prince at that. And as I said, it is a beautiful book, because it was printed by no less an artisan than Joaquin Ibarra, the greatest printer and book binder ever in Spanish history. Royal red Morocco, the covers with rich-gold gilt borders of floral rolls, raised bands, the gilt spine in seven perfect square double-ruled compartments with ornate leaf cornerpieces, blue watered silk endleaves, the paper, oh the paper, Rafe, just divine, smooth and thick, specially made for this book, with gilt, with almost no plate mark impressions, and his own ink. Each page with the prince's translation in one column, with the original Latin text underneath it in two columns in a lower font, and a vast margin. Spectacular design and craftsmanship. It is a masterpiece, Rafe."

"Yes, I know the book, Ruben, I just wasn't aware of the connection with you," said Rafe matter-of-factly. He had not interrupted Ruben's story about the book, which he knew well, because he wanted to hear Ruben's description to see if it matched what he knew.

"Oh, then you know there were only one hundred and twenty deluxe copies printed on extra-large paper making it three hundred and sixty millimetres in length."

"Yes, The Bibliotek has one."

"But, did you know there was an extra deluxe copy — a presentation copy — that Gabriel ordered from Ibarra? It was not one of the original one hundred and twenty, but it was the very next one that Ibarra made. It was a gift from Gabriel to Antonio Soler, his favourite tutor."

"Interesting, I didn't know that. And this was the book in question?"

"Yes, correct, Rafe. This was the very book I was questioned about."

"And how did you come by it, if you don't mind me asking?"

"Not at all, Rafe. I cannot give you the full story of the life of this book because I do not know it, but what I do know is this. At the end of his life, Antonio Soler was a chapel master at the El Escorial - the royal palace. I am to understand that his small collection of books was placed in the library at the palace after his death in 1783. I acquired the book from the representatives of a deceased estate in France. How it got from Spain to France in the intervening four hundred years or so, I do not know. But remember, the prince, his father the King and the rest of the family were Bourbons, and it is known that over the decades of their rule in Spain they habitually looted the library and sold or gifted the books to connections in France, so my guess is the same thing happened to my book."

"Did the seller know the significance of this particular book?"

"They certainly knew it was a first edition, but when I examined it I knew straight away it was unique and that it was not one of the one hundred and twenty. This they did not know."

"So, you got yourself a bargain, then."

"Truthfully I got, how do you say it? I got *more* than I bargained for," said Ruben.

"Your arrest? How did that come about?"

"Ah yes, the arrest. It seems I made an enemy when I acquired the book. As is often the case, he was another dealer. A French dealer; I will not say his name in case you know him. It seems he had had his eyes on the collection this book was in for some time, and he was very upset that I had gotten to it first after the collector had passed. It seems he was particularly upset that I had acquired the prince's book."

"He was beaten in the chase and he took it personally?"

"He did."

"Let me guess. When you put the book on the market for, shall we say, a reasonable mark-up, the upset dealer made it known you were selling a forgery?"

"He did."

"And he claimed it was a forgery because it was not a known copy, not one of the one hundred and twenty?"

"Not quite, but close. When I put the book on the market, he demanded to see it, on behalf of an unnamed client naturally, and to have it examined. As you know, when the price tag for a book is one and a half million Euros, as this one was, potential buyers want to know that what they are paying for is what they are paying for and before they pay for it. I allowed my esteemed colleague to bring with him anyone he wanted to examine it, by arrangement, but I would not allow the book to be taken from my office in Sevilla. Any examination had to be carried out there. This he did, and the next thing I know I am being arrested for attempted fraud, on the basis that the book was a forgery. But, not just because they discovered the book was not one of the one hundred and twenty, but because of anomalies."

"You mean your book was found to be different?"

"Yes, and I can tell you honestly, Rafe, I was not aware of any differences."

"And, they were...?"

"Before I tell you what the anomalies were, Rafe, do you know how hard it is to forge a book printed in the early eighteenth century, as this one was?"

"I would say it would be very hard," replied Rafe, knowingly.

"Absolutely! More to the point, this is an Ibarra book! A work of exceptional quality — the best — so any forger would be crazy, no, for even *thinking* they could pass off a fake Ibarra."

"Quite."

"This astounding logic was lost on my jealous colleague though, and of course the police were not nuanced enough to appreciate it. So that was my first, shall we say, line of defence."

"But you have to admit, Ruben, the most infamous forgers would see it as a challenge. To prove to the world they were better than everyone else in the book industry considered themselves to be. The best forgers always have the biggest egos."

"You are right, Rafe, absolutely right. But I am a very busy man, this is known. I am here, I am there, I have many clients, many meetings, many deals to make. Where do I find the time to devote to such a task as forging an Ibarra? Any book? To do so the first thing you need is to have a copy of the book you want to forge that is unquestionably not a fake. Not an easy thing to do. I never had such a copy. Then you need to ensure that your high-resolution photopolymer copy of each page of the real book is precisely matching the original print in every way, even down to the faintness of the block marks on the shoulder of the page from ink spills into the crevices of the typeset. Also not an easy thing to do. Then the ink on the paper itself, perhaps your biggest challenge. How do you match four-hundred-year-old inked paper? I don't know!"

"I know one forger worked out how."

"*Si, si,* you speak of... what was his name...?"

"Marino Massimo de Caro," answered Rafe.

"Ha! *Si!* de Caro! The first man to successfully pass off as real a fake seventeenth century book. And no less than a first edition of Galileo's *Sidereus Nuncias.* What a feat. A very clever man. He knew only five hundred and fifty copies were printed in the first edition and that only about one hundred and fifty of those were known to still exist, so he only made five forgeries and sold them through various intermediaries over several years so no-one could trace them all back to him. Or so he thought. Enough to recoup his costs with a handsome profit, but not too much to arouse suspicion. But five! An enormous investment of time. Yes, so the ink and the paper. He found an artisan in Buenos Aires who could create authentic looking sheets of paper with period watermarks and other features, then he found a quantity of nineteenth century India ink for sale which he bought, then had tested. It was too acidic to match paper from the seventeenth century, so after each page was inked, he baked it in his oven over a petri dish of hydrochloric acid for about fifteen minutes at so many degrees and presto! Authentic-looking pages! Brilliant."

Rafe already knew all that about de Caro, and more, but he had let Ruben speak. "Yes," he said, "but too bad he didn't take into account the cotton linters in the paper that didn't exist until a hundred years after Galileo,"

"*Si,* that is true," replied Ruben. "I see you know a lot about this case. But that was only detected a long time afterwards. After he had fooled the experts, the dealers, and the buyers. Remember, a fake book only has to look, feel, and smell like the real thing to be sold."

"So, did your book look, feel, and smell like the real thing?"

"It felt and smelt like the real thing, absolutely. Oh the feel of it. Just amazing to hold. But it failed the look test my angry colleague put it through."

"He found something you missed?"

"Ah, no and yes. He found three separate pages that were not the same as any of the corresponding pages of the other known one hundred and twenty copies."

"In what way?"

"They were perfect pages."

"Huh?"

"Ha! Yes, you see, as with all books, there will always be some printing errors. A missing full stop here, a missing comma there, a misspelled word, a missing word. Many different errors can be made in the typesetting. And even Ibarra, or one of his workers, could make a mistake and they sometimes did. My book should have had the same printing errors on those three pages that the other books had, but it didn't. Presto, my book is a fake."

"Amazing!"

"Yes, my friend thought he had me. So he informed the policia, showed them the evidence, and had me arrested and charged before I could sell the book."

"But it never got to court?"

"No, my friend the idiot had not taken into account two things. One: if I am forging a book, am I reading it? No. Why would I? I don't have to. I am not forging the grammar or the sentences, I am forging a page with text. What that text is shouldn't matter. I am making a copy. So why would I be stupid enough to read the book I am forging, take note of all the printing errors and decide 'oh, I must correct those'?"

"Yes, I see the logic."

"Good. Even the policia finally realised that. But it was the other thing my friend had not taken into account that got the charges dropped."

"What was that?" asked Rafe.

Now Ruben broke out in a huge smile. "The letter," he said.

Rafe waited for him to continue, but Ruben took his time, pouring more wine into his glass, swirling it around for a bit and letting out a happy sigh. "My *coup de grace.*"

"Yes?" Rafe said, a little impatient.

"The letter, Señor Rafe, that was still inside the front cover when I acquired the book. I could hardly believe my eyes. It was from the prince to his tutor and it was obviously given with the book. The letter explained that the book was an inadequate return for all the years of instruction his tutor had devoted to his student, but that he hoped he would enjoy reading it as much as the prince had enjoyed writing it. Then, at the very end of the letter, the prince noted that this gift was a special copy that was printed after several errors had been corrected and asked that he relay to him any remaining errors he might find for future editions."

"Wow. *Touché*. I take it you had taken the letter out of the book before allowing your friend to examine it?"

"Of course."

"Sneaky. But had not you begun marketing the book? Surely such a letter is normally included in the information to potential buyers as evidence of provenance," asked Rafe.

"That is so. But consider this: if the book was a fake, could not the letter also be? No, I expected my friend to demand to see the book and have it examined, client or no client, so I kept quiet about the letter. And that is exactly what he did; he paid for the very same authentication process that I would have had to pay for. He did exactly what I had hoped he would do — authenticate the book for me. I was very happy."

"And logic would have it that why would a forger go to the trouble of correcting typesetting errors then forge a letter about them, when it would be so much easier just to forge a real copy as is," Rafe thought out loud.

"Precisely, Rafe."

"I'm impressed, Ruben. That's a great story."

"Thank you, but my friend did not think so. First he had been beaten in the hunt, then he managed to fool himself in the revenge. All the charges were dropped when I showed the policia the letter, which fact did not get as much press as my arrest, that I am not happy about — *que sera sera* — but I sold the book for its asking price and made an enemy for life," said Ruben with a slight shrug of his shoulders. "Now, Rafe, we are only part way through our beef but we have nearly finished the de Pingus. Time to open the Teso and let it breathe."

"Sounds good to me," said Rafe, pouring the last of the de Pingus in each of their glasses. "This wine is divine, thank you."

"My pleasure, Rafe. Would you like a cigar?" asked Ruben as he pulled a case out of his inner coat pocket, opened it, and offered it to Rafe. "These are Caliqueños cigars. I smoke nothing else. They have been made in Valencia for over four hundred years. They look rough but they are one hundred percent burley leaf and very smooth to smoke. And they do not need to be humidified because they dry out in their boxes, so no need to invest in an expensive little cupboard."

Rafe could not resist; he took a cigar. It had been a very long time since he had tried one, and it had not been a good experience. But the aroma from Ruben's Caliqueños was enticing. "Smooth you say?"

"Very," said Ruben smiling, as he lit Rafe's cigar. "That is good, *si?*"

Rafe nodded in the affirmative as he took a long slow draw, which he managed to achieve without coughing. It was indeed very smooth. "I think I could start to like these."

Ruben was pleased to hear Rafe's assessment. "So tell me, Rafe the Finder, you have heard about some of the books I have found. But what about you? What have you found of late? Anything of interest?"

Rafe was by now not just relaxed, but he knew he was over-relaxed. He had dined well, very well, and had enjoyed meeting and talking with Ruben, so he told him about his finding of the Giordano Collection, a truncated version of his speech at The Bibliotek dinner.

As he had hoped, Ruben was impressed. "*Magnifico!*" he shouted, with his arms outstretched.

"*Si Señor,*" smiled Rafe before he began another long drag on his cigar. "*Si!*"

"I must tell you, Rafe, I am a little jealous," admitted Ruben.

"Don't be, it was mostly luck. And besides, you've no doubt had many great finds yourself."

"Well, yes, but not like that. And, you see, one of my specialties is rare books of anatomical studies from that early Enlightenment period, so there lies my jealousy. To find, what was it? *Seventeen* of them in the one, unexpected, place is fantastic. *Te saludo!*" said Ruben, raising his glass.

"Thank you, Ruben. Yes, it was a *good* Find."

"You should come and see my collection and tell me what you think. It has taken me many years to accumulate. Come tomorrow morning, then we will go to lunch. *Si?*"

"Sounds like a plan," smiled Rafe.

By the time Rafe said goodnight to Ruben two hours later he was glad he only had to catch the lift to his suite. After they had finished the Teso, Ruben had ordered a bottle of vintage Muscat from Malaga. Rafe didn't have to ask to know it was probably the best the restaurant had. He was now happily sozzled and replete in food, wine, and conversation. He tried not to think about the cost of the meal for Ruben, but he had the impression that Ruben was a very wealthy man and remained a dealer in antique books out of joy, not need, and it was that joy that explained Ruben's desire to meet and converse with him.

9:06am, Wednesday, 16ᵗʰ January 2205

The next morning Rafe barely remembered accepting Ruben's invitation to visit his bookstore, and only really did so when he saw Ruben's business card on the bedside table where he had left it just before falling asleep on the bed, fully clothed.

But it took Rafe some time to find Ruben's bookstore. There was one tucked away in the street which Ruben's card cited, but it was not an antique bookstore or even a rare bookstore, and the name did not match. But after some unsuccessful searching elsewhere, exasperated, Rafe returned to it and rang the phone number on the card.

"*Si* Rafe, that is the one. Just ask for me at the counter," explained Ruben when he answered Rafe's call.

This Rafe did, but even then he had trouble, for the young lady did not know of any Señor Garcia Rodriguez. "Señor Ruben?" asked Rafe this time.

"*Ah, si, Señor Ruben. Un momento!*" she happily replied before picking up a phone and calling Ruben.

Instantly a curtain at the far end of the bookstore was flung aside and there was Ruben, motioning to Rafe to come through.

Behind the curtain, which had been concealing a narrow open doorway, Rafe entered a large room with walls completely covered with towering bookcases — at least four metres high — with books crammed in every shelf. It was like a cavern, with no windows. In the middle of the room were several large old wooden tables with more books both piled and laid out. Every book was old.

"Good morning, Rafe, I hope you slept well, *si?* Thank you for visiting my little shop!" said Ruben, cheerily.

"Good morning, Ruben. Yes, I think I slept well. But I do know I had a good meal and conversation, thank you. I just don't know remember too much after that. Unlike my hotel room last night, this is a very hard place to find, and this is quite a few books you have Ruben, but where do you sit?" asked Rafe.

"Thank you Rafe, my desk is in the other room. This way." Again, Ruben motioned to Rafe to follow, this time through a small archway at the rear of the room, to a smaller one, also windowless, with only one bookcase, but again filled, and a large desk with an old leather armchair behind it and a wooden chair in front. "I keep the very rare books in here, in my office," said Ruben pointing to the bookcase, which was ornate, oak and much more heavy set than the bookcases in the main room.

"Nobody in this town is interested in old books, Rafe," said Ruben, "so there's no point showing them. And then there's the Present Sect."

"They are here, in Ronda?" asked Rafe, a little worried.

"No, I have never noticed their presence here. But in Sevilla there are those posters about. You know, *El Presente esta aqui!*"

"*The Present is Here! The Present is Now!* Yes, I've seen them."

"I wonder sometimes if the Present Sect is an issue for The Bibliotek, or if they work in your favour," said Ruben.

"You're not the first to suggest that, but no, we take account of them on the one hand and we never try to use them to promote fear and a reason to donate to The Bibliotek. That alone would make us a target."

"I guess they have enough targets already not to worry about The Bibliotek. There's been some trouble in Seville and in other parts of Spain as well, particularly Madrid; arson, that sort of thing. So, I don't advertise my real business, as you can see. Access to this part of the shop is strictly by invitation only."

"I see, that makes sense. Do you mind if I have a look?" said Rafe turning to the bookcase.

"By all means, be my guest," motioned Ruben once again.

"I'm surprised we haven't met before now, Ruben, in the normal course of my Find hunting," said Rafe as he began peering at the spines of the books.

"Perhaps because we are competitors, no?" replied Ruben. "And also I think we haven't done business together because you don't technically pay for what you acquire. That is correct, no?"

"That is correct, Ruben. We only give a Tax Certificate to the seller for the agreed value of the 'donation'. But yes, we are competitors, particularly when it's a deceased estate we are both interested in. I just don't recall competing against you."

"Oh I've been around some of those deals, just in the background. I really do prefer to keep a low profile. And besides, a lot of those deceased estates prefer those Tax Certificates because they solve a problem and don't create one by selling for cash. And if an estate prefers to deal with The Bibliotek then I don't try to argue my way back in. There's plenty of other fish to fry."

"That's very pragmatic of you, Ruben. I see what you mean about your speciality in anatomical studies," noted Rafe as he continued to examine the spines of the books in the bookcase. "Are all these books for sale?"

"Yes, everything in the shop is for sale. Though some, especially the ones you are looking at right now, I would be very sad to see go," replied Ruben.

"Yes, I can appreciate that — the curse of the bookseller. You have some beautiful ones here," said Rafe as he turned his attention to a rather large book — which he knew to be in elephant folio size — on a display stand next to the bookcase. "This, for example, is a fine copy of Mascagni's *Anatomia Universa*. In fact," observed Rafe, "it looks in better shape than the copy we have in The Bibliotek. I've not seen another copy before. This is the first edition?"

"*Si*, it is most definitely a first edition. The later editions published in Florence were much smaller and do not pay enough respect to the drawings," replied Ruben.

"I have to agree with you on that score," said Rafe as he carefully examined some of the exquisite drawings Ruben was referring to. "I have always marvelled at the detail that's been achieved. Just incredible. The most detailed anatomical drawings *ever* produced."

"You know there are rumours that some copies were hand-coloured by Canacci, but I have yet to see one," said Ruben, who was now standing next to Rafe and also looking at the drawings.

"Yes, that would be some Find for The Bibliotek," replied Rafe, as he carefully placed the book back on its stand.

"Ah yes, Landriani's air book," said Rafe, selecting a book from the shelf, Marsilio Landriani's 1775 *Ricerche Fisiche Intorno alla Salubrita dell'Aria* (*Physical Research Around the Healthiness of Air*) "This also is a fine copy. Looks like the original binding too."

"It is indeed, Rafe. I have not seen a finer example of Landriani's study, but it is not as popular as his later works. He was only twenty-four when he wrote this one. I just like it because it seems incredible that someone felt the need to study the air and conclude it is healthy for one to be in it."

"Yes, it is an oddity," agreed Rafe with a nod. "Revolutionary though at the time. It was another one hundred years before scientists finally gave up the theory of miasma as being total rubbish. I wonder how many lives would have been saved had they listened to Landriani instead of focusing on 'night air' as being responsible for cholera and whatnot."

As he spoke, Rafe continued to examine Ruben's books. "Yes, very impressive collection you have here, Ruben. Wait, what..?" Rafe looked up at Ruben, genuinely surprised, as he slipped another book from the shelf and started leafing through its pages.

Ruben was smiling. "I was wondering if you would see this one. It is special, *si?*" Rafe had picked out a 1543 first edition of Andreas Vesalius's *De Humani Corporis Fabrica* (*On the Fabric of the Human Body*). "You know he was only twenty-eight when he wrote that amazing book, Rafe, just a bit older than Landriani."

"Yes, I know Vesalius, and I know this book, which was written when he was twenty-nine," corrected Rafe. "It was only a few months ago that I secured a fine copy of the rarer *Epitome* version of this book for The Bibliotek. We already have a copy of the full *Fabrica* version, but not like this one. Ruben, these plates are coloured. There is only one known copy of the *Fabrica* with coloured plates and that was a special dedication copy given to Emperor Charles V by Vesalius himself. This is not *that* book is it?"

"No Rafe, this is not that book, and the experts — and I am sorry to say, you also — are mistaken. There are three known hand-coloured copies of the first edition. There is the presentation copy, which was acquired by the Italian National Library in Florence at Christies in New York in 1998 for more than one point six million U.S. dollars. There is also one held by the British Library. Who knows how they got it; I have not been troubled to find out. And there is this one. It acquired new by a German doctor by the name of Caspar Neefe a year after the first edition was published in 1543, by which time it had already been hand-coloured. At the time he acquired it, Neefe was the personal physician to The Duke of Saxony so he could certainly afford it. That can only mean that Vesalius had arranged for more than one copy of the first edition to be sold with hand-coloured plates, making them even more expensive than the as-printed *Fabrica*. Look here, Rafe," said Ruben as he took the book from Rafe's incredulous hands. "Look at this title illustration, see the care that was taken by the colourist, there is not a single speck of paint anywhere it should not be."

Rafe peered carefully at the page.

"Here, use my *loupe*," offered Ruben as he took off the small magnifying glass hanging around his neck and gave it to Rafe.

Rafe obliged and resumed looking at the page. It was a complex illustration of Vesalius performing a dissection of a female corpse during one of his lectures at the University of Padua, surrounded by at least a hundred peering faces of his students. Colourised it looked nothing like the original black and white illustration but also nothing like a printed colour illustration. The colourist had indeed taken great care not to overdo the richness of the colours, which were mostly tints of red, yellow, blue, and brown, including a distinct red colouring applied to the dissected part of the corpse's body, which alone helped to transform the illustration into an even greater statement than the original, because Vesalius was a pioneer of dissections and autopsies by the medical profession. Until Vesalius began doing so during his lectures, such an operation would normally have been performed by a barber under instruction by the practitioner standing next to him, and never during a lecture. The illustration was also unique in that such post-mortem operations were usually performed on male bodies not female, and this was simply because by law the cadavers used for dissection could only be the bodies of condemned prisoners, and it was rare for a female criminal to be put to death. So revolutionary were Vesalius's dissections and his accompanying lectures that the local judges in Padua's criminal courts began to consign the bodies of executed criminals directly to him, and it was this steady supply that enabled him to complete the masterpiece that is the *Fabrica* and a major leap forward in the study of anatomy. To Rafe's eye the colouring, which was performed on every illustration of the first 165 pages of the book, about half of its content, looked contemporary to the printing as he examined detailed illustration after detailed illustration, but the idea of it, for a 16th century book, seemed unreal, if not surreal, and he said as much to Ruben.

"*Si*, that is true, it does seem strange to see. But, Rafe, I have examined both of the other two known colourised copies, the one in the Florence National Library *and* the one in the British National Library and they are both *exactly* the same as this one. It is definitely the same hand holding the brush, and of course the same colours."

"And so this third copy is the only one held in private hands. How did you come by it, if I may ask?"

"Certainly, it's no secret. This book was held by the family of a medical history collector in Tyrol, for four generations. Then about a hundred years ago it was sold to a bibliophile in Barcelona for two and a half million Euros. When he died, the Spanish Government took possession of it to cover death duties, then the Great Holy War happened and the Government, facing going bankrupt in fighting its part, decided to sell this book, and many others, on the private market, quietly. Then I acquired the book from the son of the dealer who had bought it from the Government. I have all the documents."

"And it is for sale?"

"Yes, Rafe, the price is four million Euros. Thinking of buying it are you?"

"Ha! I wish," replied Rafe, deciding not to take Ruben's bait.

"You know, Rafe, before this book was published, the truth of the human anatomy was for many centuries dominated by the work of Galen, who never in his life dissected anything closer to a human body than monkeys from the Barbary coast, a fact that was revealed by Vesalius himself and which caused much scorn to be heaped upon him for daring to repudiate the knowledge of a man who promulgated, wrongly, that the human lower jaw was comprised of two bones when in fact, as proved by Vesalius, it was composed of only one. A man who pronounced as rubbish the fact undisputed for fourteen hundred years that arteries carried the best, purest, blood from the left ventricle to the brain whilst veins from the right ventricle carried less-pure blood to the lesser organs. Vesalius turned all that accepted truth — and much more — literally on its head, and he almost found himself condemned to death by the Inquisition because of it. And performing his own dissections! Why, this was *beneath* all reputable physicians, so even after Vesalius found himself appointed as the Emperor's personal physician, he continued to be treated by his colleagues as nothing better than a common barber. Even one of his old university professors kept denying the truth of Vesalius's work by claiming that the human body had *changed itself* since Galen. Can you imagine it? So, even after he published *Fabrica* it took years and years for *his* truths to take hold. And now of course, we look at *Fabrica* and know it for what it is — a work of genius — and perhaps the most important medical book ever published. And it is six hundred and sixty-two years old. Amazing."

"I quite agree with you Ruben," said Rafe, finally getting a word in. "You don't need to convince me of the importance of this book. Or its price tag. And as I said, The Bibliotek already has a fine copy of the first edition. It's just that..."

"It's just that *this* book is special," Ruben said, finishing what Rafe was going to say.

"Yes, yes it is," replied Rafe, holding the book in his hands, feeling the weight of it in far greater terms than the physical sense. "Let's talk about it over lunch. My shout."

"I would be honoured, my friend; can I recommend a restaurant? It's just around the corner, my favourite. The lamb, oh the lamb," exclaimed Ruben.

"Excellent. Just be aware though my entertainment budget is *slightly* less than yours."

A few hours later, after another good and engaging meal, enjoyed with a far less expensive tempranillo, Ruben offered to give his *Fabrica* to The Bibliotek.

"But Ruben, you said yourself you prefer cash and you know we don't pay it."

"Yes, I know that, Rafe. But I have not been able to sell it now for quite a while, so I am losing money each year I still have it. One problem is the price tag; there are not that many private buyers left at that level and I have spoken to them all. Some are interested, but until

Professor Sarkozy corrects the entry for my *Fabrica* in his census, they are wary of it."

Ruben was referring to the academic work published thirty years previously by Professor Stanislaw Sarkozy of Leipzig University which listed, according to him, all the known copies of the first and second editions of *Fabrica* and discussed all the notations made in those copies by their various owners over time. It was considered to be the first and last word on Vesalius's masterpiece and to date Sarkozy had only listed Ruben's *Fabrica* as a 'normal' copy of the first edition.

"So it's in the census, just not as being a presentation copy?"

"Correct. He's grabbed all of Neefe's notations from it, of course, but that's all. Accepting it as a presentation copy would place it front and centre," replied Ruben.

"Okay, so if you could convince him to list it as genuine, why not sell it at an auction and get paid in cash? You know The Bibliotek can only give you a Tax Certificate."

"Well, I let Sarkozy examine the book, but he still doesn't think it's a genuine third presentation copy, so there's that problem not going away quickly. I'm in a bind because if I commission a full analysis myself, people will say well of course it came it out in your favour, and then not believe it. But I cannot let the book out of my sight given its value to me. So, here is the thing, Rafe. I actually have a tax problem. A large one. It seems I have too much money, or the tax people want too much. One or the other, or both. Either way, I could really use a Tax Certificate right now instead of cash. Even at four million Euros. It will help me a lot, even though it will only be essentially forty cents in the Euro in cash terms. At least it's a sale. I've held onto it for too long already. And there is a bit of me that wants to see it go to The Bibliotek and be protected. You never know, in these uncertain times. Anything could happen."

"Hmm," pondered Rafe. "Let me get this straight, Ruben. You would be prepared to sell it, give it, technically, to The Bibliotek in exchange for a Tax Certificate for four million Euros."

"I think I would, *si*."

"And when did that idea pop into your head?"

"When I saw your eyes light up when you saw my book, Rafe," said Ruben looking straight into Rafe's eyes.

"Let me think about it, Ruben. We'll talk more about it before I leave Ronda."

This Ruben was happy about, and they agreed to meet for dinner back at the hotel restaurant the following night, Rafe's last in Ronda on this trip.

The next morning, Rafe made a few neurophone calls. One was to Professor Sarkozy, whom he knew.

"Yes, Ruben and I have been in contact with each other," said Sarkozy, "and, yes, I did go to Seville to inspect his *Fabrica*, but I am still giving consideration to revising its entry in the next edition of the census. Or not."

"So you're not convinced it is an original hand-coloured first edition copy?" asked Rafe.

"Not one hundred per cent, no, Not even eighty percent," Sarkozy replied. "I am not convinced the colouring was contemporaneous to the printing, and I am not convinced Vesalius arranged for more than one hand-coloured copy."

"The presentation copy to the Emperor?"

"Yes. If there was more than one it would tend to dilute the 'special' aspect of the copy and, more to the point, no other genuine coloured copies of the *Fabrica* have ever come to light. And nothing personal against Ruben, but the fact he is a dealer and has brought this copy to my attention immediately rang alarm bells in my mind."

"But Ruben told me that his copy is the *third* known coloured presentation one, and that the British Library and the National Library in Florence each have one."

"The one in the Florence is indisputably the presentation copy given by Vesalius to the Emperor," responded Sarkozy. "The one in the British Library however has a rather dubious provenance. I have examined it and believe it to be fake."

"A forgery?"

"Not a forgery as popularly known. It is a real *Fabrica*, that I am satisfied with, and that is why it is in the census. I just don't think it is another presentation copy."

"You mean it has been hand-coloured sometime after it was printed?"

"Exactly."

"Has it been tested?"

"Not to my knowledge. I made my assessment based on my own physical visual examination and comparison which, by the way, was a prolonged perusal not a quick glance."

"I see, but have you had Ruben's *Fabrica* tested?" asked Rafe.

"No, that I have not been able to do. Ruben would not let the book out of his office and obviously it needs to be examined in a laboratory as taking a sample is not an option."

"Okay, if we put aside the issue of there being no other known genuine coloured copies of the first edition — as far as *you* are aware, that is — what if the book were to be physically examined by my colleagues at The Bibliotek, in The Bibliotek?"

"If The Bibliotek was to thoroughly examine Ruben's *Fabrica*, including especially the paintwork, and conclude it is genuine, I would then have grounds to upgrade its status in the next edition of the census. I already have copies of the annotations throughout the copy made by the book's first owner, Caspar Neefe; they at least I know are genuine. But, for me to accept the book as a bona fide presentation copy, your analysis must look at the relationship of the paintwork to the paper. It is not enough to say it is contemporary. It has to have been contemporaneous. As you know, paint applied to freshly printed paper of that era reacted differently to paint applied years, even months later," said Sarkozy.

"Yes, I understand the distinction, and that is something my colleagues can definitely test for. I just want to be clear you would accept the results of The Bibliotek's analysis."

"I will put that in writing if you wish. The Bibliotek's set up is world class, if not world leading. Everybody knows that. And I am not so precious as to be reluctant to 'correct' the book's entry in the *Fabrica* census. Quite the opposite — it would cause a sensation. And *that* is the reason for my caution to date."

"Thank you, Professor, if you wouldn't mind putting that in writing it would be much appreciated."

6:15pm, Thursday, 17th January 2205

That evening Ruben and Rafe re-united in the hotel's restaurant. Same time, same table.

"Rafe, I am going to sit here with the wine list and wait until you tell me something."

"I've made a few calls, including to some people at The Bibliotek, and also to Professor Sarkozy. Here's the deal. I can only give you a

Tax Certificate for three million eight hundred thousand Euro. That's actually a bit more than our total annual limit for procuring Finds imposed on me by your friendly Spanish tax office, but we can handle it by reducing next year's limit. For that to happen though, you need to let me take the book back to The Bibliotek; I would personally take it with me. Our team will thoroughly examine and test the book, with a focus on the paintwork. If the results are that it is proved to be a bona fide hand-coloured presentation copy, you then have a sale. I then will send you your Tax Certificate, and Sarkozy has confirmed that he will then accordingly amend his listing of your book in the next edition of the census. How does all that sound?"

"That all sounds reasonable. But Rafe, you have offered me this deal without telling me what you think and feel about my book."

"I *want* the book to be exactly what it purports to be. I always do in these matters, that's how I operate. And personally? Well, I would be disappointed if I was required to bring it back to you — no sale — if it doesn't hold up to our examination. And our relationship would be at an end."

"Fair enough, Rafe, fair enough. So, three point eight million? I can live with that. I'd get less after what an auction house would take as commission on a four-million sale. We have a deal." With that Ruben shook hands with Rafe.

"Now Rafe, just to show you I didn't plan this all along and that I am confident my book will pass any test you throw at it, I am going to pay for dinner tonight. Time to celebrate." With those words, Ruben called the waiter over and ordered not one but two bottles of the Dominio de Pingus. Then he let his new friend-for-life Rafe decide what to eat.

Later, when they were into the second bottle of the de Pingus, Ruben said, "You know Rafe, there is another book collection lost, like Giordano's, which I have been searching for. For a long time."

"Oh? Do tell, perhaps I know it," replied Rafe.

"The Lost Library of Ivan the Terrible," said Ruben.

"Don't let a Russian hear you say that. It's actually the Lost Library of Ivan the Formidable," said Rafe, looking around at the otherwise empty restaurant. "'Terrible' is a *terribly* wrong translation of the word 'Grozny'. In the context of Ivan IV, it actually means 'Formidable,' he explained.

"So, you *do* know it?"

"Yes, I've heard of it. You say you've been looking for it?"

"*Si*," replied Ruben.

"So, you believe it exists, or did exist?"

"*Si, si.*"

"Which one?"

"I believe it still exists and is waiting for me to unearth it."

"Let me guess. You think it is buried somewhere under the Kremlin."

"Oh, I think it is buried somewhere, certainly, but not under the Kremlin. Somewhere nearby," Ruben offered cryptically.

Rafe could tell that Ruben was angling for something, but he wasn't sure what. "And you're telling me this, because...?"

"I'm telling you this Rafe because I think you are a man I can trust, that you have perhaps also been looking for the library, and that perhaps we can share what we know, just in case we are both looking at the same clues."

Rafe suddenly became alert at Ruben's words. And wary. He did not want to tell him he had also been looking for Ivan's lost library for many years, and he especially did not want Ruben to know he felt he was very close to finding the answer to the mystery; that the library had existed, potentially still existed and was waiting to be found. Hopefully by him. "Yes, you're right. I have been looking for it, but that was when I was young and hopeful. My search only helped me grow old and cynical. If I didn't give it up when I did it would have turned me into a crazed madman. So, sorry, but I can't help you."

"That's a pity," shrugged Ruben, carefully looking at Rafe's countenance. "That's a pity," he said again as he lit a Calenquenos and gave Rafe a , quick, small smile and a slightly longer stare.

END OF CHAPTER TEN

Chapter Eleven

Adcom Assesses Arcadia

*Jerry: "What is this obsession people have with books!? They put 'em in their houses like they're trophies. What do you need it for **after** you **read it!**?"*
George: "They're — MY — books!"
"Seinfeld", a popular U.S. television 'sitcom', 1994

10:40am, Wednesday, 16th January 2205

Nils Larkin had been Mads' personal assistant now for almost five months, and he had begun to understand his boss's way of doing things; and appreciate them. But he had also observed a change in the Bibliotekar's demeanour in recent weeks. He was now more serious and shorter with people than he had usually been when Larkin was first appointed to the position. And Larkin had also been on the receiving end of that change. He had also noticed that Nikka Johannson, Head of Security, had been having more meetings and phone calls with the Bibliotekar of late, and now she had just arrived for yet another meeting, this time with folder in hand. And these were not scheduled meetings they were having, Larkin had noticed. The Bibliotekar did not normally like people coming to see him without an appointment, that much he knew, but lately he seemed to have no issue with Johannson just appearing in his suite without notice, then being allowed to see him. That annoyed Larkin, so too the result of these unscheduled meetings — that Larkin no longer felt in control of Bibliotekar Ingridson's diary. Perhaps both things, and more, were annoying to him in equal measure. And now Johannson had just arrived for another unscheduled meeting which the Bibliotekar seemed not just willing but also eager to accommodate. It seemed the Bibliotekar was operating within two separate work flows with two separate agendas. One focused on 'normal business', the other on something else, unspoken and, as far as Larkin was concerned, secret.

As usual, Nikka didn't waste any time with pleasantries. "First things first, Mads. Thanks to Doctor Foote, I can confirm that Smits made a neurophone call of just under three minutes' duration on the

263

ninth of last November at four thirty-six pm to Councillor Metcalfe's neurophone," she said.

Hearing this, Mads gave a heavy sigh, got up from the chair behind his desk, walked over to the window and stared outside at the snow-covered courtyard. Nikka knew Mads well enough to wait in silence. After a while Mads turned around and faced Nikka. That was the signal for her to resume.

"Second thing is I've discovered something else about Smits, Mads."

"Yes?" asked Mads in a soft voice.

"He has continued to receive his salary from his previous job at the security company owned by Carlson, every month, without fail."

"What?! How did you find that out?"

"Well, since his connection with Carlson confirmed a few things for you, I took the initiative and dug a big deeper. For starters I accessed Smits' bank records for the account he was using to receive his fortnightly pay from The Bibliotek. I used Doctor Foote for that as well."

"Wait, was that legal?"

"Mads, you forget I am technically the Chief of Police for The Bibliotek Precinct. My powers equate to that level, courtesy of the laws enacted by the Norwegian parliament when The Bibliotek was established. So, yes, perfectly legal so long as I had reasonable cause, which I felt I had and said so to Foote. Anyway, I discovered something strange."

"Yes?"

"That account is devoid of any expenses. Smits has made no withdrawals from it — his Bibliotek salary is just accumulating in the account. That was very odd. Most employees would normally be incurring living expenses and using their Bibliotek salary for that purpose. I mean, most normal employees wouldn't be independently wealthy, would they?"

"No, indeed not," replied Mads.

"So, he had to have had other accounts. It wasn't hard to find them, and there it was, another bank account which is still receiving his regular monthly salary payments from his so-called ex-employer and from which he continues to incur his living expenses. Here is the paperwork, including the documents which show that Councillor Carlson is ultimately his employer." Nikka handed Mads a folder which he then opened and browsed through after resuming his seat behind his desk, thinking all the while he should have had enough sense to ask Nikka to obtain their bank records instead of having to rely on her to think of doing it. He noticed something else. "Another employee?"

"Yes, Mads, Doctor Foote came back to me with another name. A Senior Accountant in Michael Huntington's Finance team. Her name is Lara de Jong. She started with The Bibliotek six weeks after Smits and she came from the same company. So I checked her bank records as well, and it's the same picture as with Smits."

"Have you told Michael?" Mads asked.

"No, it did not seem prudent."

"Correct. Okay Nikka, thank you for this, it's joined a few more dots for me. It's time I gave you a full briefing, but first, can I ask you what your thoughts are about these two employees having this ongoing relationship with Councillor Carlson?"

"If it was just one ex-employee I would perhaps be prepared to accept the explanation it is a mistake on the part of the old employer. But two of them? And both Bibliotek employees? That I find hard to believe is a mistake."

"Agreed. And?"

"As far as I am concerned there is absolutely no valid reason for them to be still receiving an income from their previous employer. The fact they are receiving these payments suggests to me that they are still performing some form of services for their old company, or for someone else. Bottom line though, questions need to be asked by HR and they will need to receive good answers. And then I would sack them both, with prejudice."

Mads pondered her words before responding. "I agree, but caution for now is the key. We need to hold off taking any action until we can find out more about why they are here and what they are doing for Carlson. Here's what I know, which may go some way to an explanation."

Mads then told Nikka about the incident with Thomas, and its connection with Arcadia, and that Thomas was in hiding far away from The Bibliotek. He told her about his consequent trip to Arcadia and what he had found. He told her about the palladium and rhodium deposits on Arcadia. He told her about Dr Joyce's confession that he had been acting under the orders of Councillor Carlson when he harassed Commander Henderson. He also told her about the murder of the Viscount and its connection with Rafe and to someone at The Bibliotek, as yet a mystery as to who, and the Iceland threat. Throughout, Nikka did not interrupt. To Mads, she was clearly listening to information she had not been aware of. It felt to Mads that his instinct to trust her with what he knew was the right path to take.

When Mads had finished talking, he let Nikka think about it. Then she spoke.

"You're right, Mads, that does explain a few things. And something else: you want me to go to Arcadia; I didn't need to volunteer."

Mads smiled, "Correct."

"And I'm beginning to see that all that has been happening has probably to do with Arcadia, even perhaps the upscale of the Present Sect threats. I'm going to also assume that it was Smits who threatened Councillor Metcalfe and who took his neurophone and data pad from the Councillor's office. Actually, I don't need to assume that, the evidence points to it. And, I'm afraid to say, there appears to be something nefarious going on involving Councillor Carlson, which also explains your caution."

"That's it in a nutshell, Nikka, apart from one more thing. My instincts tell me that whatever Carlson is up to, Chair Thurldottir is right there with him, if not controlling the whole show."

"And that's because... ?"

"Carlson has been Thurldottir's attack dog ever since she took over as Chair of the Governing Council. And even before then, now that I think of it."

"I see, but Mads, why have you waited this long to tell me all this? Were you testing me?" asked Nikka, a little annoyed.

"I wouldn't say that, Nikka. What I needed was for you to find out some things for me independently of what I suspected to be the case, rather than risk second guessing them. And now we are in the same boat. You have someone in your team who is not working for you, and I have people on the Governing Council and elsewhere in The Bibliotek doing the same to me."

"And since Paul mentioned Arcadia he's potentially put himself in the frame too."

"Agreed."

"So when we go there with Finn, I should keep an eye on Paul," suggested Nikka.

"Yes, I think that would be a good idea, Nikka," replied Mads.

"Which also means I need to hold off dealing with Smits and de Jong until we find out more."

"That would be prudent, yes," cautioned Mads. He got up again and walked around to the front of his desk, sat in the chair opposite Nikka and leant forward, with the fingertips of each hand touching one another. He said, quietly but firmly, looking intently at her, "I've never experienced anything like this before, Nikka. This goes beyond mere power plays and politics. But I'll be damned if I'm going to sit back and do nothing but watch it all play out. I don't like being lied to and I don't like things happening behind my back — *our* backs. But it's new ground I'm treading on, and caution is the key word. We're on the same page on this."

"Of course, Mads. I don't like what's been going on as much as you do, especially in *my* team behind *my* back. I'll sort Smits out if nothing else but yes, I can see there is a bigger picture needing to be framed first. I will definitely be open eyes and ears on the trip to Arcadia. Is there anything else you need me to do?"

"At the moment I am trying to find out more information, and collecting evidence as I go along, which I may or may not need down the track. This..." he said, pointing his index finger at the folder Nikka had just given him, "is evidence of Carlson's involvement in whatever is going on. I also have a signed statement from Joyce that he was acting on Carlson's orders when he hassled Commander Henderson about the geosurvey team on Arcadia. What I really need is to be able to connect Carlson to Thurldottir in what's been going on. I tasked Doctor Foote to see what he could find out about Thurldottir's background and connections, but he's not having any luck. She seems to be a ghost."

"I'm happy to provide some assistance to Doctor Foote, but you do realise you are playing with fire here, Mads? We are talking about the Chair of the Governing Council of The Bibliotek. If things go pear-shaped it will be the end for you. You do know that, don't you?"

"I do know that, Nikka, but I'm not out to 'get' anyone. I simply want to find out information that is being deliberately withheld from me. I have a reasonable basis for being proactive, and to be able to do this as effectively as possible I need to be discrete and I need you to be discrete."

"What about Larkin? Do you trust him?" asked Nikka.

"No I do not. Never have. But I have no basis for that other than I just don't like him," replied Mads.

"But do you think he could be involved in keeping things from you?"

"I can't honestly say one way or another. I don't like his manner. He doesn't hide his ambition and that is something that rubs me the wrong way."

"Why don't you just replace him with someone better?" asked Nikka.

"I've thought many times of doing just that, but lately I've been using my suspicion about him to my advantage. It's getting to the point where I can benefit from the feeding of any information from him to others. Information I want them to have if my suspicions are correct. And I can put a stop to that at any time."

"I see," said Nikka. "But perhaps I should have a look at him for you, as well as Thurldottir."

Mads leant back in the chair and sighed. "Okay but talk first to Doctor Foote. I've never been quite sure how Larkin was assigned to me in the first place."

Meeting over, Nikka got up and began walking to the door. Before she left she turned around. "Don't worry Mads, we'll get this sorted, starting with Arcadia."

"You're going there tomorrow aren't you?" Mads looked up from the floor and asked.

"Yes, that's right. We're all set."

"Okay, good luck."

Nikka left Mads' office and as she walked past Larkin's desk she turned and gave him a quick but sharp 'death stare'. It was a deliberate, silent gesture, and it caused Larkin to stop saying what he was about to say. He also noticed Johannson was not carrying the folder she had arrived with.

Thursday, 17th January 2205

Paul, Nikka, and Finn exited *Nostradamus* after landing on Arcadia and stood next to the loading platform watching the automated unload/load system at work on the spaceship. The robotic mechanisms performed their tasks as a silent symphony of synchronised movement. It was hypnotic. Each fragmented step progressed fluidly and almost without sound. On this trip to Arcadia it was mostly unloading, mainly supplies for the four personnel stationed at The Bibliotek's site.

"Okay," Bradshaw said to the others after a while. "As I mentioned in the pre-flight briefing, we have to be sitting back inside the ship, strapped in, no later than two hours and forty-three minutes from now. It is a three-hour turnaround, and the doors are locked ten minutes from lift-off."

"Remind me, when do the three hours start from?" asked Nikka.

"The clock started ticking the moment the engines shut down after landing. Now, if we get separated you are on your own because there's no way I can stop this thing from taking off. Finn, is your voice app operational?" said Bradshaw.

"It's not an app, Paul, but yes, it's working just fine, as you can hear," replied Finn's holograph as he signed to Bradshaw. "I have plenty of charge on the pad, and I can set the timer." He also wanted to tell Bradshaw that he was the only reason Finn had to use his data pad to communicate on this trip, because Nikka had become almost fluent in BSL, something Bradshaw had not even attempted to do. But for now at least, he felt it prudent to hold his tongue.

"That's good, but I've also got these little boys," said Bradshaw, taking three timers out of his shoulder bag. They had straps and looked like wristwatches. "I've already set these, and they're on. They give off a thirty-minute warning of your deadline for reboarding, then a fifteen-minute warning, then a five, then a countdown from sixty seconds. Hopefully it's overkill, but it's better to be over prepared than under. Strap them on your wrist."

Nikka and Finn strapped their respective timers on, then Bradshaw continued. "Now, can we just make sure we're synced." At this, each of them held their wrists together. The timers were all on and the countdowns matched. "Okay, let's go."

The three of them exited the launch pad proper, then made their way out of the facility and stood together outside. The light outside was dusk-like. Bradshaw let his two colleagues adjust their eyes and their senses for a minute. They were experiencing an Arcadian sunset and it was spectacular. The sky was producing a light purple hue, with slowly spinning, long, thin wispy clouds that gave off smaller clouds as they spun, all reflecting a gentle mauve light. And flying around everywhere, just a few metres off the dark brown dirt and rocky ground, were many small dark-winged hard-shelled creatures, all making a soft clicking sound. On the ground were massive flat tree-like plants with branches spreading outwards along the ground. So many branches it was impossible to discern whether they had trunks.

"Wow," signed Finn.

"Yep," signed Nikka, matter-of-factly. "That's wild."

"Okay, time's running down. Can you see that line of white posts out there?" Bradshaw asked his colleagues, pointing to a row of spaced, white poles sticking out of the ground about a kilometre away from the launch facility. "That's the edge of our site. Beyond that line is the Norwegian Government's site, and over that small rise in the distance is their launch pad. They don't use it as often as we do ours, and I'm not even sure if anyone is there right now. Over on our left is our command base, and beyond that, just in front of that ridge line, is the greenhouse," said Bradshaw, pointing out the large white dome off to the side of the mainframe facility. "And that's it, basically."

"You said before there are only four staff up here usually on a permanent basis," said Nikka.

"That's right. Two in the command centre and two in the greenhouse," said Bradshaw. "They rotate 12-hourly shifts, but there are off-days every ten."

"How long does it take to get to the other launch pad?" asked Nikka.

"From here I'm told it's about a fifteen-minute walk. You want to check it out?" replied Bradshaw.

"At some stage, yes," replied Nikka.

"Well I have to go to the mainframe facility and sign us in the Visitors Log. So let's split up now and I can join you afterwards," said Bradshaw.

"Paul," said Finn's holograph, "I'm sure you know what you're doing, but how certain are you of the three hours? I mean, we don't want to miss the bus because of a wrong button."

"See that, Finn?" replied Bradshaw, turning around and pointing up to a small but brightly lit LED screen above the doorway where they were standing. "That's the launch countdown. I did look up at it as soon as we stepped outside to make sure. You can see it is now down to two hours and thirty-five minutes, and if you look at your timer you will see it is synced."

"Okay, just thought I'd ask," replied Finn. "I'm going to head over there," he signed, pointing to an open space between the greenhouse and the white poles. "It looks fairly large and open over there. And reasonably flat."

"No problem," said Bradshaw. "What about you, Nikka? Are you heading over to the other launch pad?"

"Yes, but first I'll come with you to the mainframe facility. I want to check it out."

Bradshaw hesitated before replying. Not for long, but long enough for Nikka to notice. "Okay, but you won't find it very exciting. And I need to talk to Commander Henderson about an admin issue. I believe he's on duty. Or at least I hope he is."

It felt to Nikka like Bradshaw was implying he needed or wanted to talk to Henderson in private, but she consciously didn't react to it. "Okay then, let's go. Catch you later, Finn."

Finn waved, signing "I'm off. See you later. This is some planet!"

Nikka and Bradshaw walked together to the mainframe facility, which also housed the command centre and habitat quarters for all staff and visitors.

"Finn is right, this is some planet," said Nikka.

"It sure is. Though I can't say I'd enjoy living here for any length of time," replied Bradshaw, looking around as they walked on a path in the dirt that was fairly worn and free of rocks.

"These bugs don't bite do they?" asked Nikka, referring to the bird-size creatures flying around the site, seemingly haphazardly.

"No they don't. Or at least they haven't bitten anyone yet or even looked like attacking. They just seem to be interested in feeding on smaller flying bugs," answered Bradshaw.

"And what about the sun? How much daylight do we have left?"

"Sunset stretches for about five hours or so. I think we're in the early part. The change in light is not noticeable. We should be gone before it gets really proper dark. In fact, we'll be back on Earth at The Bibliotek before that happens."

They were almost at the mainframe facility when Nikka noticed the air-conditioning units. "So we aren't open to the outside air?"

"No we're not. The smell gets to you after a while, apparently. But it's more to do with the dust. We need to maintain a secure and dust-free environment. It seems the soil has a few contaminants that are not good for any type of metal or plastic, especially our mainframe."

At the mainframe facility there was an automatic door which opened when Bradshaw pressed a button on the exterior wall. "No security as you can see, Nikka," he said.

They entered the dust lock and the door closed behind them. Instantly, they noticed the difference in the air. Then a male voice came over the intercom.

"Hello Deputy Bibliotekar, welcome back to Arcadia," the voice said.

"Hello Commander, it's good to be back. I'm here with Nikka Johannson, Head of Security at The Bibliotek. You are in the command centre?" said Bradshaw.

"Affirmative. Hello Ms Johannson, welcome to Arcadia. Your first visit I take it?"

Nikka perceived a quiver in Commander Henderson's voice. *He's trying to work out why I'm here*, she thought. "Hello Commander Henderson. It's Rolf isn't it?"

"Yes, that's right."

"Yes, this is my first visit. Very interesting so far," she answered, aware his voice had also become a little wary.

"Good. Deputy Bibliotekar, as I said, I am very much in the command centre. I will see you shortly. I have greenlit the access door."

"Thanks, Rolf," replied Bradshaw. He then muted the intercom.

"Henderson has been here a while," he said to Nikka. "He's almost at the end of his rotation, so he might be a little..."

"Off?"

"That would be a good word, yes. Off."

"Thanks for the warning."

When they finished putting on their assigned protective coats and slippers, Nikka and Bradshaw were just about to exit the dust lock and go through the vacuum routine when she gently reached out to the back of Bradshaw's neck and said, "Hang on, Paul, your collar's caught up on the coat, let me fit it... there, all good."

"Thanks. Got to look my best, I guess."

"Absolutely," Nikka said with a rare smile.

Finn walked around the area near the greenhouse in a daze. He had read the reports on Arcadia. He knew that the flying creatures and the bug-like creatures on the ground had so far posed no danger to anybody on Arcadia; he knew that the strange flat trees spread over sections of the ground were not poisonous; and he knew that the air was safe to breathe and the weather rarely turned nasty. But he was not prepared for the strangeness of it all, especially the intense purple aura in the near sky appearing in the sunset, growing deeper in colour by the minutes, and he began to struggle to concentrate. *Okay*, he thought, *I have just over two hours to do my thing. Focus, focus. Take some images, take some measurements.* Telling himself what to do helped him. First, he took his data pad out of his satchel and turned it on. *Thank goodness I charged it just before leaving The Bibliotek, the damn thing just soaks up power like nothing else.* He knew there was not much useful information to be retained by photographing what was around him because there was no context or point of reference, apart from the greenhouse. *But it's a start*, he told himself.

After taking some distance shots and some close-ups of the ground, he turned off the data pad, then took out his laser sight from his satchel and began to take measurements of the space he was in, sighting the laser on the greenhouse, the ridge beside it, and the white poles delineating the edge of the site. This took a little while as he had to take his measurements from different positions. It was quite a large area, and he determined that several warehouse-size buildings could fit into the flat area quite comfortably. The question remained, however, whether the ground was suitable for excavation and foundations. To answer those questions, Finn had a small, but nevertheless cumbersome and heavy, ground sonar system with him, and he now proceeded to take readings of the soil and what lay underneath it. He wouldn't be able to get an analysis, however, until he got back to The Bibliotek.

Just as he had finished taking his readings, he saw Nikka come out of the mainframe facility, so he waved to her and started to walk to a point where they would meet. He wanted to go with her to the other launch facility.

"How did you go, Finn?" Nikka signed as Finn approached.

"This place is unreal, it really is. Look at that sunset! But the air; phew!" signed Finn in reply. "This area," he signed, waving his arm towards where he had been measuring, "is certainly large enough for a repository to be constructed. But I won't know for certain if one is theoretically possible until I can analyse the underground measurements back home."

"Theoretically?"

"Yes, theoretically. You know I don't see any need to be doing this, apart from the issue with the Secondary Repositories. But in any event, it's all just theory until a cost-benefit analysis can be done. I also need to do some calculations based on the size of the area. These will inform any estimates of construction costs. And I need to work out if the materials we've used so far for the mainframe facility will be adequate. I suspect they won't be. But all of that won't be a problem to work out. How did you go with Paul? I got the impression he didn't want you to go with him. Looking over his shoulder, were you?"

Nikka looked at Finn as they walked and gave a little smile. She quite liked Finn. "You can be very perceptive when you want to be, Finn," she signed.

"I am always perceptive, Nikka," he signed. "It's one of the advantages of being Deaf," he continued as he smiled back at her. "So, I'm right then."

"Yes, he got more agitated the longer I hung around, so he had to ask me to leave."

"What did he say?"

"He said, 'sorry Nikka, but I need to talk to Rolf in private, if you don't mind'. So I said oh, sure, no problem, I'll catch up with you later."

"Ha! I wonder what was sooo important he needed to talk to Robinson Crusoe here in private. Anyway, how's your assessment going?"

"This place is Hicksville. The word 'security' does not exist on this planet."

"That's not surprising though, Nikka. But I guess the real question is what would it take to turn it into a secure site?"

"Now that is the question, Finn. That is the question right there."

"And I'm guessing I'm the first to ask it."

"Yep. Our friend Paul seems not to care enough to ask it."

"And?"

"The cost would be huge. It would require a total rethink of the layout and structure of the entire facility."

"So we need to talk once we get back home?"

"Yes, it would be better if your assessment included mine, or at least took it into account."

By now they were nearing the Norwegian Government's site. There was no pathway between it and The Bibliotek's and there were no lights on at all, which meant that anyone trying to make their way here during the few hours of Arcadian night would have major problems in actually finding it. There being no lights discernible also informed them that there was nobody there.

"That's interesting," said Nikka, "I wasn't aware there was no permanent presence here."

"Or perhaps there usually is, just not right now?" asked Finn.

"That's possible, yes," replied Nikka, not realising Finn was making a joke. "But let's take a closer look, shall we?"

"Wait, Nikka," signed Finn as he stopped walking. He then put his data pad under his arm and checked the timer on his wrist. "We have fifty-two minutes left. It took us about twenty minutes to get here, thanks to there being no path. Let's allow thirty minutes to get back to the *Nostradamus*, giving us max twenty minutes here, okay?"

"Sounds good, Finn," replied Nikka.

A few minutes later they were at the launch facility. As they expected, there were no signs of anybody. Nikka pressed a button next to a doorway at the small building. The door obligingly opened, so they walked in, but she immediately turned around and checked the doorway. There was an exit button and she pressed that as well, and again the door obliged by opening.

"Okay, that tells me a lot," she said matter-of-factly.

"No security," signed Finn.

"Zero," she replied, as they stood inside looking up and around. "Let's quickly check out their other building here, then head back to the *Nostradamus*."

"Agreed."

The same access system was in place in the facility building near the launch pad. The same dust lock. But there was no power being generated within the building itself, so Nikka couldn't test to see if they could access it from the dust lock. Accordingly, they left the building and began walking back to the *Nostradamus*. As they did so, Nikka opened her bag and noticed a small green flashing light on a piece of equipment inside.

"What's up?" asked Finn.

"Nothing. Just checking to make sure I have everything," she replied.

"Yes, you wouldn't want to leave anything behind. Could be a while before you got it back."

Bradshaw was already waiting inside the *Nostradamus* when they arrived. "All good?" he asked, to which they both answered affirmatively.

"Time to go home," signed Finn.

Nikka helped Finn strap into his seat, then turned to Bradshaw and checked his straps to make sure he had done his correctly. "Nice and tight!" she said to him before stowing her gear and taking her own seat and strapping herself in tight.

A few minutes later they heard the main hatch close, seal and lock. Then, after an anxious ten minutes, there was a short robotic departure announcement before the rockets ignited and with a roar the ship lifted off the ground and out of the launch facility. And then, with only another brief warning announcement, the FTL engaged. They were back in the Earth's atmosphere before they knew it and heading for landing at The Bibliotek's spaceport.

8:35am, Friday, 18ᵗʰ January 2205

Nikka sat down in one of the chairs facing Mads' desk, placing her data pad onto it, facing Mads. "You need to hear something, Mads, and please don't ask me if it's legal. It's a recording of a conversation Paul had with Commander Henderson, in private, yesterday, on Arcadia."

"Okay," said Mads, a bit hesitantly. He got the feeling he wasn't going to like hearing it. Nikka had arrived at his suite without notice, but she had insisted on being allowed to see him. As she had just come back from Arcadia, Mads was keen to see her too, but he was not expecting this.

"Here we go," said Nikka, pressing 'Play'. There were a few seconds of muffled noise, then a conversation, crystal clear. Mads recognised the voices.

Henderson: So Mr Bradshaw, what brings you here this fine Arcadian evening?

Bradshaw: We're doing a site inspection. That's all you need to know.

Henderson: 'That's all you need to know'. Great way to talk to someone living on this rock. Why is everyone so secret squirrel these days!?

Bradshaw: You had a visit from Ingridson, I understand?

Henderson: I'm fine thanks. Thanks for asking. And you? Yes, I had a visit from the Bibliotekar, what of it?"

Bradshaw: I want you to tell me exactly what you two spoke about whilst he was here.

Henderson: What's it to you? I don't report to you. I'm getting tired of all this."

Bradshaw: You may not report to me now, but you will be soon, I can guarantee you that. And you really don't want to be getting off on the wrong foot with me. Do you get my drift?

Henderson: What is your problem, Mr Bradshaw?

Bradshaw: My problem is you right now. And when I am Bibliotekar I will be getting rid of all my problems. Am I getting through to you?

[Silence for four seconds]

Henderson: What is it with you people? First some goon here for who knows what reason threatens me, then the Bibliotekar threatens me, now you. Are you a tag team or something?

Bradshaw: Hardly. What did he threaten you about?

Henderson: Who? The goon or Mr Ingridson?

Bradshaw: We'll start with Ingridson.

Henderson: He told me my rotation wouldn't be happening unless I told him why the geosurvey team wasn't recorded in the Visitors Log.

[Silence for three seconds]

Bradshaw: What did you say?

Henderson: I told him the truth. That joy boy Joyce had insisted it wasn't necessary for them to do so, and when I protested one of the guys on the team basically threatened me with physical harm if I didn't shut it. He looked more like a boxer than a geologist. So I did shut it.

Bradshaw: Now that wasn't too hard was it?

Henderson: Fuck you, Bradshaw. Next shuttle I'm on it. I've had this place and I've had you and everyone other book-loving motherfucker. I don't need your shit.

Bradshaw: Alright, Commander, calm down. No-one's having a go at you.

Henderson: Seriously? I might be paranoid from being stuck on this shit assignment for so long, but I've still good hearing. Got any more questions?

Bradshaw: Just one. What was the geosurvey team doing here?

Henderson: How the fuck do I know!? Don't you?!

Bradshaw: I just wanted to hear it from you.

Henderson: Well, you heard. Now, fuck off. I've got work to do. And make sure you sign the bloody Visitors Log on your way out. For you and your book buddies.

Bradshaw: Funny guy.

Henderson: Anyway, why don't you ask Joyce about his pals?

Bradshaw: Doctor Joyce is no longer with us.

Henderson: Eh?

Bradshaw: He resigned after he rotated back to Earth.

Henderson: Ha! Well how about that. Maybe I will too.

Bradshaw: Perhaps you should.

Nikka tapped her data pad. "That's it."

"I'm not going to even ask how you got that recorded," said Mads.

"Simple micro transmitter to a receiver in my bag. It wasn't that hard to plant it on Paul and retrieve it later," answered Nikka. She could tell Mads was troubled perhaps more about the method than the result. "Some things are best done without seeking your approval," she added. "That way if I screw up it doesn't come back to you."

"I see... Well I'm glad you got it. A very revealing conversation, that was," said Mads.

"Yes, we now know three things thanks to Paul's mouth. One: he's involved with Carlson and, possibly, Thurldottir. Two: he seems to be under the impression he will soon be the Bibliotekar..."

"Yes, that is very interesting. And definitely news to me," interrupted Mads.

"And three: he doesn't know about the palladium and rhodium. Which also tells me he is being kept on a very short leash by Carlson."

"I think you're right about that, Nikka," replied Mads. "Can I have that recording?"

"Of course. What do you want to do about Bradshaw?"

"Nothing yet. But I do want to bring Doctor Foote in on this. Can you spare me a few more minutes?"

"Yes, of course," replied Nikka.

Mads rang Justin and after he ascertained his whereabouts asked him to come to his office. A little while later Larkin called to say that Dr Foote had arrived. "Yes, we're waiting for him," answered Mads.

Justin entered Mads' office and paused for a little bit as he closed the door. "What's up?" asked Mads.

"Your assistant, Larkin, gave me a strange look," said Justin.

"Oh? What kind of look?" asked Mads as he motioned for Justin to sit in the chair opposite Nikka.

"Hello Nikka," he said to her as he sat down.

"Justin," she replied.

"He had a pained expression. Not one I had seen on his face before," Justin said to Mads.

"I see... Yes, normally he's got that stupid grin on his face — that 'I'm smarter than you but you don't know it' look. Well let's not dwell on that. Although,... neither of you were scheduled to be here according to my diary, so perhaps that's why he's feeling a bit antsy. Anyway Justin, there's something I want you to listen to," said Mads.

Mads watched Justin as he listened to Nikka's recording and noticed he maintained an impassive face but did raise an eyebrow. "What do you think Justin?" he asked.

"First I need to ask you why Henderson said you had threatened him, if you don't mind Bibliotekar?" offered Justin.

"No problem. When I was there for the dummy DRP test, I examined the outwards data log because I had been tipped off by

Nikka that Henderson was using the comms link for an inappropriate reason — sending videos of his life on Arcadia and publishing them on the internet. He knew he was in trouble for that, and as far as I am aware the sanction could be, at our discretion, a deferral of his rotation. That's correct isn't it, Justin?"

"Yes, absolutely."

"So, yes, I held that over his head and only lowered it when he decided to be honest with me and tell me what had transpired with Doctor Joyce."

"Thank you, Bibliotekar. I just needed to be clear on that because I gather this is an official meeting? I mean, this discussion we're having right now?"

"Hmm, tricky. Okay, yes, official but confidential for the time being. Is that acceptable?" asked Mads.

"Yes, Bibliotekar," answered Foote.

"Good, and the rest?"

"This conversation constitutes grounds for dismissal of the Deputy Bibliotekar, without any doubt. The threat he made to Henderson alone is an abuse of his position. On top of that, the subject matter is potential evidence that the Deputy Bibliotekar is in breach of the part of his contract that requires him to fully devote himself to actions and behaviours in fulfilling his role at and for the benefit of The Bibliotek. In simple terms he is not permitted to have a private agenda. He can aspire to be Bibliotekar — that is actually expected of him — but this conversation indicates something else is going on apart from the normal course of events which, by definition, provide no guarantee of promotion to the position, only a right to be fairly considered."

"Officially," said Mads, "am I on solid ground for holding back on taking action against Bradshaw for now, to allow myself time to investigate what that 'something else' is?" asked Mads.

"Yes, I am quite confident of that. I say that because the issue involves your position as Bibliotekar and I assume there are no questions being raised about it, officially," answered Foote.

"That's correct, Justin, and the minutes of the Governing Council will attest to that," said Mads.

"I will, however, need to make my own note of this meeting and obtain a copy of the recording, Nikka," said Foote.

"That will be done today. I won't send it on the system, instead it will be hand-delivered to you personally," replied Nikka.

"I'm okay with you making a note of this meeting, Justin, but can we keep the P&R thing out of it?" asked Mads.

"Yes I can, and will. It would appear that the Deputy Bibliotekar is not aware of it in any event," replied Foote.

"That's the conclusion we came to as well, Justin," said Nikka, to which Mads nodded in agreement.

"Okay, so I take it Bibliotekar that you are tasking Nikka to investigate the 'something else'?" asked Foote.

Mads looked at Nikka, who nodded to him. "Yes, she will handle it. Covertly, unfortunately, but necessarily so."

"Understood," said Foote. "Is that all for now?"

"Yes thanks Justin, but can you do me a favour on your way out?" asked Mads.

"Yes?" asked Foote quizzically.

"I'm going to assume that my young assistant Larkin is currently worrying that he is the subject of this meeting. Don't ask me why I think that, but as you go past his desk can you give him a look that says we were indeed talking about him?" said Mads.

Foote looked a little surprised, but said "Yes, I can do that," and proceeded to do so.

Mads was right. Larkin was thinking just that, and had it confirmed in his own mind when he got a cold stare from Foote as he walked past his desk on his way out of Mads' suite. Meanwhile, Nikka had a quick question for Mads given the conversation they had just had with Foote.

"Can I ask, Mads, if you have told Justin or anyone else in HR about Smits and de Jong?"

"Not yet, Nikka, You need to watch and wait. And just deal with me on it for now."

"Shall do."

"Now what about Arcadia, how did you and Finn go?" asked Mads.

Nikka gave Mads a rundown on what they had found out about the suitability of Arcadia as either a site for a Secondary Repository or for a partial relocation of the Central Repository.

"Do me a favour and don't hold back on the overall security cost estimate," said Mads.

"Understood, Mads. Sorry, but I need to get going. Do you want me to give your young friend another death stare?" asked Nikka as she got up and walked to the door.

"If you want," smiled Mads.

10:16am, Thursday, 24ᵗʰ January 2205

It wasn't long before Rafe received the Conservators' report on Ruben's *Fabrica*. With it came a personal note of congratulations from Violetta. Her team had given *Fabrica* a priority examination, given the circumstances, had taken note of his concerns about it, had subjected it to the usual barrage of tests, and had reached a definitive conclusion — the book was genuine. They had also taken note of the issue with the painting of illustrations done by hand post-printing and had thoroughly analysed the work performed. There was no doubt about it, it was the real deal. Rafe read the detailed report of the examination again. Then again. Then he sent a copy each to Ruben and Professor Sarkozy. A little part of him was disappointed the book was not a fake. But after a while he contemplated that maybe he had been in the job too long and he had become too cynical and too wary. This he quietly considered to himself as he made the obligatory entries for the Conservators for the Master Catalogue after completing the process of organising the Tax Certificate for Ruben. Three million eight hundred thousand Euros. Rafe was not upset at blowing the entire Spanish budget, and then some, on one book. At the end of the day, he had procured a fantastic addition to the Central Repository, without trying, and whilst having a break. *It doesn't get better than that*, he told himself. But then Rafe reminded himself. It will get better than Ruben's *Fabrica* if he managed to locate and procure the Lost Library of Ivan The Formidable. *That* would be the Find of his career, *if* he beat Ruben to it.

11:12pm, Friday, 8ᵗʰ February 2205

"**V**ie, what do you know of the Lost Library of Ivan The Formidable?" asked Mads contemplatively as he held Violetta's foot out of the bathwater and massaged it."

"Mmm, that's... sooo... nice," she cooed. "The what, darling?"

"The Lost Library of Ivan The Formidable," Mads repeated, stopping the work of his fingers and staring instead at Violetta lying at the other end of the steaming bath.

"Oh! Don't stop, Mads," she implored.

"Answer the question young lady," Mads teased.

Violetta opened her eyes and looked at Mads. "You're serious."

"I am."

"The only 'Lost Library of Ivan' I know of is the one that Ivan The Terrible somehow managed to lose," Violetta said tiredly.

"It's not 'Ivan *The Terrible*' — you don't want any Russians hear you call him that. It's 'Ivan *The Formidable*'. You're confusing the misnomer with the fact," said Mads, a little pained.

"Whatever. He was still pretty violent, even by Middle Age standards."

"Did they not teach you anything in school?" an exasperated Mads asked. "Ivan the Fourth, to give him his formal title, was born *after* the Middle Ages, and he was no more violent than any other ruler of his time. And besides, ask any Russian why the country venerates the man and it won't be because of the trite lazy label some Western translator has given him, it will be because he united the country for the first time, amongst other formidable achievements, such as introducing the printing press to Russia." Mads could see Violetta had lost interest. She had closed her eyes again. "Anyway, we're getting off track. The question was, have you heard of his lost library?"

"Whatever, Mads," repeated Violetta, without opening her eyes. "The mythical Lost Library of Ivan The Formidable, the Fearsome, the Almighty, the Great, the One and Only, the Terrible, the Whatever, is just that. A myth. A story that many want to be true, like kids and their Santa Claus and their Easter Bunny. That's what I know. Why?" she asked.

Mads shifted slightly at his end of the bath, picked up her other foot and slowly began to massage it. Left fingers pressing the sole in front of her heel, right fingers pressing the toes, one by one, in a slow sequence, in time with the left fingers. "Rafe thinks he may have discovered where it is, that's why."

"What? Don't you mean 'Rafe thinks it may exist'?" asked Violetta.

"Both."

"Explain please."

"Rafe is probably the greatest book detective the world has ever seen. I've known that for some time. He's got a long history of tracking down volumes and collections thought lost forever. To our benefit, to The Bibliotek's. To be able to do that requires a good balance of open-mindedness and scepticism. It's been a fair while since anyone has taken Rafe for a ride, that's for sure," noted Mads with a measure of pride.

"Yes, yes, so Rafe is good at his job, he's proved that just with the Giordano Collection last year and the *Fabrica* last month. Both were pretty amazing."

"Good. So you agree he knows what he's doing."

"But what's the connection with the Lost Library?"

"Rafe has never dismissed the concept of the Lost Library as a myth, which, by the way, isn't about the ruler of Russia 'losing' his library. It's about a great library of ancient Greek texts that disappeared sometime after he died. Rafe's always been of the mind that it's a negative that can't be proven. Which means he's always been open to the possibility that positive evidence exists. And now he believes he has found such evidence that points to the myth instead being a fact, and a fact that can be proven by finding the library itself. Which is to also say he thinks he knows where to find it."

"Mads, that just sounds like philosophical mumbo-jumbo," retorted Violetta. "I had the impression that Rafe was more of a realist than that."

"To you it might sound like that, but I've known Rafe for many years and I know the way he operates. So when he tells me that something he has been studying for almost as long as he's been a Finder has recently produced some tangible results, I know it's the real deal."

"Well, all I know is the whole legend is fantastic in the extreme, and the sceptic in me has always believed it is far too extreme to be taken seriously."

"I get that, but if it's true — if there is a Lost Library of Ivan The Formidable *and* it *is* the books that are said to be in it *and* Rafe does find it — that will be more than fantastic. That would be..."

"Unbelievable," finished Violetta.

"Hmm, there's no point having this discussion. You're just a closed mind," answered Mads, as he dropped Violetta's foot and made to stand up.

"Wait Mads, don't stop. Tell me more. I promise to listen. Please? I'll be a good girl," said Violetta in that voice that always worked its effect on Mads. He knew what she had in mind.

"Okay then, when Rafe gets back from the monastery, we'll see who's laughing."

"Monastery? What monastery? I thought the library was supposed to be buried somewhere under the Kremlin?" asked Violetta, suddenly interested.

"That's the myth part of the popular myth, says Rafe. No, he believes the library has been stored all this time in one of the mausoleums next to the Assumption Cathedral."

"What? The cathedral in Moscow?"

"Oh, so you *do* know something about Russia," Mads said a bit sarcastically. "No, the replica Ivan commissioned at the Trinity Lavra of Saint Sergius Monastery at Sergiyev, north-east of Moscow."

"And Rafe is going there now?"

"Soon. He's going next Tuesday."

"And then we'll see who's 'myth-taken', won't we?" said Violetta with one of her small but wicked smiles.

"Oh, that's terrible!"

"No, my darling Mads, that's *formidable!* There is a difference, you know. Now we can go to bed and I'll show you something even more formidable."

END OF CHAPTER ELEVEN

Chapter Twelve

Rafe Finds Out

"They say that Caliph Omar, when consulted about what had to be done with the library of Alexandria, answered as follows: 'If the books of this library contain matters opposed to the Koran, they are bad and must be burned. If they contain only the doctrine of the Koran, burn them anyway, for they are superfluous.' Our learned men have cited this reasoning as the height of absurdity. However, suppose Gregory the Great was there instead of Omar and the Gospel instead of the Koran. The library would still have been burned, and that might well have been the finest moment in the life of this illustrious pontiff."
Jean-Jacques Rousseau, *Discourse on the Sciences and Arts*, 1750

3:20pm, Tuesday, 12ᵗʰ February 2205

Rafe's heliojet was on its landing descent into Moscow's ambitiously-named, for now, Cosmoport Gagarin, but he wasn't as excited as he expected to be. Perhaps it was the recent events that occupied his mind. Perhaps it was because he had begun, yet again, to question the merit if not the ethics of his years-long search for the so-called Lost Library of Ivan The Formidable. Such thoughts had arisen ever since he had the first indications that not only was the library not a myth but instead had been real, that it still existed, and that its location was potentially close to his discovery. Those first indications had arisen not long before his encounter with Ruben in Spain, but now his efforts, were they to continue, had been given a new impetus by Ruben's disclosure of his similar search for the fabled library. But there were still those doubts about the efficacy of the exercise troubling Rafe. A 'lost' library implied something to Rafe that was intact and possibly safe. Safe from environmental harm and safe from the Present Sect. Safe from everyone because no-one knew its whereabouts. That could potentially be the case if *the* Lost Library, or even just parts of it, was not actually 'lost' in the literal sense but instead was being secretly cared for by someone, or something. Rafe considered this to be more of a possibility than the chance that the Lost Library was truly 'lost'; lying unforgotten somewhere, even buried.

If it were to eventuate that the library was indeed truly lost, Rafe would have no qualms about finding it, as it would potentially mean that its discovery would save whatever was left of it from the ravages of time, dust, and moisture. It was this possibility that egged Rafe on, more than the fact that Ruben was competition. But despite being excited by the chase of the fantastic truth, he had still begun to wonder as he got closer to it whether it was the right thing to do; if finding the Lost Library of Ivan The Formidable and revealing it to the world would expose it to the risk of being a target, because the more fantastic, the greater the significance of finding such a cache of ancient literature, the greater the exposure to the risk of coming to the attention of the Present Sect, and, in recent months, Rafe had been receiving signals, one more direct than others, that the Present Sect was beginning to target the ongoing work of The Bibliotek in securing the books produced by humankind.

But he needed to know, he told himself. He needed to know if some of that targeting was being assisted by someone treacherous in intent at The Bibliotek, and the mere fact that a Find such as the Lost Library of Ivan The Formidable would be a target of that treachery made it a candidate for what he had in mind. He was not new to ulterior motives, that much he conceded to himself, but this was the first time he had hidden them from a friend. More to the point his closest friend on the planet. But, as he also told himself, it was because of that friendship it needed to be done and done in this way. It made him feel like a shady promoter of a fantastic scheme. He knew it was 'out there', but he needed to make it as feasible, as real, as he could. He needed to sound, if not be, totally convincing to Mads.

And he had to admit to himself that the impetus provided by Ruben was not only to continue his search, but also to take the first steps in actually locating the Lost Library. It had been a shock to listen to Ruben talk of his own search for it. He well understood Ruben's zeal, and as much as Rafe liked him, the last thing he wanted to see was Ruben finding the Lost Library and not him. He would consider that a failure on his part, after so many years of being on its trail.

Mads had been pleasantly surprised the week before when Rafe had told him where he was going and why. "Not the Vatican?" he had asked.

"No Mads, not the Vatican," Rafe had replied.

As Mads was aware, for a long time Rafe had investigated a theory he had come up with that the books making the foundation of the so-called Lost Library of Ivan The Formidable had never actually arrived

287

in Moscow with their supposed original owner, Sophia Palaiologos, as part of the dowry for her marriage in 1472 to Ivan III, who together would become the grandparents of Ivan The Formidable. His theory was contrary to widely and long-held opinion, but Rafe had a notion that the books in question never left the Vatican, where Sophia had lived from 1465 until her departure to Moscow and marriage.

Rafe for a long time could not bring himself to believe that Sophia's dowry had included the hundreds of books that her father, Thomas Palaiologos, had apparently rescued from the Library of Constantinople in 1453, on the cusp of the fall and sacking of the city by the Turkish army of the 21-year old Sultan Mehmed II.

Rafe's reasoning was sound and even Mads could see it was worthwhile pursuing. He had listened to Rafe explain that he found it hard to believe that Pope Sixtus IV would have allowed the collection of hundreds of ancient manuscripts from the Library of Constantinople to leave the safety and sanctity of the Vatican. Rafe had argued that it was a crucial time for the Holy See, and that successive Popes had each, in their own way, sought to establish the Vatican as the world's centre of not only (the one true) religion but also of literature and the arts. It was Sixtus, Rafe had told Mads, who had formally established the Vatican Library which, a mere three years after Sophia had left to marry Ivan, held the largest collection of Greek manuscripts in the world.

Where did they come from? Rafe had asked himself. He knew that Sophia's father was not the only person to take hundreds of books from the Library of Constantinople to save them from the dreaded Ottoman hordes. The Pope at that time, Nicholas V, a longstanding bibliophile, had done the same thing and it was he who initiated the planning and designing of the Vatican Library. It was also he who had engaged the great Lorenzo Valla to translate the Constantinople Library books from Greek into Latin, and it was this collection that helped form the basis of the Vatican Library when it was finally completed just after Sophia was supposed to have departed the Vatican with her father's collection of Constantinople Library books. To Rafe it seemed very unlikely that Sixtus would have approved the inclusion of them in her dowry. In Rafe's view, there was no reason to, given the 6,000 ducats he *did* approve for this purpose.

But, try as he might, and as Mads well knew, Rafe had been consistently denied the opportunity to test the truth of his theory and this was because the Vatican steadfastly refused him permission to enter the long-closed Vatican Library to conduct his research and test his theory. Despite the ravages of the Great Holy War, or perhaps because of them, the Vatican had adopted the policy of pretending The Bibliotek did not exist. The Great Holy War had decimated the Catholic Church of its power and influence across the globe, and after the assassination of Pope Julia in 2092, the third Pope in a row to meet that fate, no successor had ever been appointed. But Rafe had kept researching and kept up his efforts, albeit diminished over time, to gain permission to enter the Vatican Library, which by now had been locked up and heavily guarded for decades. The Vatican had also long ago ceased its digitisation of the contents of the Library. That vast project was now simply beyond its resources and desire, and yet all attempts of The Bibliotek to be allowed to assist in the project's rejuvenation and ultimate completion had come to nought. Even Mads had taken it off his 'To Do List', and the Governing Council had stopped asking for updates. Rafe had finally stopped submitting requests for access to the Vatican Library when he became aware, by a judiciously accidental slip or an official's tongue, of the Vatican's suspicion of his motives. Apparently, researching the fabled Lost Library of Ivan The Formidable was too fantastic an endeavour to credit, and instead it was believed by those holding the keys to the Vatican Library that what Rafe really wanted to do was scour its contents for treasures to procure, or even steal, for The Bibliotek.

"So, what changed?" Mads had asked Rafe when his friend had told him of his impending trip to Moscow.

Rafe had replied that despite his years of research carefully piecing together a jigsaw-like puzzle, it was by mere chance that one piece of information he had come across had led him to reconsider the possibility that Sophia Palaiologos had in fact been allowed to leave the Vatican with at least a fair portion of her father's Constantinople books, if not all of them. He related to Mads that about nine months ago he had gone to Mount Athos in Greece to what was left of the Vatopedi Monastery to negotiate the procurement of a number of incunables left over after the British Library and the Bibliothèque nationale de France had already extracted the main part of the contents of the monastery's war-ravaged library. The incunables that had been left behind were damaged and Rafe offered to take them to

The Bibliotek as it had the resources to repair and thus preserve them.

Whilst he was at the monastery examining the manuscripts, he had been given access to the monastery's archives to investigate their provenance and origins, and it was there that he had discovered a bundle of letters written in the early to mid-16th century, neatly tied together in its original string binding, all apparently pertaining to the decision of the then abbot of the monastery to send a monk with the ordained name of Maximus to Moscow. This had been in response to a request made in 1518 by Vasili III, the Grand Prince of Moscow and the eldest son of Sophia out of nine children borne by her. It seemed Vasili wanted some ancient Greek religious texts in his possession translated into Slavic. Maximus agreed to go and to perform the task, which he did, but had he known that he would never be allowed to return home from Moscow afterwards perhaps he would have changed his mind. As it turned out he was eventually sent by Vasili to live at the Trinity Lavra of St Sergius Monastery at Sergiyev, not far to the north-east of Moscow, where he died in 1556 during the reign of Vasili's son, Ivan IV — otherwise known as Ivan The Formidable. And it was there in amongst the bundle of letters that Rafe found one letter in particular that had to have been smuggled out of Russia, as it had been written in Latin so as to disguise its contents. It was from Maximus to the abbot beseeching him to seek the diplomatic co-operation of the Vatican to obtain his release from Russia so that he could return home to the Vatopedi monastery. And it was in that letter that Maximus described the efforts he had been forced to make in translating not just a few, but *several hundred* ancient Greek manuscripts that Ivan The Formidable had arranged to be brought to Maximus at the Trinity Monastery.

That was the one piece of information that had galvanised Rafe's thinking. Not only that, it was new information that, until he had told Mads, only Rafe, its discoverer, knew anything about or its significance. Nobody else searching for the Lost Library, a search that had started over three hundred years ago, had been able to ascertain anything more than hints and suggestions about what Maximus had been forced to translate.

Then there was the evidence surrounding Boris Godunov.

"Boris Godunov?" had asked Mads.

"Yes, Mads," Rafe had replied. He had then explained that Godunov was the last Tsar before that terrible period that had beset Russia known as The Time of Troubles arose. Godunov's wife and son had been murdered right at the start of that period of great unrest and anarchy, and the Kremlin had been looted. Rafe explained to Mads that it was his belief Godunov took the Library of Ivan The Formidable, or more accurately by then the Library of Boris Godunov, to the Trinity Monastery for safekeeping, and that it had been there, undiscovered, ever since. Specifically, somewhere close to, or even inside, the Godunov family mausoleum in the grounds of the monastery, right next to the Assumption Church, which Ivan IV had commissioned during his reign. Godunov had built the mausoleum for his wife and son after their murder, and he was also later entombed in it several years after his death.

Boris Godunov had been a trusted friend of Ivan's. He had been appointed as counsel to Feodor I, Ivan's feeble-minded son and successor, and then became de-facto regent, then actual Tsar, so the library was his to protect and secure. It didn't just go 'missing' when Ivan died, postulated Rafe, but when Boris died Russia descended into anarchy for eight years, during which time, Rafe believed, anyone who knew about the whereabouts of the Library had died.

Mads had been interested, but not convinced. He felt it was more tenuous than the 'Vatican as keeper' line of reasoning and had challenged Rafe on it. "It's all a bit circumstantial, isn't it?" he had asked Rafe. "You really want this to be true, don't you Nags? Are you sure you haven't lost any objectiveness? Where's that cynicism I know is in you?"

"Are you finished? That's the same question, Mads, just asked in different ways," Rafe had responded. "But the answer is yes, I do want this to be true. If I have lost any of my famous objectiveness it's because after all this time spent searching and researching the primary question — did the Lost Library ever exist *at all* — I can honestly say I have not encountered any evidence, circumstantial or otherwise, that the search for its existence is a futile exercise, with no chance of success. On the contrary, there has always been that chance. Sometimes it has become less certain and sometimes it has become more certain, but it is always there."

Mads had thrown up his hands. "Fair enough Rafe, I surrender. But I thought the best line of research had been pointing to the library being buried somewhere under the Kremlin? That is, on the assumption the books did leave the Vatican with Sophia."

Rafe had then patiently responded. If that was the case, he had said (and not for the first time), it was strange that after two hundred years of searching underneath the Kremlin many artefacts had been found but nothing like any book or any indication that any books had ever been stored there.

"And in any case," Rafe had pointed out to Mads, "who in their right mind would store valuable books, or any books for that matter, in a musty, mouldy environment like that? That just doesn't make any sense and I don't know why all those countless searchers haven't factored that little bit of Physics 101 into their reckoning."

More important to Rafe, as far as he had been able to ascertain, was the apparent fact that nobody had ever examined the interior of the Godunov mausoleum or the tower of the Assumption Church it abutted.

"But I have," Rafe had told Mads.

"When?"

"Two or so months ago. Don't you remember? You rang me when I was about to fly to Moscow, to tell me about Thomas."

"I vaguely recall you mentioning something about Moscow. I was a bit stressed at the time. And?"

"The place was covered in snow and I didn't have much time to spare, just a look-see. But I did do some measurements by portable laser and guess what?"

"What?"

"The interior dimensions of the mausoleum do not match the exterior dimensions. There is a missing four square metres," Rafe had said triumphantly.

"How can there be space 'missing'?" Mads had asked.

"Mads," said Rafe, a little exasperated. He had then patiently explained, "the mausoleum's interior is four square metres less than it should be. It means there is an extra space there somewhere. A hidden room."

"Seriously? And you're going all the way back there on the strength of what your laser measurements came to?"

"Yes, I'll be there by the middle of next week. This time with more equipment."

"And you're just going to turn up with all this stuff and, what, just start digging?"

"That's the plan," said Rafe. "But not digging *per se*. This place is all above-ground, and that's important."

"You don't think maybe that some people, some of the locals perhaps, might have issues with that? Or are you proposing to do all this in the dead of night under the veil of darkness?"

"If need be, yes. But I do have a contact at the monastery, one of the few custodians left, or at least I think he is a guard, or something like that, he wears a uniform. And he seems... malleable."

"You mean willing to be bribed to let you do your thing?"

"Yes."

"Nags, I'm not hearing this."

"You worry too much Mads. And besides, what if that room does in fact hold what I think it holds. Wouldn't that be fantastic?"

"I suppose so, but what then? Have you thought that far ahead? Surely the Russian Government might want to hold onto whatever is in fact inside this secret room of yours?"

"Yes, I've thought of that, but you know as well as anybody that the way things are right now with the Tarkovsky regime, the focus is on strengthening Russia's position as the capitalist centre of the universe, and you also know as well as I do, that matters of cultural heritage have long since been pushed into the back of the regime's mind. And those in the know have told me point blank they are not interested in the fate of books that have no real connection with Russia apart from the fact they've been there for centuries. They care as much about ancient Greek literature as they do about what The Bibliotek stands for and does. So my plan is to secure whatever's there in terms of books and get them back to The Bibliotek before any announcement is made, and that the announcement will be that they were not found under the Kremlin, but elsewhere."

"I'm sorry Nags, but I'm not convinced that is a plausible plan," Mads had said in response. "Nor do I have the same level of confidence you will find anything. But,..." he sighed, "I haven't been researching this for years as you have, so I am going to let you do this, if only to allow you to resolve the issue one way or the other."

"Gee, thanks Mads, you're a peach."

"Give me a break, Nags. Now, one more question, an important one. I remember reading something a while ago that purported to be a list of the books in question. From memory, they seemed pretty amazing. Where do you stand on that?"

"Yes, I can rattle off some of that list," Rafe had replied. "Another one hundred and seven volumes, no less would you believe, of Titus Livius's *History of Rome* to add to the thirty-five that for centuries have been the only known volumes in existence, a complete original copy of Cicero's *De re Publica* to overshadow the mere fragments of four pages dispersed across the planet in various libraries including, wouldn't you know it, The Bibliotek, which holds two of those fragments, thanks to yours truly I might add, a previously unknown epic ode by Virgil, and so on and so on and so on."

"It would be amazing to find all that," said Mads.

"Yes, too amazing. All bullshit too," Nags had replied.

"How so?"

Rafe had then explained that the list Mads had referred to had come to light in the early 19th century, and at that particular time in the history of bibliophilic archaeology it just happened to be the ideal shopping list of lost ancient Greco-Roman manuscripts. "It's just too perfect of a list to be believable," Rafe had argued, "and besides, not a single manuscript in the list is mentioned in any of the letters I found in the Vatopedi archives."

"Okay then, so what exactly do you hope to find?" had then asked Mads.

"To be honest, I have no idea, but it is known that Maximus himself had taken to Moscow his own significant collection of books and these included the first books printed in Greek and other early manuscripts, and these went with him to the Trinity Monastery where he spent his last years. So even finding some or all of those would be a prize," Rafe had replied.

As Rafe's heliojet landed, he knew that a lot was at stake over the course of the next 36 hours. Mads had been right — he hadn't thought this through. And there was a lot more to think through than Mads actually knew. But at least he had given enough thought to asking Nikka to come with him, and looking across at her resolute face next to him, he was glad she had welcomed the opportunity to go on an 'exercise', as she had termed it, after Rafe had filled her in on its ulterior purpose.

Nikka returned his glance. "Rafe," said Nikka, "I am going to flash my badge at Security when we arrive, whilst you get our bags, okay?"

"Do you think that's wise?"

"Yes, I do. Call it etiquette. I am in their back yard, and even if it's for private purposes I need to let them know. Besides it will fast track our little journey through Customs and Immigration."

"Okay boss."

Nikka had been right. None of the hassles Rafe normally experienced getting out of a helioport, especially Moscow's Cosmoport Gagarin, applied to them. To Rafe's jaded self it seemed positively red-carpet, in the celebrity sense not the communist. That word 'communist' had long ceased to apply in Russia, but there were still the 'old ways' of getting things done it seemed, as was the case everywhere else Rafe travelled to.

It was late afternoon by the time they alighted from their taxi at the aptly-named Commercial Hotel, just off the Red Square. A creature of habit, Rafe always stayed there whenever he was in Moscow looking for a Find. It was a gloomy and cold day, and the mushed snow on the ground was mostly grey. It matched and blended in with the bleak yet ornate post-Communist-era façade of the hotel in the fading light.

"Nice place," observed Nikka without really looking at it. "Who's paying for this?"

"Ha, well I don't know about you, but my room's in my budget," Rafe replied.

"No problems, I have a very good friend in Accounts. You'll see me in it too," said Nikka.

"In my room?"

"In your budget," remonstrated Nikka, shaking her head. "I'm here, after all, at your request."

"Fair enough," Rafe smiled.

After checking in to their respective rooms the two met as agreed in the hotel's restaurant for dinner. Neither had wanted to venture out into the cold unless they had to, and hopefully that was not going to be the case until the following day.

At the pre-arranged time they were seated at a table in the hotel's cavernous dining room. After ordering their meal, Rafe told Nikka he had made a few phone calls.

"Okay, I'm picking up the rental hovercar at three pm tomorrow and driving back to the hotel, it's only from the next street. We'll leave after dinner."

"Why so late? Does it have to be at night?"

"Well, not that I'm looking forward to this, but if we want to test my suspicion wouldn't it be more likely that the Present Sect will show itself at night rather than during the day? They're a secretive bunch, aren't they? And besides, it gets dark around four o'clock."

"That's true, Rafe, but my concern is controlling any situation that may arise, and that's going to be much harder to do at night."

"I get that, and I agree, but bottom line is that I've been told by my contact at the monastery not to turn up before eleven pm. Actually, I was told to arrive *at* eleven, and that I would have only one hour, tops, to do whatever I planned to do.

"So we're dealing with a security guard?"

"I would use that term loosely, but yes. Custodian, security guard, something like that. It seems his shift ends at midnight. We get there at eleven, he will walk away and return just before midnight and not expect to see me."

"Does he know I am coming also?"

"No. I haven't volunteered that information and he hasn't asked if I am coming alone. But I'm not expecting it will be an issue. If it is I'll just offer him some more money. There's one more thing. This place is out of the way, and usually there's no-one there at night, so he doesn't want any of the nearby locals seeing any lights going on and off and wondering why."

"So this... 'special access'... is costing some money?"

"Ooh yeah. Euros, cash."

"How much?" asked Nikka.

"Don't worry, I have a budget for that," he replied.

"You have a budget for bribes?"

"Well, yes, don't you?"

"No, I don't! I can't believe you have a budget for that."

"We don't call it that obviously. It's called Facilitation Costs," Rafe explained, "The Bibliotek may be a not-for-profit, but we do have to deal in a for-profit world with for-profit people."

"But isn't that unethical if not illegal?"

"Nikka, I would say that in the circumstances of tomorrow night, ethics won't really be relevant from our perspective. And our access does not include any pilfering rights. That is something altogether different. I am just being allowed to make an examination, without being disturbed or questions being asked. That is all. It's not really a bribe. It is what it is— special access — as you call it."

"Fair enough. I just need to know the story."

"We drive there after dinner, like I said. We park the hovercar well outside the monastery walls, a small entry gate will be left unlocked, we go in, we find our guy, he'll be waiting for us, I pay him the money and tell him you're my assistant, he walks away, we walk to the mausoleum I told you about, we do our thing, maybe, maybe not. Depends on who is there, or not."

"That last bit is a bit vague, Rafe."

"You've heard of the saying 'play it by ear'?" he replied.

"Yes, of course," Nikka responded.

"Good," said Rafe.

"You don't speak Russian, do you Rafe?" asked Nikka.

"No, I don't, but fortunately my friend speaks fairly good English."

"What's his name?"

"Sasha."

"Do you trust him?"

"I trust him enough that he will be there at eleven and that we will get our one hour for the agreed price. Anything more than that, no. And that is why he knows me as John."

"I get the picture. I guess that will have to do. Now, draw me a diagram of the layout, from the gate to the mausoleum," Nikka said, taking a pen and a piece of paper from a jacket pocket. Rafe complied. Nikka asked him about distances, whether there were any trees around, a path, and basically anything else in order to get a feel for the place, especially as it was going to be dark. "You mentioned your friend Sasha doesn't want any lights going on and off but is there any lighting there at all that's left on at night, like lamp poles?"

"Not that I know off," replied Rafe.

"Good thing we brought torches then," said Nikka.

"Yes, but we'll need to take care how we use them. Anyone seeing torch beams must assume it is just security."

"I get that. One last thing, Rafe. Have you told anybody about this plan of yours, apart from me? Justin Foote?"

"No, nobody. We're on our own, so to speak. Is that an issue?"

"Let's hope not."

10:58pm, Wednesday, 13th February 2205

Not a sound could be heard as they walked towards the gate, apart from the crunching of the fresh snow under their feet. Rafe and Nikka had parked the rental hovercar around a corner, next to some trees and away from any houses. As they got close to the gate they could see that it was open and there was a figure standing outside it, clapping his hands slowly, either to keep warm or to hurry Rafe and Nikka along. Or both. It was freezing cold.

"Hello John, who is this?" Sasha said, motioning his head at Nikka.

"Hello Sasha, this is Julie, my assistant. Not a problem I hope?"

"No, but you should have told me it wasn't going to be just you."

"I'm sorry but you didn't ask. We still have a deal, right?"

"Yes, yes, but make sure you are gone before midnight. That is the deal, okay?"

"Okay. Here's the money," said Rafe handing Sasha an envelope.

"It is Euros?"

"Yes, Sasha, as you requested. Twenties and fifties, all old, as you also requested."

"Good. Okay in you go. I will not see you later," Sasha motioned with his hand, then closed the gate behind them but did not lock it, then started walking away.

"Just one more thing, Sasha. Is there anybody else in here tonight?"

Sasha stopped. Then he slowly turned around to face them again. "What do you mean?"

"I mean have you let anybody else in?"

"No no no, just you. And your friend. Now please go."

With that, Rafe and Nikka went through the gate, paused and turned around. Sasha was already walking away again, only this time a little quicker.

"He seemed agitated, Rafe, and not just about me," Nikka said quietly.

Rafe was keeping his gaze on Sasha's back as he disappeared into the cold dark gloom and out of hearing. "You're right. I didn't like the sound of that."

"Let's assume it means what we think it means, said Nikka, quietly but firmly. "Let's go, and remember what I said. Walk slowly and deliberately, and don't freak out if you see someone. Keep your torchlight on the ground. Whatever you do, if you see someone, don't flash your torch in their eyes. Just stand still and wait for them to move. I will be right behind you but not too close. Okay?"

"Yes, bwana."

"What?"

"Yes, Nikka. Let's do this."

It wasn't long before it became obvious to Rafe that there was a lamp post near the mausoleum, and that it was shining a broad beam of light right in front of the mausoleum door. In the light Rafe could see that it had started to snow again. He cursed himself because he had not recalled the lamp being there when he had drawn Nikka the diagram the night before. He was about to turn around to her and apologise when he saw two large human shapes appear out of the darkness beside the mausoleum and slowly walk around to the front of it. They came into the light and Rafe could see they were dressed completely in black and their faces were covered. Before he had decided what to do: keep walking, stand still as Nikka had told him to do, or turn and run, two small pops sounded behind and beside him in quick succession, and both figures in black fell to the ground. The one closer to him fell backwards, following the snap back of his head and was not moving, but the other one fell forward onto the snow and began writhing in pain, clutching the side of his stomach. It had to be a 'he' given the noise he was making.

Rafe had yet to move, frozen, when Nikka walked past him a few seconds later, holding her silenced pistol out in front of her. Rafe could smell the cordite from the shots she had fired. Nikka went over to the first body and with her pistol still trained on it she took the glove off her other hand using her teeth and checked for a sign of life with two fingers touching the body's neck. She then stood up straight again, unscrewed the silencer which she then placed in a pocket in her jacket and slammed her pistol in a shoulder holster under her jacket. "Are you alright, Rafe?" she asked, as she walked over to the second person, without waiting for a reply.

"Did you really have to do that!?" Rafe said, coming out of his shock. "I didn't know you had a gun!"

"Check the dead guy, Rafe. He has a gun in his hand and the safety is off. So yes, it seems I did have to do that." After making sure the second man she shot was unarmed, Nikka whipped off his balaclava. It was a man in his mid to late twenties. "Как зовут?" she asked as she knelt beside him and checked his wound.

"How do you know he's Russian?" Rafe asked, looking on.

"За что ты меня?!" the young man shouted at Nikka, who then looked at Rafe with a 'does that answer your question?' expression.

"Я помогу тебе, но мне нужна взамен твоя помощь. Скажи, как зовут?" asked Nikka of the man.

"How come you know Russian so well, Nikka?" Rafe asked, which elicited another exasperated expression from her.

"Паскуда! Ты же в меня стреляла! За что?!" said the man to Nikka.

"What's he saying?" asked Rafe.

"I'm trying to get him to tell me his name, Rafe, if you don't mind," Nikka said, taking one of the man's hands and pressing it against the wound. "Зажми рану вот здесь," she said firmly.

The young man complied but shouted "Ой!! боль ужасная!"

"Умрёшь если не будешь делать что говорю, этого хочешь?" asked Nikka.

"Размечталась, сука!?" he replied.

"Времени нет, ты теряешь силы," persisted Nikka.

"Анатолий... Толик Семёнов," the man replied.

Turning to Rafe, Nikka said, "His name is Anatoly Semenov. Mean anything to you?"

"No, never heard of him," Rafe replied.

"Okay, well there's a few more questions I have," Nikka said.

"Shouldn't we get this guy to a hospital?" asked a worried Rafe.

"Don't worry, he's not going to die on us, I just winged him," said Nikka matter-of-factly. "Just give me a few more minutes." Turning back to the young man, she asked, "Спасибо, Толик, ты в Секте?"

"Да, мы в Секте," he replied.

"Вы оба?" asked Nikka.

"Сказал же, да!"

Turning to Rafe again Nikka said, "Well that confirms it, Rafe. He says they are with the Present Sect. It seems you were right."

Rafe felt numb. He could feel his face instantly get hot. It seemed he had been right about Violetta but having it confirmed made him feel sick.

"А здесь зачем?" asked Nikka.

"С одним козлом разобраться," Anatoly replied.

"He said he is here to beat up some guy," Nikka said to Rafe.

"Who? С кем?" asked Nikka of Anatoly.

"Фотка в верхнем кармане," he replied.

Nikka reached into a small slim pocket in the black coat Anatoly was wearing and pulled out a 'mugshot' type photograph. She lit it with her torchlight and turned it so Rafe could see.

"It's me," he said dejectedly.

"Yes, I know it's you Rafe, but do you recognise the photo? Where it's from? When it was taken?" asked Nikka.

Rafe leaned closer and peered at the photograph. "Oh my god! That's my personnel photo. From The Bibliotek!"

"Are you sure about that?" asked Nikka.

"Absolutely. I've never liked it, and that's the one."

Nikka turned back to Anatoly. "А кто послал?"

"Да вон тот же здоровый козёл," he replied.

"Оружие где?" asked Nikka.

"А почему ты решила что оно у меня есть?"

"У дружка же есть," answered Nikka.

"Какой он мне друг, только сегодня встретил," Anatoly responded.

"Толя, А ты знал про его ствол?" asked Nikka.

"Нет! Ну всё, хватит! Кончай допрос! Не могу терпеть, вези в больницу, сука! Сказал всё что хотела!" exclaimed Anatoly, getting frustrated.

"And?" asked Rafe, getting frustrated.

"Anatoly is unarmed, he only met his friend over there for the first time today and basically was doing what he was told to do, by him," said Nikka, pointing to the body lying a few metres away. "I think he's telling the truth." She turned back to Anatoly.

"Последний вопрос, — а что он такого сделал что вам с ним надо было разобраться, знаешь?" she asked.

"Нет. Я таких вопросов не задаю, я просто исполняю заказ за который мне платят!" said Anatoly, grimacing in pain.

"He says he doesn't know why you were meant to be beaten up. He doesn't ask questions like that, he just gets paid to do what he's told to do," Nikka recounted to Rafe. "Time to get him some help."

Nikka said quietly but firmly to Anatoly, "Ну спасибо тогда! Вызываю скорую, скоро будет. Прости, Толя, что ты под мою пулю попал, но твой друг должен был застрелить вон того человека. Для этого вы и пришли."

With that, Nikka walked over to the other man's body, leant down, whipped his balaclava off and shone her torch on his face. Her bullet had struck him just above his nose. Immediately she stood up. "Shit!" she hissed.

"What? What!? Do you know him!?" asked a suddenly even more panicked Rafe.

Nikka stared at the dead face and then turned slowly to face Rafe. "Yes, I know him. He's one of mine."

"What? What do you mean, he's one of yours?!"

"His name is Smits. He is — was — on my team at The Bibliotek," answered Nikka quietly.

"Holy shit!" Rafe hissed.

Nikka said nothing. Her mind was suddenly racing back to her conversation with Mads about Smits and his call to Thomas Metcalfe.

"Nikka! What's going on!?"

"You know what this means don't you?" asked Nikka, switching back to the here and now.

"No, I don't, Nikka! Illuminate me," replied Rafe, a little sarcastically and without meaning to make a pun.

Nikka grabbed Rafe's arm and turned him away from Anatoly so he wouldn't hear what she said next. "Anatoly said 'we are in the Present Sect.' He doesn't know who Smits is. He's been played, Rafe. Just like we've been."

"You're telling me your guy pretended to be in the Present Sect?"

"That's exactly what I mean. And now we have to get Anatoly to a doctor. We can't leave him here. We need to talk to him some more, find out how he was contacted and why he believes my guy was in the Sect. Okay?"

"Yes, yes. I can see that. But we're in a foreign country. How do we just get him to a doctor? You shot him after all and he's bleeding."

"Don't worry about that. I speak Russian, or have you forgotten already? I can get us to a doctor who won't be a problem. But first we have to move the dead one. Come on, help me."

"What? Move him? Why?"

"To give us time, Rafe, before questions start being asked. The snow is our friend tonight. See that mound over there?" Nikka asked, pointing to a mound of fresh snow on the other side of the mausoleum beside a small grove of trees. "We'll put him over there and cover him," she continued as she grabbed his jacket collar and started pulling."

"What about his gun?" asked Rafe as he began to help drag the heavy lump that was Smits. "I can't believe we are doing this."

"That stays with him. Don't touch it," instructed Nikka. She ignored Rafe's other comment, and when she was satisfied with the placement of the lifeless Smits, she searched all his pockets and found a worn leather wallet which she put into her jacket pocket. Then she pulled off his neurophone and pocketed that as well. She then quickly kicked fallen snow over the body to begin its concealment.

Twenty or so minutes later the three of them were in the rental hovercar. It was now snowing heavily. Rafe was driving, Nikka was on the back seat, on her neurophone but giving Rafe directions, and tending to Anatoly, who was quiet. "Slow down, Rafe, not so fast. By the time your friend Sasha returns, Smits will be covered, and so will all the blood. They may not find him for days, or even weeks. But we need to avoid any mishaps getting Anatoly here to the doctor."

Rafe was not really listening. He was still in shock. "So close yet so far," he muttered, recalling for the first time that night since the ambush what had supposedly brought him to Russia. Fortunately, Anatoly had been able to walk to the car without too much assistance, and they had not sighted Sasha or anybody else. Nikka had given Anatoly some tablets for the pain. Rafe dared not ask what they were as Nikka was now in complete charge, but they calmed Anatoly down. From what Rafe could see from his rear-view mirror, he was asleep.

"What? What's that you're muttering? And I said slow down!"

"I said, how far?" asked Rafe, finally complying and slowing down.

"We should be there in about fifteen minutes."

"Where are we actually going? To a hospital?"

"No. We are going to somebody's house. She's a doctor. She consults from there so she will have all we need to get Anatoly patched up. And besides, we want him to avoid having to answer questions from the police, just from us. Don't worry, this won't be a problem."

Rafe was beginning to snap out of his fugue, but he wasn't convinced by Nikka's reassurance. She seemed to him to know what she was doing, and she did speak Russian, and pretty well by the sound of it, but Rafe was beginning to seriously regret the whole plan.

There was a dead body back at the mausoleum and it was fresh, and Sasha knew what 'John' looked like.

As it turned out, Nikka was right. It wasn't a problem. The doctor, a woman roughly Nikka's age, maybe a bit older, was waiting for them. It was immediately obvious to Rafe that the woman knew Nikka and liked her very much. Nikka introduced her to 'John'. Her name was Svetlana and her house was set back from the street, on its own, so there were no neighbours to be curious about the late-night arrival. They quickly got Anatoly into the surgery attached to the house, and when Rafe went back to check the car he was surprised, but very glad, to see that the back seat had almost no blood on it. Nikka had done a good a job of stemming the bleeding and Anatoly had done a good job of having a thick jacket. *Maybe the wound isn't so bad after all,* thought Rafe.

Once Anatoly knew he was being attended to, by a doctor, and not in a hospital, he spoke freely to Nikka. As she later related to Rafe on the drive back to Moscow after leaving Anatoly in the care of her doctor friend, he and Smits had been waiting for Rafe since the previous night.

"Anatoly said Smits had instructed him to pay the guard Sasha for information, and that Sasha had told Anatoly that you were coming and when. Smits then threatened to shoot Sasha if he said anything to you," said Nikka.

"But how was Anatoly contacted in the first place?" asked Rafe.

"He says he got an encrypted message from his main Present Sect contact in Moscow, who he's never met, by the way, that a senior Sect person was coming to Sergiyev, that he was to meet him, take him to wherever the man wanted to go, and do whatever the man told him to do. It seems he was used to this type of arrangement."

"So we let him go? What about Svetlana? He knows her name and where she lives."

"It will be okay. He is scared shitless and wants to make himself scarce. He wasn't prepared for any gun violence and he didn't know Smits was armed. He just thought this was going to be your everyday 'thump and scare' job. And I told him I'd do a better job of shooting him if I heard he'd been talking."

"Well, that's just great," Rafe said sarcastically. "But he was in the Present Sect, wasn't he? I mean Anatoly. It sounds like he's just your everyday crim."

"Yes, I agree, but Sergiyev is not exactly a hot spot for the Present Sect so I think he might be a crim with some ideals. Or an idealist with criminal tendencies. All talk and no walk. Lana will be fine," said Nikka, who then shone her touch over the back seat. "Good job on the clean-up. Looks like we won't have to burn the car and claim it was stolen. That would be suspicious."

"Oh yes, we wouldn't want to create any suspicions, would we?" More sarcasm from Rafe. Nikka decided to let him get it all out so that they could then focus on the task at hand. "I mean," he continued, "no more than the guy with the bullet hole through his head now lying in the snow and the local punk with the bullet hole in his belly. And by the way... Lana? That's short for Svetlana, right? How well do you know her? How do we know she's not on the phone to the police right now? Wait, what are you doing with the dead guy's neurophone?!"

"An experiment. That fool Smits didn't lock it. This is not his work phone, but I've cross-referenced all the numbers he has sent texts to and there is one, and only one, listed for The Bibliotek. Councillor Carlson no less," explained Nikka. She tapped the word 'Done' and sent it to Carlson's number.

"Wait, what?! Aren't you making a huge assumption here? Why did you just do that?"

"Listen, Rafe. This man Smits was here to put you down, permanently. To *kill* you. Not because he felt like travelling all the way from The Bibliotek to here to do it, but because he was instructed to. You wanted to prove your theory that Violetta Simpson tipped off the Present Sect by setting up a confrontation. And you kindly invited me to be here for it, as back-up. Well I backed you up, Rafe. *I saved your life.* And you got your proof, only it's not the proof you were expecting. This isn't about Simpson, it's about Carlson. He is the link between Smits and Simpson, and using the guise of the Present Sect was only a ruse. That's my theory, but I have the evidence."

Rafe looked at Nikka blankly. He was still filtering all that she had just said to him, so he focused on the last thing she had said. "So, what you are saying is there is in fact no connection between Mads' girlfriend and the Present Sect..."

"Correct."

"... and it would appear that Violetta only tipped off Carlson."

"That's my thinking," said Nikka. "And by the way, you needn't worry about Lana. She owed me big time and tonight's little visit settled the debt. Right now you need to focus on getting us back to the hotel sometime this morning!"

Mads glanced at her and was about to say something about the quality of Nikka's sarcasm compared to his own when she got in first.

"You were supposed to take that last turn on the right. It's the on-ramp to the hoverway back to Moscow."

Rafe said nothing, and turned the hovercar around at the next exit and on-ramp. The rest of the trip was covered in silence. They each were thinking about the consequences of what had occurred and what to do about them, but Rafe at least also made sure he made no more driving mistakes.

As they were walking out of the hotel car park to the lift to their respective rooms Nikka asked Rafe to meet him in the dining room for breakfast after they had each refreshed and changed.

Thursday, 14th February 2205

The hotel's dining room began serving a buffet breakfast at 6.30am and Nikka and Rafe were both there when it opened. After filling their plates they sat down at a table at the far end of the room. There were no other guests yet. Sound travelled far and wide, and for a while they only clinked their cutlery and stirred their spoons. Then Nikka finally spoke.

"Okay Rafe, here's what needs to happen before we leave Moscow," she began softly but firmly, almost whispering. "I need to arrange for a call to Mads from the Moscow police requesting he come to Moscow as a matter of urgency, and that it involves a Mr Rafe Nagy. I need to do this as soon as we finish breakfast. What's the matter, aren't you hungry?" Nikka had stopped to observe Rafe had not touched his bacon and eggs but instead was staring at his plate.

"I'm not with you, Nikka," he said, looking up at her. "You want to give my name to the police?"

"No Rafe. Snap out of it!" replied Nikka, looking around and trying not to raise her voice. "It will only appear to Mads that he is being called by the Moscow police. Do I really have to spell everything out?" she almost whispered, but forcefully.

"Sorry, go on." Rafe picked up his knife and fork and held them above his plate, as if waiting for a signal.

"Then I need to arrange for 'a body' to be found at the Trinity Monastery. When Mads arrives, hopefully in haste, we will tell him everything, in particular what it means for his relationship with Ms Simpson. Then you need to go into hiding."

"Hiding? Is that really necessary?"

"No not necessary, but helpful. Remember, someone wanted you dead, so let's let them think you *are* dead, for now. It will give us some time we badly need. And besides, they may still want you dead."

"Good point." That was the signal for Rafe to start eating. He was hungry but it felt like The Last Meal before the hangman arrived. "So we stay here until Mads arrives?"

"Correct. And there is one more thing you need to know."

"Hmm? Yes?"

"It was Smits who threatened Councillor Metcalfe."

Rafe dropped his fork onto his plate, making a loud clank that bounced around the room. In response Rafe and Nikka both glanced around as well but nobody was there to hear it except the two of them.

"How long have you known that?!"

"Not long. Mads asked me to run a check on calls made to the Councillor's phone. He only told me the reason after I confirmed it was Smits who had made that particular call."

"And now it seems he's been pretending to be with the Present Sect," said Rafe.

"Yes, and all the more reason for you to temporarily make yourself scarce."

Rafe pondered that for a while, as he resumed eating. "What about the hovercar? It's due back this afternoon."

"Call the agency and tell them you need it for an extra day or two, and that you'll drop it off at the helioport. We need to be out of the country just before it gets cleaned."

"Understood."

Just then a neurophone pinged in Nikka's pocket. She pulled it out. It was a message. Nikka opened the message, read it, then held it up for Rafe to see.

It was Smits' neurophone and the message was one word: 'Excellent'.

END OF CHAPTER TWELVE

Chapter Thirteen

Betrayal is a Bitch

"On May 21, 2001, a fire broke out in Seattle's Centre for Urban Horticulture, a biogenetics research institute. It destroyed two million dollars' worth of scientific books. The eco-activists of the Earth Liberation Front (ELF) are the top suspects, yet one of the researchers at the centre, an expert in GMOs, lamented, "All we are trying to do is improve the environment."
Lucien X. Polastron, *Books on Fire - The Destruction of Libraries Throughout History*, Inner Traditions, Vermont, 2007, page 249.

8:42am, Thursday, 14ᵗʰ February 2205

"Bibliotekar Ingridson, I believe you are on route to Moscow?" asked Thurldottir in her usual skilful way of avoiding any semblance of polite small talk. She did it so well, so consistently and so matter-of-factly, it seemed to Mads to be a physiological affliction, one which pointed to her true character.

On hearing Thurldottir's raspy question, though, Mads instantly regretted answering her call. *That was quick*, he thought, before he answered her question. He decided to replicate her avoidance of any form of salutation. "That is correct, Madam Chair. I am at the spaceport and about to board my heliojet. Is there a problem?"

"We have had this discussion before. Why did you not notify me of your intention to travel?"

"I am conducting urgent Bibliotek business, Chair Thurldottir," Mads responded in a formal tone, "and if I may ask, are you that concerned about my travel arrangements that you are tracking me?"

"I simply called your office to speak to you about another matter, but I was informed you had just left The Bibliotek without notice to journey to Moscow. You can expect to see this issue on the agenda for the next Council meeting, Bibliotekar, as I have also warned you before."

Mads tried to gauge from listening to Thurldottir whether Larkin had mentioned to her the reason for his urgent trip to Moscow, but couldn't. Neither could he ask her if he had. Instead he replied with some urgency, "The agenda for the Governing Council is your prerogative, Chair Thurldottir. What is the other matter? We are taking off soon."

"My PA has informed me he has been unable to reach Councillor Metcalfe. Do you know where he is?"

Mads had been more expecting than dreading this conversation. It seemed her patience had worn out, and he knew what was coming next. "No, I don't. But knowing Thomas that is not unusual. Do you need to speak to him?"

"That I do, it's a Phicom matter. He has now missed two meetings".

"I'm sure he's around somewhere; have you checked with Dean Coenraad?"

"Of course I have. He said he raised the whereabouts of Councillor Metcalfe in an Adcom meeting back in November." Thurldottir paused expectantly but Mads declined to take the bait and remained silent. So she resumed. "It seems he has been absent for some time; so long in fact that I am going to declare him as officially missing. We need Security to get onto this. We can't have a Councillor missing."

There it is, thought Mads, *she's finally playing her ace.* "As you wish. I am sure Thomas will surface soon but I appreciate your concern. I agree it is probably time to start looking for him," he answered as impassively as he could.

"Good, so I can leave this with you to organise?"

"Consider it done," said Mads, finishing his words just after Thurldottir terminated the call.

Moments later Mads' heliojet began its pre-take off procedures, so he quickly made the call he had been about to make when Thurldottir got to him first. "I'm sorry, Vie, but I won't be able to make it tonight for dinner."

"Oh, what's up?"

"Dr Foote and I are on our way to Moscow. In fact we are about to take off. Something has happened to Rafe and I was asked by the police to come there as a matter of urgency."

"Oh no! What happened?"

"Sorry, I don't know. I'll let you know when I know. I won't be back until tomorrow at the earliest. I'm sorry to spoil the dinner, I know you like cooking for me, I'll make it up to you." Mads didn't want to mention it was Valentine's Day — it would have been their first and he didn't quite feel it was appropriate. Yet.

"Oh Mads, don't worry about the dinner! Do what you have to do."

12:16pm

Nikka was waiting for Mads in the lounge next to reception at their hotel. She wasn't expecting to see Justin Foote with him, but as soon as they came through the front entrance Nikka arose from her chair and intercepted them before they got to the reception desk. Mads was only half-surprised to see her. "Nikka, I tried to contact you, when did you get here? What's happened to Rafe?"

"There has been an incident, but everything is okay," Nikka said quietly to them both. "Rafe is fine, he's upstairs in his room. I came to Moscow with him."

"What did you say? You came here *with* him? What's going on?" Mads asked, confused.

"Come," said Nikka, looking around and holding Mads' forearm. "It's best we all talk upstairs."

"Where are the police?" Mads asked when the three of them were in the lift.

"There are no police, Mads," replied Nikka. She was expecting the next question but hoped Mads would wait until they were in Rafe's room, behind a closed door. But he didn't.

"So you're telling me I did not get an urgent phone call from the police asking me to come to Moscow?"

"No, that was an urgent call from me. There's a reason for that which I will explain *once we get inside the room.*"

This time Mads stayed quiet until they were inside Rafe's room. A thousand questions were by then streaming through his head, but only one came out when he laid eyes on Rafe. "Excuse my language, but what the fuck is going on, Nags!?"

"Thanks for coming so quickly Mads, and I am sorry for the dramatics. But for reasons which will soon become obvious, Nikka had to create a ruse to get you here, Mads. We needed you, and Larkin hopefully, to think it was the Moscow police who summoned you here," said Rafe.

"I arranged for a call to be made to your office, knowing it would be Larkin who answered the phone, that it was 'the Moscow police' calling and it was concerning an employee of The Bibliotek, a Mr Rafe Nagy, and that you needed to come to Moscow as a matter of urgency," said Nikka.

"Okay, I think I know why the ruse. It worked, Larkin did take the call, but let's hear the rest."

"Let's sit down first," said Nikka, motioning to a lounge chair for Mads. There were two other chairs, both facing Mads, and Nikka and Rafe sat in those. Dr Foote stood by the window to their side, looking decidedly confused.

"Mads, we know now how the Present Sect was aware beforehand of my visit to Pienza and Viscount Rossellini," Rafe said quietly, leaning forward and facing Mads.

"I'm sorry, but please tell me we didn't come all this way just for you to tell me that about Larkin," Mads replied, a little irritated, as he looked at Nikka, who looked back at him and shook her head slightly.

Rafe continued. "Well we didn't know you would bring Justin with you, but I'm glad you did. We now know for certain, Mads, with absolute certainty, that it was either Carlson or Thurldottir, or both, who passed on the information," he said quietly but firmly.

Mads heard what Rafe had just said but he wasn't really listening. "That doesn't make any sense. Why would they do that? And how did they know?" said Mads, incredulous.

"Violetta told them, or at least she told Carlson," continued Rafe.

In the silence that immediately followed Rafe's words Mads looked as if he had just been struck full on by an invisible force. He opened his mouth to say something, but nothing come out, instead he sort of crumpled back into his chair. Rafe and Nikka had expected Mads to react with shock and anger at the absurdity of what they knew to be true, but instead were seeing Mads react with shock and complete devastation. It was if he had instantly accepted what he was hearing and had already moved straight onto the fourth stage of grief. He sat still, staring at Rafe, his mind racing. Then he finally broke the silent wait for him to speak.

"I told her you were going to Pienza," Mads said quietly, in resignation. "And this isn't about Larkin, is it?"

Rafe looked across at Nikka then at Justin. "Mads, I'm sorry, but yes, this isn't about Larkin, it's about Violetta. I had my suspicion after Justin told me my Bibliotek network connection had not been compromised before Pienza. You were the only person I told I was going. And there's more...."

Mads looked up at Rafe. "Yes, Nags, come on, give it to me."

"The Present Sect was waiting for me at Trinity Monastery, Mads. We were..."

"We?" Mads interrupted.

"Nikka came with me, and we were prepared this time. I had deliberately told only you, that is, no-one else apart from Nikka, about the whole thing. It was so fantastic I was counting on you to tell Violetta, I'm sorry, but we had to be sure."

"Well Nags, you were right," Mads said sadly after a few seconds, shoulders slumped. "I told Violetta all about it. That very night. You had done a very good job of making it an interesting story to tell her."

Again Rafe, Nikka, and Justin looked at each other. Silence prevailed again until Mads spoke.

"So, when you were telling me about coming to Moscow to look for the Lost Library, you already knew Nikka was going with you?"

"Yes, Mads, I'm sorry."

"So it was all bullshit, all that stuff about the Lost Library?"

"No Mads, that was all true, every word. I just didn't get a chance to find out if I was right about the Lost Library. I just used it as the means of testing my suspicion about Violetta, and on that score it seems I was right."

Once more there was silence as they waited for Mads to speak.

"Bibliotekar, I know this must be a shock, but... you seem, um, resigned to it."

Mads turned around and looked at Justin, who had just asked that question and who had more to say but was waiting for the right moment, and then at the faces of the others. Mads' face betrayed the look of someone who was trying to decide whether to say something intensely private to these people. Something that had been on his mind, worrying him. He decided to let it out. Things had changed.

"I've been a fool, my friends," he said, pausing to take some breaths. "I have succumbed to the side effects of being intimate with someone. You all know my disdain for hindsight, but I will admit it seems I missed some warning signs..."

Mads stopped and looked at the quizzical faces around him. He grabbed the arms of his chair and straightened himself. "I'm sorry, what I mean to say is that there have been subtle signals Violetta has been giving off lately that I *have* managed to notice through the veil of my feelings towards her. Notice in a bad way. In a way I've tried to ignore and not ponder. In a way that made me start to question her motives for... for... being with me," stammered Mads, looking down at his hands, which were in the process of wringing each other. He consciously stopped and gripped again the arms of the chair with each hand. "But what I am struggling with right now is the why," he said, finally raising his voice to its normal tone. "Why for fucks' sake are we talking about her and the Present Sect in the same fucking sentence. Excuse my language but can someone tell me that? She is the fucking Chief Conservator; doesn't it strike any of you as being slightly odd?!"

Mads was now almost shouting and was definitely angry, prompting Justin to speak.

"Mads," said Justin, for the first time ever using Mads' first name.

"What!?" replied Mads sternly, glaring at Justin. But then he realised Justin was not happy about something. "What?" This time it was a question.

"Now might be the right time to brief you on some things I have discovered about Ms Simpson."

"Eh? What do you mean... 'discovered'?"

"I asked Justin a few weeks ago to do a background check on Violetta," said Rafe before Justin could reply.

Mads turned back to Rafe. "When?"

"When I first had an inkling she was not who she appeared to be. I asked Justin to do it, quietly and quickly, to see if he could find out if there was anything about her we should know that might lead to her being the leak, as it were, about Pienza. And I asked him not to tell you about it."

"Why not?"

"Because I wanted to set a trap to see if she *was* the culprit and to do that I needed you to be kept in the dark."

"And?" asked Mads, turning back to Justin.

"I'm sorry, but I didn't get a chance to get back to Rafe before he set his trap, so to speak," replied Justin, who then looked at Rafe.

"I'm sorry I didn't tell you my plan, Justin. I felt it best you be kept out of it in case it went pear-shaped."

"And you went along with this?" Mads asked Nikka.

"Yes, I did, Mads," said Nikka, who then turned to Rafe. "But I didn't credit his story enough to step in and suggest something more... conventional. Sorry, Rafe."

"But you still went anyway and let him risk his stupid neck," Mads replied.

"As I said, Mads, I didn't believe there was any danger."

"But you had a gun, which you didn't tell me about," pleaded Rafe.

"You know the saying, Rafe. I'd rather have a gun and not need it than need it but not have it."

"Well the Present Sect was waiting for you, so you got it right Nags," said Mads, a little sarcastically. "But Nikka had her gun and as the two of you are demonstrably still alive I'm guessing it didn't go pear-shaped after all. So, Justin, let's hear what you have to say."

Nikka and Rafe looked at each other but didn't say anything. But Mads did notice out of the corner his eye that Nikka shot Rafe a stern look and a very short shake of her head.

"Well, to put this in context," started Justin, "you will recall, Bibliotekar, that Ms Simpson was brought on board at The Bibliotek as part of the deal with Harvard Library and, as such, HR did not conduct the normal checks for such a senior appointment of an external."

"Yes, I do recall that. After I had met her during the negotiations it wasn't an issue. Are you now saying it should have been?"

Justin coughed then said, "I know your views on hindsight, Bibliotekar, but, yes is the short answer."

"Go on. Let's hear it, and don't dress it up any nicer than it is, please."

"I was told confidentially by more than one source at Harvard that she had attained her promotions there by sleeping around and not by talent or expertise at her job. I also determined that in her final year of her undergraduate conservatory degree at another university she had filed a sexual misconduct suit against one of her professors after he had terminated their affair and failed her. The suit was settled out of court on terms that included her being awarded her undergraduate degree without further studies being required. There was also an issue with her position at the library preceding her appointment at Harvard, which she left under a cloud. Something to do with some library funds not able to be accounted for. A lot of money."

"How much?"

"Well into the six-figure range, I'm told. Nothing was proven so no charges were laid, but she had been required to resign. She was allowed to join Harvard without this issue being made known to her new employer. Knowledge of that only came later, second-hand. I was given the impression the deal involving her coming to The Bibliotek was more about getting rid of a potential problem than anything to do with her work."

By now Mads was leaning forward in his chair with his head in his hands. The others were looking at him, waiting, then watched as he got up and walked to the window, next to Justin. He looked out of the window at the cold bleakness of the snow-covered Red Square for a few seconds, sighed, then turned to face Justin. "She would never have been allowed to set foot in The Bibliotek had we known all that."

"That's correct, I'm sorry to say," Justin replied, stony-faced.

"Mads," said Nikka, "we are certain Simpson passed on the information that Rafe was going to Pienza to meet the Viscount, but it would appear she didn't pass it on directly to the Present Sect, if the Sect knew at all."

"Eh?"

"We think she told either Carlson or Thurldottir, Mads, and that they orchestrated an ambush involving the Present Sect. To make it look like the Present Sect, that is," Nikka explained.

"But ... that's just as unlikely. I mean..." Mads started to explain what he meant, but stopped, confused.

"Mads, Smits was there at Trinity Monastery, armed and pretending to be a member of the Present Sect, waiting for Rafe," interrupted Nikka.

"What? This *is* the thug in your team on Carlson's payroll we are talking about?"

Nikka nodded. "*Was* on my team, yes."

"But, how... What?" asked Mads, more confused.

"I shot him, Mads. I took no chances, I shot him once in the head, but it was dark and I didn't know it was him until I took off the balaclava he was wearing, after I shot him. I shot him because he had a gun and he was about to shoot Rafe."

Mads and Justin looked at each other with alarm.

"Mads, if Nikka had not acted quickly, I would not be sitting here today. No ifs, no buts. There were no preliminaries, no discussion.

He was there, he was waiting, he stepped out of hiding, he was going to shoot me. Nikka got in first."

"So, you are saying he was there for no other purpose but to kill you?"

"Yes, an escalation of Pienza."

"But I still don't understand. What was he doing impersonating the Present Sect?"

"We haven't got that far yet, Mads, but I did tell you he was still being paid by Carlson and I know he wasn't acting on his own behalf but was specifically instructed to do the things he did. He was carrying this," said Nikka as she pulled out a small photograph from a folder on her desk.

"What's this? It looks like a very bad mugshot of Nags," Mads said, turning to Rafe and showing a forced smile.

Rafe did not answer, but Nikka did. "It's Rafe's staff photo, from The Bibliotek. Specifically, the photo of Rafe in our security system's database, which is separate from HR's. I had it checked."

"Eh?"

"It proves Smits had identified Rafe as his target before he left The Bibliotek. Then, pretending to be a member of the Present Sect, he made contact with a man in Sergiyev who was actually in the Present Sect..."

"Was?" interrupted Mads.

"Was, is, neutralised."

"You shot him too?"

"Yes, but not to kill, to immobilise and extract information, which I obtained. Smits had told him he was there to intercept a man and give him a beating, and that he needed him to show him around the Trinity Monastery and get access. Smits had shown him the photo of Rafe and told him it was the man he was looking for. He did not know of Smits' true intention or identity, and he was unarmed."

"I see."

"And there's something else."

"Yes?"

"I've checked where Smits was on the night Viscount Rossellini was murdered, and it would appear he was not at The Bibliotek either that day or the day after. I'm told he was on sick leave, which I need Justin to confirm, discretely. I believe it was he who murdered the

Viscount and staged it to make it look as a threat to Rafe from the Present Sect."

"If that's true, then it worked, but what am I missing here, Nikka?" said Mads.

"Recall I ascertained that it was Smits who threatened Thomas."

"So you're telling me he'd been doing Carlson's dirty work?"

"Yes, and by implication, Chair Thurldottir's as well."

Mads pondered for a few moments what Nikka had been saying. "Justin, where do you stand on all of this?" he finally asked.

"I am troubled greatly by this ongoing violence involving The Bibliotek, and I am also concerned about our apparent willingness to avoid involving the relevant authorities, in particular the police. Where does one end and the other start?"

"That's a fair comment, Justin," replied Mads. "Nikka?"

"I do understand and appreciate Justin's concern, Mads, but as far as The Bibliotek is concerned," began Nikka in a calm and measured tone, "the only issue we have is one of jurisdiction. Rafe's role as a witness for what happened in Pienza has not yet been disclosed to the Italian authorities. But it will be, and it will be done by me, with full disclosure of Smits' involvement and why. The same goes for the Russian authorities and what happened at the monastery at Sergiyev. As for the delay, that is due to an ongoing investigation of illegal activities involving The Bibliotek, of which the Pienza and Sergiyev incidents are only part, and which is being undertaken by the Commissioner of Police of The Bibliotek. That would be *me*. That is *my* jurisdiction. The successful outcome of *my* investigation necessitates *my* decision not to initiate any discussions or involvement with my colleagues in Italy and Russia, *at this point in time*. I need everyone's co-operation on this."

Nikka paused and looked around the room at each of her colleagues in turn. They were all in silent contemplation. "And right now, Mads, there are two things that need to happen. First, Rafe has to play dead for a little while. He can't go back to The Bibliotek just yet. He needs to go somewhere quiet and safe that isn't The Bibliotek."

"Play dead? Dare I ask why?"

"Because for now Councillor Carlson thinks Rafe is dead, and he is sure to have informed Chair Thurldottir," replied Nikka.

"But why does he think that?" asked Mads.

"Because," said Rafe, "Smits had a neurophone with Carlson's number in it and Nikka sent a message to him from the phone that said 'Done' and Carlson replied 'Excellent'."

Mads turned to Nikka. "Why did you do that?"

"Because people start making mistakes when they think they've been successful at something. It's a fact of life, especially for the criminally-minded. And it proved to me that Smits was acting on Carlson's orders."

"And you want to see if Carlson makes a mistake, I get it," replied Mads.

"Yes, Mads. And as I said, Rafe needs to go somewhere other than Norway and The Bibliotek."

"I know just the place," said Mads. "Scotland, to join Thomas, and then bring him back to The Bibliotek with him."

"Wait, did you say Scotland? Is that where Councillor Metcalfe is?" asked Nikka.

"I'm sorry I thought you knew," replied Mads.

"You only told me he was in hiding far away from The Bibliotek," replied Nikka. "No issue. Anyway, I received a call from Chair Thurldottir the other day asking me to search for the Councillor, but I referred her to you, Mads, as I report to you not her."

Lately, every time Nikka spoke, Mads appreciated her more. This was no exception. Mads smiled. "Yes, she called me about this earlier today, just as we were about to board my flight, but she didn't mention you gave her the brush off."

"And once we all get back to The Bibliotek we need you to have a conversation with Violetta, face-to-face, it has to be very soon, and I need to be there at a certain point, if not during the entire conversation" replied Nikka. "We need to ascertain a few facts."

"Yes, and I know exactly what that information is," replied Mads. "There is also something I need to tell you. I rang Violetta straight after my call from Thurldottir. She was meant to be cooking me a romantic dinner tonight. Well, I thought it was going to be romantic. What I mean is, I had to cancel her tonight, and I told her the reason why."

"Sorry to ask, Mads," said Nikka, "but what exactly did you say was the reason?"

"I told her I had to get to Moscow urgently because something had happened to Nags. That was it. No! Wait, I also told her I had been asked by the police to come as a matter of urgency."

"Because something had happened to Rafe, as in that was what the police had told you?"

"Yes."

"That is good. I'm sorry, but let's hope she passes that on to Carlson or Thurldottir. We also need you to get Violetta to pass on some further information."

"Being what exactly?"

"Being that Rafe is dead."

"How will that help, exactly?"

"It may buy us some more time, because very soon Councillor Carlson will put two and two together when Smits fails to return to The Bibliotek and can't be otherwise reached. But timing is everything."

Mads seemed to have calmed down after listening to Nikka effectively take control of the situation, and with it, responsibility. She was definitely invested in this whole mess. He realised he had been upset at being used to trap Violetta, but he understood what Nikka was saying, and after listening to Justin's summary of what he uncovered about Violetta's past, he started to understand the potential implications.

"Lately she's been asking questions rather than just listening to me rabbiting on about my day," he said to no-one in particular. "And then there's times when it seems she really couldn't care less about The Bibliotek; she tends to get too relaxed in her time off, and the two don't go together." Mads paused, but Nikka could tell there was something more.

"And I think she read my diary one night without wanting me to know about it."

"Oh," said Nikka.

"Yes, oh!" said Mads, now looking at her. "At first I let it go, and put it down to one partner's natural curiosity about the other's private thoughts, but afterwards it started to grate on me, and I began to feel as if I needed to be wary, and that is not how I want to feel in a relationship with anyone."

"Mads, I'm sorry but if that's the case I will need to know what she potentially found out and passed onto Carlson and Thurldottir."

"Yes, I get that. First thing we do when we get back to The Bibliotek is go through my diary to see what she potentially knows and therefore potentially told Carlson."

Nikka nodded, but said, "First, though, I need to go with Rafe to Scotland. We need to leave today. You and Dr Foote should go back to The Bibliotek tomorrow, but don't arrive until late. I will meet you there with Councillor Metcalfe, and then we can have that conversation with Ms Simpson. Agreed?"

"Agreed," answered Mads resignedly. "But that doesn't leave you much time to get to and from Scotland. Thomas is holed up on a farm near Glencoe."

Nikka looked at Rafe. "Can we do it?" she asked of him.

"If we can be on a heliojet to Glasgow or Edinburgh – Glasgow would be better – within an hour, we can be at the farm tonight. It will be late, but we can contact Thomas when we land. From Glasgow it's only a two-hour drive. We can be back at The Bibliotek tomorrow afternoon."

"No, I will be back at The Bibliotek, with Councillor Metcalfe. You need to stay away from The Bibliotek for a few more days," Nikka replied.

"I can do that," said Rafe.

Nikka and Rafe both then looked at Mads, who nodded.

"Okay, let's do it," she said.

"I need to be there too, Bibliotekar, when you and Nikka have your conversation with Ms Simpson. This will need HR's involvement," said Justin. "Can I suggest one of your informal dinners?"

"Yes, I agree that will be necessary. But I won't contact her until tomorrow morning."

7:02pm, Friday, 15ᵗʰ February 2205

It would have been so easy just to let his emotions take over for a while and be done with it, Mads was thinking. Some strong words, maybe even some yelling on his part, but definitely finality of process. That was what he was telling himself, unconvincingly. He had never before experienced the sense of betrayal he felt now. He needed answers; they had to come from Violetta, and for that to happen he needed to maintain control of himself. He felt cold, cold to the core, and it wasn't the weather that was the cause. And for the first time in a long time, Mads felt old. He was going to have to be all businesslike and Violetta would probably know before long, if not immediately, that something was amiss. She would notice that the spell she had over him was completely gone. Caution was prescribed, that much Mads knew for certain. He had just finished going over his recent diary entries with Nikka as soon as she had returned from Glasgow with Thomas, who was now quietly and safely ensconced in Mads' guest apartment next door to his, and it was abundantly evident to both of them that they needed to know what exactly Violetta had read of the diary, if indeed she had done what Mads suspected. And if she *had* read his diary, they also needed to find out how much of it and what she had communicated to Carlson or Thurldottir. In the absence of extracting that information they had to assume that the contents of all of his recent notes had been disclosed. It was also now clear to Nikka after reading the diary notes that Mads had delayed being fully open with her for good reason. As for Mads, he was glad he had not caught up with Violetta on Valentine's Day as they had originally planned.

With those aims forefront in his mind, Mads had then messaged Violetta that he had returned to The Bibliotek, and if she were free for dinner a few hours hence, at 7pm, he would fill her in on what had transpired in Moscow. She had messaged back that she was free and to ask what had happened to Rafe. Mads had judiciously not replied. Now, on time, there was a quiet knock on the door of Mads' apartment.

"Hello, Mads," Violetta said quietly when he opened the door. "How's the Big Boss?" she smiled inquisitively.

For a moment Mads succumbed, without trying not to, to her aroma and presence. He let it happen, because in that instant he knew he had to welcome her in his usual manner, and that was as someone who had missed her and was looking forward to some quiet time with her. Once she was standing there in front of him, close, it wasn't too hard to do, and momentarily forget what he was about to do.

"What's up?" she asked as they finished their embrace. It hadn't worked.

"We're not alone tonight. And I'm tired. And perhaps a bit stressed. A lot's been happening."

"What about Rafe? Is he ok?"

"He's fine. Come on, I'll fill you in over dinner," said Mads quietly as he led Violetta to the dining room, where Nikka and Justin were standing, waiting, behind their respective chairs, facing each other.

"Oh!" Violetta quietly gasped, then just as suddenly recaptured her composure.

"I'm sorry, Violetta, but I completely forgot I had scheduled one of my informal dinners for senior managers for tonight. Allow me to introduce Nikka Johannson, our Head of Security, and Dr Justin Foote, Associate Director of HR. Nikka and Justin, this is Violetta Simpson, our Chief Conservator."

Formalities over, the four sat down at the round dining table, Mads facing Violetta. As they got comfortable, two waiters came from the adjoining kitchen and served the main meal — Mads' favourite — rare roast lamb and vegetables, and poured wine.

"I thought we'd skip entrée tonight and get straight into the serious part of the dinner," said Mads, a little deadpan.

Violetta sensed tension in the air. And it was at that moment she suddenly realised that she could not hear the classical music that Mads usually had softly playing in the background. She also noticed that Nikka was looking at Mads as she ate and listened, and that Justin was keeping his gaze on his plate. *Something's not right*, she thought, deciding to try to lighten the mood.

"I think I met Justin on my orientation tour, but I'm surprised I haven't met you until now, Nikka. Then again, we don't seem to have much need for security in Conservation," she said.

Nikka stopped eating and looked at Violetta impassively, then at Mads a little quizzically, who nodded slightly and sat back in his chair, looking straight ahead at Violetta.

"I'm currently investigating a violent murder and an attempted murder involving one or more employees of The Bibliotek," Nikka pointedly responded to Violetta's perception about the 'need for Security'.

"Oh, that's terrible!" she replied, visibly shocked. Or at least she appeared to be to Mads.

Nikka said nothing for a few seconds, during which time Violetta noticed that now Justin had stopped eating as well and was also looking at her.

Then Nikka spoke, in a measured, firm, tone. "Can I ask, Ms Simpson, what is the nature of your relationship with Councillor Carlson?"

"What?! What do you mean, relationship?! Why are you asking? Violetta reacted, her face suddenly betraying a *different* Simpson. It was obvious to her than Nikka's question had been prepared in advance.

"We are aware you have been feeding Councillor Carlson information given to you in private by Bibliotekar Ingridson, so that is why I am asking you to explain the nature of that relationship," Nikka said in the same matter-of-fact tone as she also continued eating as if she had just asked Violetta about the weather, or the name of the designer of the alluring dress Violetta was wearing.

Mads leaned forward and, still looking at Violetta and resting his elbows on the table, brought his spread hands together at the finger tips, in front of his face. Violetta sat frozen, with her elbows on the table and food in her fork. Her face was now white.

Nikka continued. "We know you told Councillor Carlson that Rafe Nagy was going to Pienza in Italy to visit a contact with whom he had been negotiating the procurement of his book collection, and we know you told him that Mr Nagy was going to Sergiyev in Russia to track down the Lost Library of Ivan The Formidable. And now we want..." said Nikka, stopping when Violetta interrupted her.

"So *what* if I told him?! It wasn't like a state secret," she defended herself.

"That's debatable actually, but more to the point of this conversation, you deliberately entered into a relationship — schemed to achieve it no less — for the sole purpose of spying on Mads, yes?" Nikka said without emotion. "Have I got that right, Ms Simpson?"

Violetta looked intently at Nikka, but without saying anything or moving. The shock of Nikka's words and their import had caught up with her. Then she reached for her wine glass and took a swig.

Mads could no longer contain himself. He stood up and pushed his chair in. "I'm struggling for words, Violetta. I'm struggling to contain myself. I feel like just... shouting, yelling, screaming at you. I look at the facts, again and again they swirl in my head, I can't pin them down. To you. It... just... doesn't... make... sense. But... it *is* you, isn't it? You did tell Carlson those things, and a lot more."

"Yes, Mads."

They looked at each other in silence. Mads, standing there, his hands now resting on the back of the chair, with confusion and pain. Violetta, sitting across from him twirling her fork on her plate, with palpable relief and tiredness. At last she didn't have to pretend any more. On her left and right sat respectively Nikka and Justin, both impassive and silent but looking directly at her.

"Here I am, Chief Conservator at The Bibliotek, the world's largest library. The pinnacle of my career," Violetta said defiantly but sarcastically.

"Absolutely!"

"Mads, you were lucky. You didn't get stuck there, in the Conservation Department. You had mummy to pluck you out and put you somewhere else, just a little bit higher up the ladder. Well, I'm at the top of my ladder, there's no other ladders for me! I've got four hundred and fifty-six people reporting to me. Big deal. I'm where I am because I'm good at what I do, and I'm not referring to mending bloody books. But there's nothing else. And I hate that. I want more. A lot more. And a lot more money, and that's what I'm getting."

Mads remained standing, dumbfounded, during Violetta's rant. It wasn't just the words she was saying. It was also their combination with the complete change in her demeanour and their delivery that caused him to stand looking at her, his mouth silently agape. Then he heard the words *more money* and his shock was replaced by his mounting anger. No more formalities and politeness. "You can't be serious! Is money all that this is about?!"

"Of course not! You just don't get it, do you. It's not just money. I... hate... my... job. I fucking *hate* books."

"What? How can you say that? You're a conservator for goodness sake!"

"*Was* a conservator, Mads. Past tense. I haven't done any actual work on a book for a very long time. I just manage minions who do the work, and talk about it."

Mads walked away from the table without responding and walked into the kitchen to tell the two staff they would not be needed any more that evening, after which they bid their goodnights and left the apartment. Mads came back to the table and sat down.

"I suppose you'll be wanting my resignation," offered Violetta.

"Justin?" Mads said, more as a cue than a question, as he turned to him.

"Be under no illusion, Ms Simpson," Justin began, "we have grounds to terminate your employment with immediate effect and issue a statement to staff making it clear you were terminated, on the grounds of gross misconduct. In fact, I have advised Mads to do so. However,..."

"However," interrupted Mads, "we are going to let you resign, and for personal, family, health, whatever reasons you want made public, provided you do exactly what is asked of you during the next forty-eight hours."

"Okay, I get that it's over between you and I, Mads, but why the façade?"

"I'm sorry, *you're* asking *me* why the façade?! I'll tell you why. It's because your life depends on it, that's why!"

"What, are you actually threatening me?" she said with a mock but slightly manic chuckle.

"No, it's not me you have to worry about, Violetta. It's Thurldottir," Mads said firmly.

"Chair Thurldottir? That hag, are you serious?" Violetta said, now almost laughing for real.

Mads turned to Nikka without responding and nodded his head. "Show her Pienza," he said quietly. Nikka reached across behind her to the dresser beside the dining table, picked up a folder that had been lying on the dresser and brought it back to the table, opened it, sifted through the contents, then began taking A4-size photographic prints out of the folder, one by one, each time placing them on the table, facing Violetta. Mads watched her face. He had already seen the photographs and neither needed nor wanted to see them again. Now he wanted to see how Violetta reacted to them.

There were five photographs in total, but Violetta stopped looking after the second. At glancing at the first, she exclaimed horror and put a hand over her mouth. Her eyes widened; her face still white. It was obvious to Mads and Nikka that she was shocked, probably to her core, hopefully. But neither felt sorry for her. Nikka had just shown her some of the photographs of the scene at Viscount Rossellini's house after the Carabinieri had discovered his body. Nikka had acquired them through her connections in the Norwegian Security Service.

"That's what was left of Viscount Rossellini, a resident of Pienza, Violetta," said Mads. "He had been murdered only minutes before

Rafe had arrived, and Rafe saw the worst of it. He saw the smouldering fire in the pit of what was left of the Viscount's stomach, Violetta. That we *don't* have a photograph of, but you get the picture."

"Why are you showing me this?!"

"Violetta, I was the only person who knew Rafe was going to Pienza and who he was going to visit. Until I told you."

Violetta stared at Mads, a slow comprehension beginning to show on her face.

"Then you told Carlson," said Nikka matter-of-factly. "Then he told Thurldottir and then he told someone else, and that someone else was instructed by Carlson to send Rafe a message because, like you, that person did what he was told to do by Carlson."

"Did?"

"He's dead. Shot. But not before he killed the Viscount and made it look like the work of the Present Sect, albeit without any subtlety."

"And you're saying that was the message that Carlson told him to give?"

"It was certainly the message that was given at least. The evidence speaks for itself," replied Mads.

"It also means you are implicated in pre-meditated murder, Ms Simpson," warned Nikka.

"Are you going to arrest me?" Violetta said, shakily, her defensive bravado now completely gone.

"No, Mads has already told you that you are going to be allowed to resign," said Nikka, turning to Mads, who nodded. "But what I am saying to you here and now is that if we do not get your fullest co-operation going forward over the next two days I *will* arrest you and turn you over to the Norwegian Police, no hesitation," Nikka continued, now staring intently at Violetta.

Violetta returned her stare and could see that Nikka was serious. The tone of her voice had already indicated that and her eyes confirmed it.

"And don't forget, Ms Simpson, we also know that you informed Carlson that Rafe would be in Russia, at the Trinity Monastery in Sergiyev. This is a fact you cannot deny because you were already a suspect when Rafe informed Mads of his plan to take that trip and why," said Nikka.

"I was set up?"

"Yes. The Present Sect, or more correctly someone pretending to be part of the Present Sect, was waiting for Rafe. But this time I was there as well and we were ready," said Nikka.

Mads then leaned towards Violetta. "But this time they were going to kill Nags, Violetta."

Mads and Nikka let that sink in for a few seconds. Nikka then spoke. "What are your instructions from Carlson?"

Violetta let out a long sigh and turned to Nikka. "I am to report to him anything Mads says and does that doesn't involve any day-to-day business."

"That's all, nothing else? What about Rafe? When were you asked to report on him?"

"Last October Carlson told me to inform him of any movements of Rafe that I became aware. Any. And any conversations he had with you that I became aware of."

"Did he say why?"

"Not as much. He only said there was a concern that some of his activities were attracting the attention of the Present Sect."

"I see."

"Carlson is blackmailing me," she said quietly, turning back and looking at Mads.

Mads and Nikka looked at each other. "But you told me you are being paid to spy on me," Mads responded.

"Yes, I am. But that is only half of it."

"What's he blackmailing you about?" asked Mads.

Violetta turned back to Nikka. "Full co-operation?" she asked her.

"Yes," replied Nikka.

"For how long, until you get Carlson?" she asked.

"Until we make things right at The Bibliotek," said Nikka.

"And then what?"

Nikka looked at Mads, who nodded again. "And then you get to walk away. Away from Mads, away from The Bibliotek, away from Norway. Permanently. And never contact Mads again."

Violetta looked at her unfinished meal and let out a sigh. "There was some money stolen from my place of employment — the job I had before Harvard. I was accused of the theft but wasn't arrested or charged due to lack of evidence. But I had to leave. Carlson told me he had the evidence and would disclose it if I didn't start "screwing Ingridson" — his words not mine — and getting him to talk."

"We are aware of those theft allegations. That was a long time ago though," said Justin, as if to divert Mads' attention away from what Violetta had just admitted.

"It was a lot of money. A *shitload* of money," responded Violetta.

"You read my notebook, did you not?" asked Mads, choosing to ignore her admission as well.

"Yes, it was only the once. And it was out of curiosity, not because I was on some sort of secret mission. I saw you writing in it and I thought maybe you were writing about me, or more poems about us. But then you said it was just work issues."

"What did you read?"

"Not much. I only had seconds. You stopped snoring and I thought you would wake up and notice I wasn't there."

"Snoring? I don't snore."

"For goodness sake, Mads, yes you do. A few glasses of red and off you go."

Mads went mute and was thinking what to say when Nikka spoke. "What exactly did you relate to Carlson about what you had read?" she asked.

"It was more about what I saw than what I read. Mads' handwriting is not the best, and he's not good at breaking a paragraph. Very dense writing."

"Okay, so what did you tell Carlson you had seen?"

Violetta sighed again, a longer sigh, then took a moment to recall. "I told him Mads was writing some cryptic notes. Acronyms I couldn't recall because I didn't know what they were for. Some words about 'Thomas' but I could not take them on board so I didn't mention them to Carlson, just that 'Thomas was missing'. Saw a note that Carlson is involved and Thurldottir is 'running the show'. Something about 'Bradshaw spruiking Arcadia' for The Bibliotek. Mads didn't trust Larkin. Saw 'CONSPIRACY'. In capital letters. Lots of question marks. Something about the Present Sect being an issue for Mads and The Bibliotek. Something about Deputy Bibliotekar Bradshaw and Arcadia relocation, nothing specific."

Nikka had been writing down what Violetta was saying, but now she stopped and looked at Mads with alarm, who also looked at Nikka with the same expression.

"Is that all?" asked Nikka.

"Yes."

"Did you tell Carlson that Mads had gone to Moscow?"

"Yes."

"What exactly did you say?"

"I said that Mads had been contacted by Moscow police and asked to go to Moscow as a matter of urgency. I said Mads told me that something had happened to Rafe."

"Okay. Now here is what you are now to tell Carlson. You are to say that Mads has told you that Rafe was murdered at a monastery in a city called Sergiyev, near Moscow, apparently by the Present Sect, but in order to keep The Bibliotek out of it he arranged, through my contacts, for the Moscow police to keep Rafe's identity out of the media."

Violetta stared at Nikka blankly.

"You do understand?"

"Yes."

"Then repeat it back to me."

This Violetta did. "Then what?" she asked.

"There is one more thing we need you to do."

Violetta gave an impatient sigh. It was clear she was done with any further discussion. "What?"

"We need you to come to Mads' office tomorrow morning at nine o'clock sharp. Bring your data pad so we can check to make sure you told Carlson about Mr Nagy."

"And?"

"You need to understand we need to construct a false narrative to save you from danger lest Carlson finds out the real reason he won't be getting any more information from you about the Bibliotekar. We need your help in constructing this narrative. I will explain more in the morning," instructed Nikka.

"Basically, Violetta," offered Mads, "you will tell Carlson, when we give you the green light to do so, and not before, that you want to file a sexual harassment suit against me, and when he asks you why you will tell him something like 'I've done the hard yards, and with Ingridson it was hard, he is not exactly Don Juan, and I just want the payout and leave this shithole.' Something like that. You can do that, can't you?"

"Perhaps not in so many words, but yes, I can do that," Violetta said, more than a little upset.

"Now you can leave," Mads said, without any emotion or feeling. He was empty of both.

Violetta pushed back her chair, put her hands on the table, stood up and walked to the front door without a word or even glancing at Mads, who called out to her as she walked resolutely away from the table, "Your things are in a bag beside the door."

Violetta reached the door, put her hand on the door handle, then took it off and turned to look at the bag of her overnight stay things lying on the floor for a few seconds. Then in a slow and deliberate action she kicked the bag across the floor as hard as she could. The flying bag split, the contents went spilling and sliding even further across the floor. Violetta then opened the door, stepped out, and slammed it. It had been one long, convoluted, wall of clashing sharp sounds.

"I'm sorry Mads," Nikka said quietly.

"Thank you, Nikka," Mads replied quietly, "but I daresay not quite as sorry as I am. Time for some coffee, I think."

Nikka knew well enough to stay silent for a while. Betrayal was a bitch and she well knew its bite. As did Justin.

5:10pm, Saturday, 16ᵗʰ February 2205

Abe Carlson was worried. He did not like travelling to Danuta Thurldottir's chalet, but on this occasion he had no choice. What he had to discuss with her had to be face-to-face, and there was an urgency attached to the matter.

"What is it Carlson, to bring you all the way here?" asked Thurldottir as Carlson entered her study. "I know you don't like leaving The Bibliotek."

"How certain are you that Nagy was taken care of?"

"You tell me, you're the one who got the message from Simpson that he is dead. Dare I ask the reason for your question?"

"I have not heard from Smits since I got the message that the job had been done."

"And that's an issue?"

"As you can appreciate, I have to be careful that I am not seen to be in contact with him at The Bibliotek, but it would appear he has not returned from Moscow, and he is not responding to any of my messages to his private neurophone."

"And now you are worried, is that it?"

"Yes, it's been three days. I think I should have a word to Bradshaw to see what he can find out."

"No! Don't do that. Keep that fool out of this. We need Bradshaw focused on Arcadia and nothing else but Arcadia. We do not need him asking himself — or you or me — why we are concerned with Nagy. That prick is not part of the narrative, the bigger picture. Don't lose sight of that. I have someone else close to Ingridson, someone I can rely on, unlike Smits, and who can find out more about Nagy."

"As you wish."

"It is not as I wish, it is as it needs to be. I just hope your friend Smits hasn't fucked up again. You did tell him to make this job public didn't you? I hope you haven't forgotten that's half the reason for getting rid of him in the first place. So far all we have, the Russian police have, is a body with no name attached. No attachment to Mads Ingridson is not much use to us right now. You do realise that don't you?"

"Yes, I haven't forgotten the reason we need Nagy's death to be publicly known so we can attach it to the shit list against Ingridson."

"Good. But for now, let me deal with it. And do me a favour."

"Yes?"

"Stop sending fucking messages to Smits. It's time to start using *our* people again."

END OF CHAPTER THIRTEEN

Chapter Fourteen

Rafe Makes an Offer

"One of the dreams of Western civilisation has been the accumulation of all knowledge documented in one library. It begins with the myth of the Library of Alexandria and returned strongly after the Renaissance with the growing sense that libraries could help their communities master all the questions of mankind, or at the very least offer them the opportunity to look up all the references in an important scholarly work."
Richard Ovenden, *Burning the Books – A History of Knowledge Under Attack*, John Murray Press, London, 2020, page 70.

7:16pm, Thursday, 14ᵗʰ February 2205

After their heliojet landed in Glasgow, Nikka showed Rafe a message she had just received from Svetlana. It said she hoped the next time they caught up with each other it wouldn't involve someone getting shot (smiley emoji), but that there had been no media about it.

"You see? I told you it would work out," said Nikka.

"Yes, you did. You did indeed say that."

A little while later Rafe went to collect the four-wheel drive hydrogen car he had pre-booked for the drive to Glencoe and the farm where Thomas was staying.

"Are you sure this fancy four-wheel drive is necessary? And an old hydrogen car. Not exactly conspicuous," said Nikka as Rafe pulled up in the pick-up area and started loading their bags.

"That may be the case, but it is necessary. When Justin called Thomas to let him know we were coming he said to pass on a warning about the snow on the road to the farm where he's holed up. And we're not talking hoverpath or road. We don't need chains but these big arse snow tyres will do the trick," replied Rafe with confidence.

"I take it you want to drive, again?"

"Absolutely. It's my hobby after all."

A little while later they were on the snow-slushed road and heading out of the airport precinct to the hoverway heading north.

"Please tell me you're unarmed on this trip," Rafe asked Nikka, half seriously. "Are you armed? What do they say... packing?"

"No, Rafe. I am not 'packing'. Calm down. I left my gun in safe hands at the embassy in Moscow. I will retrieve it when next I am there. Or not. It depends on how we sort out the mess created by

Smits. Thankfully my bullet went straight through his head and is now embedded in a tree trunk metres away, from what I could tell."

"Yes, I did notice it went straight through, as you say. Not something I want to see again."

"Anyway," said Nikka, ignoring Rafe's interruption, "my threat assessment for this little jaunt was very low. This trip I am just a glorified escort."

"That sounds expensive."

"Good grief! Would you like me to show you what I can do with my hands?"

"I don't know what to say to that."

"Don't say anything."

"I have to ask you something, Nikka."

"I hope you're not wanting to know if I am in a relationship."

"No, no. No! I'm not trying to make a move on you. I'm way too old for that. I mean, maybe I would if I were a bit younger. Well, a lot younger..."

"Rafe, what *is* your question?"

"Where exactly did you learn to shoot like that? I mean, two shots, bang bang, just like that. In the dark and each one right on target."

"When I was a young girl, my father taught me how to shoot. I liked it. Then when I was a big girl, the NSS taught me how to shoot to kill. That I don't like. Taking someone's life by an instant action is a big step up the behavioural ladder — or down it — depending on your view of life. There are always consequences, some immediate and direct, others not so. Some of my colleagues did not concern themselves with them, and *that* concerned me after a while. It was one of the reasons I jumped when the opportunity came up at The Bibliotek. There were other reasons as well, but it was ideal. *It's a library*, I thought, how much killing is involved?"

"Well, I'm just glad you knew what to do. I guess I owe my life to you."

"Don't worry, Rafe, I won't hold you to any favours. Just doing my job."

Rafe turned to her and smiled, then focused again on driving.

"But tell me, who made the call to Mads from the Moscow police?"

"That was me," replied Nikka.

"But, how,... I mean weren't you risking Larkin recognising your voice?"

"Not really. I have a very seductive Russian-sounding accent when I want to use it. It always gets me what I want. Men, especially non-Russian men, will do anything I ask of them when they hear it. And some women."

"Show me," asked Rafe.

She did. She repeated what she had said on the call to Larkin.

"Wow, I'm melting, said Rafe, genuinely impressed.

After a little while of quiet between the two of them, and as they left the outskirts of Glasgow and headed north to Glencoe in noticeably lighter traffic as the day's sunset fast approached, Rafe, more relaxed, turned his mind to more pressing matters. He couldn't believe it had only been the night before that they were at the Trinity Monastery.

"This is not supposed to be a violent business," he said. "It's not even a business. It's meant to be a positive and fulfilling endeavour. For the benefit of humankind. Books are books. I just can't fathom the violence; we are just repeating history rather than changing the future. I really want to believe this violence can be ended."

"I couldn't agree more, Rafe. But I think all this has nothing to do with books. There is a rationality to it, a method, and no book warrants it. Well, not to my mind at least. Then again, it seems a bullet had your name on it."

"You can be sure that has been weighing on my mind, Nikka. I must have really pissed someone off. I can probably deal with the Present Sect being behind it, but someone at The Bibliotek? That's something else entirely. So, is it really safe to bring Thomas back? I mean, right now?"

"Safety is relative, Rafe, never an absolute. But yes, provided we do this on the quiet and provided he stays in Mads' guest apartment he should be fine. Just to be on the safe side I will be assigning some discreet security presence, ostensibly in relation to Mads' overall security arrangements but specifically for Thomas's benefit. But don't worry, I honestly don't believe I have any more rogue thugs in my team. Smits was an aberration. I should have picked up on his profile a bit more carefully. He really wasn't suited for working at The Bibliotek even if he hadn't been a plant by Carlson. He made his choices though and now he's dead because of them."

"But why target me? First they send me a not-too-subtle message, then they try to deal with me permanently. What threat am I?"

"You don't have to be a threat, Rafe. And you're probably not. They only need a reason to have you out of the way. This is not some one-off event. There's a plan being played out here, and it appears to be a long term one. Not like a robbery, for example. That's a one-off crime. In, out, done. No, this is something else, and getting rid of you is just one part of it."

"That's not making me feel any easier about things."

"Put it this way, then Rafe. I don't want to get too fixated on investigating the attacks on *you*. If I do I risk not finding answers on the broader problem; the one involving the motives of Carlson and Thurldottir beyond their apparent need to have you out of the way. There's something else going on, and if we can solve *that* mystery the answers for you being targeted may well present themselves."

"I get that, I just don't like being in this situation, when I seem to have no control."

"You may have no control but you certainly can have an impact on outcomes. Provided you stay the course," Nikka responded with a little more seriousness. "Does Councillor Metcalfe know why we are coming?" she asked.

"No, I thought it best not to tell him over the neurophone. Call me paranoid," replied Rafe.

"Paranoid you are," said Nikka, turning to smile at him.

Rafe drove on without responding. After another period of quiet between them, Rafe finally got the nerve to ask the question he'd *really* been wanting to ask.

"Tell me, Nikka, how do you know Svetlana?... Lana?"

Nikka turned and looked at Rafe, as if trying to decide whether or not to answer him, but then quickly said "we were married once. When I was a lot younger," she said, then added for emphasis, "a long time ago."

"Oh, sorry," Rafe said.

"Don't be Rafe. I was sorry I thought I was turned on by women. Turns out I wasn't, after all. Well, for a while I was turned on by her at least. Then again, maybe I just changed. Whatever. There were no hard feelings. I knew I could rely on her, and besides, as I told you, she owed me big time."

"And now you're even?"

"Probably. The funny thing is I agreed to go on that trip with you in the little hope, just a little, that I could spare time to catch up with her." Nikka let out a little laugh. "Turns out I could," she smiled at Rafe.

"Well, all I can say is I am glad you did. But it begs another question."

"Let me guess. What were my other reasons for leaving the Norwegian Security Service and joining The Bibliotek?"

"Yes," said Rafe.

"Simple. Life expectancy, probabilities, injuries, age, desire, responsibility, challenge, money. In roughly that order."

"Starting with *simple*?" Rafe asked without taking his eyes off the road.

Nikka looked at Rafe and shook her head in mock exasperation. She liked Rafe's sense of humour. It was sharp and quick, though not always original.

"Fair enough," said Rafe, still not looking at her.

"And the fact it was a library," Nikka continued. "As I said, not much scope for gunplay in a library. Or so I thought."

"Let's hope it doesn't get to that. Then we'd really be in trouble," pondered Rafe.

An hour or so later, Rafe nearly missed the turnoff from the main hover road onto the farm road. The landscape was now under the heavy impression of several months of snow, rendering useless any points of reference Rafe would normally have used.

"I see what you mean about the road," admitted Nikka, as she hung onto the strap hanging down from the roof of the car as it negotiated the snow-covered and rutted dirt roads. The only way Rafe could stay on track was by keeping an eye on the snow poles lining the edge of the narrow road.

"Don't worry, it's not too far," said Rafe optimistically. "Just keep your eyes out for a stone bridge on your left. We need to turn and cross it."

It wasn't long before they turned a corner of the road and came upon an open stretch of snow-covered pasture, with the near-frozen river on their left. Despite the gloom, Rafe recognised the spot and it wasn't long before he caught sight of the bridge.

"Nearly there," he said as he slowed to a crawl in order to turn wide and steer onto it straight, given it had no barriers on it sides. After successfully negotiating their passage across, Rafe drove a few metres more and stopped in front of a closed gate.

"Are we here?" asked Nikka.

"Not quite. The farm house is over the next hill. We have to get through this gate first," said Rafe, looking at Nikka.

Nikka looked back at him with a blank look on her face.

"What I mean is, you need to get out and open the gate for us," he finally said.

"Oh, sorry" said Nikka. She steeled herself then opened the door to get out. "Shit it's cold!"

"Thomas said he'd leave the gate unlocked for us, ok?" Rafe called to her as he leant across and shut Nikka's door.

"I hope he's got a fire going!" Nikka said breathlessly as she clambered back into the car after closing the gate. "It's beyond peace and quiet here; it's next-level remote."

A minute later they were over the hill and coming down the other side, cautiously, and they could see the cottage in the early evening gloom, with smoke winding its way out of the sole chimney and some lights on inside.

"Looks like you've got your fire," noted Rafe. "Do you drink scotch?"

"Whiskey? Yes I do, occasionally."

"You really *are* in luck then," Rafe smiled.

Just then, as the car's headlights gave some light to the front of the cottage, a figure stepped out of the doorway, waved, then went back inside.

"Was that Councillor Metcalfe?" asked Nikka.

"Yes it was, and enough of this 'Councillor Metcalfe' business. Call him 'Thomas'. If you don't, he'll ask you to. Have you met him before?"

"Only once, he probably doesn't remember me."

"Well, he knows you're coming with me, at least."

As Rafe stopped the car in front of the cottage, Thomas came out again to greet them.

"Good to see you Nags, and you too Nikka. It's been a while, yes?" asked Thomas as Nikka got out of the car and Rafe grabbed their bags from the back seat.

"About two years, Councillor Metcalfe," said Nikka as shook Thomas's hand. "At a function at the Academy."

"Yes," replied Thomas, grinning and peering at her as if sizing up a leg of ham. "I believe you're right, Head of Security Johannson. Time is flying so fast these days, Faster the older I get. Now, can we agree on something? You call me 'Thomas' and I'll keep calling you 'Nikka'. Okay?"

Rafe looked at Nikka. "I told you."

"Yes, I think I can manage that,... Thomas," replied Nikka, not entirely comfortable with the informality imposed on her.

After they settled in the lounge room around the open fire, with Nikka and Rafe sitting on the lounge which was Rafe's bed for the night, but before Thomas had finished pouring each a shot of whiskey, Rafe got in first.

"Nikka, there's only one other bedroom, I think," he said.

"That's right," said Thomas. "Nikka can sleep there. You're where you are. I've got a spare blanket for you." He finished pouring and sat down in his armchair by the fire. "Now, my friends, what urgent thing has brought you both here? I gather stuff's been happening."

"When did you last speak to Justin, apart from his call earlier today?" asked Nikka.

"Cheers," replied Thomas, before raising his glass and taking a large nip. "Oh, that was near the beginning of January — the first week of the year as I recall."

"That was the call from Justin, letting you know about the Bibliotekar's trip to Arcadia and the samples of palladium and rhodium he found?"

"Yes, but as I recall Mads didn't know what the samples were until he got back to The Bibliotek," replied Thomas.

"Yes, that's correct, but the important thing is he found them in the same area you came across the geosurvey team," said Nikka.

"Oh, I didn't know that. I forgot to ask Justin that. But I did tell him the word 'palladium' sounded familiar."

"Have you been able to recall anything about that?" asked Rafe.

"I've tried, but... nuh. I may be imagining it. Just can't pin it down. Sorry."

"That's okay Coun...Thomas," said Nikka. "Yes, stuff's been happening. I can tell you that the man who threatened you was on my team at The Bibliotek."

"Was?"

"He's dead. *E morto.* Nikka shot him," said Rafe, shaking his empty glass at Thomas, who passed the bottle to him.

"You shot your own guy because he threatened me?"

"Hmfff. No," Nikka said calmly, pausing. "I shot him because he was about to shoot Rafe," she continued, glaring at Rafe. Nikka had wanted to lead into that little bit of news with some context. But now, thanks to Rafe, she had to backtrack and explain things backwards. "Shoot to kill, that is."

Thomas sat still and listened intently to Nikka as she did her explaining, with an occasional *ad lib* supplied by Rafe the only interruption. When she had finished, he spoke.

"You're saying that there's some kind of conspiracy happening at the highest levels of The Bibliotek to do with Arcadia and some very valuable minerals, with somehow an off-the-wall plan to move The Bibliotek there, plus for good measure there are spies about, one's been apparently caught, the Chief Conservator no less, plus, even better, part of that conspiracy involves people pretending to be the Present Sect and trying to knock off young Nags here? And I've missed all the fun?"

"It doesn't quite fall the way you said, Thomas," replied Nikka. She drained her glass and poured herself another. "Yes, there are several unusual things happening right now involving various parties at The Bibliotek, but I can't help thinking at the moment that it is all connected in some way. I am working on it."

"Time to pack your bags, Thomas," said Rafe. "We're not actually here just for bedtime stories. We are here to take you back to The Bibliotek. First thing tomorrow morning, in fact" said Rafe.

"I was half expecting this," responded Thomas, a bit subdued, "but half hoping not. This semi-retirement deal has been starting to feel like just the thing for me. I've made a start, can you believe, on my memoirs. If only my memory wasn't so bad."

"Your memory sounds pretty good to me," said Nikka.

"Oh," Thomas replied, smiling at Nikka. "I always have space in it for pretty women."

"Sorry to interrupt you two, but Mads needs you back at The Bibliotek, Thomas," said Rafe.

"What's happened?"

"Chair Thurldottir has officially made your absence a case of missing," said Nikka. "And that means your seat on the Governing

Council will be formally vacated with a new Councillor elected. Unless, of course, my team can locate you."

"And I'm guessing this replacement — *if* I don't return to The Bibliotek — will be someone of Thurldottir's choice?" asked Thomas.

"Hers or Carlson's," said Rafe.

"Well we can't let that happen. That would be disastrous for Mads and may tip the scales to his departure. When is the next meeting? Is it the AGM?"

"No, the AGM is on the first of April," said Nikka.

"Ha! April Fool's Day. I can't wait to see Thurldottir's face."

"But first there is a Governing Council meeting next month," continued Nikka, "and on the agenda will be a report from Mads, representing Adcom, on the progress of the Relocation Study Group."

"The what?" asked Thomas.

"The team I was telling you about which was commissioned by the Governing Council — or more accurately Thurldottir — to look at relocating part or all of The Bibliotek due to capacity and security issues. I am in the Study Group, and it's involved going to Arcadia for an inspection, largely due to the Deputy Bibliotekar's initiative," explained Nikka.

"That last bit sounds suspicious. I've never liked Bradshaw, just between us. You think he's in on this conspiracy? I've never understood how Mads came to promote him."

"That remains to be seen, I'm keeping an open mind. What I am trying to explain is that Mads doesn't want your presence at The Bibliotek to be known until you attend the AGM."

"So, what's the big rush?"

"Given more recent events he wants you safe and sound and close at hand. And he needs your help in preparing for the AGM. We're putting you in one of the Bibliotekar's guest apartments on his floor."

"So, I was right to make myself at scarce at The Bibliotek, it seems."

"No, we can't be certain about that, and I don't think so. In fact, I think the threat made against you was empty, if not a mistake."

"A mistake? It was pretty clearly made."

"Not a mistake by him, he meant it. But maybe a mistake by those pulling the strings, if they knew about it."

"How so?"

341

"It was what prompted Mads to go to Arcadia himself."

"And you knew about all this? Did you go with him?"

"No to both questions. And no to the question as to whether you contacted me about Smits' threat against you."

"Ah, yes, sorry about that. I guess I should have. But to be honest that call really shook me up. I didn't know what to think, or who to trust. I just knew I needed to get out of there PDQ."

"You're okay to go back to The Bibliotek with me, aren't you?"

"Oh yes! No problem. I've heard from Justin Foote that you were basically running the whole investigation, as you should. Can't have us amateurs fouling things up. Speaking of which, aren't you coming with us, Nags?"

"Very funny, Thomas, very funny. I am going with you only as far as the helioport. I need to avoid The Bibliotek for a little while, and besides I have Finder business to attend to in Oxford."

"Christ Church College?" asked Thomas.

"Yes, Dr Jamison sent me a message just before Nikka and I went to Moscow that he wants me to come for another face-to-face. I gather he'll tell me how it went at the Board of Governor's meeting."

"I wish I could come with you, Nags. That would be another coup for The Bibliotek, especially after these years of stonewalling. But tell me this, why were you targeted by the Present Sect?"

"That is a very good question, Thomas. We think it's just our resident thugs at The Bibliotek rather than the Present Sect, but the question as to why remains."

"I take it Nikka that you haven't officially found me?"

"That's correct, you're proving to be a very hard Councillor to find," Nikka replied with a smile. "I could lose my job over this."

"Don't you worry, I'll put in a good word for you with Mads. Now, Rafe, I don't have much in the way of packing to do, the night is still young, there's plenty of wood, and this bottle is only half-empty. Tell me more about this Ruben character and his *Fabrica*."

9:30am Sunday, 17ᵗʰ February 2205

Christian was waiting for Rafe on the steps of the Christ Church Library, at the southern end of an otherwise empty Peckwater Quadrangle. By the time he reached Dr Jamison, Rafe's face was numb from the biting cold.

"I think this time we should talk inside, in my office," offered Christian after they shook hands and welcomed each other. "It's a tad chilly this morning."

"You're not wrong," replied a breathless Rafe. "Thanks for seeing me today, I'm sorry I couldn't make it earlier."

"No problem," said Christian as he opened the first of two doors to the 18ᵗʰ century Georgian edifice that comprised the Library's main building, and beckoned Rafe to follow.

"My office is on the second floor, the stairs are this way," said Christian as he led Rafe through the foyer of the main entry.

Rafe could tell there were students about; they were sprinkled here and there amongst the massive shelves and tucked-away long wooden desks, with their intermittent lamps straining against the gloom of late winter, but he could not hear them, for it was an Oxford library and tradition still had a role to play in Oxford libraries. Silence was the rule.

Halfway to the stairs at the end of the main hall, they passed a huge, ancient, wooden pedestal. Rafe stopped walking, for he had instantly recognised the massive book sitting atop it, unopened. It was quarto size and exactly one thousand pages; an amazing publishing feat when it was first published in 1621.

"Burton's *Anatomy of Melancholy*," said Rafe as quietly as he could but still be heard as Christian leaned into him.

"You know it?" Christian whispered.

"Only too well. I studied it and Robert Burton during my time at the Academy. Well, when I say 'it' I mean the digitised version of it prepared by Project Gutenberg, with its horrible auto-generated HTML text. I gather this is *the* first edition Burton gave to the Library?"

"It is indeed. It is quite possibly our most valuable book."

"And you've got it here, out in the open, on a pedestal?" asked Rafe, a little bewildered.

"Yes, I put it there three weeks ago, not long after I received your formal proposal for The Bibliotek to procure our Special Collections.

343

It was a test, you see. We change our display books all the time, and the students are free to open them and read them at leisure, the only proviso being the book is to remain on the pedestal. I wanted to see if any student recognised the book or attempted to read it."

"Well it's a huge book. That would put a lot of people off. Opening it is a task in itself."

"Yes, but still, not one student has to my knowledge given it more than a passing glance. It's just another old book with too many pages, too many words, too much verbosity."

Rafe smiled. He knew all too well what Christian was implying. "How wrong they are. It's not just the first ever psychiatric encyclopædia, it's basically a discourse on all human knowledge then known. It was Sir William Osler's favourite book, which is saying something. As I recall, when Osler was a Fellow here at Christ Church he commenced the first ever catalogue of the five hundred books bequeathed to the Library by Burton when he died in 1640. That's almost a three-hundred-year gap, by the way."

"You know your bibliophilic history, Rafe. I commend you. Yes, the students have been remiss in ignoring the *Anatomy*. But I suspected as much, so the book has been quite safe sitting here."

Rafe looked around. "I guess you're right."

"And yes, it was Osler who decided the Library needed to finally look at and categorise the Burton collection. I daresay we lost a few volumes in the intervening centuries. Shall we?" Christian motioned Rafe to follow.

Upstairs, Christian beckoned Rafe to sit at the meeting table in his office. "Some tea, perhaps? Or coffee?"

"Coffee would be great thanks. Black."

Christian made a quick call from his desk to order the tea for himself and coffee for Rafe, then joined him at the table.

"I guess you're anxious to know the outcome of the vote?"

"You could say that."

"Sorry for the cryptic message, but I wanted to let you know in person. I have to be honest and say I wasn't hopeful going into the meeting. When I stated the case for the procurement — that is, for the Council to vote in favour of your proposal — there were quite a few questions and critical comments. But, the vote was taken and it was forty-five for, fifteen against. Which means it's been approved.

Congratulations." With that, Christian extended his hand to Rafe, who gladly took it.

"That's fantastic, Christian. I'm sure the Council has made the right decision. What do you think carried the vote?"

"Interesting question. There was no doubt that some of the features of the proposal were very favourably viewed, especially from a cost perspective. But it's true to say that the Council took into account the increased threat represented by the Present Sect. There had been a lot of agitation amongst the Oxford student cohort after the Merton College Library was firebombed and destroyed. It started with posters headed 'Positive Outcomes' and listing such things as the money saved on old and useless books for better use in the present community. Then it escalated into questioning the ongoing prevalence of libraries in the Oxford community, and suggestions that action needs to be taken. Then Lincoln College lost their library to arson, and just last year St Edmund Hall's Library was also torched. It's very concerning that such things can happen at Oxford, but the safety and wellbeing of our Special Collections is paramount."

Rafe was not surprised to hear of the Council's nervousness about the threat posed by the Present Sect, but he didn't want to say anything about the Sect, given recent events. Nor did he feel like mentioning the fact that the Christ Church Library was only one of over a hundred and twenty libraries at Oxford, each one with significant numbers of rare, ancient, and important books and manuscripts, making the odds of an attack targeting Christ Church a little long. Instead, Rafe was pleased that several years of effort was now about to be behind him and he could move on to the next project.

"I'm sure you and the Council will be pleased with the rollout of the procurement project. We are good at what we do. Are you going to be coming with the collection?"

"Well, the bottom line is I will no longer be Keeper of the Special Collections since there will no longer be any collections, special or otherwise, to keep. Hence I see no reason not to accept your offer and several reasons to accept it if you'll still have me."

"Absolutely we'll still have you. Only the job has changed a little bit."

"Oh, I see."

Just then a light knocking was heard at his office door and a young staff member brought the tea and coffee in, so Rafe waited until they were alone again.

"We'd like you to think about taking on the role of Acting Chief Conservator," said Rafe, after the staff member had left.

"Acting Chief Conservator? That *is* a little bit of a change. What happened to Violetta Simpson? She's barely been there for two years," asked Christian.

"Barely twelve months, actually. Ms Simpson has recently tendered her resignation, and is no longer at The Bibliotek."

"May I ask why?"

"I'm not privy to the specific reason, but I can tell you it was on medical grounds and nothing associated with the role itself. On that you have my word."

"I see. Well, that's a bit of an upgrade from the role we had been discussing, but is it temporary?"

"Yes and no," replied Rafe. He had talked with Mads that morning; firstly to confirm that Violetta was gone from The Bibliotek and secondly to be briefed by Mads on the exact nature of the new offer he was to make to Christian. "There are four Deputy Chief Conservators at The Bibliotek and as its turns out none of them have seniority over the others. That may be the result of bad succession planning, but the fact remains each of them are solid potential candidates for the top role. As a result, there won't be a rush to make that appointment. If you were to step into that top role as a temporary measure it would allow time for a proper assessment of the right person to be the new Chief Conservator, it would allow you to focus on on-boarding the Christ Church collection, and it would also give you the opportunity to make your case for the top role, should you choose to do so. Worst case scenario would see you come back here after twelve months, as originally discussed. But if you like working with us at The Bibliotek and want to pursue that opportunity it will undoubtedly put that little bit more pressure on the other four candidates to perform at their best."

"But wouldn't a lot of my time be taken up managing four hundred conservators?"

"Four hundred and fifty."

"Precisely. That sounds like a lot of managing and not much actual conservation work."

"The Bibliotekar, Mads Ingridson, is quite strong on ensuring every senior Conservator, no matter at what level, having the time to get their hands dirty. That's why there is an Assistant Chief Conservator whose main focus is the staff management side of things. They are the main liaison between HR and the department, so the Chief Conservator can spend his or her time more productively. This includes giving regular lectures at the Academy. Six in total during each student year, on topics of your choice. If it were you, an ideal subject of at least one lecture would the Christ Church collection project, if not more."

"I'll wait until I get something more concrete in writing from you about that role before committing myself, but for now let's assume I agree to go with the Special Collections. What happens next?"

"That's perfectly understandable. Now that I know you are definitely interested, I will get onto HR for them to get something looking like an actual offer to you ASAP. Regardless, our Lead Conservator on this project will contact you and make arrangements for our scoping team to arrive and begin the task of identification, prioritising, and packaging. Priority in everything is given to those books in the most need of repair and rectification, so we like to call this stage of the project The Triage. Before they arrive, however, we will need you to confirm all the current locations where the Special Collections are held."

"Do you want my assistance in The Triage?"

"Yes, that would be a huge benefit, especially if you already have a rough idea of the books at the greatest risk."

"I can tell you right now it's all the books currently in the storeroom. They were all in the part of the basement where we had a serious flooding problem thanks to some dodgy plumbing work that was carried out. A burst pipe happened on a Saturday night and went undetected until the Monday morning. We got all the books out but have hardly been able to do anything with them yet apart from trying to dry them out. It hasn't been easy given we don't really have the right equipment. Or manpower."

"How many are we talking about?"

"From the flooding? I'd say about three hundred and fifty books."

"We can handle that. Any more in need of urgent attention?"

"No specific group or collection, but spread around there are a number requiring some work, some a lot."

"How many of those?"

"My best guess would be several hundred."

"We can manage those too, but good to know," replied Rafe, making a note on his data pad.

"Anything else you need to know today?"

"There's another development I'd like to talk to you about," said Rafe.

"Yes? Nothing too serious I hope," replied Christian, a little off-guard from Rafe's suddenly serious demeanour.

"Serious? No, sorry, not at all. Well, serious as in important, yes, but nothing bad."

"I'm all ears then."

"Well, over the years, over the decades, every time The Bibliotek procures another collection there is a de-duping process performed."

"I'm sorry, de-duping?"

"It's a process of merely determining if one of the newly-acquired books is of an edition that The Bibliotek already has. In such a circumstance the policy is and always has been to not on-board that book into the Central Repository."

"What happens to it?"

"It gets stored in a Secondary Repository."

"For what purpose?" asked Christian. Rafe was expecting questions but not this one.

"That is a very good question, Christian. To be honest, unfortunately it has never been answered by anything other than, or better than, the 'just-in-case' argument."

"I see. Interesting."

"The thing is, there are now so many of these 'secondary' books that the time has come to look at them holistically and critically. So, we did an audit, and that has informed the decision to curate all the disparate collections in the Secondary Repositories,..."

"How many?"

"I'm sorry?"

"How many of these secondary repositories are there?

"Ah, about a dozen, I think."

"A dozen!" Where?"

"Maybe ten or eleven, I'm not exactly sure. Various places, mainly Oslo and Frankfurt."

"I see. And what exactly do you mean 'curate'? Are we talking about a stocktake?"

"No, the audit did that. What I mean by curate is that we are intending to package up as much of our surplus stock, as it were, into as many specific categories and specialties as possible, then offer them to any library or academic or research institution that wants them. Gratis."

Rafe could tell Christian was listening intently, so he continued.

"It will be a massive undertaking, will have global reach, and it will require several years of dedicated work by an as yet unknown-size workforce, if not an ongoing effort to some material degree. As such the program will require a suitably-qualified and motivated Director. This role would commence about twelve months after you would move with the Christ Church collections to The Bibliotek."

"So, you're offering me one actual job and two potential jobs, is that right?"

"Not quite. If you put it like that it's more an actual job we're offering, then another one of two after the first," replied Rafe.

"Oh, I see. Tell me this though, how did The Bibliotek manage to accumulate so many copies and why haven't I heard about it?"

"I was afraid you would ask me that. To be honest, the existence of the Secondary Repositories is not public knowledge just yet, but Mads wanted me to sound you out with full disclosure. The secrecy was initially seen as a convenience. We didn't want our donors to feel that portions of their collections were not actually wanted. And we didn't want to get rid of them. So, the answer was to store them, but now it's gotten out of hand, and we must come clean. There'll be a PR spin on it of course, but we are serious about collating all the disparate remnants of donated collections and offering them to the best home possible. I'm sure many of the surviving academic libraries around the globe, in particular, will benefit, even Christ Church if there is a suitable field of study we can bundle up for you."

"You have my confidence, that I can guarantee," said Christian. "And I think I like the whole idea, providing we don't end up getting back anywhere near the same number of books."

"And I can guarantee that," responded Rafe. "It's too remote a possibility anyway."

"Okay, but first let's focus on the task at hand."

"We shall," said Rafe, standing up. "That's all for today, thanks Christian."

"No, thank you, it's been a most productive meeting, and I am looking forward to the project very much. Let me walk you out."

As they passed the *Anatomy of Melancholy*, untouched on its place on the pedestal, Christian paused as he suddenly remembered something.

"I almost forgot — I believe congratulations are in order," he said to Rafe.

"Thanks. Um, what for?"

"For the *Fabrica*, of course. That was an amazing Find for The Bibliotek. Well done."

"Thank you. Gee, word gets around. That only happened a few weeks ago."

"Everyone knows about it, Rafe. I read about it just yesterday in The Bibliotek's fortnightly newsletter. Didn't you?"

"I must read that august publication one day," Rafe smiled.

Christian looked at him, not knowing for sure whether Rafe was joking or not. "You know, I know your friend Ruben Rodriguez."

At hearing Ruben's name Rafe stopped in his tracks. "You've met him? I had only had the pleasure of his acquaintance just before we shook hands on the *Fabrica*."

"Yes, I've met him. It was a year or so ago. An interesting fellow. Very animated, larger than life. But he knows his books."

"Yes, that about sums up my experience with Ruben. How did you meet him?"

"Well, I just remembered as we were walking past this," said Christian, gently touching the *Anatomy*. "He had contacted me asking for permission to come and inspect this very book. It seems early sixteenth and seventeenth century medical books are his speciality..."

"Yes, that's right," interrupted Rafe.

"And he had a client with a first edition of *Anatomy* of their own — there's a few still lying around, keeping doors open, that sort of thing," Christian smiled at his own joke.

"Let me guess, he wanted to come and inspect your first edition, which is without question authentic, and compare it with his client's."

"Yes, that's it exactly. His client, who he couldn't, or wouldn't, name had a suspicion his copy was a fake, so he commissioned Mr Rodriguez to find out for sure. I was sceptical I must say."

"Sceptical of Ruben?"

"Not exactly. Initially just sceptical of anyone having the bright idea of faking a one-thousand-page book. That seems an inordinate amount of effort for one fake book."

"It's funny but I had the same conversation with Ruben. He agreed with my suggestion that it is the very fact of it being so unlikely that motivates a forger, because they know nobody will be in a hurry to even contemplate a thick and many-paged book would be faked. Did you accommodate him?"

"I hadn't looked at it that way. Interesting... Yes, I let him come and inspect the book. But I had to say 'no photography' when he pulled out a camera. I only allowed him to take notes and I had one of my staff with him in the room at all times. He spent nearly an hour poring over it. I was not completely satisfied as to his *bona fides*, and I couldn't get away from the feeling, perhaps irrational admittedly, that he was making notes for the very purpose of creating a forgery; identifying all those little things that needed to be replicated that only a physical inspection would show. But as I said, I also felt it unlikely. But now that you mention that comment he made, I'm not so sure."

"Personally, I wouldn't worry. Ruben is a very smart man, and shrewd. But he's not stupid. You probably know he was accused once of forging another medical masterpiece; that's how I first came to know of him. He's most unlikely to attempt a forgery of *Anatomy* because he knows if a first edition does come onto the market and his name is in any way even remotely associated with it, questions will be asked. And just by visiting you and inspecting your copy, that instantly puts him in the frame for *any other* copy coming onto the market."

"Yes, you're probably right. I do see your point."

"Did he invite you out to dinner?"

"He did, but I declined. On ethical grounds."

"Well I can say you missed out on an unbelievable meal, and wine. Unethically speaking, that is."

"Hmm, that tells me something, I think! He also said something very interesting."

"Yes?"

"Yes, he said he was planning a trip soon to Moscow. Apparently, he discovered the last piece of information he was looking for as to the whereabouts of the Lost Library of Ivan The Terrible, would you believe!?"

"Incredible," replied Rafe, lost himself for any more words than that. But he did know one thing. He now knew it was time to give Ruben a call.

END OF CHAPTER FOURTEEN

Chapter Fifteen

The Governing Council Meets

"Biblios, members of a subgroup [of Luddites], are book worshippers. They deplore the fact that librarians, in betrayal of their name, do all they can to get rid of books... They say Universal Library technocrats have made libraries "user friendly" but hostile to book readers. Most of all Biblios resent the deportation of library books... to special ranches where bibliophagic cattle, genetically engineered by McDonald's, turn them into hamburger meat. Biblios fail to appreciate the irony that millions of novels..., mostly unread, are now eagerly devoured by a large, avid, public."
Jon Thiem, "Myths of the Universal Library: From Alexandria to the Postmodern Age", *The Serials Journal*, Vol 26(1) (1995), pp63-74, at p71

Friday, 22nd February 2205

The first meeting of the Governing Council of The Bibliotek for 2205 was scheduled to begin at 10am and Mads was going to be late for it on purpose, but not too late, he hoped, as to prompt Chair Thurldottir to begin without him; that would not have been prudent. But his want was to be just late enough to... niggle her. She brought this reaction from Mads upon herself, he reasoned, by her officiously duplicitous conduct in these meetings, most of which were held remotely in holographic format as a majority of the Councillors were usually in other countries. Mads could count on Thurldottir being either at her chalet or in her office at The Bibliotek, as she had yet to physically join Mads for any Governing Council meeting. But Mads was also going to be late because he was dreading this meeting, and that in turn was because he knew he was going to need to be very careful with his words, much more than usual in Council meetings. There was a game to be tacitly played, and Mads did not like this kind of game.

At precisely 10:04am, Mads arrived at the locked meeting room door, paused, and checked his data pad one more time for any message from *her*, but there was nothing. Notwithstanding his hurt at her betrayal, no longer getting any messages from Violetta had given rise to an empty feeling inside Mads, a feeling so painful he knew it would last for some time to come. Such had been his feelings for Violetta that he was only now beginning to acknowledge them to himself. He had been happy and comfortable with their relationship.

Its limits had suited him, including the pretence they maintained for everyone outside the door to his apartment (for he never visited hers) that the relationship did not exist. When they were alone together behind that door he never felt as if he needed to impress her; she was, or at least she seemed to be, quickly at interested ease with his ways and quiet quirks. Being told by Violetta, to his face, that it was all a ruse, a means to an end, was a hurdle for those feelings to overcome. A big, wide, deep hurdle. The last thing he wanted to be doing right now was to attend a meeting of the Governing Council, but he had no choice. Mads sighed, took a deep breath, and let it out slowly.

With that momentary lapse dealt with for now, Mads presented his face to the scan lock, which beeped and green lit him in response. The heavy door slid open, also in silence. Mads entered the short, darkened corridor to the virtual meeting room and noticed Larkin glance across at him from the control desk at the other side of the room as he approached the vacant meeting table in its middle. Within the thimble of light streaming up from Larkin's desk Mads could see that his assistant wore an apprehensive look on his perfectly manicured, clean-shaven and almost shiny face. Mads felt he knew exactly what Larkin was thinking right at that moment; that reporting to Mads was hindering his career, if not placing it at risk.

Without acknowledging Larkin, Mads sat down in his chair at the head of the large, empty, table, prompting the holographic meeting to reveal itself around the remainder of the table, with Thurldottir appearing at its opposite end, facing Mads.

"Bibliotekar Ingridson has deigned to join us," rasped Chair Thurldottir as she gave her usual death stare in the direction of what she hoped was Mads' face, "so we will begin. Can I first confirm a quorum?"

"Here" spoke each of the other Councillors' holographics in turn around the table, without any hints of irony. One seat, however, remained vacant, real and holographically.

"A quorum is duly noted, said Thurldottir. "It would appear that Councillor Metcalfe will not be joining us today," she continued, looking across to the vacant seat.

Here it comes, thought Mads.

"Some of you are aware of this already, but I need to advise the Council that the Councillor cannot currently be located and accordingly has been formally reported as missing. I discussed this earlier with Bibliotekar Ingridson and he agreed with my request that Nikka Johannson, Head of Security, personally investigate the Councillor's apparent disappearance. Also, in accordance with protocol, Councillor Metcalfe's continued absence from Governing Council meetings and general business will see his seat vacated. So for our next meeting, which as you all know is the AGM, there will be a motion put to formally declare his seat vacant, unless he is found beforehand. If made, immediately following that motion I will be introducing a candidate to replace Councillor Metcalfe."

Mads only noticed surprise on a few of the Councillors' faces. "How long has the Councillor been missing, may I ask?" asked Councillor Hans Jacobsen of the Chair.

"I'm not certain," replied Thurldottir. "You'll have to ask either Dean Coenraad or Bibliotekar Ingridson that question."

"Councillor Metcalfe has not been seen at the Academy or anywhere else in The Bibliotek precinct since early November," Mads told the Council. "He failed to attend the Academy to give a lecture on the fourteenth of that month and thereafter all other lectures he was scheduled to give, and he did not give any notice to either me or the Dean of any absence." Mads consciously refrained from mentioning Thomas's trip to Arcadia and the events subsequent to his return. He did not like holding back this information, but he felt prudence dictated doing so. "But I remain confident Councillor Metcalfe will make a re-appearance in good time," Mads concluded.

"We shall remain hopeful your confidence is well-placed," rasped Thurldottir in response, and without a pause for any further questions about Thomas, she continued, in her usual officious tone. "Let it be recorded that this is a convening of Ordinary Meeting Number Two Five Four Three of the Governing Council of The Bibliotek, and noted that my advice regarding Councillor Metcalfe be recorded in the Minutes under Other Business. Any objections?"

There were none, though Mads could feel several pairs of eyes on him wanting to see a reaction, which he did not feel inclined to give. He knew well the implication for him of Thomas being replaced on the Council by a stooge of Thurldottir.

"The first item on the agenda is an update on a project initiated by Phicom and being undertaken by Adcom — a study of the Central Repository's capacity and security issues to determine if there is a need to consider a partial or full relocation." Mads heard the Chair announce the item, making him focus again on the meeting. He quickly donned his standard 'interested face' and hoped he looked it, as Mads was also remembering that he still had no idea why Thurldottir was orchestrating secret plans about Arcadia and how it related to the Relocation Study Group.

"Bibliotekar Ingridson," Thurldottir continued, "as you are the Chair of Adcom, can you update the Council regarding this matter?" Thurldottir knew full well that Mads could do so because she had made sure before the meeting that he was going to be prepared to discuss it.

"I'm told your little study group has been making good progress on the relocation proposal," Thurldottir had stated when she called Mads a few days prior to the meeting.

"Your informant is correct," Mads had retorted. "Progress has been made, but not on any relocation proposal, as such, as you know."

"No, I do not follow you," Thurldottir had replied.

"There is no relocation proposal that I am aware of," Mads had then explained. "The Terms of Reference you gave us did a good job of keeping the study on track in evaluating the potential need for The Bibliotek to begin considering a partial or full relocation, but it is far too soon to be talking about any actual proposal."

"Sometimes I think you can't see the forest for the trees, Bibliotekar," Thurldottir had responded, just before terminating the call.

Now Mads shifted in his chair — that subconscious desire to become higher whilst seated — and spoke. He wanted to tell the Council he thought the study was a sham, but he still did not know why, so instead he had to lie.

"At this point in time," Mads began, "Adcom's report is yet to be finalised, but it is likely the report will contain the finding that moving part of the Central Repository of The Bibliotek to a new site is not only feasible, but more to the point, prudent." Mads paused, and quickly scanned the faces of Council members for reactions. Some bore the clear signs of genuine surprise. Not Carlson. He was smiling that stupid self-assured look of his, as if he were watching a rat about to set off a trap. The face of Chair Thurldottir remained however characteristically unchanged; like cold, hard, chiselled granite.

"Furthermore," Mads continued quickly, as impassively as he could manage and reminding himself to choose his words carefully, "the final report will include a discussion and preliminary analysis of a potential site for a new Bibliotek facility that the RSG has identified, in the event that the Governing Council decides to progress the suggestion of a relocation, and a recommendation that, despite not being in its stated remit, the Group be tasked to proceed to investigate the feasibility of this site."

Again, Mads paused, and this time he noticed something about Larkin out of the corner of his eye. His assistant had neither moved nor changed his expression, which, for him, was not normal behaviour. In the same instant, Mads made a mental note of Larkin's apparent impassiveness. He was taking a big risk in pre-empting, if not simply misrepresenting, the direction the RSG was heading in, and the only person who *should* be aware of this fact was Larkin, as he had heard all the doubts about the relocation suggestion at the Adcom meetings. Mads had just gone out on a limb, and he had expected at least some form of silent recognition of that from Larkin. But no, nothing.

But it was no surprise to Mads that Councillor Carlson signalled his desire to ask a question and, without waiting for Thurldottir's virtual nod — a practice Carlson always adopted which was much to Mads' aggravation and probably the reason he did it — asked in his usual patronising tone "and do we know the location of the proposed site, Bibliotekar Ingridson?"

"To be clear, Councillor Carlson," Mads answered, "there is no site yet proposed. There is merely a site the Study Group wishes to be authorised to investigate for its potential to act as a new location of part or all of The Bibliotek should, as I have said and stressed, the Governing Council decide to progress the underlying relocation proposal. At present, we, as in the Governing Council, do not know the site that has attracted the interest of the Study Group."

"But you, as in the Chair of Adcom, *do* know this site, do you not?" responded Carlson. It was obvious to Mads where Carlson was heading with his questions. Mads had to take care. "That is correct, Councillor Carlson, but..."

"I think it best we do not pester Bibliotekar Ingridson about this proposed site," interrupted Thurldottir. "For such an important decision, perhaps the single most important decision in the history of The Bibliotek, it is appropriate, if not entirely necessary, that all the procedures we have put in place to manage it are adhered to." On hearing that, Councillor Carlson smiled his usual feint acceptance, and gave the smallest of nods humanly possible, which was also, Mads believed, the limit of his face's physical capability, given how fat it and the rest of him was.

Mads' response, however, to the Chair's interruption was to grimace. Far from rescuing him from Carlson's pestering, Thurldottir had taken the opportunity to repeat Carlson's reference to the "proposed site." Her purpose in doing so was clear to Mads, and he knew it was meant to be understood by all Councillors, not just him. *So much for adherence to procedure,* thought Mads, as he resumed. "Thank you, Chair Thurldottir. I appreciate being allowed as Chair of Adcom to formally receive the final report before commenting further. Moreover, I do not wish to pre-empt any decision of Adcom to seek clarification on any issue raised by the report before formally reporting back to the Council."

"Prudent words, indeed, Bibliotekar, but I think we can safely assume the Study Group is being thorough," said Thurldottir. Yet another presumptive statement. *They're accumulating, and not in a good way,* thought Mads quickly. It was time for another voice, so he gave a pre-arranged signal to Councillor Hans Jacobson, who immediately sought and obtained the floor from the Chair.

"I've been listening to this update from Mads, Chair Thurldottir," began Hans, "and I must say I am surprised by its subject matter. So, I have to ask, why has Adcom been tasked to examine the capacity of The Bibliotek with a view to a relocation? As far as I am aware, Mads' regular reports on the capacity of the Central Repository have not ever been close to highlighting an issue."

"Phicom has been discussing the issue, prompted by the Bibliotekar's more recent capacity reports. You are not on Phicom, Hans," replied Thurldottir. "And nor is the Bibliotekar. But I am its Chair and we determined there is a trend in evidence and it was material enough to examine the capacity issue now. It was also felt prudent in view of the growing risk that the Present Sect seems to be representing to institutions such as The Bibliotek — a prime target, no less. And since Bibliotekar Ingridson does not report to Phicom, I made the formal request to Adcom to begin the project in my capacity as Chair of both Phicom and this Council. It is just a study, and whatever its conclusions and recommendations, nothing will happen without this Council's approval. Does that suffice?"

"Thankyou Chair Thurldottir, it does, for now. But I do wish to express my disappointment that the Council was not given the opportunity to discuss Phicom's concerns before Adcom was tasked with the study," responded Jacobson. Mads had already told Hans the reason why he had been directed to look at The Bibliotek capacity, but now at least it would be in the Governing Council's Minutes.

"Noted. Any *further* questions before we move onto the next item on the agenda?" said Thurldottir with a hint of distaste. There were none, unsurprisingly. Every Councillor knew that Thurldottir did not like their meetings to be prolonged by questions, and Hans Jacobson had already succeeded in pushing her buttons. If any more Councillors were surprised by the news of Mads' study of The Bibliotek's capacity they knew it was better not to ask their own questions nor make any comment until such time as Mads actually tabled the Adcom report. Such matters were best left for private conversations with Mads outside the Governing Council and away from the eyes and ears of the moribund countenance of the Chair.

"No? Then let Bibliotekar Ingridson's aural advice to the Council stand as fulfilling item one," the Chair continued more formally. "Rest assured, fellow Councillors, that whatever the work of the Bibliotekar's team produces from Adcom, there will be full and informed discussions in Council before any vote on *any* decision is moved. Now, item two, the status of the Secondary Repositories. The question being, as you all know, whether they should be consolidated with the Central Repository."

Before anyone else could, Councillor Jacobson again obtained the floor from Thurldottir. "I don't agree that the question to be considered is whether the Secondary Repositories should be consolidated with the Central Repository," Jacobson began. "I would like us instead to consider the question whether The Bibliotek should continue to maintain the Secondary Repositories *at all*, whether consolidated or not. My answer to that question, as you all know, is no, for the reasons I have consistently given. But I will say them again. By continuing with these unnecessary glorified warehouses and the desire to fill them, we not only risk losing sight of the purpose of The Bibliotek but, more importantly, our ability and ability to carry out that purpose. I am not advocating a destruction process, but I am seeking a refinement in the principles underpinning the work of The Bibliotek to exclude completely the prevailing dogma forcing us to obtain, then maintain, copies of everything. This is something for Phicom to consider."

"As usual you state your view with precision, Hans" responded Thurldottir. "But if we are to merely accept your argument and Phicom to implement it, there remains the question of what to do with the various hordes of copies of original books currently stored in the Secondary Repositories. Like it or not, The Bibliotek has, for better or worse, become responsible for them." She paused for a second before continuing. "Bibliotekar, the Governing Council has not yet had the benefit of hearing your views on the issue. In particular, what do you think should be done with the Secondary Repositories if we cease to add more copies to them? And, in particular may I ask, what is the status of the audit?"

Mads' thoughts on the issue were mostly in line with Councillor Jacobsen's and this was because the two of them had discussed the issue before the meeting, and after Mads had arranged for Jacobsen to receive a private briefing from Finn on the progress of his audit of the Secondary Repositories. More than that, Mads felt that the Governing Council should never have sanctioned the then fledging habit of Finders to procure more than one copy of any Find, should never have encouraged the growth of the practice, and should never have let that growth occur unchecked. It was as if there was an institutional desire to procure as many copies as possible of every printed record. But he did not want to say any of that.

"The audit has progressed to the point where results will be circulated to Councillors before the next meeting. Were it not for the need for Finn Mackie to prioritise the Chair's request that Adcom examine the capacity of The Bibliotek, I would have been able to table the audit report at this meeting, but I can tell you the numbers are not looking good. Several of the Secondary Repositories, namely most of those located in Oslo and Frankfurt, are nearing full capacity. Combined with that issue are the escalating costs of maintaining their book stocks in a safe condition. More than that, I tend to agree with Councillor Jacobsen. I am mindful of the fact that the occasions on which the Central Repository has had to resort to a copy held by one of the Secondary Repositories have been miniscule relative to the number of original records held by the Central Repository," Mads said. "To me, this reflects our high standards of operating the Central Repository, and it also seems to me contrary to those standards to even contemplate a need to obtain and maintain copies. For one reason, to date, with one exception, the only occasions upon which a copy has had to be sourced from a Secondary Repository for transfer to the Central Repository is when the original has been determined to be a forgery. Even then, it is policy that the forgery remains in the Central Repository and accessible. In fact, the only thing that happens when a book proves to be fake is that an annotation is made to that effect in its Catalogue entry. The single exception, as everyone would be aware, was a theft. One theft in a hundred or so years is hardly justification for the Secondary Repositories."

"What you say is probably undeniable, Bibliotekar," responded Thurldottir, "but, again, what do we do with the Secondary Repositories on the assumption nothing more is added to them ever again?"

"From an administrative point of view, I believe The Bibliotek should not continue to incur any further costs on the Secondary Repositories. Any more than that I would say is in the realm of Phicom," said Mads, mirroring Jacobson's view but expressing it as a conscious but veiled criticism of his ongoing absence from Phicom, which stemmed from the perception of many on the Governing Council that he was a mere, albeit glorified, administrator, and thus was not needed on Phicom.

The Governing Council held and exercised control over all things relating to The Bibliotek. That was the legal position at least, but despite the regularity and formality of its meetings, the real control of The Bibliotek was not held by the Governing Council, but by Phicom and Adcom.

Whilst Adcom oversaw the day-to-day operations of The Bibliotek, Phicom concerned itself with the direction the operations of The Bibliotek should take. As a rule, and as far as the Governing Council was concerned, Mads' job was to manage the operational budget for The Bibliotek, as set by Adcom and authorised by the Governing Council, and to take responsibility for giving effect to Phicom edicts as supported by the Governing Council.

Those arrangements had remained unchanged since the creation of The Bibliotek. They were examined extensively during the First Review, and whilst some minor alterations were recommended and mostly implemented, the Review basically concluded they remained appropriate. Mads, on the other hand, had never felt the structure of the control and management of The Bibliotek was "appropriate".

At times the line between Adcom's authority and his as The Bibliotekar became blurred; and, from his point of view, any blurring was confined to Adcom overstepping its authority rather than him personally. Fortunately, being the Chair of Adcom enabled Mads to rein it in whenever he perceived it to be at risk of going beyond the limits of that authority. He did this as 'softly' as possible though, because sometimes it was easier for Mads to hang difficult operational decisions ultimately on Adcom rather than solely on himself. However, that also had to be handled with care, and there were occasions when Mads made it clear that a given decision was his and his alone.

More problematic for Mads were the enduring consequences of his status as a 'mere' administrator and his absence from Phicom. It was one thing to administer without care or thought about the impact or consequences of what he called black and white decision-making. It was another thing entirely to entertain or even introduce doubt, or second thoughts, or even a care as to whether any given decision, action, or process was appropriate in the bigger scheme of things.

And it was that tired euphemism — 'the bigger scheme of things' — that tended to get Mads into trouble; when he hesitated instead of being absolute, or worse, resolute. He well knew and understood the rationale for keeping him off Phicom, so this was not his failure. Instead, his failure was in not being able to convince certain Councillors, including the Chair of the Governing Council, of the difference to his administration of The Bibliotek that would stem from him being on Phicom. He had so far failed to demonstrate the benefit of his having at least some ownership or investment in the decisions as to the operational directions of The Bibliotek.

Thurldottir could see through Mads' veiled criticism, but she chose to ignore it. "You are being too formal, Bibliotekar," she responded. "Please, give us the benefit of your *personal* opinion."

More disingenuity from the Chair, thought Mads; he wasn't welcome on Phicom, but yet again his opinion was sought on a question well within its remit. It was a mockery of his so-called status as a mere administrator which kept him from being a member of Phicom, but he had to be careful not to simply reinforce that perception in his answer. "On the assumption that a directive is issued to the effect that no more copies are to be obtained by Finders or anyone else, from any source, it would be easy to suggest that the entire contents of the Secondary Repositories be consolidated with the Central Repository. However, that course of action will raise several issues, the least of which being the current possibility the Central Repository, or some part of it, will be relocated to a preferably larger site..."

"Indeed," interrupted Thurldottir, "and what would those issues be?"

"An obvious one," Mads somewhat retorted, "would be the overt dilution of the Master Catalogue. Some entries would be confined to originals, which would need to be annotated as such, and some will become entries combining both originals and copies. The Temporary Catalogue would greatly expand, certainly by more than 500% in the relative short term."

"An enormous task!" interrupted Councillor Jacobson. "Monumental in both time and cost!"

"Indeed," Mads replied. "But well within our capacity, if not our budget, depending, of course, on the desired urgency. No, my concern lies with the outcome of such a task — the resulting everlasting dichotomy."

Several councillors, including Jacobson and Carlson, immediately asked for the floor, but Chair Thurldottir waved them all off. "A point worthy of discussion, no doubt," she said. "But let us first hear your other issues, Bibliotekar."

Mads duly resumed. "One operational issue would be the bare fact that any given copy or second or later printing of an original first edition or first printing coming from a Secondary Repository would be taking the space in the Central Repository designed for that original and dare I say more valuable book." Mads paused while he observed several heads nodding. "Another operational issue would be the impact on the Principles of Access and the Principles of Embargo. Both would need refinement. And then there's the political issue — the management of the explanation for the 'sudden' appearance of copies — tens of millions of copies — particularly in light of the fact that from the very first day that access to The Bibliotek's collections was permitted, we have placed strict limits on the extent that copies can be made of digitally-rendered items. Access to a complete copy of an actual item may easily be seen as far more preferable than having to decide which particular pages of an ancient manuscript to copy for the purposes of their study. Finally, one philosophical issue would be the relationship of those copies with the Primary Function of the Bibliotek. On that point, I agree with Councillor Jacobson." *There, I said it*, thought Mads.

"Thank you, Bibliotekar," replied Thurldottir, a little coolly and a little too quickly, Mads thought. "If we assume for the moment that consolidation of the Secondary Repositories with the Central Repository is not a viable option, has the audit progressed to the point of arriving at any recommendations?" she continued.

Mads had been hoping that question would arise. He and Finn had sat down a few days before the Governing Council meeting to finesse the recommendations Finn would include in his audit report and which they first discussed just before the last Adcom meeting. But Mads wanted to air them here and now. He knew he would get a reaction, and right now that was exactly what he needed. Something to distract Thurldottir & Co.

"Yes, Finn and I have drafted a few suggestions as to the go-forward actions. I am happy to put them on the table here and now, but only on the proviso it is understood they are *draft* recommendations and thus subject to change before the audit report is formally presented."

"Fair enough, take it as understood," replied Thurldottir.

"Okay. In no particular order, The Bibliotek should cease procuring *ad hoc* copies, and by that I mean copies not being acquired as part of procurements of collections. This is going to involve an issue of Finder management because they will no longer be paid fees for copies they procure."

"What?! We'll have a riot on our hands!" blurted Carlson.

"Quiet!" ordered Thurldottir. "Let Bibliotekar Ingridson finish!"

"Next," Mads continued without reacting to Carlson's outburst, "The Bibliotek should aim to stop procuring entire collections as the default negotiating position. Rather, we now have the critical mass of books to justify cherry-picking any given collection so as to avoid procuring copies that need to be split from the books The Bibliotek *actually* wants for the Central Repository. Next, we should consider relocating any copies of embargoed holdings to the Central Repository so that they can be accessed. The indications are there is a material number of books this policy could be applied to, but without having a material impact on the capacity of the Central

Repository. We should also consider selling or donating any multiple copies greater than two or three, and consider consolidating existing Secondary Repositories, particularly the Oslo and Frankfurt sites, and then upgrading the remaining repositories on the assumption the existing stocks are retained. Those are the current draft recommendations."

Thurldottir spoke before accepting any of the requests from other Councillors to speak. "Those are very interesting suggestions, Bibliotekar. I look forward to seeing the final report. I just have one comment for now."

"Yes?"

"The sudden appearance of accessible copies of books we have been holding under embargo of access will likely cause a high level — a very high level — of surprise and discontent, if not anger, to arise in the academic community. You most of all can perhaps understand this. One day they are being told no, they can't access a particular book, then the next day they find out we have a copy they can look at and examine. That's not a good look for us."

Mads was prepared for that objection being raised. "We don't have a PR function at The Bibliotek and nor have we ever felt the need to engage an external consultant. But there's a first time for everything, so, yes, such a course of action would need careful management from a public relations point of view. I would propose that The Bibliotek treat the disclosure of the fact we have been secretly accumulating copies as a positive initiative rather than using a defensive position as a starting point. We make the disclosure appear to be a planned event, as merely the final step in a long-term project, now being realised and brought to fruition, for the global benefit of the academic community."

"Interesting. For now," responded Thurldottir. "But, thankfully such considerations can wait."

"I would like to add one more suggestion, if I may," Mads quickly added.

"Yes?"

"I would like to suggest that Phicom give consideration to establishing a lending system for items currently held in the Secondary Repositories."

As he had anticipated, a heavy, shocked, silence occurred. It was but a few seconds, but Mads could tell that he had caught Thurldottir and the other Councillors off-guard with his suggestion. She almost appeared to struggle for words to respond with. Even Larkin looked surprised.

"I was reading something the other day," Mads continued, taking advantage of the silence, "and it occurred to me. Exactly one thousand and one years ago at the Pope's Council of Paris in 1204, Legate Dominic issued the *Second Part of the Constitutions, relating to Regular Monks and Monks.* Number 23 stated, and I quote, "*He forbids the custom of some Monks, who swore they lend out no books.*" We all know the Vatican Library ironically remains off-limits to all, and here is an opportunity for The Bibliotek to make a statement. To make a real difference. The timing is serendipitous."

Carlson could not contain himself. "Blast your historical ironies! This is a repository, not a lending library! What a ridiculous thing to suggest!"

Thurldottir immediately raised her hand for Carlson to stop, but Mads could tell she was thinking the same thing. Mads could have received the same reaction had he suggested the Governing Council be replaced by a classroom of nine-year olds.

Undaunted, Mads continued. "I appreciate such a proposal would require Phicom to make what would appear to be a radical departure from the purpose of The Bibliotek, but I would like to remind Councillors of one thing: the second of Sorenson's Three Tenets of the functions of The Bibliotek. That is, and I quote, "*It is the Secondary Function of the Bibliotek to facilitate appropriate access to all printed material under its management.*" By definition, and by virtue of this Council culpably fostering the position we now find ourselves in with the Secondary Repositories, that purpose necessarily includes their contents. So it's not a long stretch for Phicom to make after all, I would posit."

Looking around the table, Mads could sense Thurldottir was now peering at him in a way that suggested she thought he was being serious and not so ridiculous as Carlson would believe. *Or that he was up to something,* he suddenly thought. Maybe he had gone too far.

"Your point is made, Bibliotekar, but I am not sure Phicom would see it that way. In any event, I will be sure the suggestion is raised when it considers Mackie's report. Just make sure, please, that he doesn't include it as a recommendation, if you will," Thurldottir crooned.

"By all means," Mads nodded, feeling more comfortable now that he had not gone too far.

"I think we've discussed the Secondary Repositories issue more than sufficient for now. The third item on the agenda is a motion that the Bibliotekar's Terms of Office be amended to make it absolutely clear there are no circumstances under which the Bibliotekar can elect not to inform the Chair of the Governing Council of an intended absence from Norway. As this is my motion, I will address it, and then Bibliotekar Ingridson can respond before the motion is to be put to a vote," said Thurldottir, resuming her normal, officious tone. She continued, "personal safety and security is the issue here. The Bibliotekar is meant to clear with me any travel undertaken outside Norway but lately has been choosing not to. I must be given the opportunity to review the need for any such travel and weigh it against the risk that the Present Sect is beginning to represent to employees of The Bibliotek, through its increasingly violent threats and actions. It is as simple as that."

"My turn?" asked Mads.

"Proceed," responded Thurldottir curtly, waving her hand forward.

"I cannot perform my duties and responsibilities as Bibliotekar without travelling outside The Bibliotek precinct. My Terms of Office recognise this need at an operational level, which is why nobody but myself makes decisions on travel. To impose otherwise would be an impediment to the performance of my role. The limit of the Governing Council's interest in this issue is whether my travel costs remain within budget. The Chair is mistaken. I am not required to obtain pre-approval from her for travel outside Norway, and nor has there ever been any intention for that to be the case. I am meeting my Terms of Office whenever I inform the Chair, as a matter of courtesy more than anything else, of an intended journey away from The Bibliotek. By all means change those Terms. I will simply view it, though, as a conscious impediment to my job and will respond accordingly. It is as simple as that."

"Are you threatening to resign?" asked the Chair.

"I am merely voicing my objection to the motion and my reasons. How I respond to any vote in support of it is my business."

"And the security risk?"

"I think I have enough sense to gauge when any travel I undertake presents a security risk, and, to date, there has not been a single instance of any such a risk presenting itself. If it does, I am more than capable of engaging any appropriate assistance of Nikka Johannson and her security team. And now, unless anybody has any objections," said Mads, looking around the table, "I move that a vote be taken on the motion. As in now."

Amidst the murmuring that now started to flow around the table, Thurldottir spoke. "I am sorry, but I am not calling for anyone to second that."

Mads knew she was too smart to let that happen, lest the vote on her motion go against her, which was on the cards. This much he also knew from some of the conversations he had recently been having. Her motion to basically make his movements subject to her scrutiny was being viewed as petty and unnecessary, with the Present Sect threat as the excuse being overstated.

"If, Bibliotekar," said Thurldottir, directly addressing him, "you are prepared to give the Governing Council an undertaking here and now that your decisions to travel outside Norway will be taken after consulting with Security I am prepared to let the matter drop."

"So be it," said Mads, trying very hard not to exhibit the wry smile he was feeling.

Thurldottir was quick to speak again. To Mads she seemed unruffled by his bluff. "Time is moving on. That concludes the formal agenda. We now have the first item of other business which is, as I have already mentioned, Councillor Metcalfe and his ongoing unexplained absence. Let the Minutes show the procedures that will be followed at the next Governing Council meeting, as I also mentioned at the start of this meeting." Thurldottir was masterly as usual at formal language to mask what was really happening.

"The second item of other business is a question I have of Bibliotekar Ingridson," said Thurldottir. Without a pause, she continued. "Just this morning I became aware that The Bibliotek is facing exposure to a U.S. tax bill of one-point-eight billion dollars plus penalties for fraudulent Tax Certificates, that this has been known to you since November last year, and yet you have chosen not to inform the Governing Council of this exposure. Can you explain this?"

Mads was not expecting Thurldottir to raise the matter of the U.S. Tax Certificates, and certainly not in such an accusatory manner, but her long-windedness in asking her question gave him time to collect his thoughts and recall the pertinent facts. Given all eyes were now on him, his first response, however, was to emit a dismissive scoff.

He continued. "Seriously, Chair Thurldottir, there are times when I have to question the basis, if not the ethics, of your interference in day-to-day operational issues; first my business travel arrangements and now this."

Before Thurldottir could respond, Mads kept going. He felt she had just made a tactical error and he wasn't going to let her off this time. "I could just answer your question with another: who told you The Bibliotek is, how did you express it — *facing exposure to a U.S. tax bill of one-point-eight billion dollars plus penalties?*"

Mads had never before spoken to Thurldottir in such a manner at Governing Council meetings, and rarely, if ever, in private. But he noticed that all eyes were now on Thurldottir, who was not pleased with her question being thrown back at her. It was obvious though that Mads had raised a point that interested the other councillors, including Carlson. There was an awkward silence, but because he had only posed a hypothetical question, Mads proceeded to demonstrate one of the reasons why he was still the Bibliotekar – his attention to detail.

"At the Adcom meeting of 19 November last, General Counsel Collingwood advised the meeting that she had just received formal notice of an impending tax audit by the U.S. Internal Revenue Service, focusing on the Tax Certificates The Bibliotek has issued to U.S. resident donors over a seven-year period."

"Seven years, good god!" interrupted Carlson, looking around at the other Councillors as if trying to muster up the sentiment he had just expressed.

Mads let the interruption stand in silence for a few seconds before he replied, with a slightly raised tone. "What is your issue, Councillor Carlson?"

This Carlson did not expect. Normally his little bites at Mads were just that. Nips that Mads usually ignored. Now everyone was looking at Carlson, including Thurldottir. To Mads she looked a little exasperated. "Well, I mean," Carlson spluttered, "seven years is a very long period to be investigating..."

"Rubbish!" Mads interrupted. "Anyone vaguely familiar with U.S. taxation,... wait, you're a U.S. tax resident are you not Councillor Carlson?"

"No I am not. My business affairs are based in Bermuda. You know that tax haven?" Carlson triumphantly pronounced.

Bingo, thought Mads. *Strike One*. Thurldottir almost exploded out of her chair towards Carlson, or so it seemed to Mads before she regained her composure. "Anyone vaguely familiar with *avoiding* U.S. tax," Mads continued, "knows that seven years is the standard period the I.R.S. will look at during an audit. Which means there is nothing special about The Bibliotek's circumstances. And I want you to try and understand another thing, Councillor Carlson: this is not an investigation, it is an audit; a standard, semi-regular, compliance check. Anyone calling it an investigation again, I will take as an attempt to mislead the Council."

"I think we should let him continue telling us about this one-point-eight billion dollar exposure without further interruption," Thurldottir said, clearly annoyed at Carlson but using the opportunity to stoke the fire. Mads also noticed he was now "him" rather than "Bibliotekar".

"I will also consider any further mention of a 'one-point-eight billion dollar U.S. tax exposure', or *any* U.S. tax exposure, as an attempt to mislead the Governing Council," said Mads quietly but firmly. Mads knew he was perilously close to accusing Thurldottir of misbehaviour, so he quickly continued as she was about to speak. "There is *no* exposure to *any* U.S. tax or tax penalties. Period," he said quietly but as clearly and forcefully as he could, looking around the table as he said it. "This much was made clear in the end-of-year Risk Register issued under my authority to all Councillors in the first week of January. The fact of the I.R.S. audit is clearly disclosed on that register as it is a notifiable event. Also disclosed was a potential exposure of *zero* dollars, with a probability rating of ninety-five percent, the highest that can be given in the absence of absolute certainty." Mads knew the Councillors rarely, if ever, read such material as the annual update to the Risk Register. He also knew that none would admit to it.

"So, Mads, why *is* this figure of one point eight billion being raised at Council?" asked Jacobsen.

"I'm glad you asked that, Hans, I can only guess at motives. Let me explain where the figure comes from and perhaps those motives will become clearer. Councillors may recall that just over four years ago we terminated the services of our U.S. Finder immediately after it had come to light that for a period of two years he had been conspiring with certain donors to orchestrate the issue of Tax Certificates showing inflated values of relevant procurements. The purpose of such behaviour is clear: the Finder in question was getting kickbacks and the donors were inflating their tax deductions and hence lowering their tax bills. *Our* internal investigation, using a prominent U.S. law firm, concluded the amount of tax evaded by those donors amounted to a total of one point eight billion U.S. dollars."

"So the amount of the tax exposure *is* real?!" said Carlson, who couldn't help himself.

"To those donors, yes. But *not* to The Bibliotek. Have you forgotten The Bibliotek is *not-for-profit*? We have no tax exposure and nor do we have a tax presence in the U.S.. We have evaded no tax. We distanced ourselves from any criminal activity and this audit is not about that activity."

"This is about our Tax Certificate process, isn't it, Mads?"

"Exactly, Hans, pure and simple. When we discovered the anomalies four years ago, we disclosed the issue to the I.R.S., including the names of the relevant donors, the fact we had fired the Finder, and that we had reviewed and tightened our Tax Certificate procedures. And I might add, we applied those changes to The Bibliotek's procurement procedures universally, not just to the U.S.. This tax audit is the first time we have had any communication from the I.R.S., let alone a formal response to those disclosures, so we will be invoking the doctrine of administrative estoppel, which is alive and well in the decisions of the U.S. Federal Tax Court."

"Sorry, the what?" asked Hans.

"The common-law principle that allows organisations such as ourselves to rely on any ongoing inaction of government administrations as implicit acceptance of disclosed relevant practices. I want to add that there is only one thing the I.R.S. can point to, and that is the formal Tax Certificate agreement entered into with the I.R.S. by my predecessor in 2132. It's been revised a few times since, but it has always stated clearly that the agreed Tax Certificate process neither constitutes nor leads to any liability to U.S. taxation."

Mads paused to let that sink in, then said one more thing. "So, Chair Thurldottir, I now ask you, who told you we had an exposure of one-point-eight billion U.S. dollars plus penalties?"

"I was not given the benefit of knowing the identity of the person in your Finance team who passed the information to me," replied Thurldottir defensively.

In asking the question Mads had a feeling Thurldottir would give a non-answer, and he already knew who had given her the one point eight-billion-dollar figure. "So you raised this issue at Council because of an anonymous note, without at least seeking more information from *my Finance team* or *myself* beforehand. Interesting. When next you speak to this person in confidence, please do me the favour of telling him he no longer has my confidence and needs to consider his position at The Bibliotek, quickly."

Thurldottir merely gave a small wry smile and said nothing, She knew she had been snookered, and she knew there was no point prolonging it by arguing with Mads, who now predicted to himself that she would later attempt to delete the entire item from the Minutes. Instead, Thurldottir merely returned to her formal tone.

"Thank you for explaining to us the vagaries of U.S. tax law, Bibliotekar. It's been... fascinating. Before we finish up, I just want to remind Councillors once again that the next meeting of the Council is the AGM and will be held on Monday the first of April in The Bibliotek Boardroom. As you know, AGMs require attendance in-person, so have your respective PAs co-ordinate with mine on the travel and accommodation arrangements if you haven't already done so. Following the AGM there will also be a dinner in my suite. This will be hosted by Councillor Carlson, who will give a short informal presentation on what's in store for The Bibliotek over the next decade. Exciting times."

That last bit was news to Mads. He was still quietly raging over Michael Huntington's actions over the U.S. tax issue, when Thurldottir's last words hit him like a bolt thrown from afar. He felt it was more than strange that Carlson was going to present on matters that Mads should be at least aware of, if not actually driving them — he was the Bibliotekar after all — so Thurldottir's words Mads took as a thinly veiled threat, or worse, forewarning. He suspected Thurldottir had utilised Thomas's absence from Phicom to initiate such discussions.

"There being no further agenda items, I call this meeting closed," rasped Thurldottir, but she was not quite finished, "Bibliotekar, can you please remain, there is a matter I need to discuss with you."

This time Mads knew the "matter" Thurldottir wanted to discuss, and he was looking forward to hearing about it. "Larkin, terminate the recording and leave us please," he ordered his assistant.

Mads watched as Larkin impassively and silently closed down the control panel and exited the room through the door behind the panel. A sensor on his data panel confirmed he was now in an offline conversation with the Chair.

"I will be setting up a meeting to discuss your suggestion regarding the lending of items, but for now there is another matter that has been brought to my attention. I understand you recently terminated the services of Chief Conservator Violetta Simpson," she said, pausing for his response.

"That is correct. Why do you ask?"

"I ask because Councillor Carlson mentioned to me that he was disappointed to learn of Ms Simpson's dismissal."

"I'm sorry, but what is Councillor's Carlson's interest in Simpson and her dismissal?"

"You may not be aware that Councillor Carlson has been following, and sometimes sponsoring, Ms Simpson's career since her university days. This is because she is from a family that the Councillor has been close to for a long time, ever since her father was killed in The December Uprising. He feels, perhaps justifiably, partially responsible for her wellbeing and making sure she is not disadvantaged. So perhaps you can understand the concern that has been raised."

"I do not know the circumstances of her relationship with Councillor Carlson, and choose not to care," Mads responded, truthfully. "But what I have pondered on more than one occasion is why Harvard was so anxious to send her to us. So much so that a recent review of her background and career progression emphatically provided me with the answer to that question. The outcome of that review is why she no longer held my confidence as Chief Conservator."

Mads let that hang for a good moment before he continued. "I can brief Councillor Carlson and yourself on what we found out about our charming Chief Conservator should you wish it."

Thurldottir gave Mads a wry smile. She knew she was treading on his toes, so to speak, and thus she had to at least give the semblance of taking care not to get involved in a matter that was completely within his domain and nowhere near hers. But then she pulled what she thought was her ace from her sleeve.

"That will not be necessary," she retorted. "But it is my duty to inform you that Ms Simpson has levelled a serious accusation of impropriety against you." At this, she paused, probably in the hope of seeing his face betray something. It didn't. Mads remained silent, preferring instead to force her to articulate the accusation.

Thurldottir continued, resolute. "Specifically, Ms Simpson alleges that you misused your position as Bibliotekar in threatening her dismissal unless she began a sexual relationship with you, which she did under that threat, and that when she could no longer tolerate the situation you had placed her in, you immediately carried out your threat."

"That is indeed a serious accusation," Mads calmly responded. "And if it is true then I deserve to be removed from office. Do you believe it's true, Chair Thurldottir?"

Mads knew she had been caught by surprise by his reaction – her eyes narrowed to an almost imperceptibly-small slit, like a lizard's. But it was also apparent to Mads that Thurldottir sensed a trap was being set.

"What I believe or choose not to believe is not the issue," Thurldottir responded. "Oh, but it is," Mads interrupted, "My removal requires the unanimous decision of the Council to do so, and you must firstly approve the vote on such a question."

"That may be correct, but for now what I am seeking from you is a response to..."

"Has she made a formal complaint?" Mads interrupted.

"I believe that is the case," Thurldottir replied.

"Then until I receive a copy of Ms Simpson's complaint and, if necessary, seek my lawyer's counsel, here is my *interim* response," Mads said, with determination. He then quickly uploaded the video he had at the ready from his data pad to Thurldottir's screen, and it began playing.

"What is this?" she asked.

"This is a recording of Ms Simpson's last visit to my office. As you can see and hear from the footage — which, by the way, I am more than happy for you to have tested for manipulation — any non-professional behaviour during that short meeting was confined to Ms Simpson, including,..." Mads said, pausing the video, "... this bit," he added as he cancelled the pause. It was the bit where Violetta threatened to ruin Mads' career for ending their relationship, all staged for this very moment, much to Violetta's annoyance at the contrivance and being forced to be part of it, until Nikka curtly reminded her she was well-skilled in such acting and had Mads convinced her feelings for him and their relationship were genuine. The threat of arrest and jail if she did not co-operate also helped Violetta decide to play along with the new charade.

"It is my understanding that it is not permitted to make recordings of meetings without the consent of all present," Thurldottir offered vainly in response to the video. *She's rattled*, thought Mads. *Good*.

"Not correct when it concerns my office, or for that matter, yours, Chair Thurldottir," Mads responded. "As you *should* be aware, protocol provides for the Bibliotekar, that is me, to record all meetings held in my office and hold them for no longer than fourteen days before deleting them, unless a security issue arises in the interim. There is no security issue involved in this instance, but the fourteen days has not yet elapsed."

"Yes, I do recall that directive, but..."

"But nothing. Until that fourteen-day period has expired, I have the discretion as to what happens to this recording, and given the false accusation made against me by Ms Simpson, I have decided that pending my lawyer's review of her formal complaint, I will refer it to the Civil Prosecutor with a recommendation that, regardless of whatever connections she has, Ms Simpson be charged with making a false allegation of a sex-related crime."

"Apart from me, who else has seen this?" asked Thurldottir.

Mads could see she was trying not to respond to what he had just said, but he could also tell that what he said had had the desired effect. "Apart from me, just my lawyer," he answered.

"For now, I would ask you to keep it that way. I will find out more about this complaint." Thurldottir waited for his acquiescence.

"I am quite happy to agree to your request, Chair Thurldottir. Please tell Councillor Carlson that I am also quite happy to talk to..."

"No!" Thurldottir blurted, then, regaining some composure, said "I will handle Carlson" and terminated their conversation. The screen went blank.

Mads rose from his chair with a slight smile he could not repress and left the meeting room. He already knew how the whole issue with Violetta's betrayal and unearthing would play out: Thurldottir would get back to him in the next day or so and inform him that she had been wrongly advised. That it now appeared Violetta had not made a 'formal complaint' as such — as Mads had instructed — and had decided not to proceed to make one. From her point of view, that is, Thurldottir's, the matter would be closed, and Violetta would apologise for any distress Mads may have been caused. And that is exactly what happened, except for the apology. Thurldottir didn't know it, but *that* was never going to happen.

END OF CHAPTER FIFTEEN

Chapter Sixteen

Rafe and Ruben go to Russia

"Naudé's library was not planned to serve any cause short of the totality of human knowledge and opinion; his dream was that of the Pyrrhonist and universal critic, and he would by no means have shared the view expressed by a modern man of science that all books over twenty-five years old could well be placed in storage remote from the desks of students and scholar alike."
Harcourt Brown, Book Review: *Advis pour dresser une bibliothèque* (*Advice on Establishing a Library*) by Gabriel Naudé (1625), University of California Press reprint (1950), in *The Library Quarterly* Vol 21, No. 1, January 1951 at p44.

1:15pm, Sunday, 10ᵗʰ March 2205

Rafe was no longer 'in hiding', but standing on the platform of The Bibliotek's maglev station where he knew the First Class carriage of the next express from Oslo would reach. He was standing on the platform waiting for Ruben because Mads had told him it was no longer necessary to keep his whereabouts, or indeed the outcome of the failed assassination attempt on him, a secret. He had not, however, logged back into The Bibliotek network. Rafe was standing at that spot on the platform because if he knew Ruben, his new friend would be travelling in the First Class carriage. And so he was.

"*Hola, Rafe! Buenas tardes mi amigo!*" Ruben said with a big smile as he stepped onto the platform and followed up with a big hug.

"*Buenas tardes, Ruben, mi amigo,*" responded Rafe, genuinely pleased to see him. After Ruben released him, Rafe said in a mock tone, "Welcome to The Bibliotek, Señor Rodriguez. May I take your bag, sir?"

"Thank you, my friend, but be careful, it's mostly cigars."

"Excellent, that's what we like to hear — this place could do with a different aroma. Come on, I'll take you first to your accommodation — I've reserved one of our best rooms for you — then we'll head to the place where we keep some books, including your *Fabrica*."

"You lead, Rafe, I will follow."

The Visitor Apartments were a short walk from the station, and Rafe had indeed reserved one of the best for Ruben, which were all on the top floor of a three-storey typical chalet style Nordic apartment building.

"Very nice, Rafe," said Ruben as Rafe opened the door to the apartment and led him inside. "But it is very warm. Can we turn the heating down?"

"Ha! There is no heating, Ruben. It's just designed very well. Standard Nordic fare. But we can open the window for you," replied Rafe. He walked over to the square window, turned a handle and opened the thickly-glazed window a few centimetres."

"Ah, *gracias!* A window that opens. Wonderful. I cannot sleep without an open window. I am, how you say, old school."

"I am the same, Ruben. I must have an open window. And that is one of the many reasons why I love the Montelirio."

"Ah, *si*, Rafe, that is a special place, with a special view. But, forgive me, the view here is... different," said Ruben with a disconsolate look out through the window.

"Yes, it's very white, isn't it? Come, leave your bag here and we'll go to the library."

From the Visitor Apartments it was a short tram ride, deeper into The Bibliotek precinct to the Central Repository. Being a Sunday afternoon, many people were getting on and off at each station.

"This is like a small town, Rafe," said Ruben.

"Yes, and that's because it *is* a town. There are about fifteen thousand permanent residents here, three-quarters of whom work at The Bibliotek itself or the Academy or both. The rest service the town's needs. We don't really have an off-season like other places as we don't cater for tourists. In fact, we covertly discourage any but day visitors, students, and academics here to study. Okay, here is our stop."

After alighting from the tram, Ruben found he was facing a two-storey building, about a hundred metres away, jutting out from the base of a mountain, below a sloping cliff onto a plateau. Despite being only two storeys, it was stretching upwards in a curve, and was higher than a building normally five stories. How high exactly Ruben wasn't quite sure because the top of the building, its curving roof, and the ground to each side were all covered in old and fresh snow.

"The wedge shape is deliberate; for the snow coming down off the mountain; the curve pushes it to the side. It's practical and has a visual effect," explained Rafe.

"It surely does," replied Ruben. "Are those timber beams?"

Ruben was referring to the massive vertical tree trunks creating the tall façade of the building on the lower sides. "Yes, they are covering the concrete structure. Very thick concrete," replied Rafe.

There was only one entrance facing them, and at the front of it were two massive oak doors that always reminded Rafe of the doors of the Pope's Palace in Pienza. Rafe mentioned this and explained to his friend that The Bibliotek's doors were of the same 15th century vintage as the Pienza doors and had been rescued from a church in Alsace-Lorraine which had been bombed during the Great Holy War. They were always open during visiting hours, which were from 8am to midnight, every day, so the 'real' doors were a dual set of thick glazed glass sliding doors. In between, all persons about to enter were required to clean off any snow from their shoes and clothing. There were machines on the floor to serve that purpose.

As Rafe led Ruben through the set of sliding doors into the vestibule he stood back and looked at his friend. Ruben stood still. He could hardly believe his eyes or how his senses reacted. He had an overwhelming sense of space, but without feeling as if he were in an empty stadium. The ceiling was somewhere... up there... but he felt as if he had just entered a cosy... den... yet there were hundreds of people just within his eyesight. He could not work out how the effect was achieved.

"It's the floor, Ruben," said Rafe, who had been observing Ruben's reaction and well-knew it's cause.

Ruben looked down at the floor, and his jaw went further down. It was parquetry wood, the largest such floor he had ever seen. He knelt and ran his fingers over the wood and tapped. It was real wood, possibly oak, and it wasn't a veneer sheet. Each piece was a solid chunk. It seemed to breathe, and its golden colour, texture and worn sheen spoke of depth and age, and a history. And there was something else. Within the parquetry pattern there was an intermittent border between the panels, it looked like an in-lay of plastic, Ruben looked up inquisitively at Rafe.

"I'm glad you noticed that. It's a resin. In a fire situation it dissolves. Underneath it are thousands of tiny jets of angled water. I'm told anything two metres or less from floor level up will get a good soaking, but only in the immediate vicinity of any extreme heat source. It's called targeted firefighting and is just part of the whole system. If we had traditional ceiling-based extinguishers any given fire could easily result in more damage from water than from the flames it was meant to extinguish."

"Amazing. But, so much wood, Rafe."

"Not as much as it appears. The effect is achieved by the pattern. Quite brilliant, I think. I always like standing here, like you. I was the same the first time. Also notice the carpeting."

Ruben looked up and around. Indeed, there were intermittent areas of carpeting, with a colour of the same tone and texture as the floor so that it didn't seem like it was breaking up the sense of flow created by the wood.

"Just amazing, Rafe. I was not expecting this at all. And dare I say it, not so Nordic standard fare."

"You have me there."

Rafe led Ruben to the Reception Area.

"First we need to go through the main security check. Here we make sure there are no weapons or other nasty things someone is trying to bring into the Central Repository," explained Rafe.

Ruben duly found himself weighed, X-rayed, scanned, and recorded along with his purpose, which was supplied by Rafe to the guards.

"We also check you on the way out, sir," said one of the guards to Ruben, knowing he was a first-time visitor. "Any bag you take out must weigh the same as when you took it in. So must you. We do not encourage bags, though, so there has to be a good reason to have one."

Beyond the security check, there were data pads on pedestals standing like a sparsely wooded forest. Some staff were hovering. All smiling, all young. "These are actually all students at the Academy. They are all required to perform some type of work in their time-off from studies, and many choose to work here."

Again, Ruben was rendered almost immobile by the mere sight of what was before him. This time it was the sight of the open wooden bookcases lining every wall, from floor to at least three metres in height, each with a sliding wooden ladder affixed to it for the higher shelves, and every shelf filled with books. The wood of each bookcase and ladder matched that of the floor, as did the frames of the distressed leather-covered lounges and chairs sprinkled in front of them, seemingly randomly. Scores of them, probably hundreds. Many of the seats were taken up by people reading books, apparently taken from the shelves.

"It's impressive, isn't it?" asked Rafe. "Another brilliant design feature. It's meant to be a representation, a living exhibit they call it, of the essence of a peoples' library. A place where books are not only kept, but also read. So, any visitor is met with this vision, this impression. You should see this place at night. The downlights provide a targeted beam of light at each lounge and only turn on when someone sits on a particular lounge and only on each lounge. It makes each person feel as if they are in their own personal space, their own private library. And again, the wooden floor design, all meant to inspire that feeling of cosiness. There are people, many people, who will read entire books from cover to cover in this place. The creator of The Bibliotek, Siegfried Sorenson, was adamant it should not be an edifice, not something that entices people to come to do nothing but gawk and stare and then leave, but something that invites you to walk up to a shelf, take hold of a book, and then sit down and read it. Downstairs is different, but up here is the essence of a library, or at least one in the classical sense, without the edifice effect. There is nothing here to say 'look at me and see how wealthy I am.'"

"I know what you mean, Rafe, too many libraries I agree had become utterly redundant displays of ... what's the word ... ostentation, with the books having to fit in with the splendour instead of the other way around, and then only on a 'do not touch' basis. But this. This is all *about* the books, it is so clear, so different. But these books here, Rafe? They look fairly new."

"Ah, yes, this place is also a magnet. It draws our staff and visitors to come here and browse because every book you see here is new. I don't know if you are aware, but part of the mandate of The Bibliotek was that all member states of the UN agreed at the same time of approving its establishment that one copy of every new book published in their respective states must be contributed to The Bibliotek. It's the same law as you would know that many countries had in place for centuries before The Bibliotek was even proposed. So, every few days, after midnight, a new batch of books comes in, and older ones go to the Central Repository. Whilst they are here, each is processed by the librarians — you can see some of them over there by the benches — they on-board each book from here."

"So, how long does any book stay here before going to the Central Repository?"

"I think it's about one month on average before a book will go downstairs," replied Rafe. "Which means that people will keep returning here just to see and read the new books. There is always something different. With the librarians here as well it is a very dynamic place."

"But it doesn't seem frenetic," said Ruben.

"Yes, well, engagement of the mind is best done in silence," replied Rafe. "But as you can see, there are no signs to that effect. It is an unwritten rule here: de-activate your neurophone."

Ruben strolled with Rafe along the bookcases and stopped to talk to one of the librarians who, on recognising Rafe, was only too happy to show Ruben how she processed a new book. "I so enjoyed your speech at the dinner last year, sir," she said to Rafe. "Such a splendid Find for the billionth entry."

"Thank you, young lady," replied Rafe, leading Ruben away.

"What did she mean, 'the billionth entry'?" asked Ruben.

"I hate giving speeches but my so-called friend the Bibliotekar — we're having dinner with him tonight by the way — he overstretched things so that it was a Find of *mine* that was the one billionth book procured by The Bibliotek. There was a big dinner to celebrate and I had to give a speech about the book and how I had found it. He knows I hate public speaking. It's bad enough giving lectures at the Academy. The one billionth book was one of the Giordano books I told you about when we first met — an original first edition of Remmelin's *Catoptrum Microcosmicum*."

"But Rafe, that was a story that deserved to be shared to a wider audience than just conversations with me and others. I am so glad the Bibliotekar made you tell it. And besides, I am guessing there are many younger people here who wish they could be a Finder like you. Your story would have made it feel real for them."

"That may be so. I hadn't really thought of it like that. It was still a nerve-racking experience though."

"Is the Remmelin a first edition?!" Ruben asked suddenly.

"Yes, it is pretty impressive too. And it's with the *Fabrica*. You'll see them both. I'll take you downstairs now."

"This *will* be interesting," said Ruben as he followed Rafe to the mountain-side end of the hall. He could see that access was being limited. "More security?"

"Absolutely, only tougher. This is the pointy end of The Bibliotek. Special Access Only."

As they approached, one of the guards looked up and spotted a face he knew. "Rafe the Finder. It's been a long time, sir."

"I recognise you, but how do you know it's *really* me? Rafe teased, for Ruben's benefit.

"Retinal scan already done, sir."

"It has been a long time since my last visit, that's a change. This is my colleague, Ruben Rodriguez. He is with me."

"Certainly sir," the guard replied. "I have the Bibliotekar's approval for Señor Rodriguez's visit on my screen now. Just a reminder though that Señor Rodriguez must remain with you at all times. How long do you expect to be downstairs?"

"No more than an hour," replied Rafe.

This the guard entered into his data pad. "And the Level?"

"Let me double check... Level Forty-five East."

"Just a moment sir, replied the guard as he entered the information. "Okay that will be fine. Hold up your left arm now, please."

Rafe explained to Ruben that the band the guard was now placing on each of their wrists was a Locator, as a double measure, and it would be removed on their exit. "Thank you, sir, you are good to go," said the guard as he greenlit the entry panel. "Lift C is waiting for you and will take you non-stop to Level Forty-five," the guard said with a smile as he pointed towards the Lift Bay. "By the way, sir, I really enjoyed your speech at the dinner. Great story."

"Thanks," said Rafe with a small smile.

As they walked to the lift, Ruben turned to Rafe. "What happens if I rip this thing off? It's a little irritating, Rafe."

"I wouldn't advise it. You'll have Security down your throat in an instant."

"Okay, *Señor*, but did I hear you correctly, you said Level Forty-five?"

Rafe nodded.

"East?"

Rafe nodded, and they entered Lift C. "Each level branches outwards several kilometres in four different directions. North, South, East, West."

"That is unbelievable."

"Unbelievable but necessary."

"I must say Rafe, this is the most impressive security I have ever experienced. Even with this annoying band on my wrist."

"Yes, it is tight security, and all for books. See how we value them so. We estimate the market value of all the books we hold to be in the trillions if it makes sense to speak of a market, which I do not think it does. But the security is not just about their value. We are more concerned with damage than with theft. Theft is easier to deal with."

"Are you referring to the Present Sect?"

"Yes, but mostly nothing so specific. We never lose sight of the reason The Bibliotek was built — to act as the world's repository for all the world's books; the guaranteed, last resort, safest place to store a copy of each first edition. Not much more than that, and importantly nothing less. Hence the investment in security."

"Still impressive, my friend."

After a seemingly long journey down, but actually less than a minute, they arrived at Level 45. During their descent, Ruben couldn't help but notice there were another 30 levels below their destination. On stepping out of the lift, he saw that they were in a foyer, with four wide hallways branching off each side. Each was closed off by heavy-set doors except one, the signposted East Section, which was also lit at the start by a few soft downlights before its tunnel-like hallway disappeared into complete darkness. Ruben could also see some hand basins and towels and Rafe was already washing his hands. "What's that smell?" asked Ruben as he joined Rafe and also began washing.

"That, Ruben, is the smell of nothing," replied Rafe. "The entire Central Repository, all seventy-five levels, is a pure, clean, controlled, sterile environment, I'm sorry. All for the benefit of the books. The only smell you will detect from here on in will be coming from any given book you handle. And it will be enhanced."

"No gloves?"

"Neither necessary nor desirable. The books themselves have been completely vacuumed at the micro level, and so as long as we wash our hands thoroughly, there's no need to let gloves stop us *feeling* any given book that is accessible. It's a different story though for embargoed books. Those we need gloves for."

"And behind those doors, do they only open for visitors?"

"That's right. They're humidity doors. Again, for the protection of the books. Okay, now for another ride."

Rafe motioned Ruben to take a seat on the travelator that awaited them at the start of the East Section hall, and then, after seating himself next to Ruben, pressed a button on the panel at the front. Immediately but slowly at first, the travelator began its journey on a single, silent, track. As they went further into the hallway, downlights would come on to light their progress, then turn off after they had passed, and as such Ruben could see the square rooms on each side of the tunnel, filled with bookcases, and those filled with books. After ten minutes, the travelator slowed until it stopped.

"Here we are," said Rafe, stepping off the travelator. He pressed a panel on the glass wall of the book-filled room on their left and it slid to one side. It was then that Ruben noticed that the bookcases were all slim and made of pine, and there, in the middle of the room, next to a small pine table, was the *Fabrica*, on a stand with raised leaves at the top, specially designed to hold a large book of its size, with the *Fabrica* open to a double page. Against the backdrop of the shelves filled with books of the same topic, size, and age, it looked magnificent.

"The Book of the Month," Rafe said drolly. "It replaced my Remmelin, which is over here," as he knelt down to a high shelf, lifted out the *Catoptrum Microcosmicum* and carefully placed it on the table for Ruben's inspection.

"This is *magnifico*, Rafe," he said as he opened the Remmelin, "just *magnifico*. And you are right about the smell, I know it well, but it is so strong. But my head is swinging, Rafe."

"Swinging? I think you mean swimming," Rafe corrected.

"Yes, swimming, you're right. See, I cannot even speak properly. So many books, Rafe. I have never seen so many books. How far East have we come down this hallway?"

"About two-thirds."

"Goodness. You say there are one billion books here at The Bibliotek?"

"Yes. One thousand million."

"How many on this floor, this Level?"

"I am not certain, but I believe its capacity is fifteen million."

"That is incredible. And it is so quiet and still. I don't see anybody. All these books just sitting here. Alone. Sad. So far from upstairs.

From people — your 'peoples' library'. Here in the quiet black of still darkness."

"The 'quiet black of still darkness', that's good Ruben, but I know what you are saying. My view is they would have been hidden away anyway, only just in a smaller space, somewhere else if not here. And people do come down here. We do have Reading Rooms and Conservation Rooms on each level. The Reading Rooms are for researchers and the like who we approve to be in the Central Repository and for books too valuable, for whatever reason, to allow out of this controlled environment. And when I say controlled, I mean it in every possible sense. For example, when I took the Remmelin here off the shelf, Security was immediately made aware of it. Each book has a tiny, hidden, barcode imprint which allows it to be tracked. That is why we had to inform them of which level we wanted access to and which section. Well that was one of the reasons. Another reason is that the lift only goes to a nominated level. But my point is that the *Fabrica* and most of the other books on this level are not embargoed. Which means they are accessible, according to guidelines we call the Principles of Access. Designed to be a compromise between protecting each book and allowing it to be handled and, most importantly, read."

Ruben had listened intently to all that Rafe had said, taking it all in and nodding at times in acknowledgement. "I am glad to hear you say that, Rafe. So many books just waiting to be opened and their treasure revealed. It is... overwhelming."

"No argument there," replied Rafe.

Before they returned to Ground Level, Rafe showed Ruben the other books from the Giordano Collection in other rooms on Level 45. The allocated hour went by with Ruben hardly noticing, as he found the whole experience intoxicating. So taken with the experience was he that he asked Rafe if they could walk back to the Visitors' Apartments to clear his head instead of catching the tram.

"Tomorrow we embark on something that could be quite special, Rafe," said Ruben, as they walked together on the snow-covered path.

"Yes, but it could also be something quite disappointing," he replied philosophically.

"We will see. We will see," Ruben said, contemplatively. "You know, Rafe, I was not that surprised when you called me and asked if you could go to Moscow with me. You play your cards very close to your chest, but I had an inkling..."

"Inkling."

"Sorry, yes, I had an *inkling* that you too were on the same hunt."

"I get that," replied Rafe. "And since we both seemed to be close to an answer, I thought it would be a good idea to join forces."

"Of course, Rafe, of course," Ruben said with a knowing smile and a twinkle in his eye.

Rafe collected Ruben just before 7pm and took him to Mads' apartment. A uniformed steward greeted their arrival and, just as he had when he set foot in the library, Ruben stood just inside the front door and admired the book-filled shelves adorning the walls. Before too long, Mads and others came to the entry foyer.

This was Rafe's cue. "Friends, I would like to introduce Señor Ruben Javier Garcia Rodriguez. Ruben, this is Mads Ingridson, the Bibliotekar."

"I'm impressed you remembered all that, Rafe. Bibliotekar Ingridson, this is both a pleasure and an honour to meet you," said Ruben with a slight bow and then a shake of his hand.

"Both of those are mine, Señor Rodriguez, please call me Mads," responded Mads, in kind. "Let me introduce you to Thomas Metcalfe, he is a reasonably active member of the Governing Council and, believe it or not, the oldest person ever to travel in space."

"Welcome Señor Rodriguez," said Thomas, also with a slight bow before shaking his hand. "Gee, Mads, thanks for making me feel my age."

"Thank you, gentlemen. Please, call me Ruben. The oldest man in space?"

"Long story, but yes," replied Thomas.

"Ruben, I am also pleased to introduce our Head of Security, Nikka Johannson," said Mads, prompting Nikka to step forward and shake Ruben's hand.

"Welcome, Ruben, it is a pleasure to meet you," said Nikka.

"The pleasure is mine, dear lady, said Ruben, with a deep bow and then a kiss of her hand. "Rafe showed me the library this afternoon and your security arrangements are most impressive. Very thorough, and very professional."

"Thank you, we work hard on getting things right."

"Come on everybody, let's get comfortable in the lounge before dinner," said Mads.

Over a pre-dinner drink, Thomas asked "your first visit to The Bibliotek, Ruben?"

"Indeed it is, Señor Thomas, more or less a stopover," he replied.

"Nags told me about the *Fabrica*. Thank you for gifting it to us," Thomas continued.

"Nags?" Ruben turned to Rafe, slightly confused.

"That's what my so-called friends call me. Short for Nagy," Rafe replied.

"Oh I see."

"Yes, thanks for the *Fabrica*. It is a magnificent thing," said Mads.

"Thank *you* for the tax credit! It came just at the right time. Those tax people! Like leeches, only worse because they never have enough blood. And it was good to see my book amongst its friends, so to speak. It looked magnificent with them."

Over dinner Rafe made the comment that the catered meal tasted so much better than Mads' cooking.

"Thank you for your assessment Nags. This dinner is *formal* informal as opposed to *informal* informal. Your first and quite possibly your last, I understand," responded Mads.

After some laughter, Ruben changed the subject. "What books do you read, Rafe? Or have read lately?" he asked.

"I don't have time to read books."

"Are you serious?" said Ruben, visibly surprised.

"I am in serious need of one of your cigars."

"Do you *have* any books?"

"Yes, my grandmother's. She raised me. They were everywhere in her home."

"Why not read those?"

"I did. Many years ago."

"But you like books, yes?"

"It goes without saying, so I won't."

"But Rafe," Ruben persevered, "you have lost your connection have you not? You're like the man who collects fine wine but never drinks it." At hearing that Rafe turned and looked at Mads with a knowing smile. "I cannot believe you spend all your life on searches," Ruben continued. "You find, then you walk away. Reading a book is feeding the soul, Rafe, you of all people should know that. You nearly said as much just today when we were on Level Forty-five."

"Feeding is not filling. Only a good woman can do that." As soon as he said it, Rafe regretted it. "Sorry Mads," he added.

Ruben sensed something sensitive had just passed, and as it appeared to involve a woman, he continued as if he hadn't noticed as Mads gave the smallest of nods to Rafe. "A good woman never lasts, but a good book can and does. And a good book, Rafe, that can fill the soul not just feed it. This I strongly believe. But only if you read it. You know, I read the *Fabrica*."

"You know Latin?" asked Rafe.

"Of course, don't you?"

"Yes," replied Rafe.

"Well? You did at least read one page of the *Fabrica*?"

"No."

"Then I feel truly sorry for you," said Ruben, shaking his head. "You of all people. You have an opportunity nobody else has and you not only let it go past you, you throw it away."

"I repeat, I need one of your cigars."

Mads looked at his friend and he had a thought he had never had before. Ruben had stoked it. "What happens after the Lost Library, Rafe?" he quietly, but seriously, said, staring at his friend.

All other eyes also turned to Rafe, who took the cigar that Ruben held out to him, lit it slowly, just like Ruben had shown him in Ronda, drew, slowly and deliberately let out that first draw's smoke, then spoke. "Ruben, thanks, I needed this. Mads, you ask a very good question. Part of me wants to experience more of some of the places I only get to spend a few days in at a time, like Ronda," he said, winking at Ruben who smiled in return with a slow bow of his head, "and part of me doesn't want to leave The Bibliotek. Lately I've begun to appreciate my home here a lot more. And the people in it," he said, turning to Thomas and Nikka, then Mads.

"You've got a few years left in you yet Rafe," said Thomas with feigned encouragement and a faint smile.

"Gee, thanks."

"But I have to say," continued Thomas, "if you do find the Lost Library and it contains even a sample of what people say it does, it will be hard to top it as a Find."

"Yes, you're right, Thomas," answered Rafe. "But it's now or never. And besides, I'd rather be with Ruben when *we* find it than not be with Ruben when *he* finds it."

"Ha!" exclaimed Ruben, slapping Rafe on his back.

"Who owns the Lost Library, assuming it exists?" asked Nikka.

"Good question, Nikka," said Mads. "I was going to ask the same."

"Until it is found, it belongs to no-one I would suggest," said Rafe.

"The Russian Government many years ago issued a short statement that the Lost Library of Ivan The Formidable does not exist, so stop looking for it. I suppose we could hold them to that," suggested Ruben.

"Possibly, but I don't think so," replied Mads.

"Technically it should be the descendants of the rightful owner before it disappeared, if they could be found," offered Thomas. "But who really owns such books? Greece? Istanbul? What's left of the Turkish Government? Italy? The Vatican? The Russian Government? How about finders, keepers?"

"Finders, keepers!" affirmed Rafe with a thump of his hand on the table.

"Speaking for myself," said Ruben, "I am not concerned with wanting to be known as the finder of the Lost Library. I prefer to focus on the prize itself and being known as the finder is not the publicity I seek. It is personal satisfaction, and besides, there are a few dealers I do not like who will continue to waste their efforts searching for it, which is to my advantage. I have a few clients who will benefit and who I may tell the truth. So I agree, finders, keepers. Quiet finders, quiet keepers."

"Well I represent The Bibliotek," responded Rafe, "which is a not-for-profit. Who better to care for the books comprising the Lost Library? Turkey probably has a good case for ownership but it long ago gave up most of its national collection to The Bibliotek. All I care about is that Ruben and I have agreed to go halves."

"I'm not sure how that would work, but in any event, all of this is academic. I suggest we cross the ownership bridge if and when we get to it," said Mads.

A little while later, after dinner, Mads expressed a wish to show Ruben some of the books in his collection, and as the two of them discussed some of Mads' favourites, with Thomas in tow, Nikka pulled Rafe aside.

"Are you sure you know what you are doing? Going back to Sergiyev so soon may not be prudent."

"And unexpected. But I wasn't about to let Ruben have all the fun. I had no choice but to offer to go with him. But you did say you had cleared the incident with the local police, didn't you?"

"I did, but it wasn't easy. There are still some questions I need to provide answers for after I have finished my investigation," replied Nikka.

"But, for now, the case is, as they say, closed, isn't it?"

"Yes, that's true, but I can't guarantee your safety, I hope you know that."

"I do, and I wasn't asking for it. And this time certain individuals won't get a tipoff about my visit, so even if they do have someone else lined up to do their dirty work, I should be okay."

"I hope you're right, Rafe. It still seems a big risk. Are you certain you need to go?"

"If you knew how long I've been on this search for the Lost Library, you'd understand how keen I am on finding out the truth and how important it is that I be there with Ruben."

"But what about the guard, Sasha?"

"He'll be there. I do believe he was pleased it was not me lying in the snow, and I've taken care of his nervousness with twice the fee I paid before."

"But this is the last visit there, okay?"

"Duly noted. All you need to do is maintain my network status as 'off the reservation'."

"Sooner or later notice of your death will be recognised as premature."

"I get that, but Mads is pretty sure that Smits' ongoing absence has already been noted by you-know-who and two and two put together."

8:05am Monday, 11th March 2205

Courtesy of Ruben's generosity, Rafe and he were sitting in a private heliojet flying to Moscow the next morning from The Bibliotek's spaceport.

"So, Ruben, I read your notes about the Moscow Print Yard. You see, I can read after all. It makes sense to start there because, as I mentioned to you last week, my target site is an hour's drive from Moscow in case your target comes up empty, but I have to ask, really? I mean, more hidden underground tunnels? I'm sorry, but I just do not get it. Why would anyone hide or store books underground? It doesn't make sense. Look, mould is fast. When it takes hold it can destroy a book within two months, four at the most, and we are talking about centuries. But why am I telling you this? You of all people know this."

"*Si, si*, Rafe, you are absolutely right. But we are not talking about an underground tunnel, or even a tunnel. We are talking about the creation of printing in Russia, by no less than Ivan the Fourth. It was he who ordered the construction of the Moscow Print Yard, and it was there that Russia's first books were printed."

"Yes, and it wasn't long before it was burnt down by a horde of scribes a tad angry about their livelihood being made redundant by the new-fangled printing press."

"*Si si*, Rafe, that is true, if I am to understand correctly what 'fangled' means, but bear with me. The Print Yard was quickly rebuilt, but out of stone this time. And during that process a downstairs storeroom was included, which connected to a new tunnel, underground, to the Kremlin. What better place to store his library than in that storeroom, not in the tunnel? Now, fast forward a hundred years and the building was dismantled, not destroyed, and a new, bigger complex was constructed over the existing foundations and anything else that was below ground, including that storeroom. By then Ivan was dead and probably anyone else who knew. And now a friend of mine thinks he has found it, by accident."

"Okay, I'm listening."

"My friend is a researcher in Russian history at the Russian State University for the Humanities, and guess where it's Moscow campus is?"

"Let me guess, the building on the site of the Print Yard?"

"Precisely. Now, my friend was not researching the Lost Library, he was researching the history of printing in Russia, so anything left of the Print Yard is of great interest to him. But he and I have been discussing the Lost Library for some time, he's helped me in the past with getting access to research material, so when he discovered what appears to be a stone storeroom under the campus building, he contacted me. And here I am, on the way to meet him so we can try and get access to it together."

"And me."

"And you, my friend. In case I am wrong. But you won't tell me *your* target yet, will you?"

"No Ruben, not yet. Let's see how we go at your site first."

"*Si si*, as you wish."

3:35pm

Ruben looked at Rafe, a worried expression suddenly appearing on his face. His friend, Professor Igor Kavinsky, had just introduced him and Rafe to Dr Ekaterina Smirnova, an archaeologist. Igor had mentioned the institution she was with but neither heard it after hearing that fatal word 'archaeologist'. They were not expecting this at all.

"Ekaterina is here to supervise the opening of the door to what appears to be potentially your storeroom, Ruben," Igor explained, prompting Ruben to consider the term 'your storeroom' rendered moot. "It's protocol, gentlemen, in these situations, as you would no doubt appreciate."

"No doubt," replied Ruben, but thinking to himself '*típicos académicos de mierda*'.

The four of them were standing in a far corner of the basement of the University building. It was obvious to Ruben that they were alone amongst the vast dimly-lit network of benches, cabinets, shelving, and store rooms. Before them a large cabinet had been shifted away from its normal position against the wall, revealing behind it a hitherto hidden small wooden doorway flush to the surrounding concrete wall, with a recessed and corroded small iron ring in the middle of the door. Igor had obviously left it that way, unopened.

"Professor Kavinsky tells me you think this is possibly the location of the Lost Library of Ivan The Formidable," said Ekaterina, holding a large torch and alternately looking at the door and Ruben.

Right there and then Ruben suddenly hoped he was wrong, and that this wasn't the place. Right then he wished that he and Rafe were in a hovercar going to Rafe's target site. Right then he wished he had made sure Igor was a lot more careful about who he told about the hidden storeroom.

"Just one of many potentialities. I was coming to Moscow anyway as luck would have it so I thought it might be interesting to see what Igor has discovered, if anything," he replied to Ekaterina.

Rafe felt for his friend, and knew why his enthusiasm had suddenly disappeared. There was now going to be nothing 'quiet' about this discovery if it were made as Ruben had originally hoped.

"Well then, shall we begin? Igor, if you do not mind, I will start to open the door," said Ekaterina.

The door proved easier to open than she had envisaged. She pulled the ring out from its recessed position, then turned it. They all heard the locks dropping from the hinges.

Then Ekaterina pulled the ring again, this time outwards, and the door came with it. This was itself a bad sign for any 'discoveries' to be made, as it indicated prior entry, a point which she immediately advised the three men. A pungent smell and complete darkness greeted the opening, prompting each to place a hand over their mouths and Ekaterina to also turn on her torch and shine it into the opening. Suddenly they saw what looked like shelving.

Empty shelving.

One by one they entered the room, which was small and hardly fit them all. It was indeed empty. Whatever had been on the shelves, if ever, had long ago been taken away. After examining the stone walls and finding no indication of any other doorways, Ruben looked silently at Rafe, who had not spoken at all after being introduced to the helpful archaeologist.

"Well, my friends," said Ruben softly, "it seems Rafe and I have come a long way for nothing."

"Yes, it seems that way," replied a disappointed Igor. "I am sorry, Ruben, for getting you and me both excited."

"Not to worry, my friend," Ruben said, turning to Rafe. "We can at least scratch this place from our minds."

10:07am, Tuesday, 12ᵗʰ March 2205

"You couldn't have gotten a larger hovercar, could you?" asked Rafe.

"Larger? This was the biggest I could find!" retorted Ruben from the front passenger seat. "Oh, I see," he continued when he finally twigged to Rafe's facial expression, "you are perhaps joking with me?"

"Yes, it's my way of impolitely saying 'this is a very big hovercar'."

"Better to have such a car and not need it than to need it but not have it," said Ruben.

"I've heard that," replied Rafe, without taking his eyes off the road. "You seem in a better mood this morning, Ruben."

"Yes, my friend, ever since you spilled your guts over dinner last night."

"Beans."

"What?"

"Spilled my beans," corrected Rafe.

"Beans? How strange. 'Guts' sounds much better," responded Ruben.

Rafe had indeed 'spilled his guts' over dinner the previous night. After Ruben's disappointment over his 'discovery', there was no longer any reason for Rafe not to tell him the place he was now driving to and the reasons why. It had taken a little over an hour explaining all the clues he had earlier divulged to Mads as to his proposed site of the Lost Library, and that was without any interruption from Ruben, who had listened intently, occasionally smiled, and displayed a fair dose of raised eyebrows at Rafe's more nebulous dots in the drawing of his conclusions. And now Rafe was driving with intent on a now-familiar road and trying to calm the growing nervous anticipation in the pit of his stomach. He had not mentioned to Ruben the events of his most recent journey to the Trinity Mausoleum, and he had been glad he didn't when Sasha mentioned during their neurophone conversation later in the night when Rafe was alone in his room, that he wouldn't be there at the mausoleum when Ruben and he expected be there in the late morning.

"If it is alright with you, John, I will not be there so please you to leave the money in an envelope in a plastic bag just inside the door to the mausoleum and I will pick it up later. You have the money yes? You know the price has doubled?" Sasha had said.

"Yes, I have the money, all of it, plus a little bonus for your trouble. You can trust me to leave it," Rafe had replied.

"I trust you, John, like I trust that your name is John. But don't worry. If the money is there when I come tomorrow night I will not need to have another conversation with the police. You understand, Mr John?"

"Yes, Sasha. Perfectly. It's all good. The case is closed, yes?"

"I am told this yes," Sasha had answered, before continuing, "I do not know what treasure you will find there, John. There is nothing in that mausoleum except three coffins with three bodies in them. But, who am I to be troubled by what you think? Just do not make the damage, okay?"

"Yes, Sasha, I understand," Rafe had patiently said.

"And don't came back," Sasha had finished the call with.

True to his word, Sasha was nowhere to be seen when they entered the grounds of the monastery through the same gate as Rafe and Nikka had done, only this time it was bright sunshine that greeted them. In fact, there was no one to be seen anywhere, a conclusion Rafe had quickly come to as soon as they walked through the gate.

"What are you looking for, my friend?" Ruben asked.

"Just making sure we are alone," replied Rafe.

"You paid for this access, yes?"

"I did. Quite a lot."

"Then there's nothing to worry about is there?" Ruben had said, more a statement than a genuine question.

When they reached the mausoleum, Rafe looked around, trying not to focus on the tree next to which he and Nikka had dragged the limp, heavy, body of Smits that night. He was relieved to see no sign of any police tape.

"And see, there is no lock on this door," Ruben said, bringing Rafe back to the present. Before he could say anything, Ruben had opened the door and walked inside the dark, stone one-roomed cube of a building, or so it appeared to be from the outside.

By the time Rafe walked into the room, Ruben had already gone over to the wall where Rafe had said there was missing space. As with the other walls it was covered in dust.

Ruben switched on his flashlight and pointed the beam at where the wall met the floor. "It's been very dry in here for a very long time, my friend. That is a good sign. Only a little bit of old mould at the bottom," he said, moving the torch beam so Rafe could see what he meant.

"That is a good sign, and just as I remembered it the first time I came here."

"The first time?" asked Ruben as he started to move the torch light across the wall.

"Yes, when I came here and took those measurements," Rafe replied quickly, trying to make Ruben's question sound as if he had forgotten what Rafe had told him the night before, even though it had sounded to Rafe that he was asking about something Rafe had not mentioned to Ruben. Or maybe he was just being paranoid, he told himself.

"There is a something here, Rafe," said Ruben, scraping something with his fingers that his torch had picked up as jutting out ever so slightly from the wall, and who only spotted it courtesy of the tiny shadow thrown up by the torch light. "It's a hinge," Ruben added, then, shining his torch on the top and to the side of the panel, "and there is another one down here," he said as he moved the torch down along the edge of the panel with the hinge.

Rafe stood watching his friend make the discovery, transfixed. "Be still my beating heart. I had not seen that."

"It was easy to miss, my friend," said Ruben as he now searched the wall for the full lining of a door. "But I cannot find any handle, just the outline of a very low door."

"Maybe if we pushed it, it will open," offered Rafe.

"Not likely, those hinges are telling me the door opens outwards," Ruben had hardly got the words out when Rafe leant over Ruben and pushed the inside edge of the door opposite the hinges. As he did so, they both heard an almost imperceptible 'click' and Rafe felt the door move slightly inwards, before it then sprang back outwards a few centimetres. They both stood back.

Rafe then placed his index finger inside the door and pulled it back, revealing a dark space which Ruben then lit with his torch.

Before them in the torchlight stood wooden shelving that covered the far wall of the tiny space behind the door and on it, books. Many books. All with the unmistakable bindings of incunabula – pale pig skin.

They stood there, side by side, in silence.

"It seems so easy, my friend. Too easy," Ruben finally spoke on behalf of them both.

More silence.

"But what were you expecting?" Rafe finally replied. "An archaeological dig? These. Are. Books. They have been sitting here waiting for someone, like us, and here we are. Their rescuers."

More silence.

"How many do you think?" Rafe asked.

"Rough guess my friend, would be around three hundred and fifty, said Ruben as he moved the torch light from side to side and up and down. "Six shelves, no more than about sixty books in each."

More silence.

"Fifty-fifty. That's what we agreed, isn't it?" Rafe asked Ruben.

"Yes, my friend, fifty-fifty," replied Ruben.

"Fifty-fifty of what?" asked a voice behind them.

Rafe and Ruben spun around in surprise. There was the outline of a man standing there in the gloom, well inside the mausoleum.

"Shit, Sasha you gave us a fright!"

"I do not doubt it. Fifty-fifty of what? What have you found, John? Treasure?"

As calmly as he could muster, 'John' answered Sasha's demand. "I wish! No, just as you said, Sasha, no treasure. Just some old books."

"And look, John," said Ruben as he suddenly reached into the space and randomly grabbed one of the books without a care and opened it, "they're not even in Russian. Or even English. See?"

Rafe shone his torch on the opened book that Ruben now held, so that he and, more importantly, Sasha could see.

"What are they doing here?" asked Sasha, not bothering to ask Ruben his name.

"Who knows, Sasha, who knows," Rafe replied. "By the way, what are you doing here?"

"I came to get my money. I could not wait. You understand."

"Yes, no problem, here it is," said Rafe reaching into his jacket pocket and pulling out a sealed envelope, which he handed to Sasha.

"Sasha my good friend, I don't know how much John is paying you, but we need your help getting these old books to our car," said Ruben as he reached into his jacket and pulled out his wallet.

Rafe and Sasha both watched Ruben as he opened his wallet and pulled out all the money from inside it. It was a lot. "I don't know how much Euros are here, Sasha, but it is for you if you can see fit to help us in our task."

Sasha looked at Ruben for what seemed a long time. "It is very quiet here, nobody around," he finally said.

Ruben and Rafe waited. Neither were sure if Sasha had just asked them a question.

"And that is how you want it to stay, yes?" Sasha then asked. Now they knew what was on his mind.

"Yes," replied Ruben, quietly, but clearly and firmly. "We have an understanding then?"

"Yes, whatever your name is," replied Sasha, "we have the understanding. But we need to hurry. Where is your hovercar, John?"

"It's down the street past the gate," Rafe replied.

"Give me the keys," said Sasha matter-of-factly.

"Why?"

Sasha looked at John for a second before replying. "I go and get your car. I bring it here. Save much time."

"Ah, but won't you need to drive through the front entrance?" asked a sceptical Rafe.

"No, through another entrance," said Sasha, as if Rafe were wasting his time asking stupid questions. "There are many gates here. Only one for public. The rest, for employees. I am an employee. So, keys please," said Sasha, holding out his hand.

By the time Sasha returned with the car, Ruben and Rafe had piled most of the books on the floor near the mausoleum door. "John?" Ruben had asked Rafe as they made themselves busy before Sasha came back. Rafe shrugged his shoulders.

"Sometimes the utmost discretion is required. This is one of those occasions," Rafe said.

"Oh, my friend, that is not my question. I was asking why did you pick 'John'?"

"It's common and as I found out just now, easy for people to say," Rafe had replied, with a smile.

"You know my friend, we are entering the Twilight Zone?" Ruben had then said.

"The what?"

Ruben just shook his head. "You need to read more, Señor Rafe."

It was not long before all the books were piled into the rental hovercar, either in the storage compartment or spread out on the back seat in piles. Ruben had counted them all. "One hundred and seventy-six each," Ruben had announced, and, looking at Sasha, said "that's fifty-fifty."

Sasha ignored him, then said to Rafe, "Okay, you to go now. Same way you came in."

"Ah... wait, what?"

"Young Sasha here will drive the car out the same way he came in or, even better," said Ruben now looking at Sasha, "a different way he came in, then meet us outside."

"At least one of you understands," said Sasha as he got into the car and drove off.

"Come on, my friend," said Ruben putting his arm around Rafe's shoulders, "we need to close that little door and make the place nice and neat and tidy."

Just before they sealed the secret space, Ruben had a thought. He reached into a pocket and pulled out one of his cigars, which he carefully positioned on one of the shelves, at the front, where it could be seen. "You're mad," said Rafe, but he understood exactly why Ruben had done it.

Later, when Sasha met them outside he said to Rafe as he handed the keys back. "I know those books are very valuable 'John'. I am not the stupid Russian you think I am. And I know *exactly* what is happening here. You understand me?" he said with a slightly more aggressive tone than Rafe had heard before.

"But what I do not know is what is going to happen next. I do not wish to know," Sasha now said, looking at them both. "But one thing is for sure, *my friends*, I will not be reading about where your little discovery was made, or hearing about it. Yes?"

Yes, they both nodded and said, several times.

"Then goodbye 'John' and goodbye you," Sasha said to each in turn. "may your lives be as happy as mine will be from today." With that, he turned and walked away, waving his arm goodbye without turning.

6:19pm

"Ruben," Rafe laughed deliriously and raucously. He was barely able to put a sentence together. "I can tell you now, right now, there ain't a snowball's chance in Hell we have even *one* of these books!"

Ruben joined Rafe in his delirium. He realised it was an absurd suggestion. He slapped Rafe on his back and laughed harder. Rafe then got himself into a chair, gripping his chest he was laughing so hard. They had quickly drained the first of six bottles of Bollinger that Ruben had ordered from room service. It was the very first thing he had done once they had brought all the books up to his room at the hotel from the underground hovercar park. Ruben had gone up to Reception and grabbed a luggage trailer from the concierge and had to pay him a tip not to come and help him with his 'luggage', which they managed to fit onto the trailer — just — in one trip directly up to Ruben's room. Ruben walked over to another champagne bottle, grabbed it out of the bucket and in a second had popped the cork. He forgot to hold it and it flew across the room, just missing Rafe's head, making both of them laugh even harder and louder. Ruben took a swig before the champagne otherwise all poured out the bottle freely, given he was swinging it like a cat, then handed the still streaming bottle to Rafe, who reciprocated the swig, then returned the bottle to Ruben, the start of a routine they kept up until that bottle too was drained, rather quickly as well. Then the celebration began.

After a while, Rafe lifted his head from the carpet and slurred "how we gonna get this lot to The Bibliotek young Ruben? Eh fella?"

"You have a heliostrip at your spaceport" said Ruben, sprawled along one of the lounges with his head resting on a scrunched pillow, and a half-empty champagne bottle in an ice bucket on the floor next to him.

"A stripper! Yeah, let's get one!"

"No my friend, a *heliostrip*. You know, that thing you land heliojets on. You have one."

"Oh that kind of stripper. Nuh. Yes. Yeah, we do. At the spaceport. For the space cadets."

"The what? Never mind, the problem is solved, my friend. I have already arranged another private heliojet."

Rafe rolled over onto his back. "When did you do that?!"

"While you were sleeping like a baby."

"A private heliojet you say. A book heliojet? How long was I asleep?" asked Rafe as he got himself off the floor and into one of the armchairs.

"Only ten minutes. Yes, Rafe, I booked a book jet!"

Again, for the umpteenth time, Rafe and Ruben let out a raucous and loud laugh together.

"You'd make a great Finder, Ruben my man. A Super Finder! Flying to all destinations to collect books. Bring out yer books! Bring out yer books! Fly with Airbook! We promise you a good read at forty thousand feet!"

Much later still, sitting together on the floor, backs against the lounge and each holding an open champagne bottle in one hand and a cigar in the other, they stared at the books on the table.

"You know, this cigar smoke probably isn't doing them any good," offered Rafe.

"Hmm, I beg to differ, Rafe. It's better than being in a smelly tomb for a few hundred years."

"You're right, there, *my friend*, Señor Ruben."

END OF CHAPTER SIXTEEN

Chapter Seventeen

A Page is Turned

"For books are not absolutely dead things, but do contain a potency of life in them as active as that soul was whose progeny they are; nay, they do preserve, as in a vial, the purest efficacy and extraction of that living intellect that bred them... And yet on the other hand, unless wariness be used, as good almost kill a man as kill a good book. Who kills a man kills a reasonable creature, God's image — but he who destroys a good book, kills reason itself, kills the image of God, as it were in the eye."
John Milton, *Areopagitica; A Speech of Mr. John Milton For the Liberty of Unlicens'd Printing, To the Parlament of England* [sic], 1644.

11:02am, Wednesday, 13th March 2205

"So, Kaitlin, Justin tells me you've listened to the conversation recorded by Nikka on Arcadia?" asked Mads. He was talking with his Head of HR at the meeting table in his office, and at Mads' request Justin Foote had joined them.

"Yes, I have, and I must say I'm very surprised by Bradshaw's conduct. But Justin tells me it was a concealed recording, and I'm concerned about the ethics of that, if it's true."

"I'm surprised you two haven't closed that off yet. So let's do it now. Justin?" Mads said, turning towards Justin.

"The conversation was recorded by Nikka Johannson in her official capacity and was for the purposes of an ongoing investigation, in which I have been assisting both Mads and Nikka. I approved the circumstances of its production," Justin said to Kaitlin.

"Satisfied?" Mads asked Kaitlin.

That Kaitlin was most definitely not satisfied was clear to Mads from her expression and piercing eyes. "I guess I'll have to be, but what about the delay in acting on it?" she asked Mads.

"The delay was unfortunate but nevertheless necessary. Being too quick to take action would have seriously hampered the investigation," replied Mads. Justin nodded at Mads in silent agreement.

"And the comment made by Henderson about being threatened by you?" Kaitlin asked with care.

Again, Mads turned to Justin, who replied "I have discussed that with Bibliotekar Ingridson and I am satisfied that Henderson was being overly liberal with the truth."

"The truth is," added Mads quickly, "I caught the sneaky bastard misusing the comms link to create content for a private venture, being a podcast series about his work on Arcadia, and I told him his rotation off Arcadia was on the line unless he cooperated in disclosing certain information regarding other unsanctioned activities."

Kaitlin hesitated, thinking about what Mads had just said. "I'm not going to ask any more questions about what is being discussed between Henderson and Bradshaw..."

"Good," interrupted Mads.

"... But is this all to do with the special project you've had Justin working on these last few months?" Kaitlin finished asking.

"Yes, it has everything to do with it, I am afraid. As you know from our previous conversations, Justin has been assisting me with a sensitive and serious issue. Soon I will be able to fully brief you on it, Kaitlin, but for now your continued patience, and discretion, would be appreciated," replied Mads.

"Alright Mads, as you wish," Kaitlin responded, with a hint of suspicion. She was not happy about being excluded from Mads' confidence, and her unhappiness had not been helped when she only found out about Violetta Simpson's sudden departure from The Bibliotek after the event. "And Simpson? Please tell me her resignation is wrapped up in the same investigation."

"Why would you ask that?" asked Mads.

"Because I was not consulted about Simpson, and it appears to be contemporaneous with the issues involving Bradshaw."

"She resigned of her own free will," replied Mads, without expression.

Kaitlin noticed Justin ever-so-slightly shift in his chair. After a pause, she said "of course, but the question remains."

Had not Mads then told her the two events did have a connection, Kaitlin would have been even more put out. It would have potentially meant she had not only been excluded from Mads' confidence, but had lost it as well. But as it was, she was surprised by Mads' response as she could think of nothing to connect the former Chief Conservator with the Deputy Bibliotekar apart from the fact that one reported to the other. And although Kaitlin hated not knowing information she felt was directly relevant to her role, she nevertheless felt it unwise to seek a further explanation.

"And Bradshaw, your thoughts?" asked Mads.

"I agree you have grounds for his dismissal."

Mads peered at her quizzically. "Sorry, yes, sufficient grounds. More than sufficient," Kaitlin clarified. "Are you acting on it, now?"

"Very soon. Very soon."

"In the circumstances then, can I at least suggest to you that we engage outside counsel — not Bernie — to review those grounds and be present at his termination meeting?"

To Kaitlin's annoyance, Mads looked again at Justin, who gave a small nod. "I'm not one hundred percent sure that is a good idea, but given the circumstances, as you say, I will permit it on the understanding Justin is to brief the person you select from outside The Bibliotek, no-one else. Discretion is paramount."

"That will be fine," responded Kaitlin, "I have someone in mind — if that is okay with you — a senior partner from the law firm in Oslo we normally engage on HR matters. Justin knows her."

"Good, that's settled. Now, Bradshaw's replacement. I have someone in mind already, and this will be a successor appointment."

"A successor appointment? You know that means you will be putting in place a timeline?"

"Yes, I know that. It will be a five-year timeframe. That should be plenty of time for the new DB to settle into the role and it will definitely be time enough for me," asserted Mads.

"Who is it?"

"Finn."

"Finn Mackie?" Kaitlin's eyes widened. "A deaf Bibliotekar? That would be something. Our diversity rating... "

As soon as she said the word 'diversity', Kaitlin realised she had made a mistake. Mads noticed that Justin could not help himself but adopt a pained expression at Kaitlin's choice of a response, and the thought instantly occurred to him that perhaps Justin should be Head of HR instead of Kaitlin, his boss.

"Kaitlin," Mads said a little sternly, "when was the last time you and I had a conversation about The Bibliotek's diversity rating?"

"I'm sorry. I can't recall, I..."

"That's because we haven't had such a conversation. Ever. And this isn't such a conversation either. I really should not need to say this, but making Finn DB is going to be based solely on merit. Is that understood?"

Kaitlin's face by now had turned a distinct shade of red. She knew this because she could feel her ears burning. "Yes, Mads, sorry."

"Good, now *on the basis of merit*, what are your thoughts?"

"Finn is one of our better senior managers, without question. His team has the lowest turnover rate in The Bibliotek and the highest efficiency rating. And he has a total grip on his responsibilities. As you know from his recent performance reviews, he is overdue a challenge and the timing is perfect."

"Good. So, this time, you agree with my choice?"

"Yes."

"Assuming he accepts the offer, I want to review the announcement of his appointment before it is released to The Bibliotek community. And I warn you, I don't want to see any reference to his deafness, nor do I want to see any sentiments like 'overcoming adversity' or 'courageous' or 'an inspiration to us all'. Are we *now* on the same page?"

"Yes, Mads. But what about BSL? He was instrumental in its development."

"I'm fine with mentioning that, as well as the fact that he co-wrote the first BSL dictionary. But let's park that for now, as I haven't had the discussion with him yet."

"Do you need me for that conversation?" asked Kaitlin. She had consciously said 'need' not 'want'.

"I tell you what, Kaitlin, that is a good suggestion. If Finn does end up going mustang on us like Bradshaw, then we can *share* the blame for promoting him."

Kaitlin got the message. "I'm sure we won't have the same issues," she replied quietly.

"Now," said Mads, moving on. "Simpson's replacement. As you know we have four highly-motivated Deputy Conservators on our hands, and I know at least two of them won't be sad about Simpson's departure. I want this done by the book and without any haste. Am I right in saying the process of selecting the best of the four could take twelve months, to be fair to each of them?"

"Yes, Mads, I would agree with that. In some ways we are lucky to have retained all four, but as far as succession planning is concerned it is a nightmare situation, as we've discussed before. At the end of the day we don't want to lose any of them, but someone has to get the promotion."

"Agreed. And I have a temporary solution; appointing an external as Acting Chief Conservator on a twelve-month contract. This will avoid any perception of anointing a 'favourite' with an internal appointment."

"The right person could also act as a benchmark for the other four," said Kaitlin, thinking aloud. She couldn't help but like Mads' solution, and wished she had thought of it.

"Agreed, and I have someone who I believe will be an excellent candidate for taking on that role – Dr Christian Jamison, from Christ Church Library at Oxford."

"He's coming with the Special Collections?" asked Kaitlin, stating the obvious similarity with the manner of Simpson's appointment.

Mads had more than half expected the comment. "Yes, but unlike Simpson, I already arranged for Justin to do the needful on his background, and as a result I am confident he will be fine. Rafe has already informally made the offer and Dr Jamison has accepted, pending our formal offer letter, which you'll need to prepare quickly. Just keep in mind he is to be given a twelve-month contract as Acting Chief Conservator. Worse comes to worst we simply part ways after a year."

"Understood, Mads."

"If, on the other hand he proves to be a better candidate for a permanent appointment than the other four, we will cross that bridge when we come to it. But let's keep our four motivated in the meantime, okay?"

"I understand that as well, Mads."

"There's also scope for Dr Jamison to take on a new role here which is currently under development should he not secure the Chief Conservator job, but I am not at liberty to discuss that until after the Governing Council's AGM."

Kaitlin looked at Justin and straight away she could tell that he knew exactly what Mads was talking about. With that perception came paranoia once again about Mads' level of confidence in her, so she decided then and there to face it. "I'm sorry Mads, but this is just another HR matter I am being kept in the dark about. This is not something I am at all happy about."

Mads was half-pleased by Kaitlin's protest. "I hear what you are saying Kaitlin and I assure you I understand your concern. But I can also assure you there is no agenda concerning your role at play here.

I *really am* not able to be full and frank with you *at this time*, apart from making it clear that Justin has had an unfair burden placed on him. There is a level of nastiness going on that I am soon to deal with once and for all. For now though, I really do need you to trust my belief you are better off being out of it. Once all is revealed I'm confident you will see the truth in what I am saying."

Kaitlin looked at Mads in silence for a few seconds. Justin was looking pale and stressed. "Very well, Mads, I'll make no more of it." With that she rose to leave.

Mads interrupted her departure. "On a brighter note, I'd like you to be there when I have the conversation with Finn."

Kaitlin sat back down.

"I think it's appropriate to do so during one of my formal informal dinners," Mads continued, ignoring Kaitlin's desire to end the meeting. "Are you free tonight from six pm?"

Kaitlin was again annoyed, this time at the short notice, but she checked her data pad without trying to show it. "Yes, thank you, Mads, that will be fine."

"Good, I'll brief you on what I will set out for Finn as to my expectations before Finn arrives at seven." With that, Mads rose from the seat, signalling the meeting was actually over this time.

As Mads expected, Finn was right on time for his formal informal dinner. It had been a while since Finn had attended one of these dinners, but in recent months he had been too busy with work — the Secondary Repositories audit and the Relocation Study Group, on top of his normal workload — to even have much time off, let alone be keen for another invitation. But he was glad when Mads extended one for this dinner as he always enjoyed the conversation and checking out Mads' book collections, especially the black and white photography books. They appealed to his aesthetics and spoke of simpler times.

Mads had let Finn linger at the bookshelves as he checked on the progress of the dinner preparations. As he passed the dining room, where Kaitlin was already seated, Mads commented, "You see, he likes books."

Much later, after the meal was finished and coffee was served, and after the conversation had ranged from books to, well, other books, it was time for Mads to turn serious.

"I hope you don't mind me asking this Finn, but how secure is the holograph?"

"It's a flow through."

"Sorry, a what?" Mads signed.

"It has no memory, no storage capacity and no network connection or capability. It is personal to me, and to me only. It's like making a cast copy of me then breaking the cast. There are absolutely no residual relics of any conversation I have using it."

"Okay, sorry, but I just want to be sure the remainder of our conversation tonight is completely offline and just between the three of us. I don't want to talk about Arcadia or the Secondary Repositories or the RSG or any of that right now. First, and I hope you'll forgive me, there is something else I need to discuss with you."

"Yes, Mads," said Finn, genuinely curious. The fact the Head of HR was one of the three did not for a second raise any alarm bells.

"I am going to suggest something to you, Finn, but first I need to tell you that Bradshaw will be leaving us."

"When?" immediately asked Finn, looking firstly at Kaitlin, who was impassive, which indicated to Finn that she already knew about Bradshaw, then Mads. For Mads' part, he noticed the question was Finn's instant response, but he was not surprised. Neither, it seemed, was Finn.

"Very soon," replied Mads.

"And you are telling me this because... ?"

"I am telling you now because I want to offer you the position of Deputy Bibliotekar." Mads paused to let the words be taken on board and to watch for Finn's reaction, which was one of shock, judging simply by the length his jaw suddenly dropped. Without waiting for Finn to say something Mads continued. "If you accept my offer, we want to announce your appointment at the same time as announcing Bradshaw's departure. That's why we are having this conversation now. But don't say yes, or no, or maybe, right now. I want you to think it over for a day or two — no more than that, sorry — because the offer includes you agreeing to work in the Conservation Department for a few months and to also undertake and hopefully complete a part-time degree at the Academy. I also only want you to accept the position of

Deputy Bibliotekar on the basis that you will perform the role as a single step to replacing me as Bibliotekar on my yet-to-planned retirement. So what we are talking about right now is a successor appointment. I will give you a timeframe of five years until I step down, but you need to make happen your confirmation as my successor. If you do all these things, and get that degree, in my humble opinion you will end up being the best-qualified Bibliotekar we can have to replace me, and quite possibly the best we've ever had."

On hearing the words "replace me" and "Bibliotekar" Finn's entire body pushed back in his chair in physical shock. Mads let it sink in without adding to it. "I don't know what to say, Mads," Finn said when he finally was able to think of some words to string together, "this is... unexpected... to say the least. Why me?"

"Well, for one thing you are a good GM of Facilities, without doubt the best we've had in living memory." Mads quickly looked at Kaitlin, who chimed in, "I'd agree with that." Now at last she was smiling.

Mads continued. "You are on top of everything in your remit and that has placed welcome pressure on me to keep you occupied, interested, and challenged. Going forward, The Bibliotek needs a Bibliotekar who has a comprehensive appreciation of its ongoing capacity issues and you have that, better than anybody. Plus your work on the Secondary Repositories informed me of your ability to think in terms of a Bibliotekar and not just as an administrator who is good with numbers. Then there's the respect held for you by your Adcom colleagues. That is very important. I've also had some informal chats with members of your team to get a feel for your management style, and I know you've performed well in three hundred and sixty-degree reviews and responded well to management gaps, as few as they've been. I've also had quiet chats with some of the Councillors, those who know you, to sound them out and the response was universally positive."

"Thank you Mads for that feedback, especially that you feel I need to be kept challenged. I will admit to agreeing with you on that score. But can I ask why Bradshaw is leaving?"

"Several reasons," replied Mads, "but I need your discretion for now. The only other people in the know are Kaitlin and Dr Justin Foote in HR, and Nikka."

"Nikka?" asked Finn.

Mads had deliberately mentioned Nikka's name, as a hint of things yet to be revealed. "Nothing to do with the RSG," he said, rebutting what Finn was thinking. "I'm sorry but I need to leave it at that for now."

"Okay, Mads."

"Good. Now we can talk about what I *actually* propose to say to the Governing Council about the Secondary Repository audit and the relocation proposal."

11:22am, Thursday, 14th March 2205

Larkin had just put a call through to Mads from Hans Jacobsen.

"Mads, I just wanted to let you know – I've just had a look at the Risk Register you sent us Councillors — the one you mentioned during the last Council meeting — and I can't find any reference to the I.R.S. audit."

"What? That can't be right. I remember seeing it in there when I signed off on the report. Are you looking on the right page?"

"I'm pretty sure I am. I'm sending you my copy right now."

Mads perused the spreadsheet comprising the updated Risk Register that he then received from Hans. He was right. There was no listing for the I.R.S. audit. It had to have been deleted. Mads called him back. "You're right, it's not there. And I told the meeting it was fully disclosed."

"I just thought I should give you a heads up, Mads. That was a very disappointing performance by Thurldottir in trying to nail your hide about not disclosing the so-called billion-dollar exposure. Has she mentioned the fact the audit's not actually shown in the Risk Register?"

"No, she hasn't," replied Mads, mystified and miffed.

"Don't worry, Mads. Nobody on the Council reads it, least of all her. And guess what? I've also had a quick look at the draft Minutes of the meeting. There's no mention of your advice to the Council about the I.R.S. audit and its disclosure on the Register. She's made sure the Minutes merely record that a 'discussion about U.S. Tax Certificates took place, with no motions required'. So, technically, you're in the clear."

"That's all well and good, Hans, but it doesn't explain the deletion from the Risk Register of the entry for the audit. I will need to follow that up."

"That's your domain, but yes, probably a good idea. Now, there's one more thing you should know," said Hans. "I don't know if you know this or not, but your comment at the meeting about the person who you think tipped off Thurldottir about the so-called billion-dollar tax exposure didn't go down too well. The feeling is that if there is a personnel problem in your team then you need to deal with it and not let it fester. I think you know what I'm talking about."

Mads tightened. He did know what Hans was talking about. "I hear you Hans, I appreciate the feedback. I think you know who I was referring to and you're absolutely right. I can't let this go undealt with, and I won't."

Immediately after speaking with Hans, Mads called Larkin into his office.

"Do you recall being asked to distribute the updated Risk Register to the Governing Council members prior to the last meeting?"

"Yes, Bibliotekar," replied Larkin, without emotion. But Mads could see the colour start to drain from his face.

"Can you tell me then why the version of the Register you sent is different from the one I authorised?"

"Yes, Bibliotekar," Larkin replied again, before hesitating.

"Well?" said Mads curtly, raising his voice slightly.

"Before I got around to sending it, Michael Huntington came to see me and requested it be changed."

"Changed? In what respect?"

"He said that he had discussed with you the deletion of the entry concerning the audit by the I.R.S. on the basis that there were no actual dollars involved in the risk, and that you had agreed to it. You were not here at the time, and it seemed a minor thing, so I did what he told me to do."

Mads had had no such conversation with Huntington, but now he was almost certain it was his CFO who had told Thurldottir about the I.R.S. audit. "I see. You were at the Governing Council meeting. You heard me having to defend myself against the claim I had not informed the Council of a one-point-eight billion dollar tax exposure. You heard me say the I.R.S. audit was disclosed in the Risk Register and that there was zero tax involved. Why didn't you say something?"

"I'm not authorised to speak at those meetings."

"I mean straight afterwards! Why am I only hearing about this now?!" demanded Mads, now almost shouting. "And from a Councillor, no less!"

Larkin did not reply at first. Instead he moved towards Mads' desk and sat down on one of the two chairs facing it, looking directly at Mads, who stared back at him, glaring, waiting. "I was... conflicted," he finally stammered.

"What do you mean '*conflicted*'!? You are my PA, my personal assistant. Where and what was your conflict?"

"I report to Chair Thurldottir," said Larkin, again softly and deliberately.

A few seconds of silence ensued, broken by an astonished Mads. Not so much as being told that information as he was by the fact that Larkin simply volunteered it. "Repeat what you just said."

"I said... I report to Chair Thurldottir."

A few more seconds of silence.

"You had better start explaining yourself," Mads finally said, in a quieter tone.

Larkin took a deep breath. There was no going back now. "At first I was led to believe that you were under suspicion of orchestrating the RSG to hide your activity on Arcadia, and that I was being asked to assist in gathering evidence that could be used to oust you. But the longer this went on the more I came to suspect I was being used for a different purpose — the opposite of what I had been led to believe. The story I had been told at the start just stopped making sense after a while. Instead, what started making sense was a plan to get rid of you and then being able to make a bundle of money out of Arcadia. I realised they..."

"They?"

"Chair Thurldottir and Councillor Carlson."

"Go on."

"I realised they needed to construct a narrative that involved some type of approved Bibliotek activity being used as the façade for the enormous costs to date in ascertaining the nature and extent of the mineral deposits."

"Façade? How so?"

"All their costs will be allocated to the Relocation Study Group, at the appropriate time."

"And when is that, exactly? After I am gone?"

"Yes."

Mads looked at Larkin for a few seconds. He hadn't just asked him a serious question, but to Mads' surprise, Larkin was serious in his answer. He tried to ignore it. He needed to find out more.

"So the dodgy accounting has to wait. Is that it?"

"Yes, with Huntington's rubber stamp on it."

"Are you serious?"

"Yes I am. How else do you expect them to account for the multi-million Euro costs. And I know they have someone in Huntington's team to do the actual number tampering — the fudging of the accounts."

As soon as he heard that, Mads felt he may actually be hearing the truth, as Larkin may well have been referring to Lara de Jong, the other employee apart from the now-deceased Smits The Bibliotek had taken on from the company owned by Carlson's family, who just happened to be an accountant in Huntington's team. So he decided to test Larkin. "I see. And this person's name?"

"That I don't know."

"We're talking about the palladium and the rhodium, aren't we? Just to be clear."

Larkin looked at Mads for a few seconds. It was obvious to Mads that Larkin had known that Mads knew of the palladium and the rhodium.

"Yes, the palladium and the rhodium," Larkin replied. "And the ruthenium, the iridium, the osmium, the titanium, the platinum. And the rest. And when the entire relocation proposal gets canned, with your help, the real work will begin to realise that value, that enormous wealth."

"What?" said an incredulous Mads.

Larkin sighed before answering. "They need you to be out of the way so that a private consortium, ultimately owned by them, can secure a lease from The Bibliotek without too many questions being asked. Then they plan to mine Arcadia. It's worth trillions, apparently."

Mads heard Larkin's words, but only as they flowed over him like a wave. His brain seemed to stop thinking. The messages it was receiving were too unexpected and didn't make sense. His face must have reflected all this.

"You weren't to know," continued Larkin. "Your opposition to the whole relocation idea was *always* expected. They *need* you to derail it, and just enough obstacles were placed in your way to make sure you believed in what you were doing. But the whole thing was fake from start to now. The real plan is simply to get control of part of The Bibliotek's site on Arcadia without being obvious about it, and then extract the minerals. At first I thought you were the one behind the plan and that I was helping to bring you down. But then I realised you were being played, just like everyone else. Just like me. But not only being played, being set up so they can get rid of you."

"Wait," Mads finally spoke, "where do you fit in with all this?"

"Promises were made to me, to my benefit. I was placed as your personal assistant to spy on you."

"Did you tell Thurldottir that something happened to Rafe Nagy in Russia?

"Yes I did."

"This was after the call I got from Moscow police?"

"Yes."

"Why? What has Nagy got to do with any of this?"

"She knows you and he are close. The whole thing with the Present Sect and him was just a diversion..."

"A diversion? Are you serious? You're saying all the trouble we've had with the Present Sect these last six to eight months is their doing?"

"Yes."

"Why should I believe that?"

"It is my job to make sure you were going down the path of investigating the Sect, and to report back on whatever else you did in relation to the plan to relocate the Bibliotek. Their aim is to make it look as if *you* are to blame for the Present Sect's increased activity and heightened threat to The Bibliotek. It is my job to help make sure those obstacles are only temporary, that you persist, and that you defeat the so-called proposal to relocate to Arcadia. It doesn't matter to them how you achieve it, it is just vital you do, eventually."

"Stop right there," Mads instructed, as he made call on speaker. He needed back-up.

"Yes Mads," said a voice.

"Nikka, can you spare me a few minutes in my office?"

"On my way, I'm just downstairs," Nikka replied.

"Thank you, come straight in, the door is green."

Larkin continued. "They are throwing everything at you to distract you, including the Secondary Repositories."

"Just hold it there," Mads repeated, more firmly this time. Larkin was like a tap that wouldn't turn off, but this time he complied. Instead he sat wringing his hands, alarmed at hearing Nikka being summoned to join them. To Mads he seemed ready to throw up at any moment.

"When you say you were placed as my personal assistant, are you saying Kaitlin Drummond is in on this?"

"No, she isn't, as far as I know. Thurldottir had wanted me in the role for some time, and she found a way to get rid of my predecessor and parachute me into her place. It wasn't hard. My CV's pretty good on that score," Larkin explained nonchalantly, but almost choking on 'CV'.

"Go and get some fresh air," said Mads motioning his head towards the balcony. He watched Larkin stand up and gingerly walk outside.

When Nikka arrived, she was surprised to see Larkin standing alone on Mads' balcony. Mads asked him to come back inside and motioned Nikka to sit in the chair opposite Larkin.

"Larkin, I want you to tell Nikka everything you just told me. Don't leave anything out," instructed Mads, still seated behind his desk.

As Larkin repeated his story, Mads watched Nikka's face and did not avert his gaze when she turned to look at him twice during Larkin's re-telling. When he finished, Larkin looked at Mads, who spoke. "What do you think of that Nikka?"

Nikka peered at Larkin, as if trying to determine the value of a piece of physical evidence at a crime scene. "Why are you telling Mads this fantastic story?" she asked.

"I thought it was the right thing to do."

"No! That is rubbish," Nikka snapped, leaning towards Larkin. "You knew we were onto you, that you've been spying on Mads for Thurldottir right from the start, so you decided to get in first, to make it look like you're not really a person who can't be trusted, to save your slimy, oily, snake skin. That's the reason isn't it," said Nikka with measured aggression.

Mads could see Nikka had shaken Larkin. He too was a bit shaken; he had not seen this side of Nikka before. With one stroke, Nikka had wiped away Larkin's air of self-confidence, which he tried to regain.

"That is not true. I decided to admit my actions when I realised I was being lied to."

"When, this morning?"

"No, a little while ago."

"How long is a little while ago?"

"About two weeks ago."

"So you waited all that time from making that momentous decision to acting on it just now. I see. And who lied to you?"

"Chair Thurldottir."

"And the lie? How do you know it's a lie? Anything else? How many lies exactly? Are we talking about one little white lie or a whole raft of fabrications? Or something in between? Well?" machine-gunned Nikka, who was verbally well-armed, Mads noticed.

"What do you mean?"

"Is there any other reason for telling the Bibliotekar this far-fetched story other than you believing you were lied to and it's the right thing to do?"

"I have disclosed my part in good faith to..."

"In good faith!?" interrupted Nikka abruptly. "*Now* you talk about good faith? You've been the PA for the Bibliotekar for a number of months now, a position of some seniority that requires the absolute highest level of good faith and trustworthiness, and as of now you are admitting to undertaking your role with zero of both!"

Larkin was now turning pale from Nikka's onslaught. This time he remained silent.

Nikka stood up and made a neurophone call. She asked one of her team to come immediately to the Bibliotekar's office with a spare data pad. Larkin gained the impression he was being arrested. "When my colleague gets here," Nikka began instructing, "you are going to sit in the Bibliotekar's meeting room with her and make a statement, being everything you have said to the Bibliotekar and I this morning, leaving out nothing and including how you came to be working for Thurldottir and whatever you know or suspect of her activities. You will not hurry, you will take your time. You will also be crystal-clear about why you are making the statement. Then we will review what you have written and when we are satisfied with your disclosures you will sign your statement. Understood?"

"Yes." Larkin wanted to ask what would happen afterwards, but Nikka's demeanour suggested it would not be prudent to ask questions.

"How did you come to know about the real objective?" Nikka asked.

"Thurldottir told me what I was led to believe was the bigger picture only because I needed to know it in order to do my real job."

"But, how could you be trusted with all that knowledge? What makes you so special?"

"I don't know about being 'special', but I gather Chair Thurldottir feels she can trust me, given that I am her grandson."

Hearing that, Nikka sat back in her chair, temporarily lost for words. She looked at Mads with a query on her face.

Mads shrugged his shoulders. "News to me! But it does make some sense."

Nikka turned back to face Larkin. "So why are you betraying her faith in you?"

"I wouldn't call it faith."

"Well? The question remains."

"Three reasons. One, I don't like being lied to. Second, I may be ambitious, but I'd rather get ahead on my own merits. Third, I've never liked the way my grandmother has always assumed I need her help and that because of that I need to help her. It's a vicious circle I can do without."

Just then one of Nikka's team members arrived, as instructed. Mads recognised her. It was Skye. She had a brief, whispered, conversation with Nikka to the side, then took Larkin into the adjoining meeting room, closing the door behind.

When they returned about twenty minutes later, Nikka was still in Mads' office. To Larkin it was obvious they'd made some decisions.

Mads walked around from his desk to face Larkin. "Nikka here wants to either place you under immediate arrest or escort you to the next maglev leaving The Bibliotek, but I think we can avoid those options, for now. What is going to happen is this: you are going back to your desk and resume your work as if nothing happened, except for one thing. You are now working for me, me alone. That includes me telling you what to pass onto your grandmother. Is that understood?"

"Yes, Bibliotekar. But, may I ask... what about what I have just told you?"

"We'll deal with it, you can be assured of that. Until then you will continue to feed juicy little titbits to your granny, as I have said. It will be information that I tell you to disclose, and when I tell you to disclose it."

"Understood."

"One more question," said Mads. "Did you know your grandmother ordered a hit on Rafe Nagy? To have him killed?"

"What?! No!"

"Does Thurldottir think Rafe is dead? Does Carlson?"

"I don't know! What are you talking about?"

"Chair Thurldottir tried to have Rafe killed in Russia. That's what the phone call was about. She also had one of Rafe's contacts murdered in Italy and staged it to make it look like it was the Present Sect's doing."

"I don't know about any of that!"

Mads looked at Larkin for what seemed a long time. He tried to detect a lie, but couldn't. All he could see was a white face of distressed shock. "Get out and get back to your job."

A little while later, as Nikka walked past Larkin's desk she turned, leant on the edge of it, and faced Larkin. "You know, you are very lucky you told Mads what you've been up to, Larkin. But now I have to look out for you, which I am only going to do because Mads asked me to. Personally, I would have your balls for breakfast, so do me a favour — be careful." She wasn't smiling.

"That. I. will," Larkin struggled to reply.

10:20am Friday, 15ᵗʰ March 2205

"Bibliotekar, may I introduce Sigrid Gude, from Borgen and Gude, our consultants in Oslo," said Justin as the two of them entered Mads' office.

"I am pleased to meet you, Sigrid," said Mads, shaking hands with the lawyer. "It is not often I get to meet someone as tall as me. You are the 'Gude' in 'Borgen and Gude'?"

"It's a pleasure to finally meet you, Bibliotekar, and no, that was my mother."

"Ah, well that's now two things we have in common. Please call me Mads. I've given up trying to get Justin here to do so, but I insist you try. He has briefed you on this meeting?"

"Yes, I've just listened to the audio in Justin's office, and he has filled me in on the background and on the meeting we are about to have with Mr Bradshaw. Can I ask, was he given advance notice?"

Mads quickly glanced at Justin before responding. "As to this meeting, yes. As to its purpose, no. This is a scheduled monthly meeting."

"Hmm, had I known that Mads, I would have advised against an ambush."

"Yes, I've been told that before," Mads replied, glancing again at Justin, "and the advice is noted, with respect. But on this occasion, there won't be any pressure applied to the one being ambushed to do or say anything. It's a unilateral termination, nothing more, nothing less. There won't be any camouflage or faffing around, we'll be straight into it."

"So be it. I am here to observe the fireworks? As a witness?"

"Primarily yes, but please take notes as appropriate and feel free to contribute at any time should you feel it advisable."

Just then Larkin called to let Mads know that Bradshaw had arrived for their meeting. "Just a minute," Mads told him, then he called Nikka. "He's here," was all he said. Mads nodded to Justin, who bade Sigrid farewell and left the office. Mads then turned to Sigrid. "Once a month Bradshaw and I have a meeting to update each other on operational issues, but, much to my frustration, he never brings any files or even his data pad, which is right now being confiscated by our Head of Security. You'll see."

Mads then paged Larkin to let Bradshaw in, who then strode into Mads' office with barely concealed impatience, Mads quickly glanced at Sigrid as, sure enough, Bradshaw had come empty-handed.

"I'm sorry, but why are you here?" said Bradshaw curtly after being introduced by Mads to Sigrid. He was not expecting anyone else to be at the meeting, let alone an outsider.

"Sigrid is here because I asked her to be here, Paul," said Mads before Sigrid could reply.

"Really? I was under the impression this was our monthly catch-up."

"This *is* a catch-up, Paul," replied Mads. "This is when you get to tell me all about the conversations you've been having with Councillor Carlson and Chair Thurldottir about replacing me as the Bibliotekar."

The change in Paul's expression on his face confirmed everything for Mads. Bradshaw didn't need to say anything, but he did.

"What are you talking about? It's not unusual for a Deputy Bibliotekar to have conversations with members of the Governing Council, unless you're now telling me I'm not allowed to."

"Not if such conversations are about actions and behaviours that divert you from your assigned responsibilities."

"Well, they haven't."

"Really?"

Without saying anything further, Mads pressed a button under his meeting table. A second later Bradshaw's voice could be heard telling Commander Henderson he was going to deal with him once he became the Bibliotekar, which was going to be very soon. It was a carefully chosen excerpt from the recording of the full conversation he had had with Henderson.

Mads then leaned across the table towards a visibly surprised and speechless Bradshaw, whilst Sigrid tapped at her data pad. "I cannot and will not tolerate disloyalty, especially when it involves a private agenda to discredit your direct report, being me."

"How... how... where did you get that?" a shaken Paul asked.

"Surely you knew that the Command Centre is under the constant auspices of Security and, accordingly, all conversations taking place there are recorded. Henderson knew it."

"No."

"I feel truly sorry for you. You, of all people. I handed you an opportunity nobody else had and you not only let it go past you, you threw it away."

"Fuck you Mads. That was years ago. All that time you've said nothing, done nothing, about retiring. You've been long past it. Thurldottir knows it, everyone on the Council knows it. Everyone but you, in your little ivory tower. I've been more than patient."

Mads let Bradshaw have his spray, sitting back in his chair. He didn't respond, instead he waited until Bradshaw finished. Then he leaned forward again. "You've been played, Paul. Used. And it has cost you your job. Effective immediately, you are fired. For gross misconduct."

"I dispute that! One conversation with that idiot Henderson — you know how rude he was — does not stack up to a dismissible offence. You know that," said Bradshaw, looking lastly at Sigrid, who was about to say something in response.

"Your actions on the RSG were in accordance with instructions from Thurldottir instead of mine, or have you forgotten about that? We are talking about promises being made to you. And because of your impatience and your inflated view of what you are entitled to, you acquiesced to those instructions. How about that for misconduct?"

Mads had gone out on a limb with that accusation, but he felt comfortable with risking it. Sure enough, the expression on Bradshaw's face once again betrayed the truth of what he had just heard. Sigrid noticed it too. "It may be advisable for you to reserve any response to that," she said to him.

Bradshaw turned and glared at her, still in a rage. "Fuck you too!"

Just then Larkin called Mads. "Ms Johannson is here."

"Let her in," said Mads.

Nikka entered the office, carrying an open cardboard box. She looked at Mads, who nodded.

"I have here your personal belongings from your office, Paul. We have confiscated your data pad, and now I need you to de-activate your neurophone, then one of my team — she is waiting outside — will escort you to your apartment, where you will pack your belongings. Your maglev to Oslo leaves in..." Nikka looked at her watch, "... just over ninety minutes."

Bradshaw stood up, tapped off his neurophone and walked with purpose to Nikka and, barely containing his desire to yell at her, grabbed the box she was holding and walked towards the door. Stopping, he turned back to look at Mads. "You will get yours soon enough, oh Grand Poombah Bibliotekar." Then he left.

After a few seconds, Sigrid broke the silence. "That was intense."

"That was necessary," replied Mads.

422

9:02am, Monday, 18ᵗʰ March 2205

"You may notice an empty chair," began Mads in a formal tone he did not often use at Adcom meetings. "Effective last Friday," he continued, "Deputy Bibliotekar Bradshaw was terminated from his Bibliotek contract, with immediate effect. He has already left the precinct for good."

Mads paused, then spoke again. "Unfortunately, I cannot say anything more about it, until after the Governing Council's AGM two weeks from now. But what I can say is that Paul's removal was absolutely necessary, had the full backing of Kaitlin and independent legal advice, and, for me personally, was a very disappointing necessity, as I had promoted and supported him in his career at The Bibliotek, as most of you know."

Mads paused again. He looked around the table because he didn't want anyone to notice he was primarily wanting to see Huntington's reaction, which was what Mads was expecting. He was the only person not meeting his gaze. Instead, Huntington was staring straight ahead, with a blank look on his face. In that instant Mads could not help himself but to think *and you're next, pal.*

"It is a shock, Mads, to hear this news, but I think I can speak for all of us here is saying I am sure that whatever those reasons were for termination, they're completely valid, and you have our full support," offered Dean Coenraad, who looked around the table for moral support, which he got in the form of nodding heads.

"Thank you, Dom, I appreciate your words. On a far more positive note, a short statement is being issued to all staff at The Bibliotek as I speak," said Mads, turning to Larkin who nodded his affirmation. "Finn...?" Mads said, motioning to Finn, who stood up from his chair at the middle of the table, his PA following, and walked to the other end of the table and sat down, his PA likewise in the seat previously used by Bradshaw's PA. As he did so, Mads, continued. "I am exceptionally pleased to announce to you here and now, and to the rest of The Bibliotek, that, effective from this morning, Finn is our new Deputy Bibliotekar."

Without exception, and in accordance with tradition, Finn's colleagues stood up, turned to him and applauded. Mads looked around. He was pleased to see the smiles were all as genuine as his. This was one decision he was certain he was right about. For his part, Finn was clearly embarrassed by the attention but gladly acknowledged his colleagues and their congratulations, though his holographic did struggle to keep up with the various salutations.

"Onto business," Mads said after a while, prompting everyone to take their seats.

9:05am

"Ingridson has just sacked Bradshaw!" yelled Carlson. He was on a panicked call to Thurldottir.

"Excellent," she replied.

"What do you mean, *excellent*?! We need him."

"No we do *not!* He has performed his part well. This is another nail in Ingridson's coffin and we are about to nail it shut. Anyway, he's done us a favour in getting rid of that idiot."

"But they confiscated his neurophone! There are messages between him and me!"

"Well then, perhaps you should have been more careful," replied Thurldottir, just before terminating the call.

END OF CHAPTER SEVENTEEN

Chapter Eighteen

April Fools

"I had been a fool to trust implicitly so many of those closest to me at The Bibliotek and to rely on my tendency to just let things happen, but on that particular day I decided it was time to make some enemies."
Mads Ingridson, Witness Statement to the Supreme Court of Norway, 12 June 2205, p247.

6:13pm, Wednesday, 27th March 2205

It was now more than a week after the Adcom meeting and Bernadette Collingwood was still confused and a little bit angry. She had not believed her ears when she heard the Bibliotekar announce in the meeting that the final report of the RSG was to conclude that it was prudent for the Governing Council to start formulating a plan to relocate much of the Central Repository to Arcadia, and that Mads was going to present the report at the next Governing Council meeting, its AGM, in just a few days. Even worse was that the Bibliotekar had stifled all protests, including hers, against the relocation plan and any debate of the recommendations he wanted to present to the Council to give effect to it. She could not understand why the objections she thought she had clearly enunciated in her part of the draft Relocation Study Group report had apparently been arbitrarily discounted, and she could not fathom why Deputy Bibliotekar Bradshaw's sudden departure for whatever reason or reasons had not effectively killed off any notion of a relocation of the Central Repository, let alone a relocation to far-off Arcadia of all places. Bradshaw had been the instigator, and most vocal proponent of the move to Arcadia, but he had left The Bibliotek before the report was finalised. Worst of all, she couldn't figure out why Finn had apparently acquiesced to the Bibliotekar's decision, as he had said nothing in protest. And now she had been summoned by Mads to the Conservation Department without being told why, at this late hour of the working day. The 'summons', because that was how it felt to her, did not ease her mood. Instead, her memory of the last time she had been asked to come to this area of The Bibliotek, which was filled with rooms devoted to the technology of keeping books intact, exacerbated it. This was because that experience had not been pleasant. On that occasion, she had been asked to give her legal opinion on yet another book of the handful procured by The Bibliotek over time which proved to be bound with human skin. She desperately hoped this was not a similar occasion. *Something to do with Violetta Simpson's sudden departure?* she thought. *That* she could deal with; bread and butter compared to the ethics and legal consequences of cataloguing a book bound with the dried and stretched skin of a dead human being.

Clutching her data pad, Bernie followed its directions to the room she was looking for, and as she approached it she could see through the open door Nikka standing inside with Mads. *Oh no,* she thought, *whatever it is, it doesn't look good.* The thought also suddenly occurred to her that, maybe, Simpson's sudden departure was linked to Bradshaw's sudden departure. But she had no time to dwell on it.

"Bernie! I'm glad you could make it," said Mads, looking up from an old book he carefully held in gloved hands as she entered the room, which immediately struck her as being different from most of the other rooms in the Conservation Department — it was devoid of equipment, holding only rows of long tables. And on them lay, also in neat rows, many old books, hundreds of them, and all of them, thankfully, seemed at first glance to be bound in pig skin.

It was then that she also became aware of the others in the room apart from Nikka and Mads. There was Finn and his holographic, who was engaged in a close conversation with Councillor Thomas Metcalfe, there was Rafe the Finder, who had a big smile on his face, and there was Dr Justin Foote from HR, whom she barely knew. And all of them except Nikka were wearing the same gloves all the staff in Conservation wore when handling old, rare, or damaged books.

"You're not going to believe Nags' latest Find," said a beaming Mads, as he waved an arm to indicate all the books in the room, still holding the one old book in his other hand.

They were all beaming at her, which prompted her to ask "all these?"

"Nags, you tell her," said Mads, looking at his friend.

"Ms Collingwood, you are looking at half of the Lost Library of Ivan the Formidable," Rafe said matter-of-factly, "or Terrible, if you know of him by that name."

Bernie looked at him in shock. "You *found* the Lost Library of Ivan The Terrible? Isn't that supposed to be a fable, a myth?"

"It *was* a myth. Until I proved otherwise," Rafe beamed back at her.

Bernie looked around the tables and at the books upon them. "So, you found a cache of incunabula. But how do you know it's *the* Lost Library?"

"Well, it wasn't no accident I found it, it was by research focusing on the concept of the Lost Library having been in existence. And its location was indisputably linked to Ivan The Formidable. And then there's this," said Rafe as he lifted one of the books from the table nearest him and opened it to show Bernie the frontispiece. "See that mark there?" he asked, indicating a swirling scroll at the bottom of the first page.

"Yes, what is it?"

"That is the mark of one of the scribes from the Library of Constantinople," Rafe proudly revealed.

"I'm sorry, but I don't..."

"The bulk of Ivan's library was inherited from his grandmother," Rafe explained. "Her name was Sophia Palaiologos. It was her father who rescued hundreds of books — *these books* — from the Library of Constantinople before its sacking by the Turks in 1453, and Sophia brought most of them with her to Moscow, if not all of them, as part of her dowry for her arranged marriage to Ivan's grandfather."

"I see," Bernie replied. But she had not really taken in all that information. She was, however, prepared to accept the truth of what Rafe was saying. "So, what are these books? Have you had a chance to identify them? When did all this happen? And you said 'half'? Where's..."

"Whoa, hang on there, young lady. I've only managed to get this lot here today," Rafe replied. "This is half. The other half, well, that's a long story. Call this half my share."

"Bernie," said Mads, "I'll explain the 'half' bit later, but do you know how significant this Find is? I mean, putting aside the Lost Library connection?"

"To be honest, Mads, no," replied Bernie.

Mads looked at Rafe, who answered. "Okay, well, long story short, most of the Greek classics we know of are actually Byzantine copies originating from..."

"Let me guess," interrupted Bernie. "The Library of Constantinople."

"You got it," said Rafe triumphantly. "No discovery has come close to this one, ever. Not even the Herculaneum Library discovery four hundred and fifty years ago comes close, for the simple reason *that* library consisted solely of rolled-up papyrus scrolls most of which, even today, remain a mystery as to what they say."

"When you say 'discovery' am I to assume there is no paperwork, no provenance?" asked Bernie.

"No to the first, and only a connection to the Lost Library as provenance," replied Rafe.

Bernie turned back to Mads. "Are we going to have problems with this Find?"

"No," answered Mads. "I'm not one hundred percent certain of that, but I am more than confident there won't be any issues. As I said, I'll explain more later."

"Alright Mads, I'll reserve my judgment until then. For now, though, do we know anything about any of these books?"

"I have positively identified only two so far, with Thomas's help," replied Rafe, turning to and acknowledging Thomas, who stopped talking with Finn and smiled back at Bernie. "One is a copy of Eustathius of Thessalonica's original commentary," continued Rafe at a pace, "complete and in Greek, on Pinda, one of the great ancient Greek poets."

"Hang a minute please, Rafe, I'm catching up. You said E-u-s-t-a-t-h-i-u-s?" said Finn.

"Sorry, yes, I'll slow down," replied Rafe. "This commentary on Pinda alone is significant as until now only its Introduction was known to exist. The other book we have so far identified appears to be a copy of a commentary by the Stoic philosopher Hierocles on an earlier Stoic work of Cato The Younger. That also would be singularly unique. Have I got that right, Thomas?"

"Yes indeed."

"I don't know any of those names, I'm sorry, but judging by the look on your face, Rafe, and on yours, Mads, I'm guessing this is pretty major," responded Bernie.

"You said it," said Mads as the others all chimed in with nods and smiles. "Now, I'll be announcing this Find to end all Finds at the Governing Council's Annual General Meeting on Monday," Mads informed the others. "Nags, I want you there also to do a short presentation on how it came to be."

"Seriously? Again I have to present?"

"This is important Nags. Nikka will be there too," replied Mads, glancing at Nikka, who obviously knew beforehand from her return nod.

"Nikka?" Rafe looked at Mads, then at Nikka, then he realised what else would be said at the AGM. "Oh, that too."

"I'm sorry Nags, but we need to do this, we need to do it now, and do it carefully. Finn, Nikka and I will discuss this further on Sunday night with you, Thomas, and Hans Jacobsen when he arrives for the AGM. Apart from Thomas, Hans is the Councillor I can rely on the most," explained Mads. "Now," he continued, "as much as I'd like to pop a champagne cork and continue celebrating Nags' amazing achievement, there's another reason why you are all here," said Mads. Then, looking in turn at Nikka and Bernie, he said, "I know you two are wondering what happened in the Adcom meeting last week..."

"No shit, Mads," interjected Bernie, surprising herself just as much as Mads and Nikka and Finn, the other Adcom members present.

Mads smiled. "That's not like you, Bernie. But I understand." He paused. "Here's the thing..." Mads continued, spacing his words as if each one were carefully chosen, "... there will be *no* report going to the Governing Council concerning the capacity of The Bibliotek *or* Arcadia *or* anything else to do with any relocations, proposed *or* otherwise."

"What?" said Nikka, saying out loud what Bernadette was thinking.

"I said what I said in the Adcom meeting because I wanted certain people to *think* I support the notion of relocating some part of The Bibliotek to Arcadia," explained Mads.

Bernie was even more confused. "What's going on, Mads? This is not like you to play politics."

"Bernie, you are absolutely right, more right than you'll ever know. But games *are* being played, and they didn't start with me. I've briefed Finn because he is the new Deputy Bibliotekar and he needs to know the true lay of the land, but I need you all..." Mads said, looking around at his colleagues, "... to bear with me until after the Council's AGM. By then, a lot will have become public knowledge. If not, I'll be happy to answer any and all questions you might still have." Mads paused. "Now, Bernie," he continued, "what are your movements for the next two days?"

"A few meetings, nothing special, why?"

"Put them off, please. You, Finn and I are flying to Moscow first thing tomorrow morning. We have a meeting with Deputy President Yushenko. Then we fly to Reykjavik for another meeting with President Morven about the *Sagas*. I expect it will be a much more positive, and favourable, meeting than last time."

"Yes, but..."

"I'll explain more on the heliojet to Moscow tomorrow morning, and any questions about this Find. We take off at six o'clock. Make sure you're wearing your best lawyer hat because you will be drafting two Heads of Agreement tomorrow night. One to be signed by Yushenko and one by Morven and Prime Minister Magnusson, both before Monday."

10:11pm, Sunday, 31ˢᵗ March 2205

Abe Carlson was sweating. He always did when stressed. Sitting on a lounge in Chair Danuta Thurldottir's office in her private suite at The Bibliotek he was a fidgety and worried man. Thurldottir had just told him what she had learnt, separately, from Michael Huntington and Nils Larkin. "They both said that Ingridson will be recommending a move to Arcadia? That's what they said?"

"I don't like repeating myself," rasped Thurldottir in response.

"But that's not part of the..."

"And I don't like stating the fucking obvious," she interrupted.

That silenced Carlson, but only for a few seconds whilst he gathered his thoughts. "I think we need to postpone the AGM. We can't allow him to make that recommendation."

"It's too late for that. All the Councillors have arrived, including our replacement for Metcalfe."

"And Metcalfe?"

"No-one has seen him, so I'm guessing he still thinks that idiot Smits is after him."

"I don't like this. I still haven't heard from Smits, and Bradshaw — Ingridson got rid of him so why is he now on board with Arcadia?"

"Yes, that *is* interesting, isn't it? I think I smell a rat," smiled Thurldottir.

"What do you mean?"

"I suspect our good Bibliotekar only wants us to *think* he will provide a report from Adcom advocating a relocation to Arcadia. I suspect he has no intention of doing so. That he will be recommending the opposite, which is exactly what the plan is."

"I don't share your confidence, I'm afraid."

"Stop being afraid and get with the program! You are forgetting I am the Chair and I will be controlling the meeting. And that includes shutting Ingridson down if need be. We stay the course, and the course is clear — tomorrow he gets the sack. We'll have the numbers. Is your presentation ready?"

"Yes, I know my job. I'm just expressing a concern."

"Noted. Now leave."

8:52am Monday, April Fool's Day 2205

Mads was walking with Nikka. They were going to the Annual General Meeting of the Governing Council of The Bibliotek. He knew that Chair Thurldottir was planning on moving a vote of no-confidence in him at the AGM, even though it wasn't on the agenda. She had the power to do it, without notice, and from her point of view she had the ammunition: Bradshaw's failure as Deputy Bibliotekar, the debacle involving Violetta Simpson, the growing 'threat' of the Present Sect which Mads had done nothing to alleviate and the loss of the *Sagas* because of it. The list went on. It was potentially enough to sway a vote or two on the Council, and despite Thomas's return, Thurldottir would still only need to turn one of Mads' usual supporters. He knew that money would do it. He knew that not only did he need to counter each and every point of 'failure' on his part, he needed to go on the offensive before Thurldottir had a chance to even introduce her motion. He knew it was time he held his own little ambush, and accordingly he had spent the last few days and weeks planning it. It would start with Thomas's re-appearance at the AGM. That at least would make it harder for Thurldottir.

He hated having to make such a plan — it was the sort of negative behaviour which he abhorred but which Thurldottir excelled at. That he knew now, and he hated that fact even more. But it was time to meet like with like. He thought he had a good plan. Larkin's turning had spawned it and it hinged on Mads' interpretation of the protocol for the traditional first item on the agenda of the Governing Council's AGM – the Bibliotekar's report to the Council on the activities of The Bibliotek over the course of the previous twelve months. He was not required to distribute his presentation before the meeting; it was expected to be a 'Show and Tell', with an appropriate number of bells and whistles and lots of management-speak. It was also expected to be a 'good news story', focusing on achievements and the meeting of goals, only this year that particular expectation would not be met. In years past, Thurldottir had struggled to barely conceal her utter boredom during Mads' annual overview, and Mads had to admit this was not entirely due to her general narky attitude. He knew that, this year, he would have her undivided attention, but it would, hopefully, be the opposite of any degree of rapture. And that is why Mads had sought and obtained the opinions of Hans and Thomas, the two Councillors he could rely on the most, on whether his proposed 'presentation' for this year would stand up against any objections on the ground of his failure to abide by protocol. In short, Mads needed to be certain that Thurldottir could not shut him up before he had a chance to tell the Governing Council all that he wanted them to hear.

Mads was already certain that Thurldottir, and Carlson, would not want to hear it, but Hans and Thomas had both told him that what he proposed to present at the AGM was within his power to do so, and that they would support him when the inevitable objections arose. There were four other Councillors Mads could normally count on for their supportive vote, but it was a lot riskier briefing them before the meeting than counting on his planned disclosures during the meeting swinging their support to him. One or more of them might tip off Carlson and/or Thurldottir and that would spell the end of Mads' play. Then there was the question of money – whether Thurldottir had thrown any their way. She had done it to Bradshaw. There was only one way to counter that possibility: he needed to use fright as a deterrence as soon as he had the chance. He needed Nikka to do her thing.

"Why is she here?" asked Thurldottir in her usual derogatory tone when Nikka entered the board room with Mads, wearing her official uniform and her usual seriously stern yet passive face.

"Nikka will be assisting with the first item on the agenda," replied Mads with only a slight pause to his path to his chair, as Nikka took up a position standing next to the door. It was true. Nikka was going to assist Mads with his presentation.

Just as the last of the Councillors took their seats before the appointed time and Thurldottir was about to speak, Mads looked at Nikka and nodded slightly. She immediately turned and opened the door, and into the room strode Thomas as if he were returning from the bathroom. As he headed straight for his chair, he nonchalantly commented, "sorry I'm late."

"Excuse me for a moment," said Thurldottir, trying not to sound upset, but obviously caught off-guard as she arose and walked to the door.

"Going to tell your candidate to go home?" Mads called after her, without getting any response.

Within a minute, Thurldottir re-entered the room and slowly walked back to her chair at the head of the table. "Where have you been these last few months, Councillor Metcalfe, and why haven't you been contactable?"

"Do you really want me to waste the Council's time with a full explanation?"

"No, that won't be necessary," said Thurldottir, no longer concerned with not sounding upset, but also sounding tired and impatient. Returning to her 'script', she continued. "Welcome to the one hundredth and fifth Annual General Meeting of the Governing Council of The Bibliotek. I declare the meeting open. It is good to see you all here today. We must do these physical meetings more often," she smiled, or at least attempted to. It wasn't a good look.

My goodness, she cracked a joke and her face cracked, thought Mads. "Good to see Thomas back in the saddle, isn't it!?" he said loudly, or at least louder than the Councillors were used to hearing him speak, and loud enough to jolt Thurldottir, something Mads had never achieved before. He had decided to try being boisterous at the 'get go' as a means of calming his nerves. It was working.

After glaring at Mads, Thurldottir continued. "The first item on the agenda, as tradition dictates, is the Bibliotekar's annual review. The floor is yours, Bibliotekar Ingridson."

Mads was already on his way to the presenter's lectern at the front of the room, just to the side of Thurldottir's seat at the head of the meeting table before she had finished introducing him. Mads took his data pad with him, and after setting it up on the lectern, he picked up the remote and opened the holographic screens which then appeared above and behind each side of the meeting table.

The first slide merely said *Year in Review.*

"It's been a year of achievements, surprises, and challenges," he began. "Accordingly, this will mean my review will not induce slumber in any of you this year." His deadpan delivery elicited Mads some grins but no laughter. *This better go well,* he thought.

He continued. New slide: *One Billion Books*

"As you all know, these past twelve months saw the Central Repository reach the one-billionth book mark, courtesy of an extraordinary Find by Rafe Nagy, our most senior Finder."

New slide: *Secondary Repositories*

"Unfortunately, we also had cause to review the policy which gave rise to the unchecked growth of the Secondary Repositories, a situation we need to deal with as a matter of priority, as quantified and evidenced by the comprehensive audit conducted by Finn Mackie, who as you would know by now is the new Deputy Bibliotekar, and his Facilities team.

"Lost Bradshaw, didn't you," interjected Thurldottir as a statement rather than a question. "I hope you cover that and the other senior managers you've lost these past twelve months, no, wait, three months, Bibliotekar Ingridson. That's some achievement."

"I will be, and more, you needn't worry about that," Mads replied in a monotone. *Not yet anyway,* he thought quickly and almost added. "If I may continue," he said instead.

New slide: *Secondary Repositories – A Solution*

"My PA Nils Larkin is currently distributing to you your electronic copies of Finn's report, including final recommendations and actions taken to date."

"Actions taken?" asked Thurldottir.

"I'm glad you ask that, Madam Chair," replied Mads.

New slide: *Secondary Repositories - Actions Taken*

He continued. "Due to the comprehensive data produced by Finn and his team, we believe we have a significant enough, albeit disparate, mass of books to identify, consolidate and constitute specific collections, for the purpose of extricating these collections and lending them to institutions around the world."

"Wait a moment. You didn't mention this at the last meeting, Bibliotekar," interrupted Thurldottir. "We are *not* a lending library."

"What I did say at the last meeting was that our report and recommendations were not finalised. I made a point of stressing that," replied Mads.

New Slide: *Secondary Repositories – Benefits of Consolidation*

"In accordance with the second of Sorenson's Three Tenets for the functions of The Bibliotek which, again, I remind Councillors requires us to facilitate appropriate access to all printed material under The Bibliotek's management, we are going to seek expressions of interest from the remaining libraries around the world, both civic and academic, as to what collections their users would benefit from. We will then try to match those desired categories with collections held in the Secondary Repositories and then lend the matched collections to the relevant libraries." Mads paused to gauge reactions, but all were quiet and attentive, including Carlson and Thurldottir.

He continued. "We know this will benefit the libraries concerned because, over the centuries, books of common subject matter and vintage have tended to be dispersed around the globe. The rarer the books, the greater the distance of the dispersion. So, by dint of accident, The Bibliotek has effectively 'rounded up' many of these books, over time, into one place, either the Central Repository or one or more of the Secondary Repositories. So, physically accumulating such books as are held in the Secondary Repositories and making them available to libraries will enhance public access and academic study and will significantly reduce The Bibliotek's ongoing costs of otherwise maintaining them. These benefits will be maximised in the case of any book held in the Central Repository under embargo and therefore not currently accessible to anyone outside The Bibliotek. There are many such books. If any book held in a Secondary Repository is a copy of an embargoed book but cannot form part of a collection, it will be transferred to the Central Repository and added to the Master Catalogue, thus making it accessible for the first time as an alternative to the inaccessible original." Again, Mads paused, and again all were attentive. Some were now taking notes, including Thurldottir.

He continued. "We will announce this project as something that has been in train for some time and focus on the benefits to all and, of course, the fact that the project is living proof of The Bibliotek's commitment to the second of our founder's Three Tenets."

Now Thurldottir finally spoke. "You don't have the authority to implement such a program, Bibliotekar," she said in a resigned tone. "You will need to submit it as a recommendation with the report on the audit."

"I am sorry, but I *do* have the authority, Madam Chair," Mads responded. "As Bibliotekar, I make the decisions on operational issues, and given the Secondary Function of The Bibliotek, this is an operational issue. Apart from complying with that Tenet, it is also my responsibility to manage costs, and this project will see our operational costs be reduced. To steer this three to five-year project I have created the role of Director, Secondary Repositories. The Acting Chief Conservator, Dr Christian Jamison, is a natural candidate for that role should he not be confirmed as Chief Conservator in twelve months' time."

"I disagree," said Thurldottir, some of her usual officious tone returning. "I want this deferred for Phicom's consideration."

Just then Hans Jacobsen spoke. "I move that the Governing Council show its support for this initiative."

"I second that motion," said Thomas. "All those in favour?" The putting of the motion happened so fast it was as if the two Councillors had been expecting that very reaction from Thurldottir. The motion was carried 7-6, as Mads had not only hoped, but also expected, given the calls he had carefully made to certain Councillors just prior to the meeting.

"Thank you, colleagues. I am confident this project will secure major benefits for us and for our stakeholders in the years to come. Now, as I envisaged at the last meeting of Council," Mads immediately resumed, "our report includes the recommendation that The Bibliotek cease procuring copies of original books we already hold in the Central Repository. Returning to my Year in Review, we have already begun the process of consolidating the first collection within the Secondary Repositories."

Mads paused, but no-one spoke. Thurldottir sat, arms crossed, giving Mads the best 'death stare' she could muster. It was a good one, from what he could see out of the corner of his eye.

New Slide — *A Find for the Ages*

"Moving on, it is my pleasure to announce today that more recently, just last month to be exact, Rafe Nagy achieved what is without doubt the greatest Find of his career and in the history of The

Bibliotek, if not the greatest Find since the discovery of the Dunhuang Manuscripts, which included the world's oldest book the *Diamond Sutra*, in 1900." Mads paused again. He could feel the expectation in the room. "The Lost Library of Ivan The Formidable!"

Amongst the gasps, recoils, and one or two derisive scoffs, Mads could see Carlson turning to look at Thurldottir bearing an expression of sudden alarm, and Thurldottir ignore him and lean forward in her chair to concentrate her gaze on Mads, eyes narrowing to her usual lizard-like slits.

New Slide — *Secrets Revealed*

Mads continued. "And here to briefly tell you about his discovery and procurement of one hundred and seventy-six books from the Lost Library is the man himself."

With those words, Nikka again opened the door to the room, allowing Rafe to enter. As he strode to the lectern whilst Mads resumed his seat at the table, patting Thomas on the shoulder as he passed, an agitated Thurldottir spoke. "He is not supposed to be here," she said with a sharp tone. For his part, Carlson was almost beside his fat self.

"That's an interesting choice of words, Madam Chair," said Mads. "Hans?"

"This is the Bibliotekar's presentation. As far as I am concerned he can use whatever aids he likes in giving it," Hans quickly said in reply. "Besides, this is a story I very much want to hear."

"Me too," chimed Thomas. "I want to hear this. As long as it's brief, we have the time. And yes, it is indeed Mads' presentation, not yours. Proceed Nags, let's hear your story, unless of course anyone else has an objection?" Thomas looked around the table, especially at the four Councillors he knew were supporters of Thurldottir apart from Carlson who everyone knew always voted with her. None had an opinion to voice. "I thought so. Nags..." he said, turning back to Rafe, who was standing and waiting patiently.

Rafe looked at Mads, who nodded. Then he began speaking, with his arms extended forward and hands gripping the front edge of the lectern, as if about to give a sermon.

"Thank you, Mads. Good morning Councillors. Good morning, *Chair*," said Rafe cheerfully. But it was bravado. "I will keep this short and to the point. My research over the years pointed to a reasonable probability the Lost Library of Ivan the *Formidable* — or *Terrible* depending on your history — not only *had* existed during Ivan's reign but also a chance it *still* existed, hidden in a specific mausoleum at Trinity Monastery in Sergiyev Posad in Russia, not far north from Moscow. The mausoleum was the final resting place of Boris Godunov, the last Tsar of Russia before the terrible anarchy of The Time of Troubles abruptly ended his reign, his life, and the lives of his wife and young son. It was there, in the mausoleum, that I found a secret cavity in a wall after laser measurements of the inside of the room compared with similar measurements of its exterior indicated there was a hidden space behind that particular wall. Inside that cavity, which, importantly, was completely dry, we found three hundred and fifty-two incunabula, carefully wrapped and stored. That is, my associate and myself. The Bibliotek's share of this Find is half, comprising one hundred and seventy-six separate volumes. We are still in the process of identifying all of them, but I can tell you today that they do appear to originate from the Library of Constantinople as the legend of the Lost Library had ascribed, and comprise transcriptions of ancient Greek texts, most of which have never before been seen since the Middle Ages. That's basically it. I told you I would keep it short."

Mads, Thomas, and Hans immediately stood up and began applauding. They were joined by several other Councillors. Thurldottir and Carlson remained seating and did not clap. After the applause died down and seats were resumed, Rafe continued.

"Unfortunately, this discovery was not without incident."

Rafe stopped for a moment and looked purposively at Carlson, who was glaring at him, his head looking as if it was about to explode. Thurldottir, Rafe noticed, was fixated with tapping away furiously on her data pad, which, unknown to him was a clear breach of protocol for Governing Council meetings. "During the course of an earlier attempt to access the mausoleum by myself, accompanied by Nikka Johannson," continued Rafe in a business-like tone and nodding his head towards Nikka, still standing by the door, "an assassination attempt was made on my life. It was prevented by the quick actions of Nikka, who shot dead the perpetrator, who had taken pains to disguise his appearance."

"What?!" said several of the Councillors, or words to that effect.

In the stunned silence, Rafe resumed, albeit with a slightly shakier voice. "The man who tried to shoot me was subsequently and positively identified as Rikus Smits, at that time a member of Nikka's own team here at The Bibliotek."

The cacophony of voices that immediately erupted from the table prevented Rafe from continuing. Thurldottir had stopped typing and was now sitting still, arms folded again, her 'death stare' back, only this time directed at Rafe.

After a few moments, Rafe said "Smits was acting on the orders of Councillor Carlson" but no-one appeared to hear him, apart from the fat man himself, who began the difficult process of extricating himself from his chair in order to leave the room. Meanwhile, Rafe kept repeating the last thing he had said, each time getting louder until at last all other conversation stopped when he shouted "... on the orders OF COUNCILLOR CARLSON!"

At that very moment silence befell the room and all eyes turned to Carlson, who had finally managed to get to his feet and was now watching Nikka approach him, determinedly.

"Abe Carlson, you are under arrest for the attempted murder of Rafe Nagy and the murder of Viscount Visconti di Rossellini. There will be other serious charges, but those will do for starters. Come with me," Nikka said quickly, loudly, and formally, as she swiftly and deftly produced a set of manacles from the inside of her jacket and applied them to Carlson's wrists in the front stack position. It happened so fast he had no time to resist or object. Instead, he visibly reduced in statue, and meekly shuffled to the door, with Nikka holding his arm firmly. "I want my lawyer contacted" was all he said, turning his head towards Thurldottir to say it. In response, Thurldottir glanced at the ceiling, rolled her eyes, and said nothing.

Those in the room who had no inkling beforehand of what had just occurred turned to Thurldottir in silent anticipation of some sort of explanation for what they had just witnessed.

"Does she have the power to do that?" was all Thurldottir said, seemingly asking no-one in particular as she now stared downward at the desk, avoiding eye contact with anyone. But Mads knew the question was aimed at him.

"You forget, Madam Chair," Mads replied, "that as Head of Security, Nikka Johannson is also Chief of Police for The Bibliotek precinct and acts in that role under Norwegian law. It may *seem* only a title ninety-nine percent of the time, but she nevertheless retains full police powers, including those of *investigation, apprehension,* and *arrest.*" He uttered that last word a little slower than the rest but with more feeling, to make a not-too-subtle point.

"In the circumstances, I think it appropriate that this meeting be adjourned. I therefore close it," responded a now-shaken Thurldottir, who suddenly made to also rise from her chair, the potential reality of her situation having finally dawned upon her.

"I will second that motion, but not before Mads has finished his presentation," said Thomas.

"All those in favour?" asked Hans. It was now obvious to all that Hans and Thomas were acting in pre-arranged concert with Mads.

Just then all eyes turned to Nikka as she returned to the room, closed the door, and stood again in front of it. Had she been carrying a knife she could have cut the tension in the room with it, was her first thought when she saw what was happening.

"Well?!" asked Hans of his colleagues, raising his hand to vote 'yay'.

Six more hands were then raised, including Mads and Thomas.

"Motion carried." said Hans. "Please Rafe, continue."

By now Thurldottir had stopped her rise from her chair and instead resumed her seat, but she was now gripping its armrests with barely-concealed rage.

Rafe continued. "Rikus Smits had made the dual mistake of wearing a private neurophone in Russia and leaving his work neurophone in his desk drawer back in The Bibliotek. Both were confiscated by Nikka and accessed, and both contain irrefutable evidence of his and Carlson's guilt."

"Before you tell us the answer to the big question as to why this man tried to kill you, Rafe, what can you tell us about Viscount Rossolini?" asked Hans.

"*Rosselini.* Viscount Rosselini was his name," replied Rafe. He then went on to recount what had happened in Pienza and why he had arrived at the Viscount's house minutes after the murder, but he left out the gorier details. He did, however, tell the Councillors that it was obvious that someone had tipped off Smits as to his appointment with the Viscount and that, as with his actions at the monastery in Sergiyev, Smits had made it look as if the Present Sect was responsible on both occasions, even going so far as to enlist the aid and abet of an actual Present Sect member in Sergiyev. "I took the Viscount's death to be a message to me; a threat that was later acted upon in Russia. As to why, I believe it was part of a plan to target the Bibliotekar. To distract and to discredit him. It seems elaborate and over-the-top, but it worked to a degree. I was but a mere pawn in this unsavoury game and it nearly ended me. It is when the bigger picture is revealed that we see what was at stake by those behind it. Those painting that big picture. I will let Mads explain and reveal that picture. If there are any more questions, Mads will address them."

Rafe left the lectern before anyone could ask anything more, and took up a seat beside Nikka, who was still standing at the door, with her arms folded. As he did so, Mads rose from his seat and took Rafe's place at the lectern.

"Rafe has informed me that following his discovery of the Lost Library of Ivan The Formidable he is retiring from all activities as The Bibliotek's most senior, and most respected, Finder. He feels the timing is right, and, sad to say, I tend to agree. His last Find will be impossible to top and is a fitting one to finish on. As the Governing Council's Standing Orders state that any Councillor charged with a serious crime is deemed to automatically vacate their seat until at least their case is heard and decided, there is now a vacancy to be filled. And since it would itself be a crime were The Bibliotek to lose the benefit of Rafe's extensive experience, I therefore move that he be appointed as Councillor."

"I second that motion," Thomas said immediately in response.

"All those in favour?" chimed in Hans with equal rapidity. They were playing the game with a tactic previously used by Thurldottir in Council meetings, and doing it well.

"Motion carried," said Mads as soon as enough hands were raised to add to his. "Congratulations, Councillor Rafe. Would you like to take your seat at the table?" he continued, pointing to the seat vacated by Carlson.

Rafe did so, but he was clearly in some shock. He gave Mads a look that Mads knew all too well. It was a look that silently said 'you're a sneaky son-of-a-bitch' but in a good way.

As Rafe struggled with adjusting the chair to his very different height and overall size from its former occupant, Thurldottir finally spoke. "Are you now pretending to be Chair of the Governing Council?" she said, turning and facing Mads.

"No, but I will continue with my review. It's time to feature *you*," he replied.

New slide: *Conspiracy*

Mads then revealed the reason for Thomas's sudden departure and absence from The Bibliotek — that he had been threatened by Smits because he had had the misfortune of arriving unannounced on Arcadia to perform a random test of The Bibliotek's Disaster Recovery Plan at the same time as a private geosurvey team, already there for several days, was collecting mineral samples that proved that Arcadia, or at least The Bibliotek's leased part of it, contained a massive lode of extremely valuable mineral deposits. He then revealed the plot to use The Bibliotek to get control of the mineral site on Arcadia. That the CFO Michael Huntington had been bribed to make sure The Bibliotek covered the costs and the fact of the geosurvey and the preparations for exploitation. That he had signed statements from Dr Joyce, Violetta Simpson, and Nils Larkin confessing to and describing in detail their respective roles in the conspiracy orchestrated by Thurldottir and Carlson. He revealed the background to Smits and De Jong and their roles. He revealed why Deputy Bibliotekar Bradshaw had been summarily dismissed and the evidence gathered from his data pad.

All the while during his revelations Mads remained calm and did not betray any anger or other negative emotions. His presentation was thorough and without emotion, as if he were revealing the outcomes of a fiscal audit. He did not pause and he did not hurry. His audience, apart from Thurldottir, sat mostly in stunned silence. Out of the corner of his eye, Mads could detect Thurldottir sitting impassively, with her arms folded, but he thought he could feel the steam rising from her body, as if she were ready to explode at any moment. But when he finally finished, it was Thurldottir who broke the tense silence, with slow, deliberate clapping. Then she put her hands down.

"Very theatrical, Ingridson. Pity there won't be an encore in a court. None of what you have said will be admissible. Johannson here failed to 'read me my rights'," she said smugly.

"Oh, I wouldn't say that. The only inadmissible 'thing' is anything you have said, and you've said nothing of much interest in this meeting, as usual. Now, there's a heliojet standing by to take you to Oslo and a holding cell until your first appearance in the Criminal Court tomorrow. Goodbye."

"You're a fool, Mads Ingridson! We've always suspected it. Why do you think I came to The Bibliotek? Because I like books? Ha! Do you really think we went to Arcadia just for back-up systems for this shit-fuck of a morose institution? We've been planning this for years. *Years.* Do you really think a court appearance in Oslo is going to change anything?!"

"No, but this might," Mads replied impassively.

New slide: *Arcadia Sub-leases*

He quickly continued. "In my capacity as Bibliotekar, I have just signed Heads of Agreement with representatives of the Russian, Norwegian, and Icelandic governments respectively whereby they will jointly sub-lease the very area of The Bibliotek's site of Arcadia apparently filled with the valuable minerals that had been targeted by the conspiracy orchestrated by Chair Thurldottir and her as yet unknown associates."

"You did what!?" Thurldottir screamed.

"You heard me!" Mads immediately shouted back with equal force. Such was the surprise that greeted his raised voice, Thurldottir was rendered mute, and before she could compose herself Mads continued. "Our not-for-profit status and our Three Tenets dictate that The Bibliotek cannot and should not undertake exploitation of the minerals itself, and this is a fact that Thurldottir knows only too well and which was the most important part of her scheme. Wasn't it!?" he levelled at Thurldottir, who sat seething with rage.

Mads quickly disclosed that in partial return for the granting of the sub-leases, the Russian government had given its stamp of approval for Rafe's actions in procuring the Lost Library, the Icelandic government had agreed to hand over the *Sagas*, and all three governments had also agreed to fully fund the costs of all future FTL travel to and from Arcadia, resulting in a significant cost commitment being removed from The Bibliotek's balance sheet.

"You imbecile!" exploded Thurldottir. "You're giving away all that for nothing. Nothing!" she continued, then, looking around the table, said "you cannot let this idiot do this!"

"Nikka," was all Mads said in response to Thurldottir's spite, and that was all Nikka needed to hear. She had already been moving towards Thurldottir and now she grabbed her arm and pulled her out of her chair. This Thurldottir resisted, but was easily overcome by Nikka's deft arm work, and found herself quickly manacled, just as Carlson had been, and pulled towards the door.

"Be careful, bitch, you are *manhandling* a senior citizen!" the former Chair screeched. As her derogatory words were ignored by Nikka, she turned to Larkin, who was now standing at the door, which he had just opened for Nikka and her quarry. "Your mother will be horrified by your betrayal!" Thurldottir spat at him.

"I doubt it," Larkin replied, impassively. "My mother says you lied to her as a matter of course. Where lies the betrayal?"

Mads resumed his seat at the table. As his fellow Councillors turned back from the door and started muted conversations between themselves, Mads looked intently at the ones he knew had been Thurldottir supporters. On each of their faces he could see the tell-tale signs of guilty panic. He knew then that he had the Governing Council. "In view of the fact that the Chair and the Deputy Chair have just been arrested for serious crimes, this meeting cannot continue. I move that we reconvene tomorrow morning at nine o'clock, with the first item on the agenda being the appointment of a new Chair."

"I second that motion," said Thomas.

"Any objections?" said Hans.

There were none.

"Motion carried."

THE END

For now...

Terminology

Access Request, see also *Principles of Access*

Any visitor to The Bibliotek seeking access to any book held in the Central Repository is required to make a formal Access Request. If it is granted, an entry is made in the Record of Access of the person's name, institution, and date. If the request is denied, an entry is made in the Record of Denied Access of the person's name, institution, the book denied access to, date, and the reason or reasons for denial.

Alcubierre-Manning Deep Warp Drive, see *Faster Than Light Travel*

Adcom, see also *Phicom*

Adcom is a portmanteau for Administrative Committee, one of the two committees reporting the Governing Council of The Bibliotek. The other committee is Phicom, or Philosophical Committee. As its name implies, Adcom oversees all the administrative and operational functions of The Bibliotek and the Bibliotek Academy. It is responsible for implementing all policy decisions of Phicom. Adcom is chaired by Mads Ingridson, the Second Bibliotekar.

AGM

AGM is the acronym for Annual General Meeting.

Althing

The Althing is the national parliament of Iceland. Originally founded in 903 at Thingvellir, it was re-established in Reykjavik in 2168.

Arcadia

Arcadia is one of only two known habitable planets in the universe, apart from Earth. It is located in the Alpha Centauri System.

Bibliophile

A bibliophile is a person who has a love of books. A bibliophile loves to read them and/or collect them. A bibliophile is not to be confused with a bibliomaniac, who is a person with an obsessive-compulsive disorder that prompts them to collect as many books as possible, by whatever means, as objects.

Bibliotek, The

The Bibliotek is the largest library on Earth. Established by the United Nations in 2102 in northern Norway but now running autonomously, it is intended to act as humankind's repository of its written knowledge, with the aim of procuring and housing at least one copy of every book printed or published. Referred to by all who work there as 'The Bibliotek'.

Bibliotek Academy, the, aka *the Academy*

The Bibliotek Academy is a university attached to The Bibliotek and located in the same precinct. Its sole function is to train people in the various disciplines required for the operations and functions of The Bibliotek, including administration, information technology, conservation and restoration, and librarianship. The Academy also facilitates research and scholarship in books. Its current Dean is Dominic Coenraad, who also sits on Adcom.

Bibliotekar, the

The Bibliotekar is the chief librarian of The Bibliotek. The role is equivalent to that of a Chief Operating Officer of a corporation. Mads Ingridson is the current Bibliotekar. His formal title is the Second Bibliotekar. He was appointed Bibliotekar in 2154 by his mother, Ingrid Rolfdottir, who was the First Bibliotekar. The Bibliotekar is supported by a Deputy Bibliotekar.

Book Keeper, the, aka the *Keeper*

The Book Keeper is the nickname given to the Bibliotekar.

BSL, aka *Bibliotek Sign Language*

BSL is a formal language established circa 2180 that is signed by the Deaf community within The Bibliotek's 16,500 workforce who live in The Bibliotek precinct. Finn Mackie, the current General Manager of Facilities at The Bibliotek was instrumental in promulgating BSL as a uniform sign language and in the creation and publication of the BSL dictionary.

Capex

Capex is a portmanteau for 'capital expenditure', a term used to describe the category of an organisation's expenditure that is not on revenue account and thus cannot be expensed immediately but instead, over time.

Central Repository, see also *Secondary Repositories*

The Central Repository is the main facility of The Bibliotek housing its collections. It is almost entirely located underground, comprising 75 sub-levels. It currently holds more than 1,000,000,000 books.

Chained Library

A 'chained library' was one where some or all of the books were chained to bookshelves. The length of the chain would allow such a book to be taken off its shelf and read, sometimes long enough to reach a nearby table or desk, but would prevent the book from being stolen or otherwise removed from the room.

CV

CV is the acronym for *curriculum vitae*, aka résumé.

Data pad

A data pad is the main communication and network device used by all employees of The Bibliotek. Designed especially for use by employees of The Bibliotek, it is a hand-held portable, integrated, and networked device capable of connection to The Bibliotek from 95 percent of the world's habitable regions. They are used daily at The Bibliotek as personal computers and for recording and other functions, including holographics.

Disaster Recovery Plan, aka *DRP*

The Disaster Recovery Plan is the formal strategy formulated by The Bibliotek to deal with and recover from any major loss of data, either within The Bibliotek's Earth-based network, or from its mainframe at The Bibliotek or back-up mainframe at its facility on Arcadia.

Faster Than Light Travel, aka *FTL Travel*, aka *FTL*

FTL Travel was demonstrated for the first time in 2162. FTL is the common-use acronym describing the Alcubierre-Manning Deep Warp Drive, which powers The Bibliotek's spaceship the *Nostradamus* and is the sole means of interstellar space travel.

Find (noun)

A Find is the formal name of a procurement of books for The Bibliotek by a Finder.

Finder

A Finder is a book detective employed by The Bibliotek to search for, locate, and procure books (Finds) for The Bibliotek's Central Repository. Each Finder is designated a territory of Earth in which they operate.

First Review of The Bibliotek, aka *First Review,* aka *The 100-Year Review*

The First Review of The Bibliotek was an independent review of The Bibliotek commissioned by The Bibliotek Foundation in 2202, overseen by the Governing Council, and completed in 2203. Its main purpose was to examine the operations and the strategic direction of The Bibliotek to see if they were meeting the aims and objectives of its establishment, and to make any recommendations to improve those things. The broad outcome of the First Review was that The Bibliotek was "adequately performing its purpose", which led the Governing Council to cherry pick recommendations to implement, deferring or not agreeing with the rest.

Governing Council of The Bibliotek, aka *Governing Council*, aka *Council*

The Governing Council is akin to a Board of Directors, and has 13 Councillors. It's Chair is Danuta Thurldottir. Two committees report to the Governing Council: Phicom and Adcom.

Great Holy War

The global conflict generally known as the Great Holy War occurred between 2086 and 2092. It is estimated that 2.2 billion people were killed during the conflict, which is accepted as having its origins in violent incidents which occurred during and after the 2086 Riyadh International Book Fair.

Heliojet

Heliojets are the principal means of aerial flight on Earth. Fully automated, they can be used privately by groups up to 100 passengers, or commercially for cargo or up to 1,250 passengers.

Holographic

Virtual meetings are held by the Governing Council by way of holographic representation of Councillors not in physical attendance. It is also one means of audio communication by the Deaf community at The Bibliotek, using data pads.

Hovercar, see also *Hydrocar*

Hovercars are the principal means of land travel on Earth. They replaced hydrocars and can only be used on hoverpaths or hoverways, ie 99.6% of roads.

Hydrocar, see also *Hovercar*

Hydrocars are the last iteration of engine-powered land vehicles. As their use is confined to roads without hover tracks, ie dirt roads, all remaining hydrocars are four-wheel drive.

Iconoclasm, see also *Present Sect*

Now largely redundant by virtue of the Great Holy War, iconoclasm is a tenet calling for the destruction of all religious icons and objects.

Imprint, see also *Master Catalogue*

An imprint is an extremely thin and translucent unique identifier and tag attached to each book in the Master Catalogue as a means of remote monitoring of movement.

Incunable

An incunable (plural: incunabula) is the label attaching to any book published before 1501. It replaced the term 'fifteener' and was first used by the Dutch physician Hadrianus Iunius. The selection of 1501 was completely arbitrary, and books printed after 1500 continued to look the same as incunabula for a number of years. As of 2204, there were only 32,516 known incunabula, of which the majority are now held by The Bibliotek. Less than 10% of incunabula contain illustrations and most are in Latin, German, Italian, French, or English.

Induction Process

The Induction Process is the procedure by which each book procured by The Bibliotek is entered into the Master Catalogue and placed in the Central Repository. During this process the Principles of Embargo and Principles of Access are applied to the entry to determine its status. The Induction Process is carried out by the Conservation Department, which assesses each book coming into The Bibliotek as potential additions to the Central Repository.

IP

IP is the acronym for intellectual property, commonly used to describe a valuable bundle of such rights.

ISL, aka *International Sign Language*, see also *BSL*

ISL is not a formal language as such. It is instead an amalgam of recognised sign languages used by the Deaf when meeting with each other in international environments. Finn Mackie, General Manager of Facilities at The Bibliotek is deaf and fluent in Australian Sign Language (Auslan), British Sign Language, written English, written French, written German, and ISL. He was instrumental in creating Bibliotek Sign Language (BSL), which is the accepted sign language in The Bibliotek precinct.

iWrite2

First released in 2119, *iWrite2* is currently in its 96th version and is now considered the world's foremost auto word content generating software. The Bibliotek refuses to procure any book created by *iWrite2* and devotes significant tech resources to the sole task of identifying for rejection any such book included in any procurement.

List, the

The List is intended to be the primary resource for researching potential Finds by Finders. It is constantly revised and updated as Finds are made, and is the product of references found in Finds to potential Finds not yet procured by The Bibliotek. Each Finder has access to the List.

List Compilers, see also the *List*

List Compilers meticulously scan the contents of all Finds, both by the various automated means available to them and by their faithful eyes, then cross-reference all noted sources and other mentions with both The Bibliotek's Master Catalogue and its Temporary Catalogue, then "de-dupe" the results, with all sources remaining then being added to a List if not already on it. If a source *is* already on the List, its existing entry is annotated with the new additional reference. Naturally, the more annotations held by a source on the List, the more valuable it becomes in terms of The Bibliotek's desire to procure it.

Locator

The Locator is the system by which anyone at The Bibliotek can find out where anyone else is at any given time. The system also tracks the location of everyone's phone and data pad and the movements of anybody in the Central Repository. If someone cannot be found by the Locator it means they are not within The Bibliotek precinct.

Master Catalogue, see also *Temporary Catalogue*

The Master Catalogue is the main database maintained by The Bibliotek. Its sole purpose is to contain the approved entries for all books held in the Central Repository. Finders procuring books for The Bibliotek are responsible for creating the draft of the applicable Master Catalogue entry for each such book, known as the Temporary Catalogue entry. As soon as a book is given an Imprint its entry in the Temporary Catalogue is moved to the Master Catalogue. Most parts of the Master Catalogue are freely-available public information and searchable Some content is withheld for security reasons.

Neurophone

Assisted by an implant inserted just above a person's ear, neurophones are the main form of interpersonal telecommunication used on Earth.

Nostradamus

The *Nostradamus* is The Bibliotek's fully-automated spaceship. It is FTL-powered and used solely for trips between The Bibliotek's spaceport and facilities on Arcadia.

PA

PA is the acronym for Personal Assistant. Each member of Adcom has a PA.

PDQ

PDQ is the acronym for Pretty Damn Quick. Variants include PBQ and PFQ.

Phicom, see also *Adcom*

Phicom is a portmanteau for Philosophy Committee, one of the two committees reporting the Governing Council of The Bibliotek. The other committee is Adcom, or Administrative Committee. Phicom is responsible for setting all the policies under which The Bibliotek operates, and it is Adcom's responsibility to put those policies into practice and administer them. Phicom is chaired by Danuta Thurldottir, Chair of the Governing Council of The Bibliotek.

Present Sect, the

The Present Sect is a disparate group of unknown radicals intent on removing all physical books from existence, by any means. Their actions are supposedly guided by their *Manifesto For The Present* (author unknown).

Principles of Access, aka *POA*, see also *Record of Access* and *Principles of Embargo*

The Principles of Access are the guidelines by which the rights to access any given book held in the Central Repository are determined. This determination is made during the Induction Process. Under the guidelines, access is subservient to any determination of embargo under the Principles of Embargo. The default position is thus that any book not deemed to be embargoed from access is deemed to be accessible under and in accordance with the POA.

Principles of Embargo, aka *POE*, see also *Principles of Access*

The Principles of Embargo are the guidelines by which access to any given book is denied, including any exceptions to a general embargo. This determination is made during the Induction Process.

Primary Function, see *Three Tenets, the*

Record of Access, aka *ROA*, see also *Principles of Access*

The Record of Access is an ancillary database to the Master Catalogue, on an entry-by-entry basis. However, the ROA is offline to any non-network search, and is in any event only accessible by approved Bibliotek staff. The purpose of the ROA is to maintain records of all access to any given book.

Record of Denied Access, aka *RDA*, see also *Principles of Embargo*

As with the Record of Access, the Record of Denied Access is an ancillary database to the Master Catalogue, on an entry-by-entry basis. The RDA is also offline to any non-network search, and is only accessible by approved Bibliotek staff. The purpose of the RDA is to maintain records of all access requests to embargoed books and denials of access on other grounds.

Relocation Study Group, aka *Study Group* and *RSG*

The Relocation Study Group is a sub-committee of Adcom formed by Mads Ingridson, in his capacity of Chair of Adcom, to investigate and report back to Adcom on the question of whether the Governing Council of The Bibliotek should consider relocating part or all of The Bibliotek due to concerns over capacity and security. Ingridson appointed the Deputy Bibliotekar, Paul Bradshaw, to lead the RSG. The other members are Nikka Johannson, (Head of Security), Finn Mackie (General Manager of Facilities), and Bernadette Collingwood (General Counsel).

Roxburghe Club, the

Formed as initially a private dinner of eighteen friends, all bibliophiles, in 1812 in honour of the Duke of Roxburghe and the vast private library he accumulated prior to his death in 1804, the club named after him is the world's oldest society of bibliophiles. The dinner was held on the eve of a highly anticipated day of the 46-day auction of the Duke's library, which was claimed to be the greatest private library of the eighteenth century. The club's first secretary was Reverend Thomas Frognall Dibdin, and since 1839 its membership has been limited to 40. The club is also a publishing society, producing Members' books for distribution to members only, and Club books, for sale to the general public. Traditionally, complete sets of both categories of books are passed down from member to member. Mads Ingridson, the Bibliotekar, was admitted as a member in 2203, and he acquired the complete set of books of the member whose death had created the vacancy which allowed Ingridson to join the club. An attack on the club by the Present Sect in 2193 was repelled by security forces.

Secondary Function, see *Three Tenets, the*

Secondary Repositories, see also *Central Repository*

The Secondary Repositories were created to hold Finds deemed not required to be held in the Central Repository. This category of Finds includes second and later editions of first editions already held by The Bibliotek and copies of any book held in the Central Repository. The existence of the Secondary Repositories is not public knowledge as they do not technically conform to either the Primary Function or the Secondary Functions of The Bibliotek. Their capacity is becoming an issue, as is the strain on The Bibliotek's operating budget in their maintenance. All Secondary Repositories are offsite from the Central Repository, mainly located in Oslo and Frankfurt.

Subluminal Data Transmission, see also *Faster Than Light Travel*

Subluminal Data Transmission is the means by which The Bibliotek sends data to and from its backup DRP mainframe on Arcadia, by utilising the same type of wormholes as FTL but with far less energy required.

Tax Certificate

The only consideration The Bibliotek gives for procuring books is a Tax Certificate issued to the donor. The Certificate states the market value of the procurement for the purpose of the donor claiming a tax deduction. Each participating jurisdiction's tax authority has an agreement with The Bibliotek stipulating the conditions under which Finders can issue Tax Certificates and the annual monetary limits applicable to them.

Temporary Catalogue, see also *Master Catalogue*

The Temporary Catalogue contains the draft entry for each book procured by The Bibliotek. Finders are responsible for creating entries for all their Finds, and these entries are added to the Temporary Catalogue. Conservators review all draft entries before transfer to the Master Catalogue.

Three Tenets, the

Siegfried Sorenson, the proponent of The Bibliotek, formulated Three Tenets by which he submitted to the UN The Bibliotek should operate. Although the UN specifically approved of the Three Tenets, it is unclear as to whether or not the Governing Council of The Bibliotek is obliged to follow them at all times, as difficulties in applying them to all real-world situations have been experienced, given their generalist wording and despite the best efforts of Phicom to follow them in the early history of The Bibliotek. The Three Tenets are as follows: 1. *It is the Primary Function of The Bibliotek to be Earth's main repository of human knowledge, thought, and experience in print*; 2. *It is the Secondary Function of The Bibliotek to facilitate appropriate access to all printed material under its management*; and 3. *The two functions of The Bibliotek must co-exist.*

Timeline

2086   Great Holy War commences. The violence was precipitated by a suicide bombing incident at the Riyadh International Book Fair.

2092   Great Holy War ends. More than twenty percent of the world's population — over two billion people — perish in the conflict. Many institutions around the world are destroyed, including churches, mosques, temples, museums, art galleries — and libraries. Modern religion takes the blame and becomes a moot and historical concept.

2093   Siegfried Sorenson formally proposes the creation of The Bibliotek and creates its founding tenets. Later that year the General Assembly of the United Nations votes to approve the establishment of The Bibliotek. Construction work begins in a remote part of northern Norway.

2097   The respective governments of all members of the United Nations resolve to transfer their national library collections to The Bibliotek.

2102   The Bibliotek begins accepting collections. Construction of The Bibliotek continues for another five years before it is completed. The Governing Council holds its first meeting and appoints Ingrid Rolfdottir, aged 47, as The First Bibliotekar.

        Rafe Nagy is born, to a single mother, who passes away shortly afterwards. Rafe is raised by his maternal grandmother in Amsterdam.

2108   Ingrid Rolfdottir gives birth to her son, Mads Ingridson.

2133   Mads Ingridson and Rafe Nagy graduate from the Academy. Mads begins work at The Bibliotek as a Classifier and Historian in the Central Repository. Rafe begins work at The Bibliotek as an Assistant List Compiler.

2135   Rafe Nagy is promoted to List Compiler.

2141   Rafe Nagy is promoted to Finder. His designated territory is Europe, which he shares with another Finder.

2154   Ingrid Rolfdottir appoints her son Mads Ingridson as Deputy Bibliotekar.

2162   Ingrid Rolfdottir appoints her son Mads Ingridson as The Second Bibliotekar and retires with immediate effect.

        Faster Than Light travel in space becomes a reality.

2165   Ingrid Rolfdottir dies, aged 110.

2190   Danuta Thurldottir becomes a Councillor of the Governing Council of The Bibliotek. Her addition to the Council is sponsored by Councillor Carlson.

2192   Paul Bradshaw is appointed Deputy Bibliotekar by Mads Ingridson, the Second Bibliotekar.

2195   Danuta Thurldottir becomes Chair of the Governing Council of The Bibliotek, after a coup.

2196   The Bibliotek leases land in the sector of the planet Arcadia allocated to the Norwegian Government and establishes a facility at the site for maintaining its back-up mainframe and Disaster Recovery Plan System.

2202   First Review of The Bibliotek commences.

2203   First Review of The Bibliotek concludes.

        Violetta Simpson joins The Bibliotek as Chief Conservator, a position she held at the Harvard University Library before the Library's holdings were transferred to The Bibliotek.

2204   1,000,000,000th entry in the Master Catalogue. Present time.